THE HOUSEKEEPER'S DAUGHTER

Kate Bratton dreams of more. It's 1914, and her life is mapped out ahead of her: continue working as a maid in the beautiful Woodicombe House, settle down with Luke the gardener and, of course, start a family. Desperate to run away in search of adventure, Kate's plans are curtailed by the arrival of the Russell family at Woodicombe House. Tasked with becoming a lady's maid for their daughter, Naomi, Kate gets a glimpse of the other side of life. Will she return to the safety of her life before, or will the handsome Ned Russell turn her head?

THE HOUSEKEEPER'S DAUGHTER

Chapter One

Guests

Kate Bratton groaned. She despaired of him, she really did. But it was her own fault; she knew well enough that, given the chance, he'd be all over her. And here she was, pressed up against the wall, something sharp stabbing between her shoulder blades and his hot mouth on her neck. No matter how often she fought him off, he still tried his luck every chance he got. He also seemed to possess a sixth sense for the fact that, just lately, she struggled to resist him. Indeed, if he kept this up much longer, she might just give in and let him have his way.

'Go on, you know you want to.'

'No, Luke,' she said, her voice muffled by his shoulder. 'For the umpteenth time, stop it. I'm not one of those Estacott girls.'

The trouble was, he'd grown immune to her protests. She'd used every excuse she could think of but none of them deterred him. To him, they were all just part of the game.

'*I* want to. *You* want to. Where's the harm? We're as good as wed anyway.'

Wrenching a hand free from his grasp, she pushed at his shoulder, exhaling with relief when he stumbled backwards. Largely for show, she twitched the front of her apron back into place

9

and patted her cap. 'Luke Channer, we are *not* as good as wed.'

His grin, wide and lopsided, made her think of a four-year-old caught making mischief.

'Then name the day, Kate Bratton. Go on. If you want things all decent an' proper betwixt us, pick a day off the calendar and we'll go up an' see the vicar. Choose any day you like. Summer. Autumn. I ain't fussed. But let's have done with it.'

Reaching to rub at her shoulder, Kate shook her head. 'I've told you, I won't be rushed.'

'*Rushed?* Damnation, woman–'

'Luke!'

'Sorry. No call for swearing. But what's a man supposed to do? You were quick enough to say yes that day I got down on one knee and proposed. More'n a year back now, that must be. So why can't we just get it done? Can't nobody accuse you of indecent haste, if that's what you're frettin' about. After all *your* delaying, won't nobody be able to claim you must be in the family way.'

With a shake of her head, she gave an exasperated laugh. 'I should hope *not*. Although, if I let you have your way each and every time you put your hands all over me, I could easily be just that.'

He moved back towards her. Still leaning against the wall, she realized she had left it too late to side-step him. To her surprise, though, he didn't reach to touch her, instead pushing his hands into the gaping pocket on the front of his overalls. 'Happen that'd be no bad thing.'

Brushing aside a handful of hair that had fallen from under her cap, she squinted back at him. 'And how the devil do you fathom that?'

10

'Because then you'd *have* to get on and name the day.'

Oh, he was the worst! 'Luke Channer, only a man could think in such top-over-tail fashion. And trust me, nonsense like that does nothing to further your cause.'

'Faith, Kate Bratton, you're a stubborn one. What would you have me do? Tell me, I beg you, where the devil am I going wrong?'

When he ran his hand through his hair, and when, from among his sandy curls, the sunlight picked out glints of copper, russet and gold, she had to concede that to do anything truly wrong, he would have to try very hard indeed. It was just a good job he didn't know it – or know that sometimes the sight of him still made her catch her breath.

'Well, you could stop your constant pressing me to name the day.'

'And why would I do that? I want us to be wed. I thought *you* wanted us to be wed.'

'I do. It's just...'

'Just what?'

But therein lay the problem: she didn't really know what was holding her back. If she knew *that*, then she might be able to work out what to do about it.

With a long sigh of frustration, she stared beyond him across the yard. A clump of thistledown was being borne across it on the breeze. Entranced, she watched its progress. She knew how it felt to be propelled along like that, with no say as to speed or direction, for the more she thought about getting married, the more she felt as though

11

she was hurtling towards something she wasn't entirely sure she wanted. It wasn't that she had reservations about Luke himself, but rather what he was offering her. Marriage. Motherhood. Being stuck in Woodicombe. It all felt so un-imaginative and predictable – so dull.

Realizing it would be difficult to explain any of that to him, she drew her eyes back to his face. He was an earthy, honest man, a charmer: good-looking in an unkempt, unfussy sort of a way. Bright and sparky, he had it in him to make more of himself; she knew he did. And she suspected that deep down, he knew it, too.

'You ever think about doing summat different?' she asked as the thought struck her.

'My every waking moment. Though *mostly* what I think about starts with me finding you alone somewhere and ends with you not fighting me off. That'd be *real* different.'

In despair, she shook her head. 'That is *not* what I meant by *different,* and well you know it.'

With a grin, he shrugged his shoulders. 'Thought you'd want me to be truthful.'

Conceding that perhaps her question *had* been a mite vague, she turned her eyes back across the yard. The thistledown was long gone – could al-most be anywhere by now. 'What I *meant,* was do you ever think about doing something different with your *life* – with *our lives.*'

She watched him press his lips together in thought, noticing how the lightest of creases wrinkled his forehead.

'Now and again, I suppose. November-time, maybe, when I'm manuring the rhubarb and the

12

rain's coming in sideways off the 'lantic. You know, when I were a lad, I had a fancy for a life at sea. I used to stand up there at the beacon and watch the boats a-coming and a-going from Westward Quay. I fancied it'd be thrilling to sail away and leave the land behind – you know, go on an adventure. But more lately, I've started to think how I'd like–'

An adventure. Out of the blue, he'd just given her something she could use.

'Luke ... lets *us* go on an adventure.'

'What?'

'Run away with me.'

'What?'

Under his puzzled stare, she shifted her weight; perhaps she could have gone about that in a more considered fashion.

'Think about it,' she started again. 'We could go anywhere. We could go to London and make our fortunes. Or ... or to Plymouth or Bristol and join a ship bound for America to start new lives. People do that, you know. Just think: you'd get to see what it's really like to sail away from the land–'

'You been out in the sun? Either that or you've had a blow to the head.'

'Sun? Huh. When do *I* get the chance to be out in the sun? And no, nor have I had a blow to the head. I mean it, let's run away together and do something new. I'm told there's a big wide world out there.' In emphasis of her point, she swept her arm in a wide arc.

'Kate–'

'I'd marry you as soon as tomorrow if it meant the chance of starting out somewhere different.

13

Think about *that*.'

'All right, say we did *run away*, as you put it, what would you have us do when we got there? Only, so far as I can see, no matter how far we journeyed, or where we pitched up, we'd still be the same two folk we are here, toiling for them that's more fortunate than us. *I'd* still be a gardener ... and *you'd* still be a maid.'

She shook her head impatiently, more of her mousy-brown hair falling from under her cap. 'No. Don't you see? That's the whole point. We needn't *be* the same! We could do something for our own gain.'

'Like what?'

Unfortunately, there he had her. 'Well, I don't know yet. I haven't thought that far.'

'As would be clear to a blind man.'

'But other people do it, don't they?' she ploughed on. 'So why not us? Why shouldn't *we* have something ... different ... something more?'

Bringing his hands to his hips, Luke sighed. 'Kate, woman, I love you. You know that. But that doesn't mean you don't worry me with your constant fidgeting and fretting. I tell you, it's wearing – you never being content with what's in front of you. Or even with what's ahead.'

Also bringing her hands to her hips, Kate shook her head in frustration. 'That's neither true nor fair!'

At this assertion, he widened his eyes. 'Ain't it? I'll tell you what's neither true nor fair, some long time back, I asked you to marry me. Weren't a surprise, we both knew the day would come. You said yes, no surprise there, either. Then, being the

14

sort of feller I am, I tell you to let me know when you feel good an' ready. Then I wait. And, patient as you like, I've been waiting ever since. *Now, today,* you tell me you want summat different. But *different* is right under your nose, woman. Different is us getting wed and setting up home together and ... and having babes and raising them up–'

Dismayed by his response, she folded her arms and stood shaking her head. 'But all of *that* – all of them things you just said – would still be *here,* in Woodicombe.'

'Maybe. Or maybe one day not. I've no power to see beyond the here and now. Happen we *won't* always be right here. Either way, you'd be hard-pressed to find anywhere finer. Each and every sunrise, you an' me wake up in a place that brings people flocking from all over to see it. When folk from the cities want to go a-holidaying – when they want to breathe God's clean air – they come here to do it. *Here,* Kate, they journey *right here.* And, when the time comes for them to leave and go home, they don't want to. They don't want to go back to their grimy cities and their cheek-by-jowl homes in their filthy streets. And yet *you'd* have me throw all this over to take a chance in the very grime and muck all them folk come here to escape. Sometimes, I think we're too close to see what's under our own noses. To say it bluntly, what you talk of strikes me as nothing short of mazy. I can't see you've thought it through proper at all. And, if you're truly minded to hear what I think of it, I say this to you, the best thing we can do is stop right here, doing what we know and raising our children away from disease and ... filth

15

'... and ... vice.'

Disease and vice, indeed. What a narrow-minded way of carrying on! London wasn't like that at all. It was busy and shiny and prosperous. You only had to look at the Latimers, the family who owned Woodicombe House, to know that. *They* didn't look riddled with disease. Nor did they look like criminals – and *they* now chose to live in London year-round.

Stuck for how to persuade him differently, she stared down at her shoes, annoyed to see them covered in dust. Now she would have to clean them before she could get back to work. Work. She flicked her eyes to the clock above the stables: almost a half after three. She should go. It wasn't as though the only thing standing in the way of winning him over to her suggestion was a few more minutes of pleading. Although...

'Happen I don't *want* to stay *here*, raising children,' she offered into the quiet. 'Happen I want more than that.'

'Kate, what the devil is this *more* you keep on about? You can't keep talking of wanting more without being able to say what it is.'

'I can't say what it is. Some days I just feel as though there ought to be ... more.'

'And maybe I don't disagree with you, perhaps there did ought to be something more. I mean, *I'd* rather not have to be a gardener and handyman. I'd much rather drive a motorcar. But, if my lot in life is to fadge and find for the Latimers, then all I can do is make the best of it. Any road, as I've tried on so many an occasion to ram into that skull of yours, what I'm offering you *is* something

16

more. For certain it's more than some folk have. We might be stuck in Woodicombe, but we can still have a *good* life – a good and an honest one. Love. Marriage. A family. I don't know what else to say. This is who I am, Kate. But if that's not enough for you, or not what you want, then I'm blowed if I know what to do about it. I *do* know that running off to London – or to America of all places – ain't *something more.* It's madness. So, if that's the dream you have, then you'll have to chase after it without *me*. You'll have to find some other soul to go with because I'm not minded to throw all this over just to satisfy *your* itchy feet. Nor to risk getting all the way there only to find even *that's* not enough for you.'

'Luke–'

'No. I'm begging you, Kate, for once, stop and listen to yourself. Try an' hear how ungrateful you sound. And then let there be no more of this foolishness.'

'Luke!'

'No. I'm done talking about it. I've work to get back to. And so have you. If your ma isn't out looking for you already, she soon will be, any minute now and them guests will be here.' In frustration, Kate closed her eyes. He was right. She'd become so het up she'd forgotten they were expecting guests. 'But for heaven's sake, think about what I've said. And if, next time I see you, you can't tell me you've at least looked at that blasted calendar and picked a date for us to be wed, then it'll be a sorry day for both of us.' Shaking his head, he took a couple of steps backwards. Then, with an uncharacteristic glower, he pulled his cap from his pocket and pressed it onto his head.

Speechless, she stared back at him. His eyes looked colder than she had ever seen them: dark and displeased, as though daring her to say anything further.

When he turned about and started to walk away, his arms held rigidly by his sides and his gait wooden, she kicked at the gravel. Damn Luke Channer! For someone so flush with vigour and youth, he was as obstinate as an ox: a dumb ox. And he was mulish. Yes, he was as mulish as old Granfer Channer. And at least *he* had the excuse of being near-on ninety years old.

Left by herself, she spun about, swiping with her arm in frustration. She had tried her hardest to explain what was on her mind but he'd had no care to hear. By his reckoning, their lives were all neatly sewn up and pity her for not wanting the same thing. Well, she *didn't* want the same thing. Somewhere out there was a whole world of life and luck, of chances and reward. And, one day, she was going to go out there and grab some of it for herself.

Fresh air and a family, indeed! It was going to take more than fresh air and a family to satisfy *her* longing. Much more. Although, right this very minute, she'd settle for being able to creep back indoors without being seen. Yes, the last thing she needed after that little quarrel was a dressing-down from her mother for neglecting her duties.

Tock-tock, tock-tock. Tock-tock, tock-tock. With its holier-than-thou face and wearisome ticking, the long-case clock in the hallway drove Kate to distraction. Its laboured marking of the seconds and wheezy chiming of the hours ruled her every waking moment, and she loathed it more than any other piece of furniture in the entire house. Days were begun and ended by it, meals were served by it. And when, as now, the ground floor fell briefly quiet, its solemn ticking always made her feel as though someone was on their death-bed. Thankfully, on this particular afternoon at least, all that was actually struggling to draw its final breath was her will to live, as she stood waiting to be introduced to the Russell family; the people to whom the Latimers had loaned the house for the summer. The *whole* summer.

Discreetly, she cast her eyes over the three indi-viduals now stood looking about the hallway. It was all very well for *them* – ahead of *them* lay weeks of lounging around enjoying themselves, whereas all *she* had to look forward to was leaping about to their beck and call and clearing up their mess.

Although expressly forbidden to do so in the presence of guests, she sighed. But then, realizing that by allowing her shoulders to slump she was falling foul of another of her mother's rules, she drew herself smartly upright.

The woman at that moment occupying Ma's at-tention had to be Mrs Russell – the mother. A tall individual anyway, she towered over Ma by more than just the height of her hat – an elaborate and domed confection of burgundy silk. Setting eyes upon it for the first time had reminded Kate of a quilted tea-cosy, an association which, if she was to avoid being caught smirking, was unfortunate.

In an attempt to distract herself, she turned her eyes upon the woman more generally. By continually gesturing with her hands, she struck Kate as someone who liked to be the centre of attention. From her outfit, she also judged her as someone who liked to think herself still the youthful side of forty, whereas she was probably already several birthdays beyond it – and by more than she would care to have pointed out to her. Elegant, Kate conceded, taking in the softly-draped lines of her stylish frock and matching summer coat. Slender, too. But possessed of rather a shrill voice, which didn't bode at all well. In her experience, a woman with a voice like that was fond of using it. *Remove this. Fetch that. Why are you still here?* Yes, definitely the sort of woman who could make the whole summer feel like a very long time indeed.

Beyond the burgundy apparition stood her two grown-up children. In profile, their upturned noses and dimpled chins were such precise replicas that it was hard to tell which of them was the elder. On the basis of height alone, it might be the girl. Although that could simply be on account of her hat. Brimless, and woven from straw, it had the shape of the upturned hull of a fishing-smack. *Perhaps,* Kate thought, struggling not to giggle, *in London, oddly-shaped headwear was fashionable.*

With the discussion between her mother and Mrs Russell showing no signs of drawing to a close, and growing weary of waiting, Kate flicked her eyes to the young man. Reasonably tall, slim, and clean-shaven, he looked friendly, his face calling to mind that lovely silent movie actor,

Wallace Reid. Just the other day, she had seen a picture of him in an old copy of *The Stage* magazine that Mrs Latimer must have left behind. *Mmm, on second thoughts,* the harder she looked at him, the more the resemblance seemed only of the passing variety. Standing with his boater clasped to his chest and with the linen of his jacket and trousers showing signs of having been travelled in, this young man looked more earnest scholar than movie actor. Handsome enough, though, in an indoorsy sort of a way.

Her interest in the Russells wearing thin, she turned her gaze idly back to the daughter, horrified to find that she, herself, was now under scrutiny. Cursing silently, she directed her eyes to the floor; getting caught in the act of staring didn't usually end well.

'You. Yes, you – girl on the end. What's your name?'

What fearful bad luck; she hadn't even opened her mouth yet but already she was in trouble. 'Kate Bratton, ma'am,' she answered. Beside her, she could hear her sister softly tutting her disapproval. *Prig.*

With the young woman coming towards her, Kate felt obliged to look up.

'Turn about.' Drawing a breath and holding it in her chest, Kate obeyed. If *only* she hadn't chosen that moment to look at her. If only she hadn't been caught! 'Turn back.' Her heart sinking, Kate did as she was told. Then, lest she inadvertently meet the young woman's eyes for a second time, she brought her gaze to rest upon her inquisitor's lips: a perfect, blood-red, Cupid's bow. With looks like

21

those, she could sit for a cover of *The Lady* magazine. 'Did you style your own hair this morning?'

Well honestly, who else did she think would
have done it?

'Yes, miss. I mean, ma'am.'

'Very neat.'

'Thank you, miss. *Ma'am.*'

'Let me see your hands.' Again, Kate obeyed,
staring down at her fingertips, wavering under
the scrutiny. 'Clean nails.'

'Yes, ma'am.'

'You shall be my lady's maid.'

Her reaction one she couldn't possibly voice,
Kate pressed her lips firmly shut. Here was a fix
in the making and no mistake. 'Naomi, dear,' the
voice of Mrs Russell echoed around the hall. 'I
thought we agreed that, just this once, you would
manage without help.' Goodness, was she to be
spared by the girl's own mother? 'As I said to you
before we left Clarence Square, this holiday isn't
to be a formal affair – quite the opposite.'

Holding her breath, Kate flicked her eyes back
to the daughter, now turned towards her mother.

'Dear Mamma, and as *I* said to *you*, informal or
not, I have no wish to try and do without a maid.'

Discreetly, Kate continued to look between the
two women. In different ways, they both appeared
equally resolved. The daughter's light smile was
clearly meant to detract from steely determination, the mother's, from mild irritation. Of the
two, she thought it likely the mother would win
out. She certainly hoped so. She knew a girl
who'd gone to train as a lady's maid. Big mistake,
she'd said: flouncing women demanding the im-

possible, all hours of the day and night. Never a moment to herself, she'd said. Got herself married good and quick after that, she had.

'Darling, do be reasonable.'

'Mamma, I am. Surely you wish me to look presentable, especially since we're to entertain the Colbornes. From the moment you received their acceptance of your invitation to join us down here, you've spoken of little else.'

In the momentary hush that descended upon the hallway, Mrs Russell's sigh appeared to resonate with defeat. Although, to Kate's relief, she didn't appear to have entirely given up.

'You forget, my dear, we haven't consulted Mrs Bratton. Perhaps the girl can't be spared. The house isn't fully-staffed, you know. Sidney took great pains to point out to me that apart from Mrs Bratton to keep house, there's just a cook, a couple of kitchen staff and a handful of day girls who come in as general maids.'

Inwardly, Kate began to relax. The woman was right. With staffing as it was, there was no chance Ma could spare her for such frivolous duties – not for one moment.

Unfortunately, Naomi Russell didn't seem about to admit defeat. 'Nonsense. No one will notice her gone. I shall only need her two or three times a day.'

Two or three times a day? Where did this woman think she was – that new Crown Hotel along the coast, where ladies travelling without their own maid could engage one by the week? *Please, Ma, please say you can't spare me!*

'Regretfully, Mrs Russell, I hadn't been made

23

aware that the young lady would be requiring a maid...' At Mabel Bratton's remark, Kate exhaled heavily. Close shave! 'But, if it be the young lady's wish...' *What? No!* 'Then I'm sure we can all jiggle about – start earlier in the morning and work later into the evening to accommodate.'

Aghast, Kate opened her mouth to protest. Just as quickly, she closed it. What was the point? Object all she liked, it would get her nowhere. She was the *last* person whose opinion would be taken into account.

Naomi Russell, on the other hand, was already embracing her victory. Whirling back to face her, the swathes of her cape rushing to catch up with the movement of her body, she clasped her hands together. 'Excellent. You see, Mamma, it is no trouble at all. Come along then, Bratton. Or do I call you Kate?'

Weighed down by dismay, Kate couldn't get her mouth to work. Was she really to become a lady's maid – just like that?

'She'll answer perfectly fine to Kate, Miss Russell,' Mabel Bratton answered on her behalf. 'Be good and clear with your instructions and I'm sure you'll have no cause for complaint.'

'Good and clear it is then, Mrs Bratton. Very well then, Kate. Shall we go and inspect where I'm to be installed? See where you will be putting my things?'

Reading the look of warning upon her mother's face, Kate withheld a sigh of defeat. *I'm going to pay for this later,* was the thought going through her mind. *I just know I am.* Nevertheless, she nodded politely. 'Yes, ma'am.'

'Do call me Miss Naomi. *Ma'am* makes me sound like the Queen.'

'Yes, Miss Naomi.'

Even Mrs Russell was unable to change her daughter's mind. 'Naomi, dear, are you certain? This ... *girl* ... has neither the training nor the experience for such a position. She doesn't even look to be particularly–'

'Perfectly certain. Come along, Kate. Show me where I've been put. Then, while you keep a look out for the porter arriving with my trunks, I shall rest a while. Up here, are we?'

Unable to see any way out of her plight, Kate nodded. 'Yes, miss.' And then, following in the wake of shushing silk, she trailed up the staircase.

'I've been in this outfit all day and simply can't *wait* to change into something less suffocating. Our compartment on the train was stifling – utterly airless. I searched my travelling bag twice, but could I find my fan? I could not. Why Papa couldn't have arranged for us to be motored down, I don't know. On the other hand, those last few miles along that lane, well, what a bone-jarring experience *that* was! I couldn't have borne that sort of discomfort all the way down here. Tell me, Kate, why is it that all of the roads outside of London are little more than farm tracks?'

Farm tracks? Perhaps because that was what they were. 'I don't know, miss.'

Trailing across the half-landing and on up the staircase, Kate finally took the opportunity to release her sigh of dismay. Did this woman never stop talking? Did she not need to draw breath? It was a good thing they weren't in the dining

25

room: a voice like hers might shatter the Edinburgh crystal.

'I couldn't have felt more bilious had I been back on the *Mauretania* when we were stuck in that dreadful storm off Southampton. Please tell me that everything worth doing around here doesn't require being jolted all the way back up that lane!'

Slowly, Kate shook her head; Naomi Russell didn't have to be jolted anywhere if she didn't want to be. 'I'm a-feared that most of it does, ma'am.'

'Then I for one shall be staying put. Along here, are we?'

'Yes, miss, the ladies' rooms are on this landing.'

'Very well. Lead the way.'

When Kate passed ahead of Naomi Russell along the corridor, it was as much as she could do not to weep for her misfortune. Already she felt doomed; the job of lady's maid almost certain to end badly for her. In fact, at that precise moment, even the endless drudgery and mind-numbing dullness of keeping house as Mrs Luke Channer held more appeal. And that was saying something.

'It's such a shame that Papa is detained in London.'

It was the following morning and, for Kate, her first experience of Naomi Russell's daily routine. Although all the young woman had done so far was take her breakfast, she could see already that she was going to need the patience of a saint to keep her tongue in check. For a start, there was her manner of speaking. It sounded forced and unnatural. *Papa*. Was that a word for a grown woman? Why couldn't she call him *Father* or even just *Pa*, like everyone else? Not that when it came to fathers, she was an expert, her own having not even made it to her first birthday.

Catching sight of Naomi Russell staring back at her from the mirror, Kate frowned; if she was ever to avoid trouble, she had better start paying more attention. Take now, for instance: by allowing her thoughts to wander, she'd lost all track of what this woman had been rambling on about. Her father, was it? Oh, yes, that was right: she'd been rueing his absence. Clearly, then, agreement was called for. 'I daresay, miss.'

'Still, I'm sure he'll get down here just as soon as he can. In the meantime, Mamma has some friends coming to stay. Some of them are quite lively, so it shouldn't be long before there's some jollity.'

Jollity. In the servants' parlour, jollity was a word that brought about the raising of eyebrows, it usually referring to a state of affairs requiring more than the regular amount of clearing up afterwards. Even so, Kate knew it was her job to smile and appear pleased by the prospect. 'Yes, miss.'

'Now, since I am without engagements, indeed, since I am, as Mamma pointed out, *on holiday* – although Biarritz, this clearly isn't – I have decided to dispense with a morning outfit. And, since the day seems to feel as though it may become rather warm, I have decided I shall wear my lavender lawn. Yes, I know it's an afternoon

27

gown but I'm in the wilds of Devonshire. And you heard Mamma – on *this* holiday, formality is *not* the order of the day. So, since my straw hat will suffice, there's no need for you to fuss with my hair. Just brush it through for me, and then pin it into a *chignon* about here.' Raising her hand, Naomi Russell patted just beneath her crown.

Kate stared at the indicated spot on Miss Russell's head. How quickly was she to be found wanting? Not that it was *her* fault; it hadn't been *her* idea that she become a lady's maid. She hadn't proposed herself for the task; she had been singled out for it.

Perhaps it was time for honesty, though. 'I'm not sure, miss–'

Naomi Russell's reflection blinked back at her.

'You don't know how to do a *chignon?* Goodness me. They really are *the thing* now. No one wants a *Pompadour* any more – so passé. Look, fetch me that *McCalls* and I'll show you.'

Kate turned about. On the side table lay a magazine. Handing it to Miss Naomi, she waited for her to flick through the pages. Golly, her feet ached – but a glance to the clock on the mantel told her that it was barely even a half after nine. If she'd thought yesterday evening was hard work – unpacking two trunks while Miss Russell stood over her, issuing instructions – she hadn't accounted for the extent of her morning routine. And, supposedly, *this* was pared down from the way she started her day when at home in London. Or *in town,* as she insisted upon calling it.

'Look, like this. Do you see?'

Snapping her attention back, Kate stared down

28

at the linedrawn illustration.

'Oh. Yes, I see, miss. You want me to do it in a knot.'

'If you wish to call it that, then yes, a knot. I suppose, this far from London, you have different words for all manner of things. Anyway, can you do that? Or something approaching it?'

Carefully, Kate drew her hands behind her back and crossed her fingers. 'Yes, Miss Naomi. I can do that for you.'

'Good. And then I shall need you to change the band on my straw hat. There's a lilac one that tones with the trim on my dress. It will be with my gloves and so on.'

'Yes, miss.'

The exasperating thing, Kate thought as she drew the brush through Naomi's tresses, was that the woman had the most beautiful hair, as dark as ebony and as glossy as the topping on the *Sachertorte* Mrs Latimer always asked Edie to make for her.

Setting down the brush, Kate gathered Naomi's hair just above the nape of her neck and set about twisting it into a rope. Then, with a quick glance to the illustration – thankfully, just visible over Naomi's shoulder – she coiled it around and started to pin it in place.

Pushing in the last hairpin, she stood back: surprisingly good, even if she did judge as one who shouldn't. Perhaps one more pin, though, just to make certain.

'Done?'

'Yes, miss.'

'Mirror?' Reaching to the dressing table, Kate

lifted the hand mirror from the tray and held it at an angle behind Naomi Russell's head. 'Not bad.'

'Thank you, miss.' She would ignore the surprise in the woman's tone. *Not bad* was far better than the *no, no, no, not like that* she had been expecting to hear.

'Right. Fetch my dress.'

Going to stand in front of the wardrobe, Kate ran her eyes along the row of frocks she had hung there yesterday. There: that one looked to be the colour of lavender. Carefully, she unhooked the hanger from the rail and then gave it a shake.

'Is this the one, miss?'

'Yes. Help me into it and then bring my shoes – the beige pair with the double straps.'

'Yes, miss.' Pushing the tiny fabric-covered buttons through each of the corresponding loops, Kate worked her way down the back of Naomi Russell's dress. This then, she concluded, noticing how the material had next to no weight between her fingers, was *lawn*. In the palest of lavender colours, it was printed with tiny sprigs of flowers in rose-pink and cream. Oh, to own something so feminine. Oh, to have occasion to wear it! Sadly, she was unlikely to ever have either.

Lowering herself back down onto the dressing-table stool, Naomi Russell extended a stockinged foot, while, forcing herself not to shake her head in disbelief, Kate knelt in front of her and slipped on the appropriate shoe. Then she buttoned the straps. Good grief. This was worse than *anything* asked of her as a housemaid – not as back-breaking, maybe, but twice as ridiculous. Could the woman not fasten her own shoes? Some of the duties expected of her as a housemaid felt as though they had been invented solely to waste good time – like blacking a grate that was only ever going to be used for a sooty fire – but this lady's maid's business, *this* took the biscuit.

'Jolly good. Now, I'll just put some colour on my lips and then I'll leave you to it. I don't suppose you know whether Mamma is about yet?'

Kate got to her feet. 'No, miss, I'm a-feared I don't.'

'Never mind. I doubt she is. I rarely see her before eleven. Although of course, down here, she might rise a little later. We *are* on holiday, after all.'

'Yes, miss.' *Holiday,* Kate thought, lifting Miss Naomi's robe and night-gown from the chair. *What, exactly, was one of those?* With the way things were turning out, she'd be lucky to get a full night's sleep, let alone a holiday. And for that, she had her mother to blame – for not standing up to the spoiled Miss Naomi Russell in the first place!

'But Edie, I'm telling you a more dafter way of carryin' on you simply couldn't dream up!'

'And I don't doubt it.'

That her sister was unmoved, only made Kate even more exasperated. 'And such a waste of my time.'

It was mid morning the following day and, seated at their mother's desk, Edith Bratton didn't even look up from her writing. 'Don't come looking to me for sympathy, Kate. I'm fresh out of it. I spent I-don't-know-how-long yesterday writing out a list of pastries, cakes, and desserts, only to have Mrs Russell cross through half of it. "No almonds, no marzipan, no walnuts", says she. "How about lots of little meringues and choux pastry, instead? Oh, and raspberries, lots of raspberries. Everyone loves raspberries, don't they?" But do you hear *me* complaining? No. What gentry wants, gentry gets. And, same as me, you've been in service long enough to know that.'

Leaning in the doorway between the pantry and her mother's office, Kate folded her arms. 'They ain't gentry. I can tell. Got a nose for that sort of thing.'

'Makes no odds. They're guests of the Latimers and, as such, entitled to be or to have anything they want.'

Dismayed at her sister's response, Kate shook her head. Edith would walk a mile out of her way to avoid a confrontation. Or to avoid having to express sympathy. Just get on and do it, that was *her* view. Well, clearing up after people was one thing. As Ma always said, it wasn't that much different to keeping your own home, except that you were doing it for someone else and getting your board and lodgings in return. This lady's maid business, though, well this was turning out to be a different kettle of fish altogether. Apart from being a waste of perfectly good time, it was demeaning.

'But honestly, Edie,' she began, her eyes following the nib of her sister's pen as it scratched its way across the page, 'if she was a four-year-old, you'd tell her not to be such a baby and to brush her own hair and button her own clothes. She don't even fasten her own shoes, let alone find and trim her own hat.' *Scratch, scratch, scratch.* 'And *I* have to dart about, seeing to all of that before I can even make a *start* doing her room.' *Scratch.* 'And then, once luncheon's over and done with, the whole rigmarole starts all over again. More clothes, more shoes. More tidying up. And don't get me started on changing for dinner.'

Sitting back in the chair and glancing over the page, Edith set her pen on the blotter. 'Kate, I won't naysay it, but such is the way of these things. Whenever you're feeling hard done-by, just be grateful that nobody has yet worked out how to get more than four-and-twenty hours' work out of you each day.'

'Huh, if anyone ever does, it'll be Naomi Russell – you can bet your last farthing on it.'

'And another thing,' Edith said, tucking a strand of her light-brown hair behind her ear and glancing in Kate's direction, 'you'd be well advised not to let Ma hear you moaning again.'

'*Again?*'

Patting her cap, Edith returned her attention to her ledger. 'Yes, *again*. Ever since Miss Russell picked you out to be her maid, you've done nothin' but complain. We're all of us in the same boat, you know. And Ma does so hate it when you whine.'

'I *do not* whine.'

'I beg to differ. Anyway, just don't.'

Unfortunately for Kate, Mabel Bratton chose that very moment to reappear, her expression sharpening as she took in Kate's presence. 'Those new menus ready, Edith?'

'Near-on, Ma.'

'And you, Kate, what are you doing in here?'

Unfolding her arms, Kate straightened herself up. 'Nothing, Ma.'

'That much I can see with my own eyes. What I *don't* understand, is *why*. If you've taken care of everything for Miss Naomi, I'll put you to work elsewhere. We're already stretched as thin as can be, without you skiving.'

'I'm not skiving, I'm catching my breath.'

'Well, don't.'

Remembering then why she was there in the first place, Kate sighed. 'I've come to fetch some thread. She's got a loose button on one of her skirts.'

'*She?*'

'Miss Naomi.'

'Then get yourself along to the haberdashery cabinet and find what you need. And then go back upstairs and get it sorted.'

'Yes, Ma.'

'And just make a proper job of it. I don't want to hear complaints about slip-shod stitching.'

'No, Ma.'

'And stop bending your sister's ear about life being unfair. It *is* unfair, so there's no point wasting neither your breath nor your time bemoaning the fact.'

'No, Ma.'

'Very well. Now go on with you. And don't let me see you back down here this side of staff dinner.'

'No, Ma, I won't.'

Well, it was plain, then, Kate reflected as she made her way along the corridor to the linen closet: she was to get no sympathy for her plight

– not from her mother nor from her sister. She was stuck: doomed to spend the entire summer scurrying about after the privileged Miss Naomi Russell, the prospect of which was beginning to give her a very bad feeling indeed.

'Cicely, darling, you made it! Come in, come in. You must be exhausted.'

Hearing commotion in the hallway, Kate edged along the landing and peered over the bannisters. Clearly, the Colbornes had arrived. Having spent the last twenty minutes helping Miss Naomi with her afternoon change, she'd quite lost track of the time – not that the arrival of another set of guests made any difference to *her*.

'Thank you, my dear. Yes, travel these days is so wearying, isn't it?'

'Dreadfully. But a freshen-up and a nice cup of Darjeeling will soon have you feeling better. Or would you prefer Ceylon?'

Unable to hear the female guest's reply, Kate switched her attention to the older man arriving behind her – presumably, Cicely Colborne's husband.

'I say, Pamela, what the deuce are you trying to do to us with that devilish pot-holed track? Eh? Jolt us to death? Damn near broke the Mercedes! And I've not long had her–'

Either ignoring – or else oblivious to – the man's grievance, Pamela Russell greeted him warmly. 'Ralph! How lovely it is to see you.'

'–went for the *limousine* coachwork this time,' he continued, while at the same time submitting to an embrace. 'Pleased Cicely no end, no need for her to wear a dustcoat, what? She never did take to the *landaulet,* fine motor though she was.'

'Wonderful.'

'Must say, you're looking lovely, m'dear. Scarcely a moment older than the day we saw you wed that opportunist feller of yours. *Haw haw haw.*'

'How kind of you to say so, Ralph. And yes, that last stretch of road is frightful, isn't it? Still, you're here now. Did you drive yourself?'

'Drove the first stint out of Wiltshire, then the boys took it in turns. Trouble is, they only know one speed – flat-out, especially Aubrey. Lead-footed, the pair of them. Kept reminding them it's thruppence a gallon for motor spirit, you know. But do they care?'

'Aubrey! Lawrence!' Pamela Russell moved quickly on. 'Tell me you're not both still growing taller.'

Kate craned further over the bannister. All she could see, though, were the tops of heads. Or, more accurately, a squat and rather plain navy hat, a man's pink scalp showing through thinning grey strands, and two almost identical heads of dark, oiled hair.

'Aunt Pamela.'

'Aubrey, dear. Handsome as always.'

'Aunt Pamela.'

'Lawrence, what a fine man you've grown into. But please, both of you, do stop calling me *Aunt.* It was one thing when you were children but now you just make me sound so terribly old!'

When Kate realized that the next voice was her mother's – there following a discussion about luggage and the possibility of *young men to see to*

36

it – she decided it was time to retreat back along the landing. Arriving at Miss Naomi's room, she tapped on the door, but when, thinking Miss Naomi downstairs, she opened it without first awaiting an answer, she was surprised to see her seated at the dressing-table.

'Oh, begging your pardon, miss,' she hastened to apologize. 'I thought ... you were downstairs. I'm just returning your shoes after cleaning them.'

'Do you think this dress needs a necklace at the throat?'

Caught off-guard, and in any event still unused to being addressed quite so directly, Kate hesitated. But then, after crossing the room to place the shoes on the shelf in the bottom of the wardrobe, she turned her attention to the neckline of Naomi Russell's dress. 'Um...'

'As you correctly surmised, I did go downstairs. But I caught sight of myself in that mirror in the hall. I look ... *unfinished*.'

Unable to offer a meaningful opinion, Kate frowned. If there was one thing she had learned over the last couple of days, it was that, no matter the subject, mild agreement usually did no harm. 'Perhaps a little unfinished, yes, miss.'

'Then I'll wear my cross and chain. The small plain one. See if you can find it in my jewellery-box, will you?'

On the dressing table – a matter of just three or four inches from Naomi's left hand, Kate noted resentfully – was a large box covered in a striking skin. 'In here, miss?'

'Yes. And do chivvy along. The Colbornes will be here any minute and Mamma will be cross if

I'm not there with her to welcome them.'

Despite Naomi Russell's instruction, Kate hesitated. Should she mention that the Colbornes had already arrived? No, it might be safer to affect ignorance, especially given that she shouldn't have been spying on them in the first place. Instead, reaching to the jewellery-box, she turned the tiny key in the lock and, when she felt it click, raised back the lid. Inside, the lining was a luxurious cream-coloured velvet, the hinges of highly polished brass. Moving to lift aside what she thought was one of two trays sitting immediately beneath the lid, she discovered that in fact, the box had three tiers, the top two of which pulled aside on little brass arms to reveal the contents underneath. With jewels of all colours sparkling, and gold and silver glistening, Kate gave a little gasp. She'd never seen anything like it – neither the box nor its contents. 'Heavens,' she murmured.

'Beautiful, isn't it? It's crocodile skin. Mamma gave it to me when I turned twenty-one last month.' *Twenty-one:* she and Miss Naomi were the same age. Not that a casual observer would ever guess, Naomi Russell's elegance making her seem far womanlier – far more *finished*. Indeed, comparison served only to draw attention to the gracelessness of her own ways – to the gawky servant-girl she truly was. 'Inside, there was a diamond tiara from Papa, but of course, I left *that* safely at home.'

'Of course, miss.' A tiara. With diamonds in it. For a birthday present. Whatever next?

'For *his* birthday, Ned had a diamond signet-ring and a gold wristwatch. He brought the wristwatch with him. In fact, since he got it, I think he's barely taken it off.'

Kate smiled, her eyes scanning the glittering mass of jewellery for the shape of a cross. 'Which of you is the elder, miss?'

'I am. By about half an hour.'

She blinked rapidly. 'Begging your pardon, ma'am, but you're twins?'

'We are. I thought you knew. First set in the family, apparently.'

Astonished, she continued to stare into the box, eventually spotting a tiny gold cross on a chain. Carefully, she lifted it out. 'Would this be the one, miss?'

Turning her attention from her reflection in the mirror to Kate's palm, Naomi Russell nodded. 'That's the one. Put it about my neck for me and then I really must get back downstairs.'

Closing the tiny fastener, Kate stood back. No wonder it had been hard to tell which of Miss Naomi and Mr Edwin was the elder: they were the same age. She must try to get a better look at Ned, as Miss Naomi called him, to see just how similar – or different – they were.

With Naomi Russell leaving to go downstairs, Kate's eyes once again fell on the jewellery-box. A narrow slit in the cushioning along the top tier held a couple of rings: one, a tiny engraved band; the other a pale stone in a simple setting. Both looked quite old-fashioned and not the sort of thing she imagined Miss Naomi would have chosen for herself. Perhaps they had been a gift. Or, maybe, they had been passed down to her. In another section were earrings, some plain, some set with stones whose facets reflected the light. In the tier beneath were bracelets: one, a chain adorned with charms, another set with tiny pearls, and a couple that were heavily engraved silver bangles. Carefully, she lifted out the one with the inscription inside. Rotating it against the light, she read: *Min, with love from Ned.* Min? Presumably it was his pet-name for her. Was it nice to have a brother, she wondered? The bangle told her that perhaps, sometimes, it was. Was it nice to have a twin? Having never known any twins, it was hard to say. Was it any different from having any other sibling? Possibly – not that she was in a position to judge. With her own sister being so much older, she'd often felt as though she was an only child. At times, she'd felt jealous when the children at school talked of games they played at home; games weren't something you played with a sister who was sixteen years your senior. She often wished she'd known her father, too. Just this last birthday, she'd remarked to Edie that she wished she remembered something about him, to which Edie had replied – somewhat tersely, even by her standards – that the past was best left in the past. It hadn't been the response she'd been expecting, especially since Ma always maintained that he had been a good and kind man: *my lovely Thomas,* she called him.

Realizing that she still had hold of the bangle, she carefully laid it back where she had found it. Funny things, families.

Staring down at the jewellery box, she sighed. In the very bottom, she could see a leather pouch with gold lettering that read *Chatteris & Co.*

Reaching in to run her fingers over the surface of it, she fancied she could feel the raised shapes of something within – pearls, maybe? She flushed hot. She shouldn't be doing this; it was unforgivable. Quickly, she eased the hinged tiers back into place, lowered the lid and turned the key. Then she glanced about the room. Thankfully, she had tidied up earlier, in which case, she might go and see what she could learn about the new arrivals. She'd heard from one of the day girls that the room adjacent to Mrs Russell's had been prepared, along with the 'bachelor twin' on the opposite landing.

Turning the door handle, she peered out. From one of the rooms along the corridor she could hear a conversation going on: Mrs Russell's voice, clipped and precise, followed by the softer tones of an older female. Checking back to the left, she crept towards it.

'Quite a worry, isn't it?' she heard Pamela Russell saying. From the sound of it, she was in her sitting room.

'I am afraid, my dear, that with each year that passes, the circle grows ever smaller. Not *so* very long ago, one could be confident of the season throwing up a suitable match – one barely had to intervene. Nowadays, there are as many daughters of new money as old. Don't misunderstand me, Pamela, some of them aren't too far wide of the mark, what they lack in breeding made up for by a certain eagerness to *fit in,* or *do it right.* But I do miss the days when one didn't have to worry that one's offspring might *marry out.'*

'Indeed,' Kate heard Pamela Russell agree. 'As

41

I said to Mamma last time I saw her–'

'And how is Alice? Quite well, I hope?'

'Frail in body but perfectly sound of mind. Definitely not losing her hearing.'

'I said to Ralph only the other day, we should go up to town and pay a visit.'

'I'm sure she'd love to see you. I'll ask her to write.'

'Lovely.'

'Anyway, as I said to her quite recently, Naomi's line might only be old family on *my* side, but she more than makes up for it with her generous trust. Between you and me, Cicely, I've had to fend off more than one fortune-hunter since she's become of age.'

'She's not yet spoken for, then? I said to Ralph on the way down that I didn't think she was.'

Without warning, beneath Kate's weight a floorboard creaked. Brought sharply to her senses, she straightened herself up. Once again, she was doing something she shouldn't. And so, pivoting on one foot, she turned about and, holding her breath, crept quickly towards the back stairs. She really had to stop taking chances; it wasn't as though she possessed nine lives. And while, in some ways, it would be a blessing to be removed from waiting upon the tedious Naomi Russell, she could do without the fuss and recriminations that would surely follow. The Colbornes might *sound* interesting but they weren't worth getting into a scrape over. And anyway, with the whole summer stretching wearisomely ahead of her, there would be plenty of chances yet to learn all about them. At least that was one entertainment available to her: piecing together what she could about the family's various guests, especially since it seemed that if Mrs Russell and Mrs Colborne had anything to do with it, for Miss Naomi Russell, matchmaking and romance were on the cards.

'Such a desperate fuss, isn't it?'

Fastening the button at the waist of Miss Naomi's skirt, Kate nodded her agreement. 'Yes, miss.'

'I fully understand that standards have to be upheld, especially where the entertaining of guests is concerned, but the Colbornes are hardly nobility.'

'No, miss.'

'They might have a sprawling country estate but, according to Papa, it's *centuries* since they were anything of note.'

Running her eyes down the back of Miss Naomi's outfit Kate bent to tweak a section of the hem into place and then, taking a step backwards, watched as Naomi examined her reflection in the cheval mirror. 'Yes, miss.'

'So, I ask you, what's wrong with donning a gown before luncheon – especially in *this* weather?'

Aware that Miss Naomi could see her in the mirror, Kate responded with the smallest of shrugs. 'I don't know, miss.' And she didn't, either. The constant round of changing outfits had her baffled – and more than a little exasperated. As far as she could see, the many changes of attire in the course of a single day were designed solely to make more work for the unfortunate lady's maid.

'Neither do I, Kate. But yesterday, Mamma was

most disapproving of my frock.'

'Yes, miss.'

'You know, apparently, we're related.'

To this, Kate frowned; who was related? In the few seconds she'd allowed her thoughts to wander, she'd completely lost track of Miss Naomi's train of thought. 'Beg your pardon, miss?'

'Mamma's family is a branch of the Colbornes. Don't ask me how. She did explain it to me once – possibly that day we came across them at a gala. What I *do* remember, is coming quite literally face to face with their two boys and how, when one of them pinched my arm and I squealed in pain, *I* was the one to suffer a reprimand, while *they* went unpunished.'

With a smile, Kate shook her head. 'That's boys for you, miss. They get away with far more than a girl ever could.'

When Naomi Russell turned to regard her, Kate blushed. Clearly, it was too late now to remember to curb her tongue. According to her mother, speaking plainly – or, to her own way of looking at it, simply saying things as she saw them – would one day be the death of her. And yet, apparently, so would lying. No wonder she struggled to find a middle-ground. Well, if her impertinence had just landed her in trouble, there was nothing she could do about it now. With a bit of luck, Naomi Russell would be deeply offended and change her mind about her suitability as a lady's maid.

'I couldn't agree with you more.'

Slowly, Kate raised her eyes. Was she not to get a dressing down? 'Miss?'

'You're right, Kate – boys get away with murder. A single peep from a girl and it's *unseemly*. Two boys getting into fisticuffs, however, well, that's just *high spirits.*'

Pressing her lips together, Kate fought back a laugh; yes, that was about the measure of it. 'I know, miss,' she ventured, relieved that she wasn't in trouble. Nevertheless, deciding to busy herself, she crossed to the bed and picked up the two skirts rejected earlier by Naomi as being 'too warm for a day like this'. Draping one of them over her arm, she gave the other a sharp shake and examined it for creases.

'Do *you* have brothers, Kate?'

Standing in front of the walnut armoire, Kate scanned the hanging rail for either of the skirts' matching jackets. Spotting one of them, she hung the skirt alongside it.

'I *did,* miss. But he put out in the lifeboat one day to rescue a pleasure yacht in difficulties off the headland, and didn't come back.'

From the corner of her eye, Kate saw Naomi Russell's fingers fly to her lips.

'Goodness. I'm so dreadfully sorry. How awful for you.'

Running her hand over the second skirt, Kate shrugged. 'I never knew him, miss. He was a few years older than Edith and still short of nineteen when he died. I suppose by now, he'd be going on forty.'

'All the same, what a loss for your parents.'

'Yes, miss.'

'A life taken so young. And taken while trying to save others, too. Doubly cruel.'

45

Beginning to wish she'd never mentioned it, Kate glanced about the room. 'Will there be anythin' else you need, miss?'

'What? Oh, no, not for the moment. I was thinking of taking *The Lady* and going to sit on the seat under that big tree on the lawn. It was lovely and shady there yesterday afternoon. Only trouble was, no sooner had I sat down than Aubrey Colborne descended upon me like a wasp upon a fallen apple.'

The aptness of the picture made Kate smile. Although she'd only seen Aubrey Colborne in passing, he did seem to be one of those people who, wherever you went, was always there. 'Is he not pleasant company, miss?'

'Not really. Although to be fair, I barely know the man.'

'Then it was rude of him to press himself upon you like that, especially since you were alone.'

Naomi Russell smiled. 'It wasn't so much the impropriety I objected to, after all, we *were* in full view of the house. It was rather that he seemed overly eager. You know – eager to impress.' *Eager.* To Kate's mind, Miss Naomi could be describing almost any member of the opposite sex, her own Luke Channer included. 'Far too presumptuous.'

'Oh.'

'*Entitled.*'

'Oh.'

'But men are like that, don't you think? They see something they want, put their head down and *whoosh,* they go straight for it, caring little for the consequences.'

Again, to Kate's mind, Miss Naomi could be

describing Luke. 'They do seem that way inclined, yes, miss. I suppose it's how they're made. They're different to us, aren't they?'

'They most certainly are. Take Papa, when it comes to business, he's utterly single-minded – ruthless, some might say. Although, as he's always impressing upon Ned, when you start out with nothing, even becoming just moderately successful requires every ounce of one's wit and determination And he should know, from the humblest of beginnings, he's become one of the largest merchants in all of London, perhaps the whole of England.'

'Goodness.'

'*Goodness,* Kate, doesn't even *begin* to describe it. What you wouldn't know, is that *his* father was a barrow-boy.' When Kate's eyes widened in astonishment, Naomi Russell gave her a wry smile. 'It's true. At the age of twelve, my grandfather, Stanley Russell, was selling tobacco on street corners. But, unlike most boys with a few coins burning a hole in their pockets, he scrimped and saved until he had enough to acquire his first barrow. Spurred by that success, he saved for another and then another until he had a dozen or more. Then, not long after he married, he gambled everything, which, I will admit, can't have amounted to a very great deal. Nevertheless, gamble he did to take on a warehouse on the Thames. And his gamble was handsomely rewarded, because eventually, he did well enough to send Papa away to school – a good school. It was Papa, though, who had the foresight to expand into more than just tobacco.'

Kate hesitated. Miss Naomi's story might be

captivating, but something about standing there listening to it felt entirely wrong – worse, some-how, than had she been eavesdropping. 'Forgive me, Miss Naomi,' she said, turning back towards the dressing-table. 'I'm keeping you from your business.'

'Fear not. I'm not spilling the family secrets. Papa doesn't mind in the least who knows of his humble beginnings. Says a self-made man has more character, spirit and integrity than any of those born with silver spoons in their mouths.'

Her concern easing a little, Kate smiled. 'Happen he's not wrong, miss.'

'Kate, when it comes to people or business, he rarely is. Which is why someone as apparently spineless as Mr Aubrey Colborne will never suc-ceed in endearing himself to me, no matter how smoothly he tries.'

'No, miss.'

'And that being the case, I think I *shall* go and sit under the tree to read.'

'Good for you, miss. And if Mr Aubrey bothers you again, scrub him off.'

'I beg your pardon? Scrub him off?'

'Yes. You know, give him short shrift.'

'Short shrift.'

'Yes, miss. In my experience, anything other than plain-speaking is wasted on a man who wants something he shouldn't.' When Naomi Russell raised an eyebrow, Kate looked quickly down.

'Oh yes? Sounds interesting. Do tell.'

Acutely aware that her cheeks were burning, Kate raised her head only the merest fraction.

'Nothing to tell, miss.'

'Hmm. Somehow, I don't believe you. Anyway, you're right, I *should* tell him plainly. Unfortunately, since he's our guest, delicacy and tact are called for.'

'I suppose it's not done to speak plainly to your guests.'

'No matter how much one might wish to, no, it isn't. Mamma would never forgive me – certainly not *this* early in the holiday.'

When, with a smile, Naomi Russell left the room, her magazine in one hand and her hat in the other, Kate let out a long sigh. Then, in dismay, she glanced about. Weighed against other roles in the house, the job of a lady's maid sounded so genteel – and, perhaps, in a household with more staff it was – and yet, in her own situation, all it meant was that she had two lots of work to do and two masters to please. The only apparent upside she could see in this world of downs was that perhaps Naomi Russell wasn't *quite* as bad as she'd first supposed. Kept on the right side of, she might even prove to be the source of some interesting tales.

Indeed, after luncheon that same day, while assisting Miss Naomi to change into her afternoon frock, Kate found the young woman still in chatty mood.

'I told him that I was reading. And that I had been enjoying the peace and quiet.'

'But he still wouldn't leave you be,' Kate surmised.

'He would not. Although he did at least stop talking.'

'That's *something*,' Kate acknowledged, offering the sash about Naomi Russell's waist and proceeding to fashion the ends into a bow in the small of her back.

'I suppose. Although, even once he fell silent, his presence still felt intrusive. I began to imagine I could *feel* him looking at me.'

'Oh dear.'

'And *then*, when I got up to leave, he had the temerity to accompany me back indoors.'

'Quite the limpet, miss.'

'Limpet?'

'You know, them pointed shells that cling to the rocks on the beach.'

Fastening a bracelet about her wrist, Naomi Russell turned to look over her shoulder. 'Like barnacles?'

'Similar, miss, yes.'

'You know, I rather fancy he has ideas.'

Setting Miss Naomi's shoes on the floor, Kate frowned.

'Ideas, miss?'

Waiting while she slipped her feet into her shoes, Kate bent to button the narrow straps.

'Designs. Schemes. Call them what you will, but I do believe he has marriage on his mind.'

The shoes fastened, Kate got to her feet. 'Ah.'

'Precisely. But then I suppose at twenty-five years old, he would have. And Mamma certainly hasn't been slow to coo over his eligibility – her mind fastened tightly upon the fact that he's heir to Avingham Park.'

'But you're not keen on him.'

'I'm afraid I am not, no. Call me a romantic

50

but, since marriage is *till death do us part,* I should rather like the man I marry to move me. That's not unreasonable, is it?'

Kate shook her head; it didn't seem an unreasonable wish for any woman. 'Not at all, miss, no.'

'The poor soul needn't be so dashing as to rob me of my ability to think. Although, naturally, it wouldn't hurt. No. But, when all a woman has to look forward to is being a wife and a mother, surely one's husband ought to stir some sort of desire in her, oughtn't he? Or am I just being a silly schoolgirl, pining for Prince Charming to come and sweep me off my feet?'

For a moment, Kate didn't reply. *Till death do us part.* It was a scarily long time, which surely made it even more important to marry the right man for the right reasons. But just what were those reasons? And how did you know if he was the right man? Whatever your station in life, the question must surely remain: how did you know? Interestingly, with Miss Naomi mentioning desire, the picture that had come rushing into her mind was Luke, his mouth wide with that devilish grin of his and the look in his eyes suggesting he was bent on mischief. That he was handsome, she wouldn't deny; that she desired him, likewise. But was he the right man for her? Perhaps she could admit to Miss Naomi that they shared the same concerns. Perhaps it would help both of them to know they weren't alone in their quandaries. Hesitantly, she looked across at her. Leaning towards the mirror, reapplying the colour to her lips, at that precise moment Naomi Russell looked like a creature

51

from a different race: elegant; assured; clear headed. But definitely not one with whom she, a domestic, could share a confidence.

And so, with a sense of regret, the reply for which she settled was, 'No, miss, I don't think you're being silly.'

When Naomi turned towards her, it was with a thoughtful look on her face. 'Do you know, I find the fact that you are prepared to be frank with me rather refreshing.'

Taken by surprise, Kate frowned. Be frank with her? She'd thought only that she'd been truthful. 'Miss?'

'At home, in Clarence Square, my lady's maid, Wilson, lacks even a single ounce of humour. Although barely two years older than I am, the poor girl displays neither humour nor character. Frightfully good at her job but so terribly, terribly dull. Not the sort of person in whom I could ever confide. But with you, I feel entirely at ease sharing what's on my mind. Indeed, I find it hard to believe that we've only just met, I feel as though I've known you for years.'

Astounded to receive such a compliment – at least, she trusted it was a compliment – Kate beamed with delight. 'Thank you, miss.'

'And so, since, on the matter of Aubrey Colborne and his advances, we seem to be of the same mind, I have a favour to ask of you.'

'A favour, miss?' *Now* what had she let herself in for?

'No need to baulk,' Naomi said, clearly reading her expression. 'It's nothing too onerous, simply that should I one day announce to you that I've accepted a proposal of marriage from him, please lock me in this room and do whatever proves necessary to make me see sense.'

The thought of doing any such thing made Kate laugh out loud. 'Very well, miss,' she said, not even trying to control her laughter. '*Should* such a thing come about – I promise to bar the door until you agree *not* to become Mrs Aubrey Colborne.'

'Trust me, Kate, I might appear to be making light of it *now*, but, should the situation arise, I will forever be in your debt. And, while we're on the subject of marrying unsuitable men, is there anything into which *I* should prevent *you* from rushing headlong?'

Watching Naomi Russell fold a handkerchief and tuck it into her sleeve, Kate pressed her lips together in thought. As she had just that moment been reflecting, it was a good question – and one for which she never could settle upon an answer. But then, remembering Luke's constant harping about her unwillingness to commit to a date for their wedding, with a shake of her head, she said, 'No, Miss Naomi, I do not believe myself to be in danger of rushing into anything at all.'

'Glad to hear it. Right then, I'm off to keep company with Mamma and the terribly tedious Cicely Colborne. Do you know, over luncheon today, she announced that she has a *sampler* I might like to stitch!'

Kate grinned. 'Lucky you.'

'Indeed. Right, see you at the dinner-gong, then.'

'Yes, miss. See you at the gong.'

53

'Just come to say I'm done for the night.' Arriving to lean heavily in the doorway, Kate looked across to where her mother was locking the drawer to her desk. 'Very well, love.'

'Miss Naomi has retired and says she won't want anything again now until morning. That being so, I'd thought to go out for a breath or two of air afore I go up.'

'All right. Just make sure to turn the key when you come back in. And don't be gone too long – you were moaning earlier about being worn out.'

Recalling having said as much, Kate nodded. 'I was. I am.'

'Then in light of that, it might please you to learn that I've given thought to your complaint.'

Having started to turn away, Kate turned back. 'My complaint?' *To which one was her mother referring?*

'About how you can't see your way to doing two jobs–'

'Oh.'

'–and I've decided to ask Mary Bowden whether she wants to come up and help out. I doubt you'll remember her but she used to attend to the young Misses Latimer whenever they came to stay – before she stopped working to look after her mother, that is. But, with her mother passing over last year, she might be glad of the money. And she was always presentable and meticulous.'

What, unlike me, Kate found herself thinking. 'No,' she said quickly. 'It's all right.' Had Ma been proposing to offer Mary Bowden her *house-maid's* duties, it might have been different. But, with Miss Naomi having just started to take her into her confidence and share her thoughts, she had begun to feel differently about the task of attending to her – not that she would ever admit as much, especially not to either Edith or Ma. 'It's like you said,' she added, desperate not to appear overly eager, 'we're all of us stretched thin. So, why don't we see how it goes along? Happen I'll manage.'

Too late, she spotted the faintest of curls on her mother's lips. 'Very well. I'll leave it be for now – if you're certain.'

'In so far as I *can* be after just a few days,' she said, unable to backtrack now, even though, clearly, she had just fallen headlong into her mother's trap. Now, she would no longer be able to complain about the nature of her duties nor the hours needed to keep on top of them. Through being hasty to respond, she had seen to it that from now on, she would have no choice but to just get on with it all. *Clever, Ma. Very clever.*

Yes, all she could do now was hope that Miss Naomi's manner would continue to soften and that she wasn't mistaken about the unlikely alliance that seemed to have begun to develop between them – an alliance she found herself unexpectedly keen to foster.

Chapter Two

Kinships

It was hard to believe they were adults. After little more than a finger of whisky or a couple of cocktails, they took to acting like children. Although, to be fair, when it came to making drinks, Mrs Russell's idea of what constituted a measure of a spirit did seem on the generous side. Perhaps, in light of that, it wasn't surprising that the only person who still seemed sober was Cicely Colborne, her half-glass of Stone's ginger wine still largely untouched. Her husband certainly wasn't holding back, the rapidly falling level of whisky in the decanter in no small part down to him. Perhaps he thought that by replacing it in the tantalus every time he refreshed his tumbler, no one would notice. Or perhaps Pamela Russell didn't mind how quickly her guests rattled through the contents of the drinks cabinet. After all, she herself was hardly ever without a full glass in her hand.

Having been standing for some time, peering into the drawing room through the crack between the frame and its partly open door, Kate shifted her weight. For once, she didn't have anywhere else to be – not that that, by itself, was an excuse for spying upon the family and their guests. Indeed, feeling a draught around the back of her neck, she glanced quickly over her shoulder.

There was no one there. There wouldn't be: Mrs Russell had already dismissed the staff for the night. Even Ma had locked the door to her office and gone upstairs.

Squinting across the hall to the dreaded long-case clock, Kate read from its disapproving face that it was five-and-twenty to eleven – still early by most standards. It was certainly early according to Mrs Russell, now apparently proposing they all play a game.

'Yes,' she was saying as she glanced about the room, 'all we need is a blindfold and a cushion – Aubrey, pass me that large one from the sofa. Come on, it will be fun.'

As far as Kate could see, the prospect of whatever Mrs Russell was proposing was dividing opinion. A few of her guests – although perhaps more from a sense of politeness than genuine eagerness – were getting to their feet. Others were groaning and waving her away.

'I'll go first, Aunt Pamela.'

Blinking to refocus her eyes, Kate studied Aubrey Colborne as he removed his jacket and hung it over the back of a nearby chair. She had learnt from Miss Naomi that he was the elder of the two brothers. But, he was also the shorter and, looking at him now, she just *knew* it was something that irked him. She had already noticed that when he strode about, he puffed out his chest like a turkey, as though doing so somehow made up for his lack of any real stature .Yes, he definitely begrudged his younger brother that extra little bit of height. In addition to which, there was the way that, as he stood conversing with someone, he

57

repeatedly smoothed his hand back over his hair – another habit that didn't endear him to her, either. In *her* eyes, it served only to make him look shallow and vain.

She returned her attention to Mrs Russell. She was cajoling the remaining men, urging them up from their comfy positions on the sofas to fetch Mrs Latimer's ladder-back chairs from the corners of the room and arrange them in the centre. Pointing towards the rugs, she twirled about, inscribing an imaginary circle with her hand as she went. The chairs duly arranged, Mrs Russell made minute adjustments to their positions. At last, evidently satisfied, she stood back and surveyed the scene, giving Kate the opportunity to study her appearance. Dressed in a satiny fabric that wrapped across her front and then fell in soft folds to gather about her ankles, she looked like one of the fashion plates from Miss Naomi's latest magazine – one from the section entitled *In the Oriental Style*. Earlier, a furtive flick through its pages had revealed such unorthodox outfits to be the 'audacious designs' of a French couturier called Paul Poiret; his daring garments hailed by the publication as being 'the latest thing'.

Held in place by a wide sash at her waist, Mrs Russell's outfit looked more suited to her bedroom than the drawing room; indeed, were any other woman to don such a simple gown, she would look as though preparing to retire for the night. Somehow, though, with her jaw-length wavy hair partly concealed under a *bandeau* of the same fabric, Pamela Russell carried it off. To be fair, she did *more* than carry it off; she wore it with

58

style. With her languid movements and devil-may-care attitude, not only did she make it seem perfectly acceptable, she made the gown of every other woman in the room look stuffy and prim – as though designed for approval by the late Queen Victoria herself. Even the colour of the material was eye-catching: dark enough to appear black, when it moved beneath the lamplight, it shimmered the deepest of blues. Indigo. No, *midnight*.

'Now, everyone. Do hurry up and take a seat. No, not back there, Ralph, here, in the circle, you ninny. You too, Cicely, come on. That's it, Naomi, good girl. Now, I just need something with which to blindfold Aubrey.' From around her neck, she unwound her silk scarf. 'This will do. Aubrey, be a dear and stand still.'

In the half-light of the hallway, Kate shook her head in disbelief. With Aubrey now blindfolded, Pamela Russell placed the cushion in his hands and then whispered something into his ear. Pressing on his shoulders, she spun him first in one direction and then back in the other.

Unsteadily, Aubrey Colborne edged his way out from the centre of the circle, quickly colliding with the legs of his brother, Lawrence. *For certain he was aiming for Miss Naomi*, Kate thought, watching him bend to place the cushion where he evidently imagined her lap to be. From the other participants came guffaws and titters of amusement.

'Shush!' someone urged.

Sitting squarely on his brother's lap, Aubrey gave the command, 'Squeak, piggy, squeak.'

With a perfectly straight face, Lawrence drew a

59

short breath and offered a plaintive, *'Squeeek?'*

From her vantage point, Kate saw a frown crease Aubrey's forehead. Clearly, that wasn't the response he had been expecting. 'Squeak, piggy, squeak,' he once again instructed.

'Squeeek.'

By now the room was in uproar and, with no desire to be discovered, Kate quickly pressed a hand to her mouth.

'I say, what's going on?'

Startled, she turned sharply about. Oh, dear Lord, Mr Edwin! Now she was for it. Quickly, she straightened up and directed her gaze over his shoulder. By chance, it landed on the clockface. Ten minutes before eleven. Not that it mattered.

There being little point trying to disguise what she had been doing, she cleared her throat and, at half her usual volume, said, 'A parlour game, sir.'

'Can you see which one? I shouldn't mind knowing which particular humiliation I'm about to let myself in for.'

Not the sort of response she had been expecting, she froze. 'Um...'

Deciding to look for himself, Ned Russell leant across to peer through Kate's spy-hole. 'Aha! Squeak, piggy, squeak, one of Mother's favourites. *Breaks the ice,* or so she'd have it.'

'Breaks the ice, sir?' In the circumstances, it seemed only polite to respond, especially since it was *he* who had addressed *her.*

'Yes, you know, gets people to relax and let down their guard – stops everyone standing about like stuffed shirts.'

'Stuffed shirts?' Fearing she was beginning to sound like a parrot, Kate hurried on. 'Forgive me, sir, but I don't understand.'

'Oh, yes, sorry – it was a favourite expression of one of my professors at college. It's used to describe someone who's stiff and starchy and entirely lacking in … well, in character or interest.'

With a polite smile, Kate nodded. 'Oh, I see.' Although Mr Edwin sounded reassuringly ordinary, she nevertheless felt it expedient to excuse herself and slip away. No sense in letting a harmless encounter end in trouble. 'Well, begging your pardon, sir, but I'd best be getting back along. I only came to–'

'–to see what all the commotion was?'

Was he sparing her embarrassment? Was he presenting her with an excuse for having been there when, clearly, there could have been none? If so, what a gentleman he was. 'Yes, sir,' she opted to agree. 'That I was.'

'Then please be assured that all is well. It is only Mamma trying to ensure that everyone enjoys themselves. Despite the shrieking, there is no cause for alarm.'

Carefully, she exhaled with relief. 'Thank you, sir.' But, just to be sure there was no chance of this misfortune catching up with her later on, she decided to risk making doubly certain of how things stood. To her mind, trouble was always best nipped in the bud, especially where her mother was concerned. 'That being the case, sir, might you be inclined to … *overlook* … that I was even here?'

Despite the murkiness of the hallway, she could

see a row of white teeth showing between parted lips.

'In this light, it would be hard to be certain that *anyone* was here – let alone speak as to their identity, even were it to be at the insistence of the local constabulary.'

He had a sense of humour, too. What luck! 'Then I bid you goodnight, sir.'

'And I you, *faint apparition*.'

Having scarcely dared to breathe throughout their entire exchange, when Kate turned to slip away along the corridor, she gulped with relief. What a perfectly polite and reasonable young man he seemed. And what a lovely soft voice he had – not in the least shrill, like his mother's.

Faint apparition. What a lovely thing to be called!

'Did you enjoy yourself last evening, miss?' It was the morning following Kate's encounter with Ned and, gripping Miss Naomi's breakfast tray tightly, she was negotiating her way between the pieces of furniture in the still darkened room

'It was certainly a long one,' Naomi Russell replied, raising herself up from beneath the bedcovers and stretching two pale arms above her head. 'Goodness, we were late to bed.'

With Naomi settled, Kate placed the tray across her lap, thinking rather belatedly to make a quick check of its contents. Cup, saucer, teaspoon. Milk jug, sugar bowl, strainer. Tea in the pot. Butter dish, marmalade, spoon, knife. Two lightly-boiled eggs. And, in the rack, toast with the crusts removed – the latter striking her as pitiful given that Miss Naomi was neither an infant nor an invalid.

'But you enjoyed yourself, miss?'

'It was mildly diverting, I suppose. Mamma's very good at getting people to join in, even when they don't really want to. Incidentally, I learned yesterday that in a couple of days, Aunt Diana will be down to stay. If you think Mamma is lively, wait until you meet her sister. She's incorrigible. When we were growing up, Ned and I always used to think she was the perfect aunt. She would show up at our schools and take us out for tea. And she would buy us lots of tuck to take back with us. Ned used to love her for that. I used to give a lot of mine away, but Ned, well, I remember him saying that despite trying every trick he could think of to stop himself eating it all at once, by the end of the next day he had always finished every last ounce of it. And then, of course, for ages afterwards, he would feel horribly sick.'

Watching Miss Naomi adjust her napkin, Kate smiled. And then, in the name of conversation, she asked, 'Was your school far from home, miss?'

'Not *very* far, no. We boarded in Kent.'

With no idea of where that was, Kate nodded. Moving across to the window to draw the curtains a little wider, and hearing Miss Naomi scraping butter across a piece of toast, she asked, 'Was it odd being apart from him?' She knew that by asking so many questions she was risking a reprimand but, ordinarily, guests of the Latimers were old people, usually well into their forties, not young and interesting like Miss Naomi and Mr Edwin. And that was another thing, having never met any twins before, she found herself intrigued. At least Miss Naomi seemed untroubled by her curiosity.

'It was rather odd, yes. The hardest part was that *he* went away first – the autumn after we turned eight – whereas *I* had to remain at home with a governess until I was eleven. He always came back so full of tales of the fun he'd had that I couldn't wait to be allowed to go away. It was horrible being left behind at the start of every new term.'

Turning back into the room and looking about, Kate went to the dressing table and started to tease the hair from the bristles of Miss Naomi's hairbrush. If she continued to tread carefully, there was no reason why she couldn't find out even more about these Russell children. The world they inhabited was certainly an unfamiliar one. 'And then Mr Edwin went to university,' she said to that end.

'He did, yes. Oxford. He didn't think he'd be accepted, but *I* knew he would be. He's terribly smart and dreadfully committed. Whatever he does, he gives it his all.'

Carefully placing the brush back on the vanity tray, Kate decided it safe to ask one last question. 'And what will he do now, miss?'

Naomi Russell dipped the corner of a triangle of buttered toast into her egg. 'He's supposed to be joining Papa's business. Naturally, it's been the plan all along. But I have to say–' Looking quickly to the door, Naomi Russell lowered her voice before going on to add, 'Between you and me, he's not that keen. On the other hand, neither does he wish to incur Papa's wrath, which he surely would were he to announce that he wanted to do something else. Either way, I've begged him not to upset either of our parents with the matter whilst we're down here. Mamma's talked of nothing but this holiday for months. I think she sees this as her last chance for us all to be together.'

'Yes, miss.'

'And she won't thank him for causing ructions. Although, with the way things are going, it might not be Ned who causes those. If Mamma keeps foisting Aubrey Colborne upon me, I might just raise a few of my own.'

'Yes, miss,' she agreed. The few snippets she had uncovered about the Russell children were fascinating but perhaps, before she could put her foot in it, she should withdraw. No sense over-stepping the mark when, generally, things were going along quite nicely. 'Well, if you will excuse me, miss,' she ventured to that end, 'I'll leave you to finish your breakfast in peace.'

'Very well. Incidentally, these eggs are delicious – just like those we used to have when I was finishing in Switzerland. They came from a little farm up the valley.'

'Glad you like them, miss. I'll tell Edith. And I'll be back in a while to help you dress.'

Slipping from the room, Kate closed the door behind her and stood for a moment in the corridor to reflect upon what she had just learned. For all of their apparent freedom, the Russell children seemed rather without purpose, neither of them having much idea of what they were going to do with their lives. Well, obviously, Miss Naomi would be getting married – and to Aubrey Colborne, if her mother had anything to do with it. Being pressed to marry was something they had in common. Beyond that single coincidence, though, two more different lives it was hard to imagine. Would she swap places with her? Not if, in doing so, she would be faced with having to marry Aubrey Colborne. No, thank you very much. If those were the terms, she would rather stay where she was. That aside, of course she would swap places. Offered the chance to become part of the Russell family, she would leave the drudgery of service in a heartbeat. And she doubted there was a maid in the land who wouldn't say the same.

'So, what're they like, then?'

It was later that same day and, having washed out the little squares of muslin Miss Naomi used to remove the cosmetic preparations from her face, Kate was pegging them to the clothes-line in the yard.

'Happen she's not as bad as I'd feared,' she replied to Luke's question.

'The daughter, you mean?'

'Miss Naomi, yes.'

Leaning against the wall of the laundry, he stared across at her.

'And the rest o' they?'

She shrugged. 'Very different folk from the Latimers, that's for sure.'

'Suppose they would be,' he acknowledged, 'the Latimers are gentry – this lot are just folk with money.'

'Mm.'

'Any rate, reckon you'll be free later to walk out with me?' Without even stopping to think, Kate

66

shook her head. 'Chance would be a fine thing.' Even as the words left her mouth, though, she felt mean. She was almost certain to have a few odd minutes to herself at *some* point. At least, she would if she was crafty. Yesterday, she'd realized that being Miss Naomi's lady's maid had an unforeseen upside: it wasn't always possible for Ma to know where she was or what she'd been asked to do. So, if she wanted to avoid being given more housekeeping duties, all she had to do was say that she was already engaged on a task for Miss Naomi. As long as she said it with conviction, Ma was unlikely to be any the wiser. But, where Luke was concerned, after their little spat the other day about getting wed, she didn't feel inclined to risk her ruse for *his* benefit.

Glancing up, she noticed that he was wearily shaking his head.

'Truthfully?' he said. 'You're that busy you can't even spare ten minutes to step out with me?'

Still feeling mean, she made her smile a deliberately warm one. 'Sorry,' she said, going across and slipping her arm about his waist. 'But this lady's maid business is never ending. If I thought I never had a still moment as a housemaid, I hadn't counted upon having to one day work for the likes of madam.'

He pulled her closer. 'Running you ragged, is she?'

Carefully, she disentangled herself. 'And then some.'

'All right. Well, happen you'll have some time tomorrow.'

Starting to move away from him, she nodded.

'With a fair wind, aye, who knows? But, right this moment, I'd best be getting back indoors – caught her heel in the hem of her skirt, didn't she? Wants it stitching, don't she?'

'Aye,' he said, the shake of his head a rueful one. 'And I'd best get back to pinching out the side-shoots on them tomatoes. Again.'

Watching him go through into the main yard, Kate felt a prickle of unease. She hadn't *lied* to him, not really. On the other hand, she hadn't been entirely truthful, either. She probably *would* have some free time later, it was just that she didn't really feel like spending it with *him*. If, later on – and at a loss as to know what else to do with herself – she had a change of heart, she could always seek him out. It wasn't as though he would be hard to find.

With a shake of her head, she turned towards the tradesman's porch. Once inside though, she was brought to a halt by something of a commotion in the kitchen corridor. After the dazzling brightness of the yard, she strained her eyes to make out a young woman with a small child tugging at her skirt. In her arms appeared to be a swaddled infant and, tearing back and forth over the same few yards of corridor, his bare feet slapping upon the stone floor, was a small boy.

She frowned. *Gypsies, again?*

'Stop that, Frankie,' a weary voice pleaded. 'Unless you be a-wanting another clout.'

Liddy Beer? Was that really Liddy Beer – or, as she had more properly become, Liddy Tucker? What on earth was *she* doing back at Woodicombe?

Squinting in disbelief, she went towards her. 'Liddy?' she ventured. 'Is that you?'

Swiftly, the young woman turned about. 'Saints alive! Kate! You're still here! I thought you'd be long since wed and gone.'

Before she knew it, and with no care for the fact that her sleeping baby was being squashed between the two of them, Liddy Tucker was giving her a one-armed hug, filling her nostrils with earthy aromas, with perspiration and the scent of milk.

Struggling to conceal her shock at Liddy's bedraggled appearance, she carefully extricated herself from their embrace. 'Whatever are *you* doing back here?' she asked.

In the days when she had been a housemaid, Liddy Beer had always been most particular about her looks, her light brown hair regularly washed, her complexion clear and her figure trim. Where was that fastidious girl *now?* What had happened to reduce her to this state of dishevelment? Her face was puffy, her eyes heavy, and her hair was in need of a good lathering with some *Castile* soap. To cap it all, the mean row of lace around the neckline of her greying blouse was coming unstitched. And if she *was* wearing a chemise beneath it, it had to be of the most threadbare and worn-through fabric imaginable.

'Frank Tucker, stop that this minute,' Liddy raised her voice in the direction of the little boy still charging up and down the corridor. 'Sorry about 'im,' she added with a hapless shrug. 'Never stops, that one. On the go from morn till night. Even a good strapping from his father don't slow 'im down.'

'And how is...' What on earth was the first name of that fellow Liddy had married? 'Charles?' Yes, that was it: she had gone from being in service at Woodicombe to marry Charles Tucker, a stitcher at the glove factory. Smitten with him, she'd been.

'Laid-off from Pilton's three weeks back, him an' half a dozen others. Factory manager said winter orders from the big shops in London have dried up. Don't make sense to *me*. Like Charlie said, gentry folk will always have need of kid gloves. Either way, end of his shift, he was out on his arse. Left with no choice but to try for odd jobs down at the harbourside. Trouble is, there's plenty of others doing the self-same thing. Even when he *is* lucky enough to get summat, 'tis just the one trip at a time; tedn't steady work. It's what brings *me* back up *here*.' Gesturing over her shoulder with her head, she went on, 'Young girl from the kitchen's gone off to find your Ma. I've come to see if she can see her way to giving me some work. I don't mind what I do, honest to God, put me to work in the kitchen, you won't get no complaint out of *me*. Maid-of-all-work? I'll make a good job of it.' Down at their feet, the second of Liddy's three children had begun to grizzle. 'For heaven's sake, hold your noise, Clementine. Carrying on like that won't do neither of us no good.'

Kate exhaled heavily. Did Liddy really think that Ma would give her a job? Had she not looked in a mirror lately? In that state, Ma would send her away with a flea in her ear. 'How old are your little ones?' she asked feeling guilty at the speed with which she had rushed to judgement.

'Frank turned three a month or so back, Clemmie will be two come September, and this one, well, truth to tell, I've lost track, what with the lack of sleep. Must be nigh-on ten weeks now, near as makes no odds.'

'Goodness.' It was the only thing Kate could think to say. Three children in four years. *Three.*

'Look, Kate,' Liddy lowered her voice to say, 'you remember how hard I used to work, don't you? Well, I ain't changed. An' I'll do anything, honest. Please, speak for me to your ma, will you?'

With much difficulty, Kate contained a sigh. What on earth did she say? 'You, as well as anyone, know how Ma can be,' she said softly, uneasy that Liddy should put her in such a position. 'No one was ever able to persuade her against her own mind. Least of all me.'

'*Please,* Kate. If Charlie don't chance upon some proper work soon, he's said he'll be left with no choice but to go over an' join the Devonshires an' go soldiering. And some folk do say there be a war coming. So please, I beg you, just remind her how hard I used to work. Not too much to ask of you, is it?'

'All right,' Kate said, trying to conceal her reluctance. 'I'll do my best.'

'God bless you, Kate. I shan't let you down, honest to goodness I shan't.'

'Liddy Tucker? Or do my eyes deceive me?'

With her mother now coming along the corridor towards them, Kate felt Liddy grasp her fingers and squeeze them tightly. 'Thanks ever so, Kate,' she whispered and then, turning away from her

71

and hitching her baby higher in her arms, rushed to say, 'No, Mrs Bratton, 'tis no mistake. It's me, all grown up and with three of my own now.'

Grown up or grown old, Kate wondered as she took the chance to slip away. Ducking out of sight into the still room, she stood shaking her head in dismay. Who would have thought that in the space of four short years, Liddy Beer, scarcely six months older than her and always the prettiest of the housemaids, could so quickly have lost her looks and ended up so worn-down and desperate?

Leaning against the stone bench, she shivered. While she wouldn't recognize Charlie Beer from Adam, word among the housemaids at the time had been that he was quite a catch, opinion being that by marrying him, Liddy was doing quite well for herself. He didn't come home covered in dung from a day spent labouring in the fields, nor did he go to sea and come back reeking of fish. He wasn't even in service; he'd had a job in a factory that came with the chance of one day being made up to overseer. But now, seemingly, he was forced to try his luck down at the harbour, presumably in the hope of helping out on one of the day-boats. But that wasn't even the worst of it. The worst of it was poor Liddy herself, who seemed to have slid into a state of slovenliness and been worn to shreds by the demands of three small children. What on earth sort of life was that for a woman of barely two-and-twenty years old? One she had to make good and sure of avoiding for herself, that's what it was.

'Yes, I had a most pleasant afternoon, thank you.'

72

It was later that same day, and Naomi Russell's reply was in response to what had, by now, become Kate's customary enquiry at that hour.

'That's good, miss.'

'Indeed,' Naomi went on to elaborate, 'it was made all the better for the fact that Aubrey took the Colbornes' motor and went exploring with Lawrence and Ned. For once, I was able to sit in peace. Well, until Mamma summoned me to take tea with her and Aunt Cicely. Honestly, you can see where Aubrey gets it from – his dreariness, I mean.'

Picking up the hairbrush, Kate began to draw it carefully through Miss Naomi's hair, her mind once again back on Liddy Tucker. Not surprisingly, Ma *hadn't* offered her a job.

'But what would you do with the little ones, dear?' she was reported by Aggie, one of the maids in the scullery, as having asked. To that, Liddy had been overheard to reply, 'Oh, they'll be all right in the stables a few hours at a time.' Shortly afterwards, Liddy had been seen leaving in tears.

Determining to stop thinking about Liddy and her plight – after all, she could do nothing for her – she snapped her attention back to the matter of Miss Naomi's hair. 'How would you like me to style it this evening, miss?' she enquired.

Turning her head this way and that, Naomi appeared unable to decide. What poor Liddy Tucker would give to have the styling of her hair as her only concern, Kate found herself thinking as, shifting her weight from one foot to the other, she waited for Naomi to make up her mind.

'To be honest, I'm not especially fussed,' Naomi Russell eventually replied, the accompanying wave of her hand an airy one. 'That said, one daren't risk displeasing Mamma with anything *too* casual. Pin it high, if you will. I've decided to wear the plum-coloured silk and it has rather a fussy neckline.'

'Yes, miss.'

'As gowns go, I find it rather matronly, which is a shame because it cost Papa a small fortune. So far, I've only worn it for Henley. Do you know the Henley Royal Regatta?' Understanding very little of Miss Naomi's question, Kate shook her head. Gowns. Hairstyles. Fortunes, small or otherwise: all a far cry from Liddy's plight and the likelihood of her husband now having to join the Devonshires. 'No, why would you?'

Yes, why would she? 'No, miss.'

'Well, simply put, it's rowing races on the Thames, with lots of spectators bobbing about in other little boats to watch. Although, to be fair, it's rather grander than I've just managed to make it sound. Anyway, after the races, there are balls to enjoy, hence the new gown. It was on account of Henley – well, *and* through Mamma deciding at the last minute to go for a week to Marienbad – that we couldn't travel down here any earlier. There's an hotelier in Henley with whom Papa does business and so, every year, he reserves rooms for us. In the days beforehand, there's always a tremendous fuss and sense of anticipation but, this year, the event itself turned out to be rather a let-down. One couldn't complain about the weather, that was perfect. But, almost to a man, the English rowing crews were beaten by foreigners. And the balls seemed more subdued than previous years, too. Papa said it probably had to do with how unsettled things have become since the assassination of that archduke and his wife. Apparently, it's almost certain to lead to war. Either way, I shan't mind if I don't go again.'

Go again? Presumably, Miss Naomi was referring to this Henley place, rather than to war. 'No, miss.'

Pinning the final strand of Naomi Russell's hair in place, Kate stood back. The evening sunshine slanting through the window was giving it an especially deep lustre.

'I do declare you're becoming quite proficient at this,' Naomi Russell remarked, angling her head to examine the finished effect. 'Easily as good as many of those women who do it for a living. Or the men, with their made-up French names and put-on accents.'

Kate smiled. It was rare for her to be complimented for her efforts. 'Thank you, miss. But it's easy with your hair. I'd be happy to get mine just to shine as nicely as yours, let alone to stay in place. Real lovely is how it looks in this light.'

Through the mirror, Naomi Russell looked back at her and then, lowering her voice to a conspiratorial whisper, said, 'I do have a little help. I use the same balsam by which Mamma swears. Don't ask me what's in it, but she gets it from an old-fashioned apothecary in Bond Street. It's terribly expensive. Thankfully, a little of it goes a long way.'

Having been hoping to learn that Miss Naomi

used something she could put to work on her own lacklustre strands, Kate gave a sigh of disappointment. How typical that only women of privilege got to have pretty locks.

'Well, it certainly does its job, miss. Worth every penny, I'd say.'

'It does, doesn't it? Although I have heard that rinsing with a little apple-cider vinegar can be just as efficacious.'

Effie-what? Presumably, that meant it was a good thing. 'Vinegar, miss?'

'Apparently so. One or two of the girls I finished with swore by it. Rather cheaper, too, I should imagine. *And* more easily come by.'

For a moment Kate stood, motionless. There was bound to be some vinegar in the pantry. Whether or not it was of the apple cider variety, she had no idea. But, if she waited until after the dinner-service, she could go and take a look. Even if she could only make her hair look *half* as shiny as Miss Naomi's, it would be an improvement. After all, no harm was ever had from looking nice.

And so, much later that evening, with the Russells and their guests gathered on the terrace to enjoy the sunset, and with the kitchens having fallen still for the day, Kate stole down to the pantry and stood scanning the shelves. There. *Sarson's:* that was vinegar. She reached for the bottle and peered through the glass at its contents, the decidedly murky shade of brown hardly reassuring. Well, it would have to do; if she dallied too long she risked getting caught and having her entire plan go awry. And anyway, surely even the wrong sort of vinegar was better than none at all?

As was later to become apparent, procuring the vinegar was merely the first obstacle in her path to shiny hair. The second, was where to go about her task such that she wouldn't be discovered, every bathroom on every landing having been assigned to a guest or guests. After much deliberating, the safest place seemed to be the sink in the laundry. With that decided – and having managed to cross the kitchen yard unseen – the next obstacle was a rather more vexatious one: what to actually do with the vinegar? Should she try and wash her hair with it? Rinse it with it? Rub it on and leave it to soak in? Resting against the edge of the sink, she stared at the bottle – not that the label was going to offer step-by-step instructions for the use *she* was about to put it to. She peered more closely at it anyway. Badly smudged, it appeared to offer advice only for *How to Make a Pickling Brine*. Not much help there, then.

In the end, dismayed and irritated by her lack of progress, she pressed the plug into the sink, turned on the tap and unpinned her plait. Watching the dribble of water creeping slowly up the side of the sink, and growing fed up with waiting, she bent her head directly under the tap. Gasping at the shocking cold of it, she immediately shot back up, striking her skull on the tap as she did so. Cursing loudly, she swung about to check that she was still alone.

Rubbing at the back of her head, she cursed afresh. So far, all she had to show for her trouble was a wet patch on the front of her skirt and a dull ache to the back of her head. Damn her impetuousness! Why couldn't she have thought this through properly and waited for a better opportunity to carry it out? Because patience wasn't one of her virtues, that was why. Never had been. Probably never would be.

Turning off the tap, she stared at the inch or so of water in the bottom of the sink. It would have to do. She had a clump of cold wet hair dripping on the floor and a damp skirt; she had to get on with it.

Doubling over the sink, she made the remainder of her hair as wet as she could. Then, reaching for the vinegar bottle, she undid the cap, the pungent fumes making her feel as though she was going to sneeze. *Well, here goes. Miss Naomi had better be right about this.*

Bent over the sink, she started to pour the liquid over the back of her head, feeling the chill of it trickling down her cheeks. Good job it was a big bottle, she thought, engulfed in a cloud of bitter fumes, because her hair seemed to be soaking it up. The bottle feeling almost empty, she set it on the side of the sink and ran her fingers down through her hair. With a crick in her neck and her eyes running, she could only hope that all the discomfort was going to be worth it.

When holding her head upside down became too uncomfortable to bear any longer, she reached about for the tap, turned it on and let the water run over her head. With no idea how much rinsing was required, she persisted for what felt to be several minutes. Then, finally, she wrung the water from her hair and, winding it into a rope, held it to the top of her head Careful this time to avoid the tap, she raised herself upright, felt about for her towel, and wrapped it about her wet hair. Now to make her way back upstairs without being seen.

Eventually, arriving back in her room, she stood puffing lightly. Stripping off her skirt and blouse, she hung them over the bedstead in the hope that they would dry of their own accord. Then, pulling open the top drawer of her chest, she gathered together her curling rags and laid them in a row.

The process of twisting her hair, rolling the lengths up to her scalp and then securing the ends of the rags was laborious and, quickly wearying of the task, she remembered why, some time back, she'd vowed not to bother with it any more. Having started, though, she now had to stick at it and, eventually, with the last section tied in place, she heaved a sigh of relief. Of course, now, on account of the knobbly lumps fastened to her head, she would probably have difficulty sleeping. Well, a few hours of slumber could be caught up on any old night, whereas nice hair was important; poor Liddy Tucker all too plain a reminder of what happened when you didn't look after yourself.

The following morning, dragging herself out of bed after a night of rather broken sleep, she drew back the curtain to find that it was a glorious day, dewy and fresh with clear skies that hinted at the prospect of a proper summer's day ahead. Not a single cloud threatened the unbroken blue of Mother Nature's ceiling, not a breath of breeze disturbed the green of her summer mantle. It was a joyous discovery: on nice days, it always felt as though anything was possible.

Still drowsy, she set about the tedious business

of unravelling the rags from her hair. Then, holding her breath, she peered at the tiny mirror propped up on her chest of drawers. She needn't have worried: rewarding her wariness was the most unlikely mass of glossy waves. And for that, she had Mr Sarson and his vinegar to thank.

Her problem now, she realized, unable to draw herself away from the mirror, was how to show off her shiny locks without drawing attention from the wrong quarters – namely, Edith and Ma. Were either of them to notice anything different about her appearance, she would be left facing all manner of questions, which would, in turn, require an equal number of lies.

Ruing that she couldn't simply wear her hair loose, she decided to settle for the next best thing. She would carefully draw it back to the top of her head and tie it into a high ponytail. Then, with the ends of her ringlets loosely pinned, the shape could be made to accommodate her cap but the style would still be soft and loose.

Once complete, to her own eyes at least, the result was startling. Later that same morning, she even caught Miss Naomi studying her in the mirror.

'You're wearing your hair differently,' she remarked. And, when Kate offered her best attempt at a light and unconcerned smile, Miss Naomi went on to say, 'It's very fetching – glamorous, almost.'

For Kate, though, it almost turned out to be a case of pride preceding a fall. Just before the dinner-gong later that same day, as she was about to make her way up to Miss Naomi's room to finish readying her change of outfit, she was waylaid by her mother stepping purposefully into her path.

'Everything all right?' Mabel Bratton asked.

At the uncharacteristic vagueness of her question, Kate instantly suspected a trap. Indeed, the familiar tautness gripping her insides – an unfortunate side-effect of practicing deceit – reminded her of being about ten years old and the scrapes she and Luke used to be reprimanded over. Heavens, the adventures they'd had.

'Fine, thank you,' she answered as lightly as she could.

'Nothing out of the ordinary to report? No unusual requests been made of you?'

She frowned. To what was Ma alluding? Stuck to think of anything, her conscience, for once, relatively clear, she shook her head. 'No, nothing unusual,' she replied. The question burning away at her was 'unusual how?' Experience, though, told her that it was usually better not to take the lids off any cans of worms; the creatures having a habit of wriggling their own way loose without any help from *her*. 'Well,' she said, smiling brightly, 'I'd best go and finish getting Miss Naomi's change ready.'

'Before you do–'

Damn: so close. Re-affixing her smile, she turned back. 'Yes, Ma?'

'You wouldn't happen to know anything about this, would you?' From behind her back, Mabel Bratton produced the vinegar bottle, holding it out in front of her as though it was a fine wine requiring her approval.

81

She stiffened. How on earth...? 'It's a bottle,' she chose to observe. 'From the look of it, an almost empty one.'

'I didn't ask you what it is. I can see that plain enough. What I asked, was whether you know anything about it, by which I specifically mean whether you know anything about its being in the laundry?'

Unable to help it, Kate burst into laughter. 'The laundry?'

'One of the day girls found it there this morning, abandoned on the edge of the sink.'

Oh, please don't let my face give me away, Kate willed. *But why, oh why, didn't I think to take it back indoors?* As questions went, it was moot. The fact was that she hadn't thought to. And now, the damage done, all she could do was feign ignorance. Thankfully, it was something at which she was most proficient. 'Maybe someone wanted to try and get a stain out of something. I've known vinegar to lift grass stains from gentlemen's flannels–'

'So I'm to believe you know nothing of how it came to be there?'

Practised at thinking on her feet, Kate knew to avoid telling an outright lie. 'I haven't been asked to remove any stains.'

To her answer, Mabel Bratton gave a weary sigh. 'Very well. Go and see to Miss Naomi.'

When her mother turned sharply and walked away, Kate started in the opposite direction. She *hated* lying. It made her feel sick. So, why did she do it? Climbing slowly up the stairs, she knew why. She did it because in this house – and with both her mother and her sister being the sort of people they were – she didn't have an ounce of privacy. Nor did she get to control much of her own life, her mother still treating her as though she couldn't be trusted to know her own mind. Indeed, a dispassionate individual might reasonably contend that Mabel Bratton brought most of their disagreements and conflicts upon herself. If, instead of meddling, she trusted her daughter to just get on with her life, maybe she wouldn't be lied to quite as often.

Reaching the top of the stairs and rounding the half-landing, Kate sighed. To that same dispassionate individual, though, Mabel Bratton would most likely offer a simple rebuttal: if her daughter would stop dallying and get on with marrying her fiancé, then she, her long-suffering mother, would have no need to meddle in the first place.

'Oh, good, you're already here.' Coming briskly through the door, Naomi Russell tossed her parasol onto the bed and bent to ease off her shoes. 'Goodness I'm in need of a freshen up. And somewhat late getting up here, too. I'll just slip out of this frock and then pop along to the bathroom.'

'Yes, miss.' To Kate's eyes, Naomi did look rather warm. 'I'll fetch your robe.'

In the time since narrowly avoiding trouble with her mother, Kate had busied herself readying Miss Naomi's change for dinner. Earlier that day, learning that she proposed to wear the dreamy gown of lilac satin, she had already laid out the matching gloves and bag, along with stockings and shoes, the latter of her own choosing. Staring down at the outfit now, all set out just so, she realized that she had come to like this work. It was nice to handle such fine clothes and dainty possessions. And, contrary to her initial expectations, Miss Naomi wasn't proving that difficult to please.

On her way to the door, and catching sight of the garments on the bed, Naomi paused to look them over. 'Good choice of shoes,' she said. 'You're learning.'

'Thank you, miss.'

'And I find myself looking again at your hair. Has it held like that all day?'

It was something of a surprise to Kate, too. 'Yes, miss. It has.'

'*Well done.*'

'Thank you, miss.'

With Naomi gone, Kate found that she couldn't stop smiling. To have been praised for her efforts was gratifying, and gave her an idea. Crossing to the dressing-table, she hesitated for a moment before reaching to open the top of the jewellery box. It was something she shouldn't do – not uninvited – but, suddenly, she had an urge to demonstrate to Miss Naomi that she knew what she was about – that she could be relied upon to choose things to suit the occasion or, in this case, to suit an outfit. Easing aside the tiers of the jewellery box, she picked out a pair of crystal-drop earrings and searched for the matching necklace. Taking the greatest of care, she polished them on the corner of her apron and laid them on the dressing table. Then she sought the bracelet she'd seen the other day – the one with the stones that, while not a precise match, did look remarkably similar to those in the pieces she had already chosen. Placing it alongside the others, she turned to look at the dress and then went to the drawer containing what Miss Naomi referred to as her *bits and pieces.* There, among her hat-bands and gloves, was a narrow length of ivory-coloured silk that would sit nicely in her hair. If Miss Naomi thought it an odd choice, she would try to convince her otherwise.

As it turned out, Naomi pronounced the choice of headband *inspired.* 'Quite brilliant,' was what she said of it.

Watching her appraise the finished effect in the mirror, Kate smiled, on the verge of thanking Miss Naomi when there was a light tap at the door.

'Naomi, dear?'

'Come in, Mamma.'

In a cloud of heavy scent that put Kate in mind of the depths of a thundery summer's night, Pamela Russell crossed the room and kissed her daughter on the cheek. Then, standing so as to admire her own appearance, she said, 'Darling, I should like you to spend more time with Aubrey.'

Now standing at the laundry basket, folding undergarments, Kate hesitated. Behind her, the conversation sounded like one for which perhaps she shouldn't be present. On the other hand, Mrs Russell could see well enough that she was there. And anyway, from a purely selfish point of view, it sounded like exactly the sort of conversation that might prove interesting. And so, setting the garments upon the top of the chest of drawers, she proceeded to inspect and fold them with the utmost care – but absolutely *no* haste.

'Oh, Mamma, really? Must I?'

'Darling, you'll never get to know him – or he, you – if you don't even make the effort to talk to him.'

Behind her, Kate heard Mrs Russell move across to the window, from where she pictured her looking abstractedly down to the garden.

'Perhaps I don't *want* to get to know him. He's terribly dull.'

'Nonsense, my dear. The Colbornes are a good family. An *old* family. And what you need to remember is that one day, in the not so distant future, everything will pass to Aubrey. *Need I say more?*'

'But he's boring and loud. Lawrence, on the other hand – with whom I had a perfectly pleasant conversation over luncheon – is far nicer. Unlike his brother, he doesn't bawl all the time. Nor does he go overboard to impress.'

'Naomi, listen to me. There's no point bestowing your favours upon Lawrence. He's the spare: he won't inherit a thing. Bat your eyelids at Lawrence and trust me, you'll live to regret it. Imagine – missing out by so narrow a margin. Such a frightful mistake and one that I simply cannot allow you to make.'

Motionless at the laundry basket, Kate couldn't believe what she was hearing. It would be bad enough if Mrs Russell was joking but clearly, she wasn't.

Seated back at the dressing table, Naomi leant closer to the mirror to examine her chin. 'The mistake, as you put it, Mamma, would be to end up married to the most boring man in the land.'

Pamela Russell turned back into the room. 'Naomi, darling, all I'm asking is that you give him *a chance*. To that end, I've seated him next to you at dinner.'

'Well, I shan't create a fuss,' Naomi replied, rising from the stool. 'On this occasion, I shall respect your seating arrangement and sit next to him. More than that, I do not promise you.'

Slowly, Kate turned about. With a light smile, Pamela Russell was moving to kiss her daughter's cheek.

'I assure you, my dear, one day you'll thank me for it. One day, when you're installed at Avingham Park, running that vast house and entertaining goodness-only-knows-who, you'll look over at Lawrence Colborne, seated with his plain and meanly-dressed little wife and think, *but for Mamma, that fate could have been mine.*'

'If you say so, Mamma.'

'I do. Trust me to know of what I speak. Oh, and by the way,' she added as she went towards the door, 'Diana has arrived. So, do try and be downstairs in time for drinks on the terrace before we go in to supper.'

With that, Pamela Russell swept from the room, her daughter left shaking her head. 'So,' she said wearily, 'I am to spend an entire meal seated next to the most boring and boorish man Mamma has ever invited to dinner. And believe me, Kate, that's saying something. Between you and me, he's the sort of man I shouldn't like to be seated next to at *someone else's* wedding, let alone at my own!'

When Naomi then turned to check her appearance in the mirror, Kate went across to the window and raised the sash. Pamela Russell's scent seemed to have been left clinging to everything in the room, something about the smell of it making her think of desperation.

The window opened, she stood looking out. For certain, given her mother's forceful nature, Miss Naomi was going to need every ounce of her determination to avoid the fate lined up for her. And that was *without* reckoning upon the quiet steeliness of Cicely Colborne, whom Kate had overheard only yesterday, discussing with Aubrey the attractiveness of Naomi Russell and her *generous trust*.

Drawing a breath of the fresh air blowing in beneath the open sash, Kate sighed. Had someone, even as recently as a few days ago, told her that she would come to feel a sympathy for – even a certain kinship with – the privileged Naomi Russell, she would have laughed out loud. But the more she found out about her, the more she realized how they shared some surprising traits – one of the reasons she felt minded to help her resist her mother's attempts to marry her off to the ghastly Aubrey.

'Perhaps all you need do, miss, is humour her,' she said as the thought occurred. It was what *she* would do in the same situation.

Naomi Russell fell still. '*Pretend* to enjoy Aubrey's company, is that what you mean?'

Kate gave a little shrug. 'If she sees you appearing to do as she's suggested, happen she might leave you be.'

'Hmm. Mamma's no fool. But I suppose it's

worth a try. Even so, I shall still hold you to our agreement, if I even *look* as though I'm about cave to her wishes and marry the man, you're to knock some sense into me – vast Colborne estate or no.'

Drawing herself upright, Kate smiled. 'Yes, miss. Rest assured, I shall be as good as my word. I shan't let you be married off to him.'

'Good. Because I have absolutely no desire, whatsoever, to become shackled to that braying ass, Aubrey Colborne!'

'No, miss.'

'Mamma may coerce, bully or bribe all she likes but eventually, the power to say, or *not* to say, *I do*, rests solely with me. And the same applies to you, Kate. When the time comes, don't let anyone persuade you against your better judgement.'

With a picture of Luke bearing an expression of frustration coming to mind, she smiled. 'No, miss, I shan't.'

'Heed your conscience.'

'I will, miss.'

When there was then a further knock at the door, the two women exchanged guilty looks, Kate praying as she went to answer it that it wouldn't be Pamela Russell, returning because she had overheard what they had just been discussing.

On the other side of the door, though, was a sight that left her tongue-tied for a different reason. Leaning against the frame, her thin fingers entwined in a necklace of amber-coloured beads, and most of her hair concealed beneath a turban of gold lamé, was a woman so flamboyantly dressed as to put Kate in mind of a character from *Ali Baba and the Forty Thieves.*

Behind her, Naomi gasped. 'Aunt Diana! You're wearing trousers!'

'Naomi, darling. How lovely to see you.'

'You *are!* Aunt, you're wearing trousers!'

While the two women went on to exchange greetings, Kate withdrew to the far side of the room. Miss Naomi had warned her that Aunt Diana was *a character,* but she hadn't been expecting her to look as though she'd come straight from performing on the stage. Her outfit alone was so unlike anything she'd seen before that she was finding it hard not to stare. The outermost layer, although an unusual shade of russet, was a fairly ordinary wrap. Beneath that, however, was an ivory-coloured tunic that fell to just below her knees, where it was gathered into a wide and heavily embroidered band. Below *that* was the garment of black silk that Miss Naomi had thought to be a pair of trousers but which was, Kate could see now, a skirt, ruched and stitched so as to suggest a separate column of fabric about each leg. *Quite ingenious.* Unfortunately – to Kate's mind at least – when viewed from the side, the outfit resembled a lampshade. It also seemed a rather daring choice for a woman whose age, if the greying of her hair was anything to go by, had to be at least fifty.

Remaining unremarked upon in the corner of the room, she continued to steal the occasional glance. Even had she not known that the newcomer was Pamela Russell's sister, she would have been able to guess as much. The two women shared the same shape of nose, identical, as it happened, to those of Naomi and Ned. But, where Pamela Russell was ebony-haired like her daughter, Diana appeared to be lighter and sandier. Her complexion wasn't as flawless as that of her sister, either. Peppering her cheekbones and banding the bridge of her nose were pale freckles, while at the corner of each of her eyes was a fan-shape of wrinkles. Her mouth, though, was an exact match to Miss Naomi's – small and neat.

'Terrible shame about Henley this year, wasn't it?' Diana observed, releasing her niece from her embrace. 'I blame the good weather, it brought far too many people, most of them entirely the wrong types.'

'*You* can't complain, Aunt, *you* only stayed a single night.'

Going to perch against the side of Naomi's bed, Aunt Diana set down her beaded handbag and, noticing her reflection in the mirror, reached to adjust her turban. On the front of it was a jewel-studded oval, not unlike a brooch, from behind which sprang a single, fluffy black feather. By nodding in time with every movement of Diana Lloyd's head, it had Kate transfixed.

'This dreadful business with Austria-Hungary didn't help,' Diana Lloyd went on. 'At least half the ministers of His Majesty's Government were absent – did *you* see Sir Humphrey, or Sir Richard? No. And yet, since the summer of my coming-out, neither of them has missed a single year. You know–'

There was something about the wistful air with which Diana Lloyd then sighed, that made Kate hold her breath in anticipation, and led Naomi to ask, 'Know what, Aunt?'

'Oh, nothing, darling. It's just that every time I think about Dickie Rathbone – Sir Richard, as he is now – I find myself wondering what my life would have been like had I done as Mamma wanted and married *him*. He was so dreadfully keen on me. And Mamma adored him–'

'But *you* didn't?'

Kate lowered her head. It was a very private conversation to be overhearing, which just made her hope all the more that they wouldn't suddenly remember that she was still there.

'No, I *was* keen on him. But that was before I fell for Kingsley. Mamma despaired of me, I know she did. But we had a wonderful marriage. Anyway, what were we talking about? Oh, yes, Henley. Well, I still contend that if one wants to apportion blame for the wretchedness of the thing, one should look to events in Sarajevo.'

To Diana Lloyd's pronouncement, Naomi groaned. 'Oh, please, Aunt, not you as well! I've had quite my fill of that dreary business, the men in this house talk of little else. I'd been pinning my hopes upon *you* arriving and cheering things up.'

Getting to her feet and reaching for her handbag, Diana Lloyd gave a sharp nod. 'Understood. Shan't say another word on the subject. We'll make up for the disappointment of Henley by having some fun of our own, right here.'

'Thank goodness. Now, where have they put you?'

'A couple of doors down.'

'And are you unpacked? Or shall you borrow Kate?'

'I shall borrow no-one. I'm not decrepit and I travel light – as well you'd know. You're aware, of course, that I brought the Fillinghams with me?'

With a look of surprise, Naomi shook her head. 'I didn't even know they'd been invited.'

'Moot point now they're here. Just Anthony and Cordelia – not the boys. I suppose they're too grown-up now to want to go about visiting with their parents.'

'Yes, I suppose so,' Naomi agreed.

'Well, I shall let you finish getting ready and then see you downstairs for drinks. Later, we shall have some fun. Anthony mentioned getting up a couple of fours for whist but I shall do my best not to get roped in. I say, I don't suppose there's a phonogram, is there?'

For a moment, Naomi appeared to think. 'I haven't seen one. But I'll find out.'

'Good-oh.'

Once Aunt Diana had left, Kate thought how dull the room seemed without her. Miss Naomi certainly hadn't been wrong to say that she was a character. She was also someone of whom Ma would completely disapprove. But then Ma disapproved of anyone who rocked the boat – unsettled the order of things – upstairs *or* down.

'Is there one, would you happen to know?' Naomi asked.

Kate frowned; while she could guess the matter to which Miss Naomi was referring, it would be better that she didn't appear to have been eavesdropping. 'Is there one of what, miss?'

'A phonogram. Aunt Diana is minded to jolly things up with some dancing.'

'Mr Latimer *did* have one, miss. But last I heard, it was broke.'

'Oh well, never mind. At least I shan't have to be waltzed around the floor in Aubrey Colborne's hot and sticky grasp. Although, were a waltz the only alternative to a tango, then I suppose I could grit my teeth and bear the discomfort.'

Covering her mouth with her hand, Kate tried to conceal a laugh. 'So, if it turns out that it *does* still work, miss – the phonogram, I mean – you'd prefer I didn't let on, even if it did mean you missing out on a chance to dance with Mr Lawrence?'

Naomi gave a wry smile. 'Faced with the determination of his brother, I shouldn't think poor Lawrence would get a look in.'

'No, miss. It does sound unlikely.'

'Actually, do you know what?' Naomi said, unexpectedly spinning about to face her.

Plumping the cushions on the easy chair, Kate shook her head. 'No, miss?'

'I do believe the time has come to take a leaf out of Aunt Diana's book. She's never given a hoot for other people's opinions and so, neither shall I. Listening to her talking just now has made me realize that where Aubrey is concerned, I've had quite enough. I should like to get to know Lawrence. And I'm not going to let either Mamma *or* the dogged determination of his brother prevent me. This evening, I shall, of course, abide by Mamma's request. But, tomorrow, I shall make a plan. Indeed, I shall enlist you to help me with it.'

'Me, help you, miss?'

'Yes, you strike me as a resourceful girl. So, tomorrow morning, you and I shall put our heads together and work out not only how best to give Aubrey the slip but also, how I might respectably go about spending some time with Lawrence.'

'Very well, miss,' Kate replied, flattered that Miss Naomi should think to call upon her for help. Plotting such a thing would certainly liven up her days. Not only that, but who knew when having Miss Naomi feel indebted to her might prove useful? One day, she, too, might need help. Besides which, it sounded like fun. 'Between us, I'm sure we will come up with something,' she said, determining not to let Miss Naomi down – nor let her see quite how much she was already looking forward to it.

'Good. I knew you would understand. But now, I suppose I had better go down and act as though fascinated by Aubrey.'

'Yes, miss,' she said, holding open the door for her to depart and then closing it behind her.

Contrary to her initial impressions of Miss Naomi Russell, and irrespective of their different stations in life, she realized that she had begun to warm to her; she admired her spirit and her determination, both traits she wouldn't mind more of for herself. It was true that, as young women about to make their way in the world, their lives were as different as chalk and cheese, but since insistent men and over-bearing mothers were something they seemed to have in common, perhaps they would benefit from sticking together. Moreover, if Miss Naomi could set her sights on something and go after it, then

95

why couldn't she do the same? The truth of the matter was that she probably could. Unlike Miss Naomi, though, the biggest hurdle *she* faced was not only deciding whether or not she wanted to spend her life wed to Luke but, if she didn't, what it was that she wanted instead.

Chapter Three

The Chaperone

'So, what do you think? Is Aunt Diana's idea a helpful one?'

Lifting the breakfast tray from Miss Naomi's lap, Kate withheld a sigh. Last night, she had lain awake for hours, her head filled with fledgling thoughts of how Miss Naomi might get to know Mr Lawrence, only to learn this morning that Aunt Diana had already come up with *the perfect plan*. Yes, as ideas went, it did sound like a helpful one. But it was also annoying, Aunt Diana's ingenuity having denied her the chance to impress Miss Naomi with her own inventiveness. Moreover, it probably removed any chance of a role for her in the unfolding excitement.

Setting the tray on the side table, she fought to conceal her frustration. 'I suppose her plan could be made to work.'

Heedless of Kate's disappointment, Naomi swung her legs over the side of the bed and slipped her feet straight into the slippers waiting

96

for her on the rug. 'I mightn't go so far as to call it a plan just yet – more the bones of an idea. At the moment, it rather lacks finesse. I mean, while Aunt Diana's suggestion of going into the village on the pretext of buying a new hat is fine as far as it goes, clearly, it isn't something I can do alone. Nor does it explain where Lawrence comes in.'

No, Kate thought, but, when it came to finding a suitable chaperone, the full-of-ideas Aunt Diana, whose *incredible* scheme this was, would surely be the perfect choice. After all, she was Naomi's aunt – Pamela Russell's own sister. Who could possibly be more suitable? And, once *that* was agreed upon, Diana Lloyd's 'bones of an idea' would almost certainly go ahead, leaving no part for her in the adventure at all – curse the woman.

'No, miss,' she belatedly agreed.

'But neither can I really go with Aunt Diana.'

Holding out Miss Naomi's bathrobe and waiting while she pushed her arms down through the sleeves, Kate frowned. 'You can't, miss?' With luck, Miss Naomi would go on to explain why – not that it was likely to alter the outcome.

'Not really. You see, whoever comes with me will be complicit in the thing. And, while it's one thing for Aunt Diana to offer to buy me a hat, it's quite another to ask her to deceive Mamma. And anyway, talk about putting the carriage before the horse, we don't even know whether Lawrence would entertain being party to such a ruse.' *But he will,* Kate thought. 'After all,' Naomi continued, tying the sash of her robe about her waist, 'he's terribly decent.' *He's also a man,* Kate thought but decided not to say. 'Even the very thought of doing such a thing might horrify him.'

To Kate's mind, Miss Naomi couldn't have it more upside down. But her observation did trigger an idea. 'Maybe he needn't know that you even *have* a plan.'

With a thoughtful look, Naomi sat back on the side of her bed. 'He needn't *know?* I don't understand. If he doesn't *know,* then doesn't the whole thing fall apart before it even starts?'

Handing Miss Naomi her toiletries bag, Kate began to smile, what had been little more than a fleeting thought was now beginning to feel more properly formed. 'No,' she said, 'it doesn't.'

Naomi patted the space beside her on the eiderdown. 'Come. Sit here. I'm intrigued. Explain to me what it is you have in mind.'

Kate sat down. 'Mr Lawrence needn't know of the plan at all. All *he* needs is to be in Westward Quay at the same time as *you.*'

From Naomi's face, Kate still read only puzzlement. 'But...'

'In fact,' she said, warming to her idea, 'it might be for the best if he *didn't* know.'

'So that he might not feel uneasy about the deception, is that what you mean?'

'That's right, miss.' More importantly, Kate realized, so that he could neither decline to go along with the idea in the first place, nor change his mind at the last minute, the latter possibility feeling downright cruel.

'Hmm. So ... precisely how, then, do you propose we go about this?'

Having secured Miss Naomi's interest, Kate sensed that she might now have the chance to make it sound as though the whole plan had been her idea all along. 'Well, you'd set off with your chaperone to go to the milliner's–'

'Where I proceed to buy a hat.'

To Kate, the purchase of a hat – or not – was neither here nor there; it was the rest of her plan that was of the greatest interest to her. But she knew to remain calm and present her scheme as dispassionately as possible: *nonchalantly,* as she'd heard Diana Lloyd saying of someone yesterday evening. At the thought of such an unlikely word applying to *her,* she laughed. 'Well, you did say your aunt has offered to buy you one. So, why not let her?'

'Why not indeed? One can never have too many hats, especially not during the Season.'

Slowly, Kate nodded her agreement. 'And it *would* back up the story of why you'd been to Westward Quay – if, later on, someone was to ask.'

'Such as Mamma, did you mean?'

Kate shrugged. While years of practising subterfuge had made her something of an expert, advising someone else on how to go about it was new to her. And it was beginning to make her feel uneasy. 'I suppose so, yes.'

'All right. Go on. Then what?'

Naomi Russell's growing enthusiasm for a plan that was nowhere near ready for scrutiny made Kate wish she'd kept quiet until she'd properly thought it through. That she hadn't done so was hardly surprising: how often, just lately, had she opened her mouth and spouted something half-baked, only to instantly regret it?

'Well,' she ventured, still struggling to picture

the rest of her plan, 'as I said, you go with your chaperone—'

'*Not* Aunt Diana. As I said a moment ago, it can't be her. Nor Mamma.'

Heaven forbid. 'No, neither of them,' Kate said. Unexpectedly, she spotted the missing piece of the plan. 'Miss Naomi, do you trust your brother?'

To her question, Naomi Russell raised an eyebrow. 'Of course I do – utterly. But *he* can't be my chaperone—'

Growing impatient, Kate laughed. 'But he *could* be Mr Lawrence's.'

'*Lawrence* doesn't need a chaperone!'

'No, I know that. But you see, I've had a thought.'

Naomi Russell nodded. 'Go on.'

'Confide your plan to your brother. Then, while you and your chaperone go to the milliner's, Mr Edwin suggests to Mr Lawrence they make an outing to the village – perhaps to take a look about. Westward Quay is quite interesting, you know – there are some pretty sights around the harbour and whatnot.'

'Right...'

'And then, since your brother knows where you'll be—'

'At the milliner's.'

'—it shouldn't be too hard for him to accidentally bump into you.'

'Kate, that's it! Then, when, apparently quite by chance, we come across one another, I tell him that we were thinking of going to take afternoon tea.'

'Yes. At Mrs Hunnicutt's Harbourside Tea

Rooms. They're by far the nicest – not that I've ever been, of course. But Mrs Latimer always used to say they were most acceptable.'

'Ned could say that he's starving – because he always is – and then suggest they join us.'

Surprised by the satisfaction she felt, Kate smiled warmly. 'Yes. Yes, that's it.'

'Kate, you're a genius.'

'Thank you, miss.'

'Very well,' Naomi went on, her expression thoughtful, 'I'll ask Aunt Diana whether she might loan me her motor and her chauffeur for the afternoon. I'm sure she'll agree.'

'Good idea, miss.' It was then that in Kate's mind, the final piece of the plan slotted into place. She'd need to be careful, though: she couldn't afford to appear too pushy. And so, to that end, she said, 'But you still need to decide who to take as your chaperone. Without that, Mrs Lloyd's car and driver will be neither here nor there.'

For a moment, Naomi Russell looked puzzled. 'I don't understand.'

'Without a chaperone, you can't go anywhere–'

'Oh, my dear Kate, I've already decided *that*. *That* was the easiest part of all.'

Crestfallen: that was probably how her face would look if she could see it at that precise moment.

'Oh. Well. Good,' she said anyway. After all of that effort, it seemed she was *still* destined to miss out. 'Then you're all set.'

'Kate, you ninny – it's *you*. I've decided *you* shall be my chaperone.'

Kate swallowed noisily. Dare she trust her own

101

ears? '*Me*, miss?'

'Of course, *you*. With whom else might I embark upon an undertaking of such daring?'

'Umm...' *Goodness*. Now that this was really going to happen, she felt petrified.

'Please, Kate, do say you'll do it. I promise you nothing will go awry – Ned and I will make certain of it. In any event, *were* there to be any sort of ... repercussion, I should see to it that none of the blame fell upon *you*. *You* would merely be following my instructions – an entirely reasonable state of affairs. And anyway, as far as everyone else is concerned, we will simply be going to see about a new hat – one being given to me by Aunt Diana as a generous gift. And *she* never lets us down.'

Despite feeling thrilled by this turn of events, there was one more thing of which she felt it best to make certain; having now claimed the idea as her own, what she couldn't afford was for it to fail. 'And Mr Edwin will go along with it – play his part?'

'Of course he will. Ned and I would do anything for each other.'

'Then, yes, miss. I shall gladly accompany you.'

Still marvelling at the relative ease with which this had finally come about, Kate allowed herself the briefest of smiles. She was going on an outing – for once, she was going to be a part of something colourful and exciting!

Oh, if only she didn't feel so fidgety!

It was the day of the trip into Westward Quay, Kate having awoken with the sunrise to face the prospect of having the entire morning – with its myriad distractions and grievances – to get through first. And deceits, too – the worst of which arose at staff dinner when, across the table from her, Edith kept staring at her as though suspecting that something was afoot. Surely, she couldn't *know*, could she? Surely, her trembling wasn't so obvious that her sister had deduced she was up to something?

Directing her attention down to the unwanted food on her plate, she took her fork and stabbed distractedly at a pea. 'What?' she asked, looking back up and catching her sister glancing in her direction yet again.

'Nothing,' came Edith's reply. 'I was merely wondering what could be making you look so uncommonly flushed.'

'Not that it's any business of yours,' Kate responded, placing her hands in her lap to conceal just how much they were now shaking, 'but I've got the bellyharm.' *More lies.* And they were making her so nervous that if she wasn't careful, she would give herself away! She had to do something. And then she was struck by an idea. 'Ma,' she said tentatively, looking along to the head of the table, 'might I be excused. I need some air.'

When her mother merely nodded her agreement, Kate gathered up her plate and cutlery, scraped back her chair and fled along the corridor, dumping her unfinished meal by the scullery sink. Golly, she felt sick! How she had got herself into such a state, she didn't know. It was only an outing to Westward Quay, albeit one she had to keep secret for fear of both her and Miss Naomi being forbidden to go. Yes, she reminded herself:

103

pull yourself together. This is important, Miss Naomi is relying on you.

Taking a few steps away from the yard, she raised her hand to her eyes and surveyed the lawns. There was someone on the bench under the cedar tree; it looked to be Cicely Colborne, getting to her feet and opening her parasol as she did so. Nevertheless, to avoid any chance of being seen, she ducked back out of sight.

'Seems you found the chance to get away, then.'

Having considered herself to be alone, she felt her shoulders sag. Luke: someone else she was going to have to deceive. Slowly – and with the greatest of reluctance – she turned about and let him draw her into an embrace. Against her face, the unyielding canvas of his overalls smelled of earth and vegetables and sweat. 'Hello,' she said flatly.

'Funny I should just be thinking about you.'

It didn't strike *her* as funny; by his own frequent admissions, not a moment went by when he *wasn't* thinking about her.

Despite not wanting to talk to him, she did her best to feign interest. 'Oh?'

'Aye, just this very minute.'

'Oh.'

'You had your dinner?' he asked.

'Wasn't hungry.'

'You? Not hungry? Ordinary times you're starving.'

'I've got the cramps.'

To this, she felt his embrace loosen. 'Ah.'

'I've been excused for a moment to try and walk it off.'

His arms loosened further still. 'Ah.'

'That being so, if you don't mind, I should like to take a few more steps before I have to get back indoors.'

''Course,' he said, releasing her entirely. 'Everything else all right, though?'

Her impatience getting the better of her, she tapped her foot. 'Perfect.'

'You've not been put to helping out in the kitchen?'

She frowned back at him. 'In the kitchen? No? What would make you say so?'

'On account of your hair smelling like you've been picklin' cucumbers.'

Her hair smelled of pickles? Oh, good grief.

Withdrawing her eyes from his, she tried to think how best to explain it away. 'Must have picked up the smell from walking through.' To her unconvincing offering, she saw him raise an eyebrow.

'Must have.'

Mercifully, it would be difficult for him to prove otherwise.

'Anyway,' she said lightly, 'I can't dally. Happen I'll see you later, though.'

His exasperation was unmissable. 'A man can but hope.'

When he started back across the gravel, his stride long and loping, she stood watching him go. Poor soul. She did hate being mean to him. Truth was, at that precise moment, she simply didn't have the wherewithal to fend off his advances; remaining calm and acting normally was taking all of her powers of concentration.

Even an hour or so later, calmness was still in short supply, helping Miss Naomi – in *her* state of nervousness – serving only to heighten her own apprehension.

'Do you not think it too dreary?' Naomi asked of her chosen frock: a simply-cut, linen batiste affair with a lilac stripe on an ivory background.

'It's very flattering, miss,' Kate observed of the summery, but admittedly rather ordinary gown. 'After all, you're not supposed to be dressing for tea, are you? You're supposed to be going to choose a new hat. Going for afternoon tea is an afterthought, if you will.'

Naomi Russell let out a long sigh. 'You're right, of course. But, if I only dress for the milliner's, might I not be doing myself a disservice?'

With a smile, Kate shook her head. 'Mr Lawrence already sees you several times a day, miss, including when you're all done-up in your finest for dinner.'

'I suppose...'

'And anyway, isn't this afternoon supposed to be just the start?'

Drawing her eyes away from the looking-glass, Naomi Russell turned slowly about. 'The start? I'm afraid I don't follow.'

Taking a step to the side – so that Miss Naomi could no longer see her reflected in the mirror – Kate hesitated. By no stretch of the imagination was she the best person to offer advice on sweethearting, her own situation having lately fallen into complete disarray. And that was without all the rules and considerations for a young woman from a family like the Russells. So yes, what did

106

she know of these things?

She glanced to the night-table and Miss Naomi's travel clock: five-and-twenty minutes after two. The appointment with the milliner was at three. And, as yet, neither of them was any-where near ready to leave.

'What I suppose I mean,' she ventured, 'is that this afternoon's little meeting is supposed to let you find out whether he's the person you think he is. And whether you would like to get to know him proper – or even, at all. That being the case, you'd want him to be himself, wouldn't you? His normal, everyday self, I mean – not the sort of polished-up, best-behaviour self you'd get at a dinner or some such.'

'That's true,' Naomi said, turning to look over her shoulder at her.

'So, you should be the same? Shouldn't you be *your* ordinary self?'

'You really think this dress won't make me look too dull?'

With another glance to the clock, Kate shook her head. 'No, miss. If we pin one of your silk flowers to your straw hat–'

'The little sprig of lilac blossom, that one, did you mean?'

In a single movement, Kate turned to the chest and pulled back the top drawer. 'That's the one. And if you wear these lace gloves and carry your parasol–'

'Yes...'

'And maybe that nice pearl brooch of yours–' Quickly, Kate gathered the various items and fixed or fastened them to Naomi's outfit. Then,

107

panting lightly, she stood back. 'Just right, don't you think?' Thankful when Miss Naomi nodded her approval, Kate went to the wardrobe and, glancing along the rows of Miss Naomi's shoes, selected the beige pair with the twin straps. 'And these. You remarked the other day upon how comfortable they are to wear – and you might need to cover quite a distance on foot.'

Without question, Naomi slipped her feet into the shoes. 'Well done. For someone with no training in this sort of thing, you've turned out to be very good at it. But then I knew as much when I saw your hair that first day. *There's a girl who takes pride in how she looks*, I said to myself. And you haven't proved me wrong. In fact, I would go as far as to say that we have surprisingly similar tastes.'

Having buckled the straps of Miss Naomi's shoes, Kate shot upright, galvanized into saying, 'Then if you're all set for the moment, might I be excused to go and freshen up before we go? Only–'

'Good Lord, yes. How selfish of me not to think of that! Please, do run along. I *was* going to suggest that you might like to change out of your uniform but, were someone to see you, I suppose it might raise suspicions.'

'Yes, miss, I suppose it might.' Damnation. She'd been hoping to shed these dowdy garments in favour of her Sunday best. Oh well, she could still tidy her hair and trim her straw hat. *In which case,* she thought, glancing again to the time, *there wasn't a moment to lose.*

108

'Oh, *I* don't know.'

The two young women had been at the milliners for almost an hour, Mrs Nancy Giffard, the proprietress, ferrying hats of all descriptions, Naomi Russell turning this way and that to study her reflection in the over-sized triple mirror as she tried them on. To Kate's ears, Miss Naomi sounded weary, her mind not on the matter of hats at all. Given the circumstances, she supposed it was hardly surprising.

'Does madam have a particular occasion in mind?' Mrs Giffard enquired, her voice striking Kate as matching Miss Naomi's for apathy.

'Not as such. As I said to you earlier, the hat is to be a gift from my aunt.'

Seated on a hardback chair in the corner of the room, Kate stifled a yawn. If Miss Naomi didn't get on with it, Mr Lawrence and Mr Edwin could easily grow tired of wandering around Westward Quay and go home. And she would hardly blame them.

'If I may say something, miss,' she said, rising from the chair, and crossing the couple of steps to where Naomi Russell was fingering an outlandish turquoise creation of gauze and feathers. 'I thought the first one you tried on most fetching.'

Absently, Naomi Russell looked back at her. 'That little one?'

'Yes, miss. That soft pink colour would be most...' she hesitated. She had been on the point of calling it *serviceable*. But serviceable headwear was for people who could only afford a single hat – hardly a description to win over someone who already had a dozen or more. So, what *would* convince Miss Naomi to look at it again? *Useful* was hardly compelling, *wearable* no better. 'Flattering. It would look most flattering on you.' Going across to the counter, she removed it from its stand and held it out, aware that Mrs Giffard was eyeing her with mistrust.

'Flattering, you say? Hmm.'

At Kate's involvement, Mrs Giffard's expression changed to a glower. Well, she could glower all she liked. On this occasion, Miss Naomi needed shepherding towards a decision – and quickly.

'Yes, miss. Knowing your wardrobe as I do, this pretty colour would suit a number of your outfits … and its neat little shape could be made to sit very nicely in your hair.'

'Hmm.'

Oh, dear Lord, do come on. It's only a hat. And a hat you don't even need, at that!

'Just enough of a brim to shade your face but not so much as to lift in the breeze.'

'It *is* rather breezy down here, isn't it?' Naomi Russell remarked as though noticing for the first time.

'It's being on the coast that makes it so, madam. Many of my ladies like to keep their hats small for that very reason.'

Finally, Kate thought, a helpful contribution from Mrs Giffard. For someone with a good many hats to sell, thus far she had been rather slow in making a case for any of them.

'I'll take it.'

'You don't wish to try it on again, madam?'

'No, no need, thank you.' At this sudden decisiveness from Miss Naomi, Kate's eyes widened. Was that it? Were they done? 'Please box it up for me and I'll send someone to collect it. I'm afraid I'm running late for another appointment.'

'As you wish, madam.'

With that, Naomi Russell turned briskly about. 'Come along, Kate. I've just seen the time. We've not a moment to spare.' Striding in unlikely fashion across the little shop, Naomi Russell arrived at the door well ahead of Mrs Giffard, where, to the tinkling of the bell, she stepped briskly out onto the pavement. When, trailing in her wake, Kate caught up to her, she added, 'I had no idea it was so late. Why didn't you say something? Look, there they are, coming along that harbour wall.'

Kate turned her head. 'The mole, miss. We call it the mole.'

'Mole? How ridiculous. Anyway, Ned appears to have seen us. So, which way do we head for this tea-room?'

To Kate, Miss Naomi's sudden purpose was unsettling. It reminded her of the day of the Russells' arrival, when she had stood in the hallway, inspecting her suitability as a lady's maid. *Determined. Not to be crossed.*

'Further along here, miss. It's the building with the bow window next to the Custom House.'

'I see it. Don't walk *too* quickly then – we need to afford them the chance to catch up.'

'Yes, miss.'

That particular afternoon, the town's narrow and uneven pavements were teeming with holiday-makers. In light summer shirts and straw hats, the men all looked red-faced, the women, sticky and short-tempered, their children either whining for ices or already letting them melt down their hands and onto their clothing. To avoid a particularly broad gaggle of them, Kate stepped down into the gutter and, once on the cobbled roadway, skipped a pace to catch up.

'Are they still behind us?' Naomi glanced down at her to ask.

When the crowd on the pavement thinned a little, Kate risked a glance over her shoulder. 'I can't say for certain without making it too obvious that I'm looking,' she said. But then, noticing that they were less than fifty yards from the tearoom, she added, 'Let's stop and look in this window for a moment.'

Naomi Russell surveyed the shopfront in question, its window stuffed with knick-knacks, most of them inscribed – fittingly or otherwise – with the word *Devon*. 'But it's a souvenir shop,' she said.

'Yes, miss.'

'Why would *I* be looking in a souvenir shop?'

'It's only for a minute,' Kate replied. 'You don't really have to look.' Over the last few days, she'd forgotten how rapidly Miss Naomi could become displeased or irritated. Perhaps, this afternoon, her tetchiness had been brought on by nerves; she certainly felt apprehensive herself – and Miss Naomi's grouchiness was doing nothing to help. 'But we don't want to arrive at the tea room without them.'

'Min! I say, Min, I *thought* it was you!'

Thank goodness. Wearing almost identical cream

linen suits, with colourful cravats at their necks and straw boaters in their hands, Mr Edwin and Mr Lawrence looked very … *London.* Mr Edwin in particular, with a new touch of summer colour to his face, looked healthy and relaxed.

'Ned! Lawrence!' Naomi remarked, to Kate's ears, her attempt at feigning astonishment surprisingly passable. 'What are you two doing here? And how odd you should be here at the same time as us.'

Now, though, she had overdone it: did she know nothing about subterfuge? To most people's reckoning, to draw attention to the coincidence of a situation was to immediately render it suspicious.

'Miss Russell,' Lawrence Colborne acknowledged Naomi with a polite nod.

'Lawrence, this is Kate, my lady's maid. She's been helping me to choose a hat. Kate, this is Mr Lawrence Colborne.'

Having stepped back from the gathering, Kate smiled in Mr Lawrence's direction. For some reason, though, she couldn't bring herself to face Mr Edwin.

'Was she dreadfully bad at choosing?' he nevertheless leaned towards her to enquire.

Bother. Now she *had* to look at him, ready or not. Mischievous, that was the nature of the expression she gleaned from her quick glance to his face. 'Not too bad, no,' she answered him.

'Kate and I were minded to partake of some refreshments,' Naomi announced, to Kate's mind, rather too eagerly. 'She tells me there's a tea room along here. I say, you could join us – if you'd like to, that is.'

How suddenly all the sweetness had returned to Miss Naomi's manner, Kate noted, flushing, and directing her eyes to the pavement.

Above her head she heard Mr Lawrence reply. 'Yes, I'd like that.'

'I should say. I'm starving!'

At Ned's response, Kate had to smile; Miss Naomi had predicted he would say just that. But, being twins, they must almost be able to read each other's minds.

'Shall we, then?'

'Yes, let's.'

'Kate, be a dear and remind me where it is.'

At Miss Naomi's command, Kate nodded. Her throat felt dry and her palms tacky. And, despite having been able to think of little else for the last couple of days, she suddenly felt sick with panic. What on earth could have possessed her to think that *she* could take tea with gentry? How on earth had she not worked out before now that it was bound to end badly?

Sensing that Miss Naomi was waiting upon her response – and recognizing that it was too late now anyway – she gestured somewhat stiffly with her arm. 'Just along here,' she mumbled.

'Then please, do lead the way.'

When they stepped inside the tea room, it was to the chinking of porcelain and the humming of conversations. Waitresses moved noiselessly between square tables at which were seated ladies in cloche hats and sprig-printed dresses. To Kate's horror, though, not a single table was free. Of all the misfortune...

'Heavens,' Naomi whispered in her ear. 'Just

our luck to find it full.'

'By the look of things,' Ned observed generally, 'the party at that table in the corner have just requested their bill.' And then, to his sister, he added, 'I'll go and see whether I can speak for it.'

Before long, the foursome was being seated at the corner table, Kate somehow having the presence of mind to side-step Miss Naomi so that she might end up seated next to Mr Lawrence.

Settling into their places, she took the chance to study their surroundings. The large room was much as she would have imagined it from the outside: well-worn floorboards, polished to a shine; beamed ceiling – badly stained above the fireplace and so low as to force any man taller than Mr Lawrence to stoop; dark wheel-back chairs at tables with gingham cloths and, upon them, bud vases containing single pink carnations. The other customers, she noted, were mainly older and rounder, the tips of their noses pink from the sunshine – matronly types, for the most part, tidily dressed and of the genteel class for whom taking tea with friends was a regular occurrence. None of them were housemaids, of that she was certain.

'Since we're in Devon,' Lawrence announced, bringing Kate's attention back to their own table, 'might I suggest cream teas all round – my treat.'

Next to him, Naomi Russell was peeling off her lace gloves. 'That sounds lovely. Thank you, Lawrence.'

Entirely unaware of the etiquette in such instances, Kate settled for nodding. While they had been waiting to be seated, she'd seen a cake stand being delivered to one of the tables by the door.

On the lower tier had been tiny sandwiches and soft rolls with interesting looking fillings. Above those had been scones and, on the top-most tier, miniature iced-fancies. She'd been hoping for something like that. But never mind; eating wasn't the reason they were there.

When their waitress arrived – a young woman with a long plait hanging down her back, whose elder sister, Kate felt certain she had been at school with – she was bearing a tray of bone china that rattled alarmingly as she proceeded to set it down on the table. Noticing that it was the same Aynsley pattern as the tea service they had in the dining room at Woodicombe, she smiled.

Moments later, their waitress returned with two tea plates, each bearing two modestly-sized fruit scones. She then brought two little wooden platters – to Kate, like miniature chopping boards – onto each of which she placed two tiny china pots: one of jam, the other of clotted cream. Setting them nervously in front of Naomi and Kate, the waitress disappeared to return moments later with the same for Lawrence and Ned.

'If you can't eat both of yours,' Ned said to his sister, 'I shan't mind helping you out.'

Kate tried to smile. Unfortunately, she had become terrified of putting a foot wrong – or rather, a knife or a spoon – and looking like a country bumpkin.

Her head lowered – apparently in admiration of her tea – she watched Naomi use her fingers to twist apart one of her scones and replace the two halves side by side on her plate. Grateful to have observed such a thing, she carefully set her knife

116

back beside her plate, picked up a scone and followed suit. Then, just as Naomi was doing, she spooned a small amount of cream, spread it with her knife onto just a corner of her halved scone, and topped it with a modest dollop of jam. And then she stared at it. Good grief, this was unnerving. Who would have imagined that eating something as humble as a scone could, in polite circles, be so fraught? But then it was widely held that the King ate peaches with a knife and fork. Anyway, she reassured herself, trying not to giggle, she seemed to have the measure of it now, with which she finally raised the scone to her mouth and took a bite. It wasn't as large a bite as she would have liked but she was in the company of gentry: seated to either side of her were Mr Lawrence and Mr Edwin. Just wait until she told … but no, she could tell no one. As much as she would love to tell Edith, she couldn't breathe a word to a soul; Miss Naomi trusted her – she had said as much the other day. And then there was her position as her lady's maid to consider, not to mention the fact that Ma would have a fit if *she* found out. She could imagine her now, her stare icy and her movements clipped. And that was *before* she considered her voice, raised just enough to convey her complete dismay.

'Are you not terribly hungry?'

The question was whispered so softly and in such conspiratorial tones that at first, Kate imagined it not to exist outside of her head.

'I seem not to be,' she replied equally softly, realizing that the enquiry had come from Mr Edwin.

'You know, I think the scones at Woodicombe

117

are better,' he whispered.

She smiled politely. 'I shall make sure an' tell my sister.'

'I also prefer mine properly cold so they don't go soggy under the cream.'

'Me too,' she said, casting her eyes quickly towards Miss Naomi. She, though, had *her* attention firmly on whatever Mr Lawrence was saying. 'Though they mightn't be warm on purpose,' she continued as the thought struck her.

'No?'

'They might have been only just this minute pulled from the oven, especially given how busy it is in here.'

Watching him glance about, she realized she'd never been within a hair's breadth of a gentleman before – at least, not in broad daylight, and certainly not to one so similar to her in age. 'You might be right,' he said. 'The jam's jolly good, though. And it's hard ever to find fault with clotted cream.'

Taking care to keep her lips pressed together, she smiled and then forced down her mouthful. 'Yes. I could eat it every day. And not just on scones, either.'

'On baked apples?'

'Blackberry and apple crumble.'

'*Rather.* And, of course, on strawberries.'

'Or raspberries,' she said. 'Never thought of that.'

'But they're perfect together.'

'I'm sure they are.'

Momentarily stuck for anything else with which to pair clotted cream, she gave a little sigh. Seen this close-to, it was surprising just how faithfully his features resembled those of his sister. Eyes, nose, chin – all looked familiar to her. That being the case, how had it taken so long for her to notice? And to notice also that he was actually quite handsome?

With their conversation having come to a halt, and suddenly desperate for him not to turn away, she said, 'Have you been able to do much exploring yet?'

'Some,' he replied, quite ordinarily. 'Although not as much as I should have liked. The little cove is rather lovely, isn't it?'

She nodded her agreement. 'Proper. And 'tis a good starting off point for some real nice walks, too.'

'Oh yes?'

'Yes,' she said, the tension in her limbs beginning to soften. 'If you go to the right and follow the path far enough, you end up here in Westward Quay. There's one steep climb on the way back but, to my mind, the views more than repay all of the puffing.' When she saw him nod, his expression one of interest, she went on. 'Go to the left instead, and it'll take you around the headland. Once you've climbed that first stickle path, it flattens out and from there, the walking's easy. Mind you, on a blowy day, it can be terrible windswept.'

'When I should imagine it's all very dramatic.'

Dramatic. If that meant to fear being blown from your feet, swept over the cliff edge, and dashed on the rocks below, then yes, she supposed it *was* dramatic. 'Yes, sir,' she agreed anyway. 'Best

119

choose a still day. And go when the tide's down, if you can. That way, you can watch oystercatchers picking about in the rock pools at the foot of the cliffs. And, if you go early of a morning, in the pasture away to the left, you might spot hares. Or, if you're *really* favoured, the odd deer.'

'Deer?'

Her earlier unease now largely forgotten, she nodded. 'A long time back, there was a herd of them in Woodicombe Park, but after the house burnt down and the estate fell into ruin, most of them escaped. At least, so Granfer Channer would have it.'

'And now they roam as free as nature intended.'

She frowned. According to Granfer Channer, a good number of them had quickly been poached. But there was probably no need to lead him to thinking that she was descended from generations of ne'er-do-wells and crooks. 'Some of them do,' she said instead.

'Then I shall follow your advice and make a point of exploring properly in both directions.'

'If you be so inclined, sir,' she said, worried lest he think she was trying to tell him what to do.

When, raising an eyebrow at her, he popped the final piece of his scone into his mouth, she smiled. How on earth was it possible to talk to him so easily? They had nothing in common – less than nothing, if that was possible – and yet here they were, conversing as though they had known each other for years – much in the same way as Miss Naomi had remarked only the other day.

At that very moment, across the table from her,

Naomi was patting at the corner of her mouth with her napkin. 'Delicious,' she said, addressing the table in general. 'But I fear we had better not tarry. Aunt Diana will think we've kidnapped her driver and forced him to take us back to town.' And then, turning to Lawrence, she said, 'I would offer you a ride back, but I'm not sure how it would look.'

Lawrence Colborne smiled politely. 'That's terribly kind of you but I drove us here in Father's motor.'

'Oh. Oh, I see.'

'He doesn't enjoy driving on the roads down here – says they're too rough and too narrow, fears coming around a bend straight into a herd of sheep. Or a farm cart.'

Across the table, Kate crumpled her napkin and placed it carefully on her plate. With hindsight, she wished she hadn't eaten all of her second scone. Or, more correctly, all of her clotted cream. Hopefully, Mrs Lloyd's chauffeur wouldn't drive too quickly on the way back. Unused to travelling by motor car, she'd felt queasy enough on the way there – and that had been on an empty stomach.

'Well, thank you, Lawrence, for a most lovely tea.'

With Miss Naomi making to get to her feet, and Mr Lawrence assisting her, Kate stiffened.

'May I?' Mr Edwin asked, gesturing to the back of her own chair. With a gulp, she nodded. 'Thank you for your charming company, Kate. From now on, I shall be forever on the lookout for foods that might benefit from a great dollop of clotted cream.'

When they reached the door to the pavement and Lawrence Colborne held it wide, Kate heard him ask, 'Miss Russell, might I accompany you back to your motor? I don't know about you, but I shouldn't mind a short stroll before the drive home.'

'Thank you, yes,' Naomi agreed. 'I should like that.'

And so it was that Kate found herself strolling along the quayside in the company of Mr Edwin, while ahead of them, Miss Naomi walked beside Mr Lawrence. Out in the open, though, her mind seemed to empty of things to talk about. Perhaps it was because they had already brought the occasion to a close and it now became necessary to start over. Thankfully, Mr Edwin seemed happy just to walk.

'Where is Aunt Diana's driver waiting for you?' he enquired after a while.

'Along by the green,' she answered. But then, realizing how that probably left him none the wiser, she added, 'You might have noticed it on the way in, at the bottom of the hill.'

For a moment, Edwin Russell appeared to think. 'By the church?'

She nodded. 'Directly next to it, yes.'

'I remember. We left Uncle Ralph's motor on that stretch of road behind it.'

'Oh. Yes. It's shady there.'

'Yes.'

How badly she longed to be back in the relative security of Mrs Hunnicutt's little tea room, seated at their discreet corner table with its way of inviting conversation and the sharing of confidences.

Ahead of them, though, she could already see Mrs Lloyd's motor. She sighed. Was she foolish to imagine that Mr Edwin had been doing anything other than being polite occupying her like any gentleman would so that his sister could converse with Mr Lawrence? Probably. No doubt, as far as he was concerned, the charade was now over: his duty done.

But, throughout the journey home, as she sat listening to Miss Naomi recount details of her conversation with Mr Lawrence, and heard how she thought him 'sincere and amusing', she began to change her mind. In the tea room, Mr Edwin – *Ned* – *could* have ignored her; after all, to him, she was no more than his sister's servant. That he had spoken to her courteously and with interest, suggested that perhaps she was wrong. Maybe he had genuinely enjoyed talking to her. And why shouldn't he have? She wasn't altogether un-attractive. Nor was she unintelligent or lacking in a sense of humour. She might be in servant's uniform but that didn't make her brainless and dull. She'd certainly tried her best not to be.

Beyond the windows of the motorcar, fields and hedgerows sped past, while, inside, Miss Naomi kept up her retelling of her conversation with Mr Lawrence. Occasionally, she offered a smile of either sympathy or delight, whichever felt in keep-ing with the tone of her remarks. But mainly, she sat deep in thought about Mr Edwin. He had been so easy to talk to, leaving her feeling as though she had known him for years. There was more to it than that, though, the sensation inside her undeniable. Try as she might to ignore it, their encounter had left her feeling quite giddy. *He* had left her feeling quite giddy. She might even go so far as to say that she felt *lovesick*. It was ridiculous – even to her – but true. In those few brief moments with him, she felt as though she had fallen in love.

The realization making her flush hot, she turned her face sharply towards the window. How nonsensical! No one fell in love that quickly. And anyway, she was overlooking that he was gentry and wouldn't for one moment feel the same way about her. Things like that just didn't happen. Of course they didn't: what was the matter with her? She should pull herself together and stop entertaining such taffety ideas, as her mother would say of them.

Mortified by her own foolishness, she hung her head and stared into her lap. Her feelings, though, were not to be easily dismissed. And anyway, who was to say that entertaining such thoughts was folly? Pamela Russell had married the son of a barrow-boy. So, why shouldn't a lady's maid be courted by a gentleman? It wasn't *entirely* unthinkable.

Hearing the sound of gravel under the motor's tyres, Kate looked up; already, they were drawing alongside the front porch. And there was Diana Lloyd, getting up from the seat under the cedar tree, waving as she came towards them and then waiting as Miss Naomi was handed out.

'Aunt,' she heard Naomi Russell respond as the two women embraced. 'Thank you awfully for the loan of your driver.'

'Safe to deduce from your face that the afternoon was a success?'

'A great success, if I am any judge.'

'Well done, girl. That's the way, decide what you want and set out to get it. No shilly-shally-ing.'

Decide what you want and set out to get it. Well, if it was true for Miss Naomi, then why couldn't it be true for her, too?

Feeling uncomfortably hot and not a little conspicuous to be standing on the driveway, she looked quickly about. There being no one in particular from whom to excuse herself, though, she simply turned and set off towards the servants' door at the back. There was time yet before she needed to get Miss Naomi's change ready and so, she would go and freshen up: run her wrists under some cool water and splash her face to calm what she felt was probably an unfortunate glow.

Barely halfway there, the sound of purposeful footsteps brought her to a halt. Expecting to see either her mother or Edith scrunching towards her – intent upon demanding to know where she'd been – she spun about. On the warpath on this occasion, however, was Pamela Russell, her sights fixed firmly upon her daughter.

'Naomi Russell, have you taken leave of your senses?'

Carefully, Kate continued on across the drive until reaching the corner of the house, she slipped out of sight and stood, waiting to hear was going to happen next.

'Mamma, I was just saying to Aunt Diana–'

'Whatever made you think it acceptable to

travel into town on your own?'

'I wasn't *on my own*. I took Kate.'

'You took Kate.' Even at her considerable distance, Kate detected the contempt in Mrs Russell's tone. 'By Kate, I suppose you mean that country schoolgirl you insisted upon taking as a lady's maid.'

Incensed, Kate pressed a hand hard against the brick wall. How dare she!

'She might be a country girl, but she's loyal and clean and hardworking. And when we leave here, I've a good mind to take her back with me to Clarence Square.'

Just to annoy you, seemed to Kate the only omission from that statement. She did wonder, though, whether Miss Naomi meant it: would she really take her to London? It would be one way to continue to see Ned...'

'Petulance doesn't become you, Naomi. It hasn't for some time,' Pamela Russell continued. 'Think what people must have thought to see you about like—'

'Mamma, I don't care a fig for what people thought. They no more know who I am than I do they.'

'And you, Diana, whatever were *you* thinking to allow her to – no, to *facilitate* her going off like that?'

In contrast to the tautness of Pamela Russell's voice, Kate thought Diana Lloyd sounded unperturbed. *Nonchalant,* even. 'Pamela, surely I needn't remind you of the things we got up to as young gels? Remember that time—'

'Diana, you're not helping.'

'Pamela, if I promise not to abet your daughter again, will you give me your word that you will forgive Naomi this one transgression?'

'Please, Mamma. I assure you I did nothing to bring shame – had no part in anything of which you would have disapproved.'

Overhearing Naomi's plea, Kate hoped she had her fingers crossed; Pamela Russell would in fact be appalled by what had transpired.

'Hmm. In future, try to remember that in your present state, and by which, I mean without a marriage settled, my only concern is for your reputation.'

'Yes, Mamma. I know. I apologize for upsetting you. It won't happen again.'

Hearing movement across the gravel, Kate peered around the corner of the wall; Miss Naomi was going indoors Something, though, made Kate remain where she was, her instinct rewarded when she heard Pamela Russell say to her sister, 'Sometimes that girl astounds me. What she needs, of course, is her own household and a husband – someone firm, someone she wouldn't dare disobey.'

With the matter of Naomi's dressing-down brought to a close, Kate's mind returned to the more urgent business of how to see Mr Edwin once again, something she was still mulling over when, arriving at the gate into the yard, she opened it back and then turned to fasten it behind her.

'Your ma's been looking for you. In a real fret, she is.'

She looked over her shoulder. Not surprisingly,

127

it was Luke. And he looked deeply unhappy.

'I'll go and see her,' she said, despite having no such intention.

'Where the devil have you been, Kate, without a thought to tell anyone?'

Turning about and starting to walk towards the back door, she said simply, 'I've been on an errand with Miss Naomi.'

'All afternoon?'

She shook her head: where she had been – in the course of her duties – had nothing to do with him. 'Not *all afternoon*, no.'

'Then where else have you been? Because no one's seen you since dinner.'

She could feel the tension creeping into her shoulders; if Luke had noticed how long she had been missing, Ma couldn't fail to have done. Still, she would deal with Ma only when she had to: no sense trying to cross that bridge before she had even reached it. And anyway, it was typical of Luke to be jealous: he never liked to think she was beyond his control – never liked it when he didn't know what she was up to every minute of every day. 'Nowhere else,' she replied. 'Like I said, she went on an errand and took me with her.'

'Into Westward?'

Where Miss Naomi went was none of his business and well he knew it. 'I'm not at liberty to say.'

Already tiring of his manner, she reached to open the door. He wouldn't follow her inside, not in his gardening boots, nor would he bar her way. Well, not twice, he wouldn't.

'You'd better make yourself at *liberty* to say, if not to me then to your ma. Spitting nails, she is.'

With her fingers folded around the door-handle, Kate paused. 'Then perhaps she should spit them at Miss Naomi, for *I* was only doing as I was told. And, since it was Ma who made me do this job in the first place, it would serve her to bear that in mind.'

His response was to make a scoffing noise. 'And any road,' he went on, starting to reach for the door-handle before seeming to think better of it, 'what've you done to your hair?'

Instinctively, she raised her fingers to where it billowed softly from beneath her hat. 'My hair? Now you're just being daft.'

'I am not. And you know it. Ordinary times, it's all coiled up beneath your cap – won't let it down even if I beg you to. But today, it's all sort of ... fluffy and ... loose.'

Beneath her uniform, she could feel her chest reddening and hoped her face wasn't doing the same. It didn't *feel* flushed. But, under his pro-longed scrutiny, she certainly felt horribly warm; time to get herself indoors where he couldn't follow.

'I don't know what you mean.'

'You do, Kate,' he said as he watched her examine the soles of her shoes and then step over the threshold. 'I know what it is, you know, you're trying to wear it like *she* does.'

'You're mazed,' she retorted, bent on wounding him for the perceptiveness of his remark.

'Well, it don't suit you. You look like ... well, like...'

Bending to unlace her shoes, her face moment-arily hidden from his view, part of her longed to dare him to say exactly what it was he thought she looked like. But, in truth, she could do without the further aggravation. Not only that, but she wasn't sure she wanted to hear. It was bad enough that, if what he said was true, her mother's wrath awaited her.

Leaving him to fume on the doorstep and latch-ing the door quietly behind her, she peered along the corridor. From the kitchen came the sounds of chopping and of water running into pans: dinner being prepared. With a bit of luck, there might be sufficient commotion to cover her slipping past her mother's office – as long as Ma didn't choose that moment to look up from her ledgers.

As it happened, she was able to steal past and arrive at the foot of the stairs without incident. Now all she had to do was make it to her room, wash her face, put on her pinafore, and get along to Miss Naomi's room to ready her change for dinner.

Taking the stone stairs two at a time, and with a feeling of relief, she rounded the half-landing, her thoughts still on Luke. Curse him. With his petty jealousy, he had sucked all the warmth from her afternoon. Worse still, he had left *her* feeling bad about it.

'Where in God's name have *you* been all after-noon?'

She stopped in her tracks. Ma. Well, she wouldn't look up; she would continue calmly on her way, as though coming across her on the servants' landing was perfectly normal. As, indeed, it was.

'On an errand with Miss Naomi,' she said levelly. Best to keep to the same story she had told Luke, which, in any event, happened to be the truth.

Her mother, though, wasn't to be mollified. 'An errand? More like wormed your way onto a spree.'

'That's neither true nor fair. Miss Naomi had to go into the village and ... since she couldn't go alone, she asked me to go with her–'

'For the whole of an afternoon? Without it occurring to you to check first whether you could be spared – *for a whole afternoon?*'

A single step short of her mother, Kate shrugged. 'I just do as I'm bid. I couldn't have known how long she would be out. It's not as though you would have gone against what was asked of me anyway. So, why *would* I think to mention it?' *You can't have it both ways,* was what she longed to add. *The rough with the smooth, and all that. Either I obey* her *or I obey* you.

'Well, next time Miss Naomi wants to whisk you off with her, have the common decency to mention it to me *before* you go, or so help me God, I'll put you to work in the scullery. Don't think just because you're my daughter I wouldn't do it, either. I knew no good would come of this arrangement – giving you ideas, that's what she's doing. Well, I won't tolerate such flagrant disregard. Take one more step out of line and you'll wish you hadn't, that much I promise you.'

Unable to help it, Kate shrugged. 'As you wish.'

'*As I wish?* I'll tell you this, young lady, if it

wasn't for leaving Miss Naomi in the lurch and for upsetting her mother, I'd march you down to that scullery right this very minute and set you to the dishes so fast, your feet wouldn't touch the ground. You're *that* close to it. Heed my warning and do not wear my patience this thin again.'

Feeling as though biting her tongue was completely beyond her, it was only the memory of sitting next to Ned and watching as he devoured his cream tea that made her realize how Ma had the power to destroy her chances of seeing him again. On nothing more than a vindictive whim, Ma could confine her to the kitchens – or worse still, the scullery – so that she would never catch so much as a glimpse of him again.

'I'm sorry,' she said, the upright bearing of her head betraying that she was anything but. 'From now on, I will check before obeying any unusual instructions from Miss Naomi. But now, if you will excuse me, I must go on up or risk making her late for dinner.'

Breathing heavily, Kate skirted her mother's rigid form and went along the corridor to her room. On the other side of her closed door, she sank onto her bed, her teeth gritted and her head shaking slowly from side to side. She had done nothing wrong – nothing at all. But, unless she wanted to spend the rest of her summer stuck in the scullery, showing a little remorse, and keeping out of her mother's sight, might not be a bad idea. And, while she had absolutely no desire to show contrition, if it meant having the chance to see Ned again, it would be more than worth it.

Chapter Four

This Business of War

It was too early to take Miss Naomi her breakfast: she hated to be disturbed before nine o'clock – had made that quite plain at the outset. On any other morning, Kate wouldn't have found that irksome. But, this morning, she was forced to wait around, kicking her heels, all the while desperate to discover whether, yesterday evening, Ned had made any mention of her. He wouldn't have, of course. But she could always hope.

From where she was standing in the corridor, she glanced through to the kitchen clock. Ages yet. Plenty of time if she wanted to wander past the morning room and see whether he was still at breakfast. It would mean taking a risk but all she needed was a passing glimpse. Trying to weigh whether or not it was worth it, she yawned. Sleep hadn't come easily to her last night, her mind bent on replaying snippets of the conversations from afternoon tea. Unable to settle, she had made matters worse by fretting over the question of whether Ned had just been acting politely or whether, as he had intimated, he had found her genuinely interesting. If she was to avoid another sleepless night, it was something she owed herself to find out – and that could only be achieved by putting herself in his sights and waiting to see

133

how he acted towards her. Well, for that, she would have to wait until later in the day – perhaps as late as the middle of the afternoon, when nothing much was required of her and when most of the guests chose to take it easy after luncheon.

Taking a step backwards, she craned for another look at the kitchen clock: *still* too early for Miss Naomi's tray. But, on the other hand, just enough time to casually stroll through the hallway and past the morning room.

'If you ask me,' she heard a man's voice saying as she neared the open doorway, 'the lull in activity over the weekend has served to dampen the fervour for war.' Trying to place the speaker, she stopped where she was. Despite the accents of most of the men sounding much alike, she had learnt to tell the voice of Ralph Colborne from that of his sons by the way he always sounded as though he needed to clear his throat. Perhaps, then, it was Dr Fillingham speaking, his voice being one with which she was less familiar.

'To my mind, any dampening of fervour, as you put it, is merely an illusion,' another voice observed. 'An illusion brought about by the fact that it was indeed the weekend.' Ralph Colborne, Kate surmised – definitely. 'It says here that in Downing Street, and likewise at the Foreign Office, all the government officials were either on their country estates or else playing golf, a solitary clerk being the only one left to receive the telegrams from our diplomats all over Europe.'

In response to this, one of the other men guffawed. 'Heaven forbid the threat of war in the Balkans should spoil their weekends.' That, she

134

knew without a doubt, was Mr Aubrey.

'Is it not possible that our Government has simply decided to let everyone east of Berlin handle their own affairs? As, in my opinion, they should.'

Aunt Diana? She was up already? When Miss Naomi mentioned that her aunt wasn't one for lying in bed and having breakfast brought to her on a tray, she hadn't pictured her breakfasting alone among the male guests. But then Miss Naomi had also said that her aunt was quite likely to be seen walking barefoot across the dewy lawns well before anyone else was about, only to return and eat a breakfast that would overwhelm the appetite of most men. *Well, good for her.*

'You'll join your grandfather's regiment, of course.' Ralph Colborne again – presumably to one or both of his sons.

In the hallway, she shifted her weight. She couldn't really dally much longer: getting caught would be a disaster on all fronts, but especially given that she didn't know whether Ned was even in the room. In fact, he could come up behind her at any moment. As could her mother.

'Nothing less than my duty, sir.' That was Mr Lawrence, although to what or to whom he was replying, she could no longer remember.

'That's because *you're* expendable, little brother, whereas *I* bear the weight of the great legacy resting upon me – the continuation of our family line.' And clearly that was Aubrey speaking, betrayed, again, by the very pompousness for which Miss Naomi detested him.

Miss Naomi! Remembering with a start that she

135

still had her breakfast to prepare, she pivoted on one foot and stole away. One day, she would be the architect of her own misfortune – one of the few things her mother ever foretold that stood a reasonable chance of coming true.

With Miss Naomi's breakfast tray almost ready, Kate watched the big hand on the clock edging closer to the hour. It took almost three minutes to walk from the kitchen to her room, and four minutes of boiling to produce the perfectly runny yolks to her eggs; a further moment or two to go before she needed to lower them into the water.

Across the room, the door from the scullery creaked open and, imagining it to be her mother, she stopped lolling against the table and readied a defence as to why she appeared to be idle. The person who in fact appeared was Edith, wiping her hands on a cloth. Nevertheless, in precise imitation of their mother, she looked Kate up and down and shook her head. But, instead of questioning her, she continued on to the pantry. 'Luke's outside,' she called back, seemingly as an afterthought. 'Wants you to go out and see him a minute.'

Containing a sigh, Kate pressed her hands hard onto the surface of the kitchen table. He could want all he liked. 'I'm just about to boil Miss Naomi's eggs.'

'I'll see to those. Go out and see what he wants. Go on.'

She *could* dig in her heels – refuse to go – but that would just make her look like a five-year-old. And, since Edith was only truly happy when she was meddling, it might be better not to give her grounds for thinking that something was properly amiss between her and Luke. Allow her to believe that, and she'd poke and pry and poke some more until she had found out what it was. 'Fair enough. Nice runny yolks, mind.'

'Go on with you. I think I can manage a couple of soft-boiled eggs.'

Out in the yard, Kate found Luke pacing about, his look nevertheless one of surprise when she opened back the door.

'Didn't think you'd come out 'n see me.'

'Wouldn't have, but for Edith offering to see to Miss Naomi's breakfast,' she replied to his observation. 'Fine time you've picked. What do you want?' This morning, it was hard to miss that his face wasn't set with his usual grin.

'To ask you to forgive me for speaking out of turn yesterday afternoon.'

It wasn't what she'd been expecting. Indeed, with her fingers curled tightly into the palms of her hands, she'd been steeling herself for more of his displeasure. 'What?'

'It's just that when no-one knew where you was, I fretted. Tedn't like you to go off like that, without so much as a word to anyone.'

She drew her gaze away from his eyes. Looking at them made her feel all hot and twisted inside – wretched. Instead, she confined herself to looking at his boots; today, rather than being caked in mud, they were merely coated with dust.

Still unable to look at his face, when she lifted her head she made a point of staring across the yard. On the farthest side, under the eaves of the

137

old coach house, the eggs in the swallows' nest must have hatched because both birds were darting back and forth with insects and grubs in their bills. Not much longer and, without so much as a backwards glance, the young would fly the nest. Did the parent birds remain together afterwards, she wondered, or did they, their job done, go their separate ways, and come back next year to start afresh with a different mate? *A different mate*. Hmm.

'I didn't have time to tell anyone,' she said, the continued need to lie only adding to her discomfort. 'Trust me, no one was more surprised than me when Miss Naomi said I was to go with her.' At least that last part was true.

'Well, anyway, I don't like it when things betwixt us aren't ... well, you know ... right.' Inadvertently meeting his eyes, all she could think to do was shrug. 'But I say again, Kate, I want us to be wed. And with this war comin', I don't want us to tarry over the doing of it, neither. When the call comes for men to go and fight, I want to be ready. I shall want to go off, knowing things between us are sorted and settled.'

When the call comes for men to go and fight? Would he really go a-soldiering? How could he speak of wanting things settled between them and then, in the very same breath, talk of going away to fight? Would he really leave her? Just like that? Her face screwed up in puzzlement, she risked a glance to his expression. From the ordinariness of it, he appeared to be serious.

With her thoughts spinning, and not a little hurt by the realization that he would leave, she drew a breath. 'You'd go and fight?' she said, her tone barely concealing her alarm. 'In a war?' When he looked back at her, his eyebrows were raised in surprise. ''Course I would. 'Tis every man's duty. For king and empire.'

'You'd kill people? Other soldiers, all of them men just like you?'

'To protect the folk I love? In an instant. Kill or be killed, that's how I see it.'

As though caught in a draft of cold air, Kate shivered. Suddenly, the prospect of Luke – and young men like him – marching off to war was alarming, while people like Aunt Diana, who apparently held that the country should have nothing to do with it, seemed to make a sensible point. *Luke would leave her to go and join the army?* 'Some folk say it won't come to that,' she said, grateful to recall one of the more comforting opinions she'd overheard. 'And others say they'll have nothing to do with it if it does.'

'Aye, I've heard folk say the same. But those who think war won't come be a-burying their heads. And those who won't fight if it does, are cowards. Me, I won't be found wanting. I'll do my duty. Happen *I* think some things are worth fighting for. Happen I think *you're* worth fighting for.'

Feeling tears welling, she spun away from him and started back towards the door. 'I have to go,' she said. 'Miss Naomi don't like her eggs hard-boiled.'

'Well, just think on it,' he added as she fumbled with the latch. With the door closed between them, she leant back against it. He was prepared to go to war. And seemingly, *for her.* Whatever did she do now? Let him go off to fight – if need arose – thinking that when he got back, she would marry him? Or did she simply do what everyone else would be expecting her to and marry him regardless? What if *that* was his plan? What if, tired of pleading with her, he was trying to frighten her up the aisle?

Back in the kitchen she stood, shaking her head, willing her thoughts to settle; she had Miss Naomi to face and couldn't do that all a-fluster. But, even were she to succeed in calming her mind, she knew that the sickly feeling in her stomach would not be so easily settled. Nor would her conscience; in the flurry of excitement over Ned, Luke had slipped from her thoughts. And now, this morning, she had learned that not only was he prepared to put himself in harm's way and go and fight, but that he was prepared to do so for *her.* Her: the woman whose thoughts had turned to another.

Well, curse Luke Channer and his patriotism. And curse this blessed business of war for putting such thoughts into his head to start with.

It was taking a risk, she knew that. By trying to catch even a glimpse of Mr Edwin, she was risking all sorts of trouble. But she felt drawn to see him. And if there was one time of the day when the risk of getting caught was about as low as it could possibly be, it was now, immediately after dinner, when the family and their guests would be withdrawing from the dining room to make merry. It was something that, since Pamela Russell had issued an edict to that effect, had become their nightly habit.

'No, no, no,' Mrs Russell had commanded on that first evening, 'we ladies shall not be withdrawing separately from you men. Ralph, Aubrey, and you too, Lawrence and Ned, you shall not desert us for the remainder of the evening. We have no desire to sit spouting dreary tittle-tattle, thank you very much. We wish to amuse and be amused. So, if it's cigars and cognac you want, bring them through. Take them out on the terrace, if you must, but then return indoors and be sociable.' And to Kate's knowledge, not one of the men had protested – at least, not within earshot of Pamela Russell, they hadn't.

And so it was that the newly-expanded party was now decamping to the drawing room, the women gravitating to the sofas to sit fanning at their faces, the men drifting out onto the terrace to *take some air* before Pamela could coerce them into some or other parlour game.

For her part – once again concealed in a dark corner of the hallway – Kate strained to catch their conversations. At that moment, she could see Diana Lloyd talking to Ralph Colborne, the expression on the face of the latter suggesting that he was put-out. Indeed, his remark, as the pair of them left the dining room and crossed the hallway, confirmed as much. 'My dear Mrs Lloyd, I'm afraid you couldn't possibly *be* more mistaken.'

Diana Lloyd appeared unmoved. 'Ralph, I disagree. Just because Britain has a mighty empire, doesn't mean she need meddle in the affairs of others. And, since in this instance there would appear to be no immediate threat to king or empire, I say spare the effort and let the Balkans sort it out among themselves.'

Good grief: all anyone talked about these days was this bloomin' war.

'Dangerous talk, madam. For, if we simply sit back and leave others to *sort it out,* as you would somewhat naïvely have it, how are we to ensure that the consequences don't prove disastrous? Far better, surely, to play a part in shaping the outcome than to be bound by a deal fashioned by others, primarily to their own advantage.'

'Were we under any real threat, then I *might* agree with you, but–'

And then, there he was: Mr Edwin. *Ned.* Her wait had been rewarded. With his jacket slung over his shoulder and a finger loosening his bow tie, he emerged from the glow of the dining room as though appearing to her in a dream. Pressing herself even further into the narrow space behind the jardinière, home to an immense aspidistra, she hardly dared to breathe. Ordinarily, she hated the monstrous plant with its dust-gathering leaves that snagged at her cleaning cloths. This evening, however, she was grateful for the cover provided by its hideously overgrown mass.

From what she was able to see, Ned's resemblance to the picture she had been holding onto in her mind was uncanny. That he was shorter than Luke didn't matter; Luke was unnecessarily tall. That he was less muscular didn't trouble her, either. That he had less colour from the sun only made him appear more refined and less ... earthy. And yesterday she had noticed how, in comparison to Luke's hands, Mr Edwin's looked small and neat. To the touch, she supposed they would be soft and smooth and lacking in scars and roughness.

All too soon, Edwin Russell had sauntered from her view to take his place among the throng in the drawing room. But at least she had *seen* him. At least she had a fresh picture in her mind – one that would serve her while she made up her mind what she was going to do about ... well, about *him*.

'Hello, there.'

Startled from her thoughts, Kate shot upright. It was after luncheon the following day and, having first checked that Luke was nowhere in sight, she had gone to the cutting-border to pick a small posy for Miss Naomi's dressing table. Enclosed among the towering wigwams of sweet peas, their perfume, combined with the warmth from the sunshine, had been making her feel drowsy. Surprised by Mr Edwin's voice, she now felt even hotter.

Turning slowly, she smoothed a hand over her cap. 'Forgive me,' she said of her disarray. 'I didn't see you a-coming.'

'Then it is I who should apologize for creeping up on you.'

'No,' she said, still recovering her breath. 'I was miles away in my thoughts.'

Against the bright sunshine, he narrowed his eyes. 'Pleasant ones, I trust.'

Feeling no need to lie to him, she shook her head. 'Not really. My mind was all a-wrestle with thoughts of this war that everyone says is coming.'

'Ah.' Standing with his jacket hooked over a finger, he cocked his head. 'I should imagine the prospect fills you with concern.'

She nodded. And then, staring down at the dozen or so long-stemmed sweet-peas she had cut, she said, 'Is it going to come? War, I mean.'

She watched him shrug. Rather than a gesture of careless disregard, it struck her as one of genuine doubt.

'If one believes what's written in some of the newspapers, one would say it is almost inevitable. Listen to others, and one might think there's still a chance it can be avoided.'

Hardly what she had been hoping to hear. 'Oh I see.'

'I read this morning that Sir Edward Grey – he's the Foreign Secretary – wants Britain and Germany to mediate between Russia and Austria-Hungary. The newspaper was rather dismissive of his chances of success, though, intimating that there are those in Germany who would rather like to see Austria crush little Serbia.'

'So, it's more likely to come than not?' she said, grateful that for once, someone thought her worthy of an explanation. 'Only, since I know nothing of the matter, I struggle to know *what* to think.'

'I should like to be able to reassure you,' he said. 'But for the moment, that's rather beyond any of us to do.'

'It's just that some people – around here, I mean – are already talking of going to fight.'

'I know. Unsettling, isn't it?'

She nodded. 'Horrid. I don't even like it when people have a falling-out, let alone having to think of them setting upon each other with guns and … things.'

'Me neither. I like it best when everyone just gets along. Alas, we're not all destined to see eye-to-eye.'

Inside, she had a question burning away at her, driven in part by the memory of the earnestness on Luke's face as he told her of his own intentions to go and fight. Ordinarily, she would never have the courage to raise such a thing with someone like Mr Edwin but, since he was already talking so freely, she summoned her courage. 'Would *you* go and fight?' she asked. When all he did was raise an eyebrow, she flushed and hastened to apologize. 'Forgive me, sir. That's none of my business.'

'On the contrary,' he replied, shifting his jacket to his other hand. 'The prospect of war makes it everyone's business. Would I go and fight? I would almost certainly have no choice. My conscience would not allow me to stay at home while others went willingly to defend the realm. Would I relish the task? No. Would I have it in me to kill another human being? That, I cannot say. Until any one of us is faced with such a dilemma, who among us can know? Standing here on such a golden afternoon, the prospect makes me sick to my stomach. But, if a soldier from an enemy army shot the man standing next to me, or came rushing out of that copse, bayonet fixed, intent on killing both of us, would I feel differently? I should imagine I would.'

When he finished speaking, Kate let out a long

145

sigh. In many ways, it was a perfect answer: a carefully weighed argument between an ideal and the rather harsher reality. Curiously, it also felt far more reassuring than any of the brave talk that Luke had spouted.

'When you put it like that, I understand,' she said. But then, feeling the sun burning the lower half of her arms and suddenly remembering where she was, she looked about. Heat was shimmering up from the pale and newly-mown lawns, while the indigo shadow under the cedar tree looked cool and inviting. 'Forgive me,' she said again. 'I'm keeping you from going about your business.'

'*You* are keeping *me* from absolutely nothing,' he said earnestly. 'I am the one who, with little consideration to the fact that you were going about your duties, came across to talk to *you*. With hindsight, I realize now that it was remiss of me, but I will admit to finding your company most enjoyable – so unlike that of the young women one ordinarily has occasion to meet – like a breath of fresh air after a stuffy dinner.'

Horrified by the extent to which she was blushing, she ducked her head and scrabbled about in her mind for something to detract from her discomfort. 'I was just picking some of these for Miss Naomi,' she said, offering the bunch of blooms towards him. 'I noticed this morning how the little bar of soap she likes to use is called Sweet Pea, and so I thought to put some on the dressing table for her.' Oh, good Lord, now she was rambling; now he could be forgiven for thinking her mildly dotty.

'That's very thoughtful of you,' he said, nevertheless. 'I'm sure she'll think so, too. By the way, I hope you didn't get into trouble yesterday – you know, for your part in our little charade.'

Beginning to breathe more normally, she managed a smile. 'Not too greatly, the trouble I did land in being of my own making.' When he looked quizzically back at her, she forced herself to explain, 'By not saying where I was going aforehand.'

'Ah.'

'But all is smoothed over now.'

'I'm glad to hear it. Well then, I shall retreat into the shade until it's time to go and see what's for afternoon tea. And then I shall attempt to determine whether any of it would benefit from a dollop of Devon's finest.'

Unable to help it, she laughed out loud. 'After yesterday? I wouldn't have thought you could find room for no more of it. I know *I* couldn't.'

'Oh, I have room for a smidgeon,' he said, before pressing his hat squarely back onto his head, nodding politely, and setting off in the direction of the house.

When he had left, she stood twirling the stems of her little bunch of sweet peas, watching absently as the pinks and purples swirled into a single, lilac-coloured mass. Fancy *him* coming over to talk to *her!* A breath of fresh air, he had likened her to.

Perhaps, then, he had deliberately sought her out. In which case, happen it wouldn't be overly-daft to imagine that he had found himself thinking about *her* in much the same way that she had been thinking about *him*. Good gracious: what a joyful state of affairs that would be!

Remembering then the task that had brought her out there, she stooped to pick up the pair of scissors she had dropped to the grass. And then, with a definite feeling that she was being watched – and by someone other than Mr Edwin – she glanced about. Apart from a blackbird scratching about in the leaf mulch, though, everywhere was still. She looked towards the house, but even that showed no obvious signs of movement. It had to be her imagination. Or maybe, just maybe, it was her conscience urging her to think long and hard before letting her feelings run away with her. And definitely before doing anything rash.

'Now, darling, tonight, I've seated you next to Aubrey.'

It was just before dinner that same day, and Kate had just been putting the final touches to Miss Naomi's hair when Mrs Russell had entered. Bringing with her a cloud of her heavy scent, she had gone to perch on the window seat.

In response to her mother's announcement, Naomi groaned. And then, with a conspiratorial look towards Kate and a despairing raising of her eyebrows, she said, 'Not again, surely, Mamma. I sat next to him only the night before last.'

At the window, Pamela Russell raised the shade that had been lowered against the afternoon sun and stood looking out. Something about her presence always made Kate feel hot and bothered, especially when she was attending to Miss Naomi. This evening was no exception. 'Ouch!'

'Sorry, miss,' Kate apologized for her heavy-handedness with the last pin. 'But doing it higher up on your head needs more pinning than normal. You know, just to be sure.'

In front of the mirror, Naomi Russell angled her head. 'I like it. Very stylish. Very elegant.'

'Thank you, miss.'

'I've put you next to him for a reason,' Pamela Russell went on, at which both Naomi and Kate turned towards her. 'This never-ending talk of war has me quite beside myself. We are on holiday, we are supposed to have left such things behind. But apparently, I am the only person who understands that. So,' she said, turning more fully back into the room, 'this evening, you are to help me.'

In the mirror, Naomi and Kate exchanged brief glances. 'Help you how, Mamma?'

'By being lively and interesting. You'll have Aubrey to your left – your ally in our little fight-back – and his father to your right. So, until I signal the turn, you're to spend the first half of the meal distracting Ralph with any subject of your choosing – apart from one that might lead him on to discussing politics, of course – by which time, *I* will have ensured that his claret glass has been re-filled so often that all thoughts of war will be forgotten. After that, you may talk with Aubrey. For my part, I shall do the same with Anthony Fillingham. And dear Cordelia, who is quite of a mind with me on the matter, will entertain Lawrence. If we women take the initiative and don't allow our attention to waver, the evening stands a chance of passing in jollier mood.'

With a light shake of her head and a sly smile to Kate, Naomi turned to her mother. 'But what about Aunt Diana? She crusades for peace even before anyone else has had the chance to *mention* war, which, as you can't fail to have noticed, has all the men itching to point out the flaws in her argument.'

'Let them itch. Diana, since you ask, will be seated next to Ned, whom I have already placed under strict instruction to keep her glass filled, and her conversation on other topics.'

While Pamela Russell paused for breath, there came a sharp rapping sound. And when the door opened swiftly back, it was to reveal Diana Lloyd herself.

'*Darlings,* there you are,' she said, striding in.

Tonight, the garment that Naomi had mistaken for trousers was being worn with a gold-coloured jacket edged with purple. Wrapped across her front and held in place with a matching purple sash, it fell to an asymmetric hemline just above her knees. On her head was her favoured gold turban.

'Aunt Diana,' Naomi rose from her stool to greet her aunt. 'We were just talking about you.'

'No doubt your mother was warning against allowing me to goad the men with my opinions on this war.'

'Something like that.'

'For goodness sake, Diana,' Pamela Russell rounded on her, while at the same time kissing her on the cheek and fingering the satiny sleeve of her tunic. 'Very stylish by the way. *Poiret,* again, is it?'

150

'From that same visit to his *atelier,* yes.'

With a nod of approval, Pamela Russell resumed. 'Anyway, there won't *be* a war. Those who say otherwise are overlooking the fact that Kaiser Wilhelm and our own dear King George are cousins.'

'And families never fall out, is that what you're saying, Pamela? That blood is thicker than water, and that family always sticks together, papers over the cracks, no matter what?'

'Please don't take that tone with me, Diana. I happen to think that's how it *should* be, even if you don't.'

In the silence that followed, Kate shivered. She never knew how to behave when this sort of thing happened, usually resorting to doing nothing that might draw attention to her presence and make an uncomfortable situation even worse.

'Mamma,' Naomi began, taking the opportunity of a lull in her mother's diatribe. 'Did you ever meet Lawr– I mean, did you ever meet Aubrey's grandfather?'

Proceeding to tidy the dressing table, and grateful for the change of subject, Kate smiled at Naomi's cunning, her interest in Lawrence still firmly a secret.

'Hector Colborne? I remember being introduced to him the year I came out, but I would hardly say that I knew him, no. Why do you ask?'

'Oh, only that Lawr– *Aubrey* was talking of him this afternoon. Apparently, he was the youngest something-or-other to graduate from Sandhurst and be given his own command. Also, *Lawrence* said that if he's accepted into his grandfather's regiment, he might be able to put in a good word for Ned.'

'Have I just completely wasted my breath! Did you not hear me specifically instruct that this evening, there is to be no talk of war?'

At Mrs Russell's outburst, Kate slipped to the furthest corner of the room where she busied herself straightening the cushions on the easy chair and then tidying the curtains at the window. Ned was going to join the army? How had *that* come about? Only a few hours ago, he had suggested to *her* that he wasn't in the least hurry to go off and kill people. *Now* what was she supposed to think? Had he just been placating her? She didn't think so; his horror at the prospect had seemed entirely genuine.

Across the room, ignoring her mother and taking one last look in the mirror, Naomi simply fixed her usual smile in place and then said, 'Well, come along, both of you. Enough of that – dinner awaits.'

When the three women had left the room, Kate closed the door quietly behind them and then slumped into the chair. This business of war had her so confused. Ought she not be proud that Luke and now seemingly, Ned, too were willing to do their duty? Surely, she should be, especially given how she felt about Mr Aubrey and the squirmy way *he* seemed to avoid the issue altogether. But she didn't feel proud at all. That Luke was so eager to go and fight had caught her by surprise; how had she never known that he would be willing to kill someone – albeit an enemy someone? And then there was what she

152

had just heard about Ned. That he should be considering which regiment to join – especially when he had so recently indicated to her that he would rather not – filled her with panic.

Getting up from the chair and feeling utterly lost, she went back to the dressing table. Carefully, she returned to the jewellery-box the three sets of earrings Miss Naomi had chosen not to wear. Then she replaced the string of pearls she had worn that afternoon into its leather pouch. She put the remaining hairpins back into their box and set the brush, comb, and hand-mirror neatly alongside one another on their tray. She gathered up Miss Naomi's discarded undergarments, put them in a laundry bag, drew the string at the top and dropped it into the basket. Then she cast about the room. She might as well turn down the bed, top up the jug of water on the night-stand and lay out Miss Naomi's nightdress. She wouldn't draw the curtains yet, though; the room needed the air, the evening showing all the signs of turning into an unpleasantly sticky night.

With all of that done, and with a heavy sigh, she went to stand in the bay-window and look out over the gardens. Although there were still a couple of hours until sunset, the shadows had begun to lengthen and, from their various hidden perches about the garden, culver birds could be heard cooing sleepily. All told, it was a perfect summer's evening. *Almost* a perfect summer's evening. Come dimpsy on an evening such as this last year, she would have been sneaking out to see Luke and then fending off his advances as they sat laughing in the tallett, or lolling about in the long

153

grasses up at the beacon, choosing names for the children they would one day have. How things had changed. How *she* had changed. How Luke hadn't. One year on and while *he* still wanted all those same things, *she* didn't. And, now that she'd started to get to know Ned, she seemed to want them even less.

She looked across at Miss Naomi's clock. Ned would be at dinner now, either obeying his mother's command and doing his best to keep his Aunt Diana from discussing political affairs or else ignoring his mother's instructions altogether. Probably, while yearning to do the latter, he would in fact be doing the former.

Turning away from the window, she caught sight of Miss Naomi's latest copy of *The Lady*. It lay opened at a page bearing a drawing of a young woman in a dark uniform and cap, much like her own, except that on the bib of her pinafore was an emblem of a red cross. Staring down at the expression on the illustration's face, Kate felt a stab of envy: the young woman looked serene and fulfilled. While perhaps not so very different from being a housemaid, she knew that young women who went to become nurses did so because they felt a calling to, not because they had stumbled into it, trudging without much say up the drive to the big house, directly in the footsteps of their mothers, aunts, and older sisters. Service was something you had no say about being born into – a bit like being born into the gentry – whereas becoming a nurse was something you did by choice.

She lifted the magazine from the side table and

examined the picture more closely. When war did come – because now, despite Mrs Russell's belief in the power of family ties, she was almost certain that it would – perhaps with it would come opportunities. If Luke could join the army – and Ned and Lawrence, and all of the others – and be trained to do something new and useful, might not similar chances arise for her? She didn't particularly fancy nursing – too much blood and gore and sadness – but there might be something else she could do. Yes, there was a thought. If Luke and Ned had a duty to the realm, didn't she have one, too?

The idea of doing something fulfilling was an appealing one. The biggest problem she could foresee was how to go about it. Woodicombe was so very far from anywhere sensible. And Ma and Edith would be of no use. Miss Naomi might prove of *some* help, but, as usual, it seemed that if she was to get anywhere, she would have to rely on her own resourcefulness, something she did at least have by the bucket load.

Heaving a long sigh, she wondered what to do with herself. It was far too early to go to bed as well as far too lovely an evening. So, she would take a short stroll around the grounds, taking care to stay well out of sight of the house and anyone who might challenge what she was doing. And then, once dinner was over, and the guests removed to the drawing room – or perhaps, tonight, out onto the terrace – she would take a circuitous route back and see whether a glimpse of Ned was to be had. Then, in the morning and with a clear head, she would give proper thought about how to further her idea and turn it into a proper plan. Howsoever she decided to go about it, she would do so in secret. She wouldn't even tell Miss Naomi yet – just in case. But, if a suitable occasion arose, she *might* tell Ned, who might even have some advice to offer.

Kate rubbed her arms. After the warmth of the day, the light breeze felt fresh, the skin on her arms rippling with gooseflesh.

Finding herself at something of a loose end, she had wandered as far as the beginning of the path down to the cove, where she was now sitting on the stump of a tree, long since felled by a January gale. She could just about remember it – a lofty pine, whose crown had shushed and swayed in the merciless winter winds that blew straight off the Atlantic. In its time, it had been home to a poorly-sited rookery, whose nests, as often as not, were upended before the eggs could hatch, and to the drey of an oddly-coloured squirrel.

Unsurprisingly, she had been thinking about Ned and the matter of whether or not to try to enlist his help with her plan. Unable to say for certain why, she nevertheless felt that he would have some valuable observations. Well, coming from him, of course they would be valuable. And anyway, without a helping hand from someone, she was stuck to know where to start.

Sensing then that there was someone behind her, she turned sharply looking over her shoulder.

'Well, good evening to you.'

With no care to avoid catching her skirt upon

the roughly-hewn stump, she leapt to her feet, her heart skipping what felt to be several beats. Ned!

'Good even' to you, sir,' she muttered, embarrassed by the fact that she had been thinking about him and confining her eyes to a line well below his own.

'Out taking the air?' he asked.

She risked meeting his look. 'I am.' By rights, she should really continue to address him as 'sir' but, having taken tea with him, and having had him refer to her as a breath of fresh air, it no longer felt strictly necessary. That, and the fact that she didn't want to remind him that she was a servant.

'Me too,' he said. 'The other fellows are on the terrace with their cigars, and the ladies have gone to powder their noses.'

She smiled. 'You don't like cigars?'

'I can take them or leave them. On an evening such as this, I prefer to take the air. And, having enjoyed a couple of glasses of claret, I find I have no need of a cognac.'

'I've never had claret,' she said. 'Nor cognac.'

'No, I imagine not. Some clarets can be quite nice, others not so much. There's an awful lot of nonsense spoken about wines, nonsense about the types of grapes and so on – about the different types of cognac, too.'

'Oh.'

For a while after that, neither of them spoke, but then, he said, 'You know, I had a feeling I might find you out here.'

Aware that she had been lacing and unlacing

157

her fingers, she drew her hands behind her back. He had been thinking about her? *Again?* This was better than she had dared hope – not that she could let it show. 'Oh?'

'From the dining room, I saw a form slipping through the shadows. I had an inkling it might be you.'

'Guilty, your honour,' she said, regretting it almost before the words had left her mouth. 'Guilty for sneaking away, that is.'

'It occurred to me you might be slipping away to see someone – a sweetheart, perhaps.'

A sweetheart? Was he trying to establish whether she was promised to someone? Was this his round-and-about way of enquiring whether she would welcome his advances? Because she would. She most definitely would!

'No,' she said, grateful to be able to answer him without lying but ruing how much she was suddenly trembling. 'No, I wasn't slipping away to see anyone–'

'But how foolish of me! There's bound to be a long line of young men on your doorstep!'

'No,' she said, aghast at how fast her heart was beating but somehow managing to affect a light laugh, 'I assure you there is no line of suitors on my doorstep – trust me, I think I'd have noticed such an unlikely thing as that! My mother and my sister certainly would have.' Oh, dear Lord, now she was babbling!

What she *wanted* to do was examine his expression – gauge his reaction to her answer. But she couldn't bring herself to look.

'You do surprise me.'

Instinctively, she scoffed. At the same time, however, she spotted an unlikely opportunity. And so, slowly unfurling her fingers from where she had been pressing her fingernails into her palms, she asked, 'What about you? Do *you* have ... someone special?' She was being woefully forward, although no more so than he had just been.

'I do not, no. Although I daresay it won't be long before Mamma does with me as she's lately started doing with Naomi.'

Her spirits tumbled. Had she, in her state of hopefulness, read too much into his question: was the matter of sweethearts and marriage on his mind only because his mother had set her sights on Aubrey as a suitable husband for his sister? She was minded to think not; his enquiry could barely have been plainer.

'I do *want* to be wed,' she said, lest her earlier answers had led him to thinking her set against the idea. It was also safer than blurting the thought in her mind, which was *yes, please, I should welcome your attentions with open arms.*

'Me too,' he seemed quick to agree. 'Eventually, that is. To the right person.'

'Of course,' she replied, 'to the right person.'

'I say, I hope my sister appreciated the sweet-peas.'

She blinked several times. Was he satisfied with her answers then? Or was he regretting speaking of the matter in the first place? Indeed, had she misunderstood the whole thing? It was more than possible. But why ask her about sweethearts unless it was his intention to establish her situation? All she could do, it seemed, was confine

159

herself to answering his questions.

'She didn't mention them.' Now she just sounded miserable.

'How very remiss of her.'

'But I expect she liked them,' she said, making an effort to brighten her tone. 'They filled the room with their lovely smell.' At least, they *had* done until his mother had come bowling in, over-powering everything with a scent that while different to the other evening, had still put her in mind of the depths of a dark and sultry night.

'No doubt they did.'

'Was there anything at tea that was in need of clotted cream?' she asked, desperate that he shouldn't think their conversation at an end and take his leave. There might still be a chance for her to reassure herself as to his motives.

Having moved a pace or two further away from her, he was now taking off his jacket and loosening his bow tie. That done, he stepped further away still to lean against the trunk of a birch tree. 'Alas, no. But there *was* a cream sponge with strawberries on top.'

'Bit late in the year for strawberries,' she observed, immediately wishing she hadn't. What was the matter with her? *Daft question.* Among other things, the thudding of her heart was making her feel light-headed and, every time her mind returned to his possible reasons for raising the matter of sweethearts and marriage, she came over all panicky.

'Is it? They *were* quite small.'

'We're more into summer raspberries now.' Oh, but this was hopeless. Here she was, alone with

160

him, the matter of marriage clearly on *his* mind, a plan in hers that could do with his help, and yet she was droning on about soft fruit. 'After we spoke this afternoon,' she said, this time forcing herself to meet his look, 'I thought more about the war, and what you said about it being your duty to go and fight – whether you were really for it or not.' There. That was better. For the moment, she would set aside the matter of his advances – or otherwise – and see whether he might have any advice to offer regarding her plan to volunteer. After all, if she was clever, the one might bring about the other. Yes, now *there* was a thought!

'Oh, you shouldn't pay too much heed to *my* ramblings,' he said. 'Just because *I* have doubts, doesn't make the underlying need for it flawed.'

Unsure what he meant, she frowned. But, with the subject now out in the open, she determined to press on. 'And so, I came to wondering, why does the duty of doing the right thing, you know, for king and empire, fall only upon the menfolk? What about the women? Shouldn't they do something, too?'

'I do hope you're not thinking of taking up a rifle!'

Blushing, she shook her head. 'No, of course not.'

'Forgive me, I meant that as a joke but it was in poor taste. Tell me what bothers you and I will listen sincerely. What did you have in mind to do?'

In response to his question, she shrugged. 'That's just it, I don't rightly know. How do women like me, with no training at anything,

161

become of any use?'

For a moment, he seemed to think. 'Well, do you mean to pursue this as an occupation, or just in your spare time?'

'Since I don't have no spare time – not to speak of – I was thinking perhaps there was something I could do on a proper footing. Although heaven only knows what.'

'I see.'

'And you've no idea how useless that makes me feel.' There, she'd said it. All of it. Curiously, she now felt less jumpy.

'There's no shame in being stuck to know how to help. After all if everyone who wanted to help but didn't know how to go about it gave up because they felt useless, we'd be in a real fix. No, the reason I ask what you had in mind, is because Min and I have a cousin, Elizabeth, who is an organizer for something called the Voluntary Aid Detachment. Every time we see her, she presses Min to go and help out. From the little I remember of it, it's run by the Red Cross and comprises young women volunteers, whom they train in things like cooking, and caring and nursing. I also recall that before we left London, she was saying how, with the threat of war looming, she was hoping to try and recruit more volunteers. If you like, I could write to her and see what it's all about. I can't promise it will suit what you want to do – you know, with it not carrying any remuneration – but she's certainly in the right place to know of other organizations, much more so than I.'

'You'd do that for me?' Oh, but how gushy and

breathless she sounded! 'I should be truly grateful,' she said more levelly. 'But only if it's not too
much trouble.' There: that was better. It was true
that she'd been hoping for something more than
just being a volunteer but, whatever it turned out
to be, she would join up anyway. As he himself
had intimated, one thing had a habit of leading to
another. It would also show people that she was
serious in her ambition to do something with her
life.

'I shall write to her tomorrow. I would offer to
telephone her but I don't know that I'd succeed
in getting through to her – she's frightfully busy.'

'Of course. I understand.'

'Well, I suppose I had better return to the fray
– only so long I can be away without mother
noticing. I saw her with a great box of props
earlier, so I imagine we're in for another spell of
parlour games.'

Watching him start to walk away, she beamed
with delight. This evening, she had done an
astonishing thing: she had taken the first step to
bringing about the changes she so badly craved.
At the very least, she had let it be known that she
wanted to do something different – something
valuable and fulfilling. Even if she did have to
start somewhere close to home – to be trained
and what-not – it would still be a step in the right
direction. And anyway, if she came recommended
by the Russells, this Elizabeth woman might get
to hear of her and want her for something in
London. More importantly even than *that*, she
had let it be known to Ned that she was free to
respond to any advances he might care to make.

Now, it was just down to him to make them.

She sighed heavily. How fortunate that she had ventured out. How equally fortunate that he had seen her! She looked up. Already he was halfway back across the lawn and turning towards the terrace, from where he no doubt hoped to blend, unnoticed by his mother, back among their guests.

Still scarcely able to believe what had come about, she glanced to the sky; she should go in, too. Although not expected to be anywhere at that precise moment, after the trouble following her trip to Westward Quay, it would be better not to give Ma reason to come looking for her or to suspect that anything was afoot; no point dashing her chances before they had even amounted to anything.

Letting herself in at the back door and still elated at how things had turned out, rather than head straight upstairs, she went along the corridor and peered into the servants' parlour. Only Edith and her mother were there: Edith bent low over something she was darning; her mother reading a letter, probably from one of her cousins further down the county and with whom she kept up a regular correspondence.

'*There* you are, love. I wondered whether you'd come down and make yourself a Horlicks.'

'It's much too hot for that,' Kate replied to her mother's observation. 'I'll just take up a glass of water.'

'It's from Fanny,' her mother said, motioning with her head to the single sheet of paper in her hand, 'Frederick's been poorly, but he's on the mend now.'

Struggling to remember which one was Frederick, Kate nonetheless nodded. 'That's all right then.'

'But now she's worried about her other two – what with this war business.'

'Mmm. Seems more people think it'll happen now.'

In response to her observation, Edith looked up. 'People? What people? What people do *you* talk to?'

Puzzled by the uncalled-for sharpness of Edith's tone, Kate frowned. Was this a trap? Had she been seen talking to Ned? Trying unsuccessfully to will away a flash of panic, she shrugged her shoulders. 'I don't *talk* to anyone, as well you'd know. But, like it or not, I do get to overhear *other people* talking. And to my mind, some of them seem quite well informed.'

'Ooh. *Some of them seem quite well informed.* As if *you'd* know.' Feeling herself tensing, Kate stared at her sister, whose head was once again bent over her sewing. 'Look, I don't know who's got you all sour-sapped, but I *do* know it wasn't me. So just have a care to be a bit less crabby.'

'Huh.'

'Enough, you two,' Mabel Bratton directed. 'I don't know what's got into the pair of you.'

Standing stiffly, Kate shook her head. 'Nothing's got into *me*, Ma. It's *her*.'

'Kate, I said enough. Your sister's probably tired. Leave her be.'

'Yes, Ma.'

'And Edith, have a civil tongue in your head.'

'Yes, Ma.'

165

'That's more like it.'

Even though, until that very moment, Kate had intended breathing nothing of her plans to anyone, Edith's pettiness had given her an urge to put her in her place. Besides which, since a change to her circumstances *could* come about quite suddenly, it couldn't harm to start paving the way for her eventual announcement. Not about Ned, of course. But, if anything, coming across Edith and her mother, grouchy and exhausted and passing their evening with only each other for company, she felt even more certain that getting herself out of Woodicombe was the right thing to do. If this was what awaited her as Luke's wife – an evening spent mending rents in garments by the light of a single gas-lamp – while people like Naomi and Ned dressed up to eat fancy dinners and play parlour games, then she felt even more inclined to do everything in her power to get away. And, if that meant making her plan known in order to have to stick by it, then so be it.

'I've been thinking...'

'Yes, love?'

'With this war comin'–'

'Not that business again.'

'Edith, have the grace to hear your sister out.'

'Sorry.'

'With this war coming, and all the boys and men talking about joining up and doing their bit for king and empire, I thought *I* should like to do something too.'

When her mother put down her letter, and Edith stopped pulling her darning needle through the cloth of her skirt, Kate swallowed.

'What do you mean, *do something too? You* can't join up.'

'No, I know that, Ma. I didn't mean join the army. I just meant do something useful, maybe get trained so that I can be a volunteer, you know, should the need arise.'

For all the comprehension it showed, Mabel Bratton's face suggested that Kate might as well have been speaking in German.

Edith on the other hand, had her mouth half-open with disbelief. 'You? And what could *you* possibly be trained to do?'

Stay calm, Kate urged herself. *Don't bite*. It was a sentiment easier to think than to see through, though. 'That's the point of being trained. You start by knowing nothing about a thing and end up knowing how to do it well. Think, Edith, even *you* weren't born already knowing how to make pastries and puddings.'

'Stop it, you two,' Mabel Bratton warned absently, her attention once again on her letter.

'*She* started it,' Kate said. 'Again.'

This time, her mother looked up at her. 'Look, child, be sensible–'

'Ma, I'm not a child. And I haven't been in ages.'

'Even so, dear, I have to agree with Edith – what could *you* possibly be trained to do?'

'Pretty much anything I'm minded to, I should think. I've two hands, two eyes, two ears, and plenty of practise at using them. I should say that's enough to learn to do almost anything, wouldn't you?'

'And what does Luke say about all of this?'

Responding to her mother's question, Edith didn't even look up from her darning as she said, 'Doubtless she hasn't told him.'

'As it happens, I haven't – not that it makes any odds. This is about *me*. It's about what *I* want to do. He's already made it quite plain – without, I might add, a thought to talk to me – that when the war comes, he's going soldiering. So, why shouldn't I do something too?'

'Look love, if this is because Luke will be going away–'

'It isn't about Luke. I told you, it's about me.'

'–and you're worried he might not come back to you, well, that's easily set to rights.'

'Ma, for the final time, *this isn't about Luke*. And the sooner you accept that, the sooner you'll understand why I want to do something to help.'

'Why don't you go on up to bed, love – take that Horlicks anyway? I know it's a warm night but it'll help you nod off nice an' quick.'

'*I don't want a Horlicks!*'

'*Lower your voice.* I will not have you bawling like a fishwife. Remember where you are, for heaven's sake.'

'Then please just listen to me for once,' Kate said. '*Your* lives may have passed *you* by, but that doesn't mean mine has to. Whether you like it or not – *and you, too, Edith* – I'm going to *do* something. Something for the war and something with my life. It might take a while, and I might not know for certain what it is yet, but mark my words, I'm going to do it. And can't neither of you stop me.'

Sweeping from the room – and making a point

168

of slamming the door behind her – Kate stood in the corridor, her teeth gritted and her hands clenched. If, before that precise moment, she'd had any lingering doubts about her plan, she didn't now.

Now, she was adamant: she would let nothing and no one stand in her way.

The following morning, Kate awoke to find that she had a headache. As she stood pegging Miss Naomi's little squares of muslin to the line in the laundry yard, her eyes felt like squares in round sockets and the sunlight taunted her with its brightness. She'd hardly slept at all last night – mainly because, after her confrontation with Ma and Edith, she'd gone to bed feeling cross and unable to calm down. At times, the two of them treated her like a wayward child and showed a complete disregard for her opinions and views. Just because *they* didn't want to do anything differently from how they'd always done it, didn't mean she had to live her life in the same fashion.

Pegging the last of the cloths to the line, she groaned; she was doing it again, going over and over in her mind how unfairly they'd spoken to her and how, with hindsight, she should have gone about it differently. For a start, she wouldn't have said anything at all to them yet. As it was, it might be a couple of weeks before Ned heard anything from his cousin. A couple of *weeks*. In that amount of time, the war could have come and gone.

'You all right?'

Just when she thought her day couldn't get any more tedious! 'Fine, thank you,' she muttered, fielding Luke's enquiry.

'Your ma said I might find you out here, said she'd heard you in the laundry a while back.'

Unable to ignore him without inviting comment, she turned to face him. 'And here I am. She was right. There's a surprise.'

'You look … cross.'

Well, it was brave of him, she'd give him that.

'No,' she said, lowering her shoulders, and immediately feeling the tension starting to drain from her neck. 'No, I just didn't sleep well.' There was little point rankling *him*, as well.

'Aye, a touch warm, weren't it?'

'Very.' Looking back at him, she sighed. None of this was really his fault and yet, sooner rather than later, he was the one whose life – along with all his hopes and his plans – were going to be turned upside down, his dreams tossed about and then cast aside like flotsam on the returning tide. But, even though he was standing between her and her dreams, she didn't hate him. She just knew now that she no longer wanted to marry him.

'Day before yesterday, I got talking to that Mr Colborne.'

Determined not to let him see that this piece of news piqued her interest – after all, this could still be a trap of some sort – she drew a long breath and then said, 'Which one?'

'Eh?'

'Which Mr Colborne? There's three of them.'

'Oh. Aye. The lightly-built one.'

'Mr Lawrence.'

'That'd be him.' What she mustn't do now, was show *too much* interest. She must wait for him to

170

go on and explain, which, being Luke, he was bound to do. 'He were having trouble starting that motor of theirs. Fine job, she is.'

'Aye?' *How was she unaware that this had happened? Luke had been talking to Mr Lawrence and she hadn't known about it?*

'Any road, as you know, back in the winter, I went up and helped out on Abe Pardey's farm – him having not long since picked up that tractor from that auction over at High Barns.'

Unable to help it, Kate yawned. 'Sorry. I'm just dead tired. Go on. You were saying.'

Creasing his forehead with a deep frown, Luke continued. 'Well, more 'n one occasion, she wouldn't fire up. And him and me had to see what to do about it. He knew a bit about motors but I knew nothing. Even so, betwixt us, we always got her going. So, I offered him – Mr Colborne, that is – the benefit of what I'd seen previous.'

'And did you get it started?' she asked. Much to her own surprise, she was genuinely interested now.

'We did that.'

'I bet he was pleased.'

'He were. So much so that when I said I'd always wanted to have a go in such a fancy motor, he offered to show me how to drive her. Up the drive we went, all the way to the lane. First him, then me. Then me again. In truth, tedn't that much different to Abe Pardey's tractor. And I told him as much. Course, he laughed at that – said not to tell his father, given the sum it had cost him.'

'Mmm.'

171

'Any road, the thing is, he said to me that being able to drive a motor is a real useful thing to know how to do – what with the war coming and everything. I told him I'd never thought of that. But, it's like he said, Kate, this war ain't going to be just about rifles and bayonets, like the wars gone before. It's going to be about mecker ... mechanized guns and ... armoured fighting vehicles, the likes of which have never been seen on a battlefield before.'

'But if no one has seen them, how does he ... oh, never mind.' There were times to pick holes in facts and times to just let them go. As her mother often said, *if you're not minded to hear the answer, don't ask the question in the first place.*

'So, I says to him, I shouldn't mind that. And he says to me, maybe I could speak for you. All sorts of regiments are going to need men who know how to drive.'

'Ned... Mr Edwin knows how to drive. By all accounts it's no big deal.'

'You're wrong there, Kate. It's a real tricky thing to master. And it's a proper responsibility, going along at such speeds.'

'Hmm. So, you'll be off soon, then?'

'What?'

'I said, you'll be off to join up soon.'

'Well, once war is *formally declared,* as Mr Colborne put it.'

She shook her head. Ten minutes with one of the Colbornes and Luke Charmer had a mouth full of big words. *Formally declared,* indeed.

'And I suppose now that you're hobnobbing with the gentry, you'd know when that will be.'

172

'Won't be long now. I doubt you've seen the papers this morning but, two days back, Austria-Hungary declared herself to be in a state of war with Serbia. And then there's that grisly business in Ireland. Newspaper said within days there could be civil war *there*. So, the way I see it, it's begun – we're already at war – or as good as.'

Not having been expecting such an informed answer from him – but having no reason to believe him wrong – she stared back at him. It was still worth checking that he wasn't toying with her, though. 'And that's the God-honest truth?'

He nodded. 'God's honest. Mark my words, by the end of this week, if not before, one way or another, we'll be at war.'

She swallowed. It wasn't just talk then; it was real. Even so, she would make a point of finding Ned to see whether he agreed. But if it *was* true, perhaps she would be needed for this volunteer thing sooner than she'd thought. Lord – there was a thing. And her not in the least bit ready, either.

'I see,' was all she managed to reply, her mind whirling.

'Look, Kate, marry me, will you? Let's not hang about no more. Give us the nod and I'll go up the church and get a special licence. Vicar'll give it us. He'll understand our haste; like everyone else, he'll know war's a-coming.'

And then it struck her: this was her mother's doing. It had to be. While everything Luke had just said might indeed have its roots in the truth, it was her mother who had put him up to this. On the back of her announcement to them last night, Ma must have nabbed him and pointed out that as far as getting married was concerned, it was now or never. Well, she wouldn't be herded like a wilful ewe.

'What does Ma say to it?' she asked, not blinking as she watched his face for the slightest sign that she was right.

But he didn't blink either. 'She thinks it a good idea. She's of the same mind as me – that we shouldn't wait on the off chance that all of this will go away.'

Curse him. He wasn't even going to attempt to deny it. 'You've spoken to her then.'

'Spoke to her first thing – soon as I heard tell the latest about the war.'

'Then my answer's no.'

'*No?*'

'That's right. You heard. No. I will not have you and my mother – and no doubt my sister, too – scheming behind my back and deciding when *I* get married. *When* I want to get married, it will be *me* who decides. Me and my husband-to-be.'

'Your husband-to-be? Kate–'

'And now I really must go back inside. I've stood here listening to you telling me your long tale about motors and Mr Colborne and driving in a war when all along, all you were trying to do was trick me–'

'Trick you? Bloody hell, woman, is that what you think this is – a trick?'

'It's underhand, that's what it is. And I'm surprised at you falling for it. Told you I'm acting strange, did she–'

'Well...'

'I knew it! Told you she was worried about me,

did she? Said you could make me see sense – that I needed to be settled down. Need a babe to fill my days, do I? And a husband to put an end to my taffety ideas? Is that what she said? Because trust me, I don't need either of those things until I say I do. And so, when you look at the calendar and wonder why there's no day ringed for us to be walking up the aisle, stand in front of the mirror and look at yourself long and hard and then, go and take a good look at my mother because, between the two of you, you've set back your chances...' It was on the tip of her tongue to say *altogether* but something made her think better of it. '...even further.'

Spinning away from him, she finally drew a proper breath. How dare he! How dare her mother! Well, if that's how they wanted it. If *they* weren't going to respect *her* wishes, then she wouldn't give a fig about theirs, as Miss Naomi would say. She would go ahead with her plan. Ned respected her opinions, and that was all that mattered.

'Kate–'

'No, I'm done,' she called over her shoulder as she stomped back across the yard. 'And if you know what's good for you, you won't breathe another word about weddings.'

Seething, she returned to the laundry and slammed the door shut behind her. Marriage? Well, if that was how her opinions and her dreams were to be run rough-shod over, then marriage could wait. Those three schemers had just seen to it that now, no matter how much Luke pleaded, there would be no naming of the day at all.

175

Chapter Five

A Fateful Evening

Kate stared into the bowl. The knob of soda she had dropped into it a moment ago seemed to have dissolved and so, extending her forefinger, she tested the temperature of the water. Just right. Holding Miss Naomi's hairbrush by its silver handle, she carefully lowered the bristles into the liquid. Taking care not to wet any of the silver surround, she stood for a moment, waiting for the soda to do its job.

Shifting her weight from one foot to the other, she wondered about Ned's plans for the day. Would she get the chance to see him? Hopefully, *he* would be thinking about seeing *her.* She'd fussed with her hair, just in case.

Deciding that she had waited long enough, she lifted the hairbrush from the liquid and gave it a shake. An examination of the bristles, though, made her return it to the solution; she might as well ensure that they were completely clean.

She sighed. Yes, she was rather hoping to bump into him because she wanted to see how he would behave towards her. Since their shared confessions, the suspense of waiting to see him was becoming unbearable, leaving her with a constant feeling of being strung out on tenterhooks.

Growing impatient, she lifted the hairbrush

from the bowl, turned on the tap and held the bristles under the stream of cold water. Idly watching as it splashed into the sink and gurgled down the plug-hole, she fancied she heard footsteps. Turning off the tap, she listened, the purposeful nature of them making her stiffen; by the sound of it, Ma was on the warpath. From force of habit, she made a quick check down the front of her uniform and readied a general denial. And then, when the footsteps came to a halt behind her, she fixed a smile and turned briefly over her shoulder.

Standing with a pile of table-linens in her arms, her mother surprised her by smiling back. 'You look a lot brighter today.'

Brighter? *That* wasn't the sort of accusation she'd been expecting. More used to denying things, she wasn't even sure how to respond. Perhaps the best thing was to remain vague – at least until she'd had a chance to spot the trap. There was bound to be one. 'Umm…'

'Had a chance to think things over, have you?'

There. That was it.

'Happen I have,' she replied, shaking the water from the bristles of the brush and then laying it on its back on a piece of cloth on the drainer. Reaching for the scrap of towel hanging on the nearby peg, she dried her hands. No matter how strong her desire, she *must not* let her mother know anything more about her plans. She'd already made that mistake once. Nor must she let slip anything to Edith. In fact, it was Edith's treachery she feared the most.

'Then no wonder you look less grumpy.'

Even that sort of dig wasn't going to provoke her; she would let the words wash over her. She would console herself with the fact that her plan showed all the signs of coming together nicely.

That she chose not to offer a reply meant that eventually, her mother turned and walked away. Priding herself on having managed to keep her mouth shut, Kate also set off, making her way up the stairs and along the landing to Miss Naomi's room. Further along the corridor, on the curve of the main landing, she could tell from an oblong of brightness that Mrs Russell's door stood open. She could also hear voices – although, where Pamela Russell's shrill tones were concerned, it was hard not to. 'I have to concede that your plan worked.' *That* voice belonged to Aunt Diana.

'Of course it did.' And that was Pamela Russell answering her. 'And wasn't the atmosphere all the better for it? Wasn't it? Wasn't conversation at supper on both evenings far more civilized? And I thought the picnic-tea on the lawn a triumph – everyone was present and yet no-one fell out. Given the unsettling nature of the current situation, that was no small achievement.'

'But how many more distractions do you have up your sleeve, Mamma?'

Realizing that Miss Naomi was also there, Kate decided it was safe to stand and listen a while longer.

'As many as prove necessary to keep the peace until your father arrives.'

'*Still* no word from Papa?'

'The only word he sent, was to say that he has – and I quote verbatim – *his fingers in several new and lucrative pies,* which, for the moment, he dares not desert. An indication of when he is likely to join us, however, was conspicuous by its absence. This evening, I shall telephone him.'

'May *I* speak to him?'

'If you wish. I intend being quite straight with him. *He* agreed to this gathering, and so he should jolly well show up. And sooner rather than later. I can't do it all single-handedly.'

'That's most unlike you, Pamela. As often as not you tell him, in no uncertain terms, not to meddle – that you have everything under control.'

'That's different. That's when we're in Clarence Square, where I can rely upon things to happen in accordance with my precise instructions. Down here, it's all rather more haphazard.'

'So, what further amusements *do* you have planned?'

'A party. Out on the lawns, under the stars – food, entertainments, music–'

'And you can pull that off, Pamela, out here, in the middle of nowhere, with only the minions you've just described as being haphazard?'

'Of course not, Diana. Don't be ridiculous. I have no faith in those bumpkins whatsoever. But I *do* have faith in my address book.'

Since she was one of the *haphazard bumpkins* in whom Mrs Russell had just expressed no faith, Kate felt it time to slip away. And so, turning carefully about, she crept back along the landing to where, taking every care not to make a sound, she returned Miss Naomi's hairbrush to her dressing-table.

A party. Under the stars. That meant at night,

with the cover of darkness: opportunities aplenty to keep watch on proceedings. She might even have the chance to sneak away and see Ned. Yes, on the evening in question, she would see to her hair and change out of her uniform. From the sound of it, Ma and Edith would be too busy to bother about where she was and what she was doing. And, to improve her chances further still, next time she saw him, she would let slip that there was nothing she liked more on a pleasant evening, than a stroll down through the woods to the cove. He probably wouldn't think it odd; he'd already come across her wandering about the grounds. But if he did, he did: she couldn't help that; in a couple of weeks he would probably have left. Gone was the time for hesitation, or for standing about letting the grass grow under her feet.

Five-and-twenty minutes to seven. If she didn't hurry up and get this done, she wasn't going to have time to get herself into her hiding place before proceedings got under way. The trouble was, the ring of salt around the soles of Miss Naomi's navy-blue kid-skin shoes was proving laborious to remove. She had scraped away the worst of it with the blade of a paring-knife. Then she had dabbed at it with a scrap of cloth soaked in white vinegar, watching with relief as some of it dissolved. Unfortunately, traces remained, stubbornly resisting her attempts to pick it from the stitching, grain by grain, with the end of a meat-skewer. It didn't help that she was standing in her own light, straining her eyes to see. Still, it was her own fault for not having seen to them yesterday, the minute Miss Naomi had come back from walking down at the cove and pointed out to her their condition.

Eventually, too weary to concentrate any longer, she gave up. It was a task she would finish in the morning; there would be plenty of time before Miss Naomi was up and about and able to notice that the shoes weren't back in her wardrobe.

Relieved by the chance to stand upright, she straightened her back and rolled her head in circles. Golly, her neck felt stiff. Her feet ached, too. Today, she had been on them even longer than usual, the number of times she had run up and down the stairs impossible to count. On any other night, she would be looking forward to sitting with them in a bowl of Epsom salts dissolved in warm water, last thing before bed. But not tonight. Tonight, she had plans to watch the fun.

It was the evening of Pamela Russell's party. And, throughout the day, there had been so much kerfuffle surrounding costumes and outfits – the fittings conducted secretly in an unused bedroom – that she was itching to see the results. Even now, with things about to get underway, she still didn't really know what was going to happen. The only things she did know had been gleaned from catching snippets of conversations and from glimpsing a hand-written card left lying on a side table: *Fête Champêtre* – A Diverting Evening of Costumes, Food and Rustic Amusements.

Even Miss Naomi, retiring earlier than usual to her room to change, had been unusually tight-lipped.

181

'Can you manage ringlets, do you think?' was all that she had asked.

Taking cover now amid the rhododendrons at the edge of the lawn, she sighed. All things considered, she was fortunate to have made it down there in time; now she would at least be able to watch everyone coming out of the French doors onto the terrace and proceeding down the steps.

When she drew a breath of anticipation, her nostrils filled with the smells of the shrubbery: damp earth; leaf mould; the bitter aroma from the leathery foliage of the rhododendrons themselves. Hearing distant voices, she carefully lifted aside one of the branches obscuring her view. Already, something was happening.

With her eyes not knowing what to settle upon first, she gasped: Miss Naomi, in a gown of deep blue silk, was on the arm of ... Ralph Colborne. *Ralph* Colborne? Not Lawrence, for whom she would surely have been hoping? Not even Aubrey, for whom she wouldn't have? In military uniform, Ralph Colborne looked distinguished, the scarlet of his jacket a blazing contrast to the silver of his hair, the gold of his buttons glinting in the evening sunshine. But where on earth could Mrs Russell have found such costumes, especially at such short notice? And particularly here, in Devon. It defied belief.

On Mr Colborne's arm, Miss Naomi looked like a princess and she could see now why she had asked for ringlets, her appearance suggestive of the young woman in the oil painting that hung, forgotten, in a dusty frame on the staircase. Entitled simply *Amelia*, it was said to be one of only four paintings to have survived the fire that, almost forty years ago, had destroyed the manor house. Studying Miss Naomi's appearance – as best she could, given the distance – Kate sighed. The blisters to the ends of her fingers from the curling iron had been worth it, the smell of scorching, too; her painstakingly created ringlets perfect for that gown.

From behind Naomi Russell came further movement: Cicely Colborne on the arm of Lawrence, the latter also sporting military uniform. Tonight, Mrs Colborne's thinning grey hair looked to have been expertly styled but her frail frame appeared even more petite than usual, dwarfed as it was by yards of lilac silk, a full skirt falling in tiers, each of them edged with a contrasting lace. Added to that, the low angle of the sunshine was doing her complexion no favours, picking out the wrinkles around her eyes and across her forehead to add at least a decade to what Kate supposed to be her true age. It was widely held among the staff that she was younger than her husband by some margin, also that she was his second wife, her husband's first choice having died in childbirth, the infant tragically passing with her. Terribly sad, really. But sad also, surely, to be someone's second choice.

When, for a while, no one else seemed about to appear, Kate redirected her attention through the branches of the rhododendrons to the lawn. The transformation from formal gardens to rustic pasture was startling Little more than a few hours previously, all manner of props and materials had still been arriving, most of them unimaginable in this remote part of Devon. From where had they all come? All anyone below stairs knew was that Mrs Russell had spent ages calling on the telephone and then issuing precise instructions to Edith about desserts and cakes that were to be prepared. But *only* desserts and cakes: the other courses, she had disclosed, were being prepared elsewhere by a proper *chef de cuisine.*

Almost from first light, a stream of visitors and deliveries had begun arriving. No one could recall anything like it – not even Ma in the days before the old manor had burnt down. Clearly, Kate had determined, watching as a dozen or so pitch torches had been unloaded from the rear of a delivery van, when it came to throwing a party, Pamela Russell took no chances with the arrangements, nor, seemingly, did she spare her husband's money.

'She's doing it to get back at him for not being here, you know,' Kate had overheard Miss Naomi comment to Aunt Diana. At the time, she had failed to comprehend her remark. Now, though, it made sense.

From her sideways viewpoint among the gnarly trunks, she tried to look along the terrace. Nearest to, at the foot of the retaining stone wall, a canopy of canvas had been tethered to the lawn with ropes and poles, the effect being like a tent without sides. Beneath it stood four chairs and four music-stands. Earlier in the day, the words *string quartet* had been muttered, mainly by those with no idea of what one was. Quartet, she knew, meant *four,* and so, presumably, there was to be an orchestra, albeit a small one. Several yards from the front of the canopy, bales of straw had been arranged in a semi-circle, which she supposed were intended to serve as benches. How odd, though, for an event where money was clearly no object, to expect the ladies, in all of their finery, to sit upon straw.

Beginning to tire of waiting for something else to happen, she let her eyes wander to the far end of the terrace, where, earlier in the day, she had watched four men in overalls erecting a tent about a central pole. At the time, she had been unable to glean its purpose. With its flap now fastened against prying eyes, she was still none the wiser.

Other items of interest that had appeared since her earlier covert visit included oversized blankets, spread on the ground as though for lounging or picnicking. At one corner of each them, smaller blankets had been stacked in twos and threes, perhaps for use against the late-evening chill. She gave a wry chuckle: at that very moment, with perspiration trickling down into the small of her back, it was hard to imagine there being demand for such a thing. And anyway, dotted about the lawn were braziers, fashioned from metal to look like baskets and so laden with logs that, once alight, were sure to give off a blistering heat.

The downside of choosing to conceal herself in the shrubbery, she now realized, was that she had no idea of the hour. In any event, it might not be a bad idea to let herself be seen indoors. Last time she had looked into the kitchen, Edith had been bent over a tray of tiny pastries spun with sugar. And Ma had been talking to the mustachioed man with the thick notebook, who had been present all day. From what she'd been able to determine, he was in charge of ensuring that Mrs Russell's instructions were carried out to the letter, Ma having apparently been reduced to passing on his orders and then watching as he scribbled notes or ticked off things on his list. Either way, in the general busyness of below stairs, no one had noticed either her arrival or her departure – which was just how she liked it.

She looked back to the French doors. How much longer before Ned came out? Having stood for so long on the uneven ground, her feet were beginning to ache but, knowing *her* luck, if she left now, she would miss seeing him. And she was desperate to know which of the women would have the good fortune to be on his arm. She *had* thought it might be his sister but, since it wasn't, perhaps it would be Aunt Diana.

Again, she sighed. It had been a peculiar sort of a day, the upheaval to the normally smooth running of the household disorienting. All day, a trail of strangers, some of whose roles she had been able to deduce from their livery – chefs, waiting-staff, and so on – had sought out the stubby little man with the ornate moustache, waiting while he flicked backwards and forwards though the pages of his notebook before being directed to their place of work.

She glanced again to the doors. Finally, movement. She strained to see, disappointed when it was only the musicians, already looking rather sticky in their stiff evening dress. With nothing more exciting to occupy her, she watched them

186

step from the terrace onto the lawn and then cross to their seats under the canopy. Several moments of settling down and rearranging things followed: the heights of their stands; the pages of their music; the distances between their chairs. When they finally took their seats, there came the sound of strings being plucked.

Then came the examining and tweaking of bows, and finally, the humming of a single note, easily a match in resonance for a swarm of bees.

Carefully, she shifted her weight, unable to risk that the leaf debris beneath her feet might crackle loudly enough to draw attention. It was bad enough that her nose was itching, making her feel as though she was in continual danger of sneezing. Settling into a marginally more comfortable position, she brought her hand to rest on a nearby branch and once again peered out through the foliage: someone was just inside the French doors. It was the little man with the notebook, and he was leading out a stream of liveried waiters bearing wicker picnic-baskets, each one carried to one of the rugs. There, the waiters unfolded and laid out linen tablecloths. That done, with a flourish, the lid of each basket was unfastened and opened back. By now gathered upon the terrace to look down upon the spectacle, the assembled guests applauded and, from their midst, Pamela Russell stepped forward. Ned: she was on the arm of Ned.

Although it was to see him that Kate had been suffering such discomfort, it was Pamela Russell's gown that caught her eye. Off-the-shoulder and extraordinarily low-necked, it had a full skirt, beneath which she could only imagine there to be all manner of hoops and petticoats. Devoid of the ruffles and frippery adorning the gowns of the other women, it was stunning in its simplicity, its colour as rich as, but more scarlet than, blood. To Kate, it seemed a dress chosen purely for its ability to draw attention, rather than for any particular historical accuracy.

Her curiosity as to Mrs Russell's outfit satisfied, Kate turned her attention to Ned, only partly visible beyond his mother. He, too, was in military uniform, except that where every other man wore crimson, Ned was wearing blue. His jacket was trimmed with a collar of gold, so high that it looked most uncomfortable to wear, and gold epaulettes that made him seem very square of frame. Drawn to studying him, she realized that he had been dressed in blue in order to act as a backdrop to his mother's gown; Mrs Russell hadn't chosen that jacket to make *him* stand out from the other men but in order to display her own appearance to best advantage. Had Ned worn a crimson jacket, the colours of the two out-fits would have clashed, whereas the blue set off his mother's gown nicely. She had to hand it to Mrs Russell, it was a very clever idea. Miss Naomi might maintain that her father was shrewd, but seemingly, her mother didn't miss a trick, either.

Returning her eyes to Ned, something about the vision of him as an army officer made her shiver. She didn't like to think of him going off to war. And so, she wouldn't. Tonight, she would just look at him and hope that, later on, she would have a chance to talk to him. Scarlet or blue, the colour and nature of his uniform altered nothing; he was still, by a country mile, the most handsome man in sight.

Kate smiled. Her decision to creep away from proceedings in the garden and let herself be seen indoors had proved worthwhile. Casting no more than a single glance in her direction, and with her arms full of napkins, Ma had merely nodded at her, her mind clearly on other things.

Edith, likewise, had barely looked up from her work.

'My, Edie, they're beautiful,' she'd said, making a point of remarking about the creations to which her sister was putting the finishing touches.

'Aye,' Edith had absently replied. 'Damned fiddly, though.'

With that, Kate had been left free to slip along the corridor and up the stairs to her room. Since no one needed her – and she had given them every chance to say otherwise – she felt it safe to change out of her uniform and into her own skirt and blouse. The rest of the evening was hers.

Having freshened her face with soap and cool water, she angled the small mirror to check her appearance. What she saw made her shake her head with dismay. If she wanted to look ... well, comely ... having her hair pinned ordinarily back was no good at all. While she couldn't wear it loose about her shoulders, she *could* fasten it more softly. Pulling it from its knot, she stood brushing through the length of it until she had counted one hundred strokes. Even in the murky light of her attic room, she was quite pleased with

189

the way it shone.

With her hair re-pinned in a style similar to that favoured by Miss Naomi, she turned about, trying to peer over her shoulder at the reflection of the back of her head. Unable to see anything, all she could do was trust in her pinning. At least as the evening wore on, the failing light would disguise any waywardness.

When she arrived back at the bottom of the staircase, she hesitated. Sounds from the scullery suggested that clearing up had started, which probably meant that, outside, the guests were now eating. The question thus became one of what was going to happen next? What, precisely, were these 'rustic amusements' that Mrs Russell had planned? The only way to find out was to go and look. But, for that, creeping about among the rhododendrons would be pointless. For a start, it would soon be too dark to navigate a path through their twisting limbs: much better to go out through the scullery and head for the far end of the lawn. From there, she ought to be afforded a reasonable view.

'Ladies and gentlemen, may I beg your indulgence.' Arriving at the corner of the house, Kate could see Pamela Russell, posing on the terrace as though on a stage. From the picnic blankets on the lawn, her guests had turned towards her, while, back against the house, apparently concealed from their sight by the shadows, stood a figure Kate didn't recognize. All she could tell was that it wasn't one of the guests. 'Thank you, everyone,' Mrs Russell continued. 'Now, I should like to introduce to you one of the most intriguing women I have ever had the good fortune to meet.' Although none of her audience would have been aware of it, at Mrs Russell's announcement, several of the men sat more upright. Hardly surprising, Kate thought, deciding that most of them looked tipsy: their hostess had mentioned an intriguing woman. 'Ladies and gentlemen, I give you Madam Sybil, seer, mystic and prophetess *extraordinaire!*'

From down on the picnic blankets came murmurs of puzzlement, although, from politeness, there was also light applause. On cue, the figure in the shadows stepped forward. Wearing a long gown, dark in colour and formless in style, she stood erect, on her head a turban almost identical to the one favoured by Aunt Diana – but black.

From somewhere down on the lawn, a man's voice called out. 'Prophetess? Ha!'

Without even a glance to Pamela Russell, Sybil the prophetess proceeded slowly down towards the lawn, the hem of her robe slinking down the steps behind her. Not knowing what was going to happen, Kate held her breath.

'Among you this evening,' the woman stopped a few steps short of the grass to announce, 'is one whose offspring keep her from peaceful sleep.' Kate gulped. She hadn't been expecting anything like that. Nor, from the bewilderment on the faces of the guests, had they. With everyone's attention secured, in a clear and commanding voice, Sybil continued. 'She is blessed with sons, two of them, similar in appearance and age, both on the cusp of manhood. But the younger one troubles her,

191

the younger one...' From one of the blankets on the grass came a little gasp followed by the sharp turning of heads towards it. Cordelia Fillingham? Was it *she* with her hand over her mouth? Looking back to where Sybil was partially silhouetted by the light from the torches, Kate willed her to go on. The younger one *what*?

'My God, Pamela! What is this business?'

Although the observation surely came from Cordelia's husband, Sibyl was undeterred. 'Rest assured, sir, I reveal my prophecies only to those for whom they are intended.'

'Hogwash, I say. Bunkum, all of it!' And that, Kate knew without a doubt, was Aubrey Colborne. And, already he sounded the worse for drink.

'I have a strong sense of you, too, sir,' Sibyl turned to him to respond, a hush once again coming over the blankets. 'The path you choose is a dangerous one. Mists swirl about you. You would wear them like a cloak. But I caution you to beware. I urge you, seek my counsel – be willing to hear it.'

Kate blinked rapidly. This woman, this stranger, had the measure of everyone present? How could that be?

'Ladies and gentlemen,' Pamela Russell stepped forward to say, 'Madam Sibyl will now take private consultations. Who shall go first?' When, in the startled silence, no one answered, she went on. 'Nobody? Come along, now. Don't be shy. Who among us is not intrigued?' As she continued to stand, awaiting a response, her arm held wide, it was as much as Kate could do not

192

to leap forward and volunteer. What an opportunity to learn her fate! Oh, if only! As it was, it fell to Mrs Russell to say, with Kate felt not a small amount of irritation, 'Then while *you* all gather your courage, *I* shall show you that not only is there nothing to fear, but much to gain.'

For a while afterwards, and to Kate's disappointment, nothing much seemed to happen. With Mrs Russell having accompanied Sybil into the tent, most of the guests remained seated on their blankets, one or two of the men moving about to confer and glance uncomfortably towards it.

'She's gone too far this time,' a male voice opined loudly enough for Kate to hear.

'Devilish thing, what?' his companion seemed to concur.

But, just as Kate was debating whether she could wait around any longer on the off chance of seeing Ned, the flap of the tent opened back and, from the gentle glow within, Pamela Russell emerged, smiling and serene.

'Marvellous,' she murmured, to Kate's mind, a little too loudly to be entirely genuine. Swiftly, Cordelia Fillingham went to her, her manner hesitant, furtive almost. 'Of course, my dear,' Mrs Russell said. 'Allow me to introduce you.'

And thus began what was to become a steady trail of female guests to Sybil's tent, each of them remaining for what felt to be around ten minutes before reappearing, their expressions ranging from surprise through pensiveness to, in one case, what Kate could only think of as alarm.

'What do you think? Do we have a fraud on our

hands?' With Ned's voice coming out of the darkness, Kate jumped. How had she neither seen nor heard him approaching? And what must he think to find her once again spying on his mother and her guests?

'Umm...'

'It seems none of our guests can quite decide.' At least the cloak-and-dagger nature of her presence didn't trouble him. 'Those who would chance a reading seem to feel she is entirely genuine. Their husbands, I suspect, feel differently.'

'Only to be expected,' Kate replied, her initial surprise at his arrival slowly subsiding.

'Please, do explain to me why you think so.'

In the darkness, Kate frowned. If *he* had spotted her, then who else might also have done so? Who else might, at this very moment, be watching them conversing?

'Well,' she said, deciding to worry about that separately, 'seems to me, men prefer to rely on the things they can see with their own eyes or touch with their own hands – real things that they can ... poke an' prod. Whereas women strike me as thinking that oftentimes, there be greater forces at work – ones not always so easily explained away.' Feeling as though she had revealed rather too much about her own way of looking at the world, and catching sight of what looked to be mild amusement on his face, she hastened to add, 'Leastways, that's how it seems to me. And I can only say it as I see it.'

For a moment or two, he didn't respond. Despite the cooling of the evening, she thought he looked warm, his blue jacket abandoned and his hair bearing the signs of having been swept, repeatedly, away from his face. In addition, the sleeves of his shirt had been rolled back and the neck of his shirt unbuttoned: highly inappropriate for an army officer.

'So,' he eventually said, 'when it comes to … well, shall we call them *unearthly forces,* is it your contention that we separate into believers and cynics along the line of the sexes?'

It was *precisely* how she saw it. Men even called women fanciful for it. But, rather than give him the chance to deride her, she was struck by a means with which to lend her idea weight. 'Will *you* be going in?' she asked him. 'For a reading … or an audience or whatever it is?'

'Hardly. Will you?'

'Were I at liberty to, then yes, I should jump at the chance.'

'And with which I suppose you rest your case?'

She smiled. 'I do stand by my belief, yes.'

Less than two paces away from her, he reclined against a tree. It seemed beyond her to accept that she was there with him, the mantle of the night allowing them to once again converse, free from the usual conventions. *Blissful,* Kate thought, *that's what it was.* If only it didn't have to end.

'Hmm.' When she looked across, his faint smile bore a suggestion of mischief. 'It seems to me, Miss Bratton, that your case, while not entirely without merit, flounders for want of more participants – a broader sample, if you will.'

In the same vein, she rose quickly to her own defence. 'It don't need no more. I know what I've seen with my own eyes.'

195

To this, he inclined his head, his expression a mixture of amusement and consideration. 'As reliable a source as any, I suppose.'

Her point seemingly won, they fell to stillness. To Kate, the silence felt comfortable. Even so, she would prefer that they continued to talk. And so, to that end, she asked, 'Are you enjoying the evening?'

'Mamma seems to be. And that's the main thing.'

'Ah.'

'And, despite the manner in which she has just unsettled some of her guests, tomorrow morning, they will all rush to compliment her upon the marvellous spectacle – the imaginative theme – and thank her, profusely, for a most enjoyable evening.'

'Why are you the only man not rayed in crimson?' she asked She knew that conversation-wise, she was leaping about but, since she didn't know how long he would remain, she wanted to make the most of this unlikely chance.

'On account of Mamma changing her mind. It was her wish that the men be colourful and dashing, so the uniforms supplied by the theatre company–' *A theatre company,* well that explained it! '–were those of infantry officers. But, at the last minute, she changed her mind about her own gown and, since I was to be her escort, and the colour of my costume clashed with hers – or so she would have it – something had to be done. At that late stage, the only other uniform to fit me was for an officer of a lancer regiment, which just happened to be blue. Intolerably stiff collar, by the way. Don't know how the original chap stuck it, dress uniform or no.'

In the darkness, Kate smiled. His explanation was much as she had expected: it was all about Pamela Russell and how she appeared to her guests. But then it *was* her party. 'The scarlet uniforms are striking,' she said. 'But the blue is nicer.' *The blue is nicer on you.*

'Hmm.'

'May I ask you something?' she ventured, recalling something she wanted to know.

'Of course.'

'What exactly is a *fett champetter?*'

'A *fête champêtre?*'

At his correcting of her pronunciation, she blushed. 'Forgive me my ignorance. It's how it looked written down.'

'I'll tell you what it's *not,*' he said, unbothered. 'It's not what you see before you here tonight, which is more a *faux champêtre.*' It wasn't the answer for which she had been hoping. In fact, it didn't feel like an explanation at all. Besides which, from him, the sarcasm was unusual. 'I'm sorry. That wasn't very helpful,' he said, immediately contrite. 'It's just that sometimes, mother should ... oh, never mind.' With a shake of his head, he sighed. 'The words *fête champêtre* don't translate terribly well into English, but the term usually describes a sort of pastoral or rural celebration or festivity. At the end of the last century, it was the thing – especially, for a while, among the gentry of France – to don the dress from earlier times and fashion an idealized rural setting in which to make merry.'

'Oh. I see.'

'It was imaginative of Mamma, I'll grant her that. And, given that we're so very far from the people she would ordinarily summon from her address book, no mean feat. It's just that she *could* have settled for a far simpler affair. People would have been just as happy. But no, she always has to try and outdo her last great event, fearing if she doesn't that people will no longer speak of her gatherings with the same awe.'

Unsure how to respond to this frank admission from him, she settled for, 'Mmm.'

'By the way, I've written to Cousin Elizabeth, making enquiries on your behalf.'

'Thank you,' she said, determined to remain calm even though it was as much as she could do not to grin with delight.

'I walked to the letter-box at the crossroads yesterday morning.' Opening her mouth to tell him that there was a box on the hall table for letters requiring posting, she decided against it: perhaps he had wanted the walk. 'Of course,' he went on, 'I have no way of knowing how long it will be before she replies. As I think I said to you, her volunteer work keeps her very busy.'

''Course,' she said, feeling her cheeks colouring under his gaze. She realized then that this was the first time she had seen him since the evening before last. Yesterday, after lunch, the entire group – family and guests alike – had decamped to the cove, where rugs had been set out and elaborate sun shades devised so that no possible discomfort could spoil a picnic tea. Hampers of provisions had been ferried, drinks had been cooled, and bundles of towels had been supplied for those tempted to risk a dip in the sparkling water.

His time on the beach, Kate thought, had given him a glow and made him look even more relaxed – if such a thing were possible, something that prompted her to ask, 'Was it nice down in the cove yesterday afternoon?'

That she had thought to enquire seemed to please him. 'Do you know, it *was*. It was delightful. For once, everyone seemed calm and agreeable. But, with the sun shining and the location so picturesque, it would be a soulless creature whose thoughts kept returning to war, would it not?'

Shifting a little, she nodded. 'It would.'

'Not that the likelihood of war recedes just because a dozen people on a beach in Devon refuse to talk about it for an afternoon.'

'Although perhaps,' she ventured, in two minds whether to continue, 'if *everyone* were to spend an afternoon on a pretty little beach, they'd *all* be more calm and agreeable, and then they *might* think twice about the need to go to war.'

'I say, what a charming idea! Perhaps I should write and suggest it to Sir Edward Grey. Sir, rather than watching as Russia mobilizes her army and navy, might you not suggest to St Petersburg that they spend a week at the beach instead? While you're at it, suggest it to the German Chancellor, too, salt water and sea air a proven tonic for calming all manner of hysteria.'

For a moment, she wondered whether he was mocking her. His face, though, seemed to suggest only amusement.

'Just a fanciful notion, sir. Ma says I'm full of 'em.'

'No harm in that, Kate.' *Kate! That was the second time he'd called her Kate. Not Miss Bratton, but Kate!*

'Aha.' He straightened up. 'Aunt Cicely emerges from her audience. She looks shaken, do you not think?'

Straining to make out the expression on Cicely Colborne's face, Kate nodded. 'She does. I wonder what was said to turn her so pale?'

'Charlatans play on people's emotions. It's part of their power – their hold over their subject, if you will.'

Wanting desperately to believe that Sybil's gift of foresight was genuine, his remark disappointed her. 'You'd still have her a fraud?'

To Kate, the little snort he gave suggested whole-hearted agreement, even before he had replied.

'Almost certainly.'

'Oh.'

'But *you* still don't?'

Unexpectedly, she saw her chance. Although hanging wraith-like in the night air, it nevertheless felt worth trying to grasp. 'I shouldn't venture to judge either way, not without having first seen for myself.'

'You would have an audience?'

Nothing ventured, nothing gained. 'I would. I should like to hear what she has to say and then decide for myself. The way I see it, if all she does is spout bromides and speak of things so general that they might be made to fit any woman on earth, then I should agree with you that she is a fraud. But, should she know something about

200

me, some detail that no one else could have told her, then I should hold otherwise.'

'And what would you ask her to bring that about? How would you go about your investigation so as not to *lead the witness,* as it were?'

Having not expected to be so deeply questioned, she frowned. 'Since I shan't be seeing her anyway, I must confess to not having thought so far ahead.'

Throughout their conversation, he had been leaning idly against the tree but now, pushing himself away from it, he stood looking directly at her. 'What if I could get you in to see her? Would you go?'

Goodness. Had her ploy worked? 'In an instant.'

'Stay there.'

Before she could enquire as to his intention, he was striding across the lawn towards where his mother was talking to Miss Naomi. When he arrived alongside her, barely a dozen words seemed to pass between them, the gesture accompanying Pamela Russell's response suggesting deep disinterest in whatever he had said. Clearly, then, he hadn't asked his mother whether she, Kate, might be granted an audience.

Puzzled, she watched, as, turning towards the house, he went indoors. Now what should she do? His parting instruction to her had been *stay there* – but she was no longer certain that he was going to return.

For what felt like ages, she repeatedly scanned the lawn and the terrace for sight of him. More time passed with still no sign. But then, hearing someone coming through the trees towards her, she spun about, her heart thudding in her chest. 'Oh! I was thinking you'd forgotten me.'

Although, in the darkness, it was hard to determine his precise expression, her remark appeared to surprise him. 'I wouldn't do that. But I did have to be careful. You see, I asked Mamma whether, when whoever is with Sybil at the moment has finished, *I* might take a turn.'

'You? But I thought you said–'

'A ruse. I didn't think you'd want me to ask whether *you* could go in–' Relieved to hear it, she shook her head. 'So, while I go in through the front of her tent, you are going to slip in through the back–'

'I'm going to do *what?* Oh, no, I couldn't–'

'Don't worry, I have it all worked out. I shall go in, explain to Sybil what is happening, unfasten the back of the tent, let you in, and then go out the same way. When you're done, I shall slip in through the back and exit through the front. No one will be any the wiser.'

All Kate could think was that she felt peculiar. Was he really proposing to do this for her? Would they get away with it? Would Sybil even agree to go along with such deceit? What if this Sybil woman told Mrs Russell? Would they get into trouble?

So many questions!

'You definitely don't want to go in – for yourself, I mean?'

In answer to her question, Ned shook his head. 'I don't need someone to tell me what lies ahead. My belief is that almost without exception, one

202

gets the future one deserves, endeavour generally bringing its own reward. Aim for what you want, strive diligently towards it, and generally, success will come.'

'That's always been my thought too,' she said, astounded to think that while they were so completely different, they should hold such similar views. 'It's just that I never thought to meet another person who felt the same. Most folk around here hold either that things are *meant to be,* or else that they're not.'

'Like you, I disagree. But, if you want an audience with Sybil, I have every faith that my plan will work. Just don't be too long making up your mind. Whoever is in there at the moment is unlikely to be much longer.'

Unexpectedly, Kate was beginning to regret showing her hand. 'Do you think me foolish to be curious – to want to see what she has to say?'

'As it happens, I don't. Mamma brought her here for entertainment. Why not let her entertain you?'

At that moment, she realized she was no longer sure what she wanted. But, if Ned was prepared to stick his neck out for her, then it behoved her not to appear ungrateful. 'All right,' she said. 'Thank you. Tell me what to do.'

It wasn't what she had been expecting. Inside Madam Sybil's tent there were just two easy chairs and a low table with a hurricane lantern from within which, a stubby candle was giving off a yellowy light. No crystal ball, no deck of cards featuring sinister drawings – not even saucers with tea leaves. To Kate, it was a bit of a let-down.

'The young man tells me you specifically requested an audience,' Sybil said once she had bid Kate sit down.

'Umm ... yes. I mean, yes please.'

The prophetess smiled. This close-to, she was younger than Kate had imagined. Her complexion was evenly-coloured – in this light, slightly golden – and her eyes unusually large and dark and rimmed with black. Her nose was prominent – hooked, even – and her lips full and painted scarlet. Apart from that, she wore no embellishments; her fingers were uncluttered by rings, her throat was free from collar or necklace, her ears devoid of gold or stones. Not at all what she had been expecting.

'Sit quietly,' the woman instructed her. 'Remain still, keep your eyes upon mine and let me speak of what I see. Do not utter a sound, for to do so will break the connection.'

Again, Kate had to force herself to swallow. 'I understand,' she said, her voice barely registering. And then, doing as she had been told, she stared back at the pair of dark eyes, feeling as though they were searching her soul, picking over her innermost thoughts, and uncovering her secrets.

'You have questions about your future,' Sybil began. 'A natural state of affairs: you are young and still seeking your path through this life. But, I have a strong sense that what burns away at you most, is the question of whom you shall marry. Well, my dear, the answers to those questions and more are there for you to see. Your future is already written and, once you master the art of seeing it for yourself, you will become mistress of your own destiny. You will see your true path.' Briefly, while trying to make sense of this, Kate lowered her eyes. Remembering Madam Sybil's instruction, she quickly raised them up again. 'Are you destined to remain in service or is there a Prince Charming in your future? The answers are there for you to see.'

Momentarily forgetting Madam Sybil's instruction about remaining quiet, Kate couldn't help herself. 'But how do I do that? See my future, I mean.'

'Time, you must understand,' the woman continued regardless, 'is an inexact ideal, existing within us and without, in many forms. The past, the present, the future, no one single notion of it can ever be entirely separated from the other two. For that reason, determining your future is straightforward.' At this, Kate straightened herself up in readiness to remember what she was about to be told. 'Choose a clear day and a quiet place. Calm your mind from its busyness. Then, look deep into your heart. Look first to your past, then to your present. From such honest examination will your future gradually emerge. Were you to beg me to guess at what you might see, I believe it would be two paths diverging in front of you. While both will seem within your grasp, you must beware, for, one of them, while promising much and glittering brightly, will bring only heartache. While you alone must choose which path to follow, I would offer to you this advice – consider both paths with equal care. Do not be too hasty to dismiss the one that is flat and even and well-trodden. Though you might crave a new direction – for it is only human nature to do so – the path that hints at the unfamiliar is littered with twists and turns. Its pull upon you will be hard to resist, its very foreignness hinting at great excitement. But know this, such paths are always slippery and wont to end suddenly and without warning, leaving you cast adrift far from all that you know.'

When Madam Sybil unexpectedly fell quiet, Kate shivered. That was it? She had finished? Seemingly aware of her quandary, Madam Sybil looked towards the rear of the tent. 'That is all. Be about your business now, girl, but have a care, those by whose side you would walk may not be what they seem.'

When Madam Sybil rose to her feet, Kate had no choice but to do likewise. 'Umm ... thank you,' she muttered, moving to the rear of the tent and feeling about for the open section of flap. *Those by whose side you would walk may not be what they seem?* What did *that* mean? More to the point, who did she mean by 'they'?

While fumbling with the canvas, her hand unexpectedly met Ned's fingers reaching in from the other side. In shock, she recoiled.

'All right?' he enquired, bending to look at her face, his expression one of mild amusement.

She nodded stiffly. 'Yes. Thank you.' But then, lest he attempt to suggest discussing what had happened, she hurried on, 'But I'd best be getting back along. I can't afford to be caught out here.'

'Of course,' he said, smiling and holding aside the canvas flap. 'And I had best make a point of being seen back among our guests.'

Grateful to have avoided being grilled on what had happened, she took a few steps into the trees, where, for a moment, she simply stood in the darkness. She wished she could make better sense of what Madam Sybil had said. She hadn't been expecting riddles; she had been hoping for guidance. On the bright side, she *had* learnt how to see her future. And it was pleasing to discover that she could take charge of her own destiny. But, at that precise moment, she was far too weary to do either. She would try it in the morning. Now, though, all she truly wanted was her bed.

Careful to remain away from the light of the torches, she took the long way back across the lawn, arriving at the corner of the house and flattening herself into the shadow against the wall. So far, so good. Now all she had to do was make it to the back door.

While she stood catching her breath, the stillness all around her was broken by the sound of scuffling, and then muffled voices, one of them seemsingly female. Bother: someone was further along the path. But who? And what were they doing? It was hard to imagine two gentry folk pressed up against the wall like a sailor and a harlot but, with so much drunkenness about, who knew what might be going on? The problem was, to use another door brought the risk of being seen.

Preferring to wait and see what happened, momentarily, she remained where she was. Having let herself become so tense about seeing Sybil, not only did she now have a headache but also a sense of disappointment. To her credit, Sybil hadn't seemed the least perturbed to have a

207

servant-girl sitting before her. But to say that it hadn't turned out how she had been hoping, was to grossly understate it.

'Will you stop it!'

Startled from her reflections, Kate stiffened: the voice sounded like Miss Naomi's. Puzzled, she peered in the general direction from whence it had come but, away from the glow of the torches, everything was utterly black. If it *was* Miss Naomi, was she in genuine distress? Or would she be embarrassing everyone involved by going to investigate? She tried to think what to do for the best. Surely, it had to be better to be safe than sorry.

'Miss?' she called, her enquiry leaving her lips as little more than a whisper and making her shake her head in exasperation; no one was going to hear a call as pathetic as that! She drew a breath down into her lungs. *'Miss Naomi!'*

'Kate, oh, thank goodness. Do come and help me.'

Unable to see anything more than a few yards of path stretching ahead of her, she edged towards the sound of Naomi Russell's voice. 'Where are you, miss?'

'Here. It's Aubrey. He's got me ... trapped.'

Mr Aubrey? He was heavily built. She wouldn't be able to fight *him* off. 'I'll go for help,' she called over her shoulder and then sped away.

Haring back towards the terrace, she raced up the steps, only to arrive at the top and smack straight into a warm shirtfront.

'Whoa! I say, Kate, is that you? You're in a bit of a—'

'Quick,' she said, only then looking up to see that it was Mr Lawrence. 'Quick,' she said again, grabbing at his arm. 'It's Miss Naomi. She's... Mr Aubrey, he's—'

'What the deuce?' When she pointed back the way she had come, he sprinted ahead of her to the short flight of steps. 'Down here?'

Catching up to him, she nodded. 'Further along...' How fortunate that of all the people into whom she could have run, it was Mr Lawrence. Now, whatever the fuss, no harm need come to Miss Naomi's reputation.

'Naomi?'

'Miss Naomi?'

Above the sound of their calls came a heavy grunting and Miss Naomi's muffled voice. 'Thank God. Lawrence, please, get him off me!'

As they drew nearer, shapes became apparent. Pinned against the wall, with Aubrey's head upon her shoulder, Naomi was one-handedly trying to push him away.

'Good God, Aubrey, you fool, get off her – this very minute!' When Lawrence grasped his brother's arm to pull him away, Aubrey staggered heavily backwards, his arms flailing as he attempted to remain on his feet.

Naomi, breathing rapidly, rushed to Kate's side. 'Thank goodness you came. He was crushing me.'

Grasping Naomi's outstretched hand and feeling how badly it was trembling, Kate blew out a long stream of breath. Apart from having slightly dishevelled hair, Naomi looked otherwise unharmed, Kate's fear of finding her with her garments awry thankfully unfounded. 'Are you all right, miss? Has he hurt you? Ought I to fetch Dr Fillingham?'

'No, I'm not hurt – although no thanks to *him*. I heard the stitching of this dress rip and I think one of my stockings has laddered, but I don't need Dr Fillingham. More than anything, I simply feel rather shaken.' And then, turning to Lawrence, she said, 'I'm so very grateful, Lawrence. Thank you.'

'What happened?' he asked her, still wrestling to subdue his brother. 'Did *he* bring you down here?'

Naomi didn't hesitate. 'No, no. No, I realize now it was a stupid thing to do but, when I saw him heading towards me across the terrace, and when I saw how drunk he looked, my only thought was to give him the slip. He looked terribly unsteady on his feet and I didn't think he'd go to the effort of following me. Unfortunately, he did. He came after me and ... and lunged at me. That's when I heard Kate calling.'

Pushing Aubrey with sufficient force that he stumbled backwards and fell to the ground, Lawrence moved to Naomi's side. 'Please tell me that he didn't harm you, or so help me I'll…'

Naomi Russell gave a little laugh. 'No, he did nothing. Although his intention was plain enough. And, had he been sober, then I suppose the threat might have been rather more real. But no, he just pressed me up against the wall and tried to put his hands all over me.'

'Good God. Whatever can have possessed him?'

'Whisky, from the smell of him,' Naomi Russell remarked.

'Look, I should probably take him indoors and try to sober up him up before anyone sees him in this state. But I'll only do that if you promise me you'll let Kate take you inside, too.'

'I'll be fine, Lawrence, truly. I just need to compose myself and tidy up a little.'

'Very well. If you're sure. Kate, would you attend to her, please?'

Still holding Miss Naomi's hand, Kate nodded. 'I will, Mr Lawrence.'

'Thank you. And I don't suppose you could arrange for some strong coffee to be brought to ... well, where would you suggest I take him – preferably where no-one will come across him just yet?'

'The morning room would be quiet now,' she said.

'And Naomi, are you *certain* you're all right? You wouldn't prefer to have a quiet word with Dr Fillingham?'

'Lawrence, please, I'm fine.'

'All right.'

Unexpectedly, Kate felt herself warming to Mr Lawrence. She had always thought him the more pleasing to look at and the more gentlemanly of the two brothers but now, this evening, she had come to properly like him. Although authoritative, the way he gave instructions – without any hint of arrogance – made her want to do precisely as he said.

'Come away inside, miss, and let me tidy you up. Then, if you like, you can come back down to the party and no one need be any the wiser.'

But, just as Naomi opened her mouth to

211

answer, a growl, the like of which might more usually be expected from a wild dog, rose up from the form of Aubrey, until that moment in a heap on the ground where his brother had left him. His attention given over to Naomi, Lawrence had dropped his guard, so that as two arms wrapped around his throat, he was easily pulled to the ground.

With a yank of Naomi's hand, Kate drew her beyond reach of the two sets of kicking boots.

'Lawrence! Oh, Kate, do something!'

Do something? What would Miss Naomi have her do – wade in and break them up? 'I'll go and fetch help,' she said, the idea slow to occur to her.

Leaving behind the struggling and grunting brothers, Kate ran back along the side of the house to stand at the top of the flight of steps, her eyes narrowed against the brightness. Hoping to see Ned, she scanned from left to right, but the nearest man was Ralph Colborne. Well, he would have to do. At least he was alone.

'Mr Colborne, begging your pardon, sir–'

At her approach, Ralph Colborne blinked several times as though trying to focus his eyes. 'What the devil...?'

'–please, might you come with me? There's a bit of a to-do and–'

He peered down at her. *Oh, please,* she willed, *please don't let* him *be drunk,* too.

'Who are you?'

'Please, Mr Colborne, sir, there's a fight. Your sons are fighting.'

Continuing to peer down at her, his expression didn't change. What was the matter with the man?

Was she no longer speaking the King's English?

'What, girl? What's that you say?'

Oh, this was ridiculous! Of all the people she could have come across! 'Sir, your son Aubrey is beating the living daylights out of your son Lawrence. Down there. Along the side of the house.'

'Well, why the devil didn't you say so?' Finally, he started to move. 'Down here, you say?'

'Yes, sir.'

Even before they had drawn close, the sounds of scuffling and groaning alerted her that the skirmish continued.

'Hie there, the pair of you. Get to your feet. This instant.'

Down on the ground, the two brothers gradually fell still. Then, each ignoring the other, they got slowly to their feet, Lawrence dusting down his clothes, Aubrey cursing and holding his ribs.

'Are you all right, miss?' Kate whispered to Naomi.

'Fine, thank you. I'm fine.'

'Take yourselves indoors, the pair of you,' Ralph Colborne ordered his sons. 'But *do not* go across the terrace. Find another way inside. I will *not* have you ruin Pamela's evening. Nor will I have you bring disgrace upon your mother and me. Clean yourselves up and wait for me to come in and see you. In the meantime, you are to speak to no one. Do you hear me? Not to a soul.'

'Yes, sir.'

'Yes ... sir.'

As Lawrence and Aubrey disappeared into the darkness, Naomi stepped forward. 'Mr Colborne, please may I assure you that Lawrence's only part in this was to come to my aid. Aubrey was the one who–'

'Young lady, I suggest that you, too, say nothing of this. And you, girl,' he said, turning to Kate, 'for the sake of your employment, would be sensible to do likewise.'

'Ralph? Ralph, darling, is that you? And did I hear you talking to Lawrence and Aubrey? Ralph?'

In despair, Kate exhaled a long sigh. It was Mrs Russell. And, from the sound of it, she, too, was on the drinky side of sober. Just what they didn't need.

Turning stiffly aside, Ralph Colborne started towards her. 'It's all right, Pamela. It's nothing. Just a bit of high-jinks between brothers. You know how young men can be once they've a tot or two inside them. A hot-headed disagreement, that's all it was.'

'And is that Naomi? Naomi? Is that you?'

'Come along, my dear,' Ralph Colborne coaxed, offering Pamela Russell his arm. 'Let's get you back to your guests, shall we?'

'But what–'

'Come along, that's right.'

With Mrs Russell being led away, Kate felt Naomi's grip on her fingers slacken. 'That was close,' she whispered. 'We don't need Mamma involved.'

To Kate, that felt like an understatement. 'No, miss,' she agreed.

'He didn't believe me, you know – Mr Colborne, I mean, when I tried to tell him what happened. Poor Lawrence, despite being blame-

214

free, he'll be reprimanded just as severely as his brother. Aubrey's their favourite, their great son and heir. Well, he's no better than an animal. And I shall make sure Mamma gets to hear of this.'

To her surprise, Kate started to shiver. 'Perhaps we should get indoors, miss,' she said. 'You and Mr Lawrence know what happened, that's the main thing. And Mr Aubrey, too, if he remembers come light of day.'

'Yes, very well,' Naomi agreed. 'I suppose you're right. Let's go inside.'

When the two women arrived back at Naomi's room and Kate lit another lamp, Naomi went to sit on her bed. To Kate, she looked rather forlorn.

'There, miss. Now, shall I fetch out a new pair of stockings and take a look at your gown?'

'You know, Kate, I think perhaps I have no wish to return to the party.'

Offering her a smile, Kate nodded. 'I understand, miss. All that nerviness leaves you feeling drained, don't it?'

'Yes, I think that's it. I feel quite exhausted – certainly too wearied for any sort of confrontation with–'

'Naomi Russell!'

Together, the two women spun about to see the door shuddering on its hinges and Pamela Russell teetering in the empty frame.

'Mamma–'

'How ... could you? How *could* you upset the Colbornes ... of *all* people?'

Quickly, Kate stepped aside. And then, alarmed by the expression on Pamela Russell's face, she backed further away still.

'*Upset them?* Mamma, you weren't there. You didn't see–'

Having retreated all the way to the corner of the room, Kate didn't know what to do for the best. Through her mind flashed thoughts of fetching someone to help, but when she'd done that earlier, it seemed only to have made matters worse. And anyway, unless instructed to the contrary, a maid was never supposed to interfere – no matter the calamity. Besides, who on earth would want to try and reason with a woman in Pamela Russell's state? Having taken several unsteady paces into the room, she had come to a halt and was now leaning for support upon the back of the easy chair.

'Oh, that's to be your claim, is it? You had nothing to do with ... Lawrence setting upon Aubrey ... and beating him black and blue?'

So many objections lay stuck to Kate's tongue. Miss Naomi had done nothing wrong. And Mr Lawrence *hadn't* set upon Mr Aubrey. It was quite the other way around. If Mr Aubrey was *black and blue*, then so had to be Mr Lawrence, Mr Aubrey having set upon him unprovoked. Seemingly, though, there was nothing she could do to make matters right. It wasn't worth the risk of losing her job to argue with Pamela Russell.

'Mamma, with the greatest of respect, I don't know what Uncle Ralph said to you but it seems there's been a mistake–' When Pamela Russell raised an arm, apparently to wave away her daughter's response, despite her feet appearing glued to the rug, the upper half of her body swayed. Her eyes seemed to be causing her distress, too –

blinking far too frequently and flitting about the room. Strands of her hair had come unpinned and the heavy layer of foundation on her face had sunk, unflatteringly, into her wrinkles.

'You do know ... why I invited the Colbornes?' she said. 'You do *know*, why I went to all this trouble?'

Kate shot Miss Naomi a look of concern. What were they to do? Very shortly now, Pamela Russell was almost certain to collapse in a heap on the floor.

Naomi returned her look 'They are your old friends,' she began uncertainly, at the same time taking a very small step towards the chair. 'You've always said they are old family friends.' She took another step, careful to make it small enough for her mother to remain unaware of her approach.

'And they are. More than that, they are your way back into a life of ... a life I gave up ... to marry your father.' Catching the look Miss Naomi gave her, Kate edged in the same direction. 'But *do you see that?*' Pamela Russell demanded. *'Do you?'* For a moment, Naomi Russell stayed where she was.

'Mamma, really, I–'

'You do not. Instead of doing as I say ... and charming Aubrey, you play fast and loose with his brother and then ... and then *somehow* set them against one another. Why would you do that? Tell me. Why?'

'Mamma, I don't know what–'

'Well, I will not stand for it! I will not.' With one of her shoes apparently becoming caught in the petticoats of her gown, Pamela Russell collapsed into the chair. But, just as both Naomi and Kate

217

took a couple of steps closer, Mrs Russell heaved herself back to her feet. 'You will *marry* Aubrey Colborne. You *will.*'

'You're tired, Mamma,' Naomi ventured, her voice soft and her movements gentle. 'You've had a dreadfully long day. Why don't I help you along to your room, and then, once you're settled, I'll go downstairs and explain to our guests that you're not feeling well?'

To Kate, Miss Naomi's suggestion sounded like the perfect plan. She was even on the verge of approaching further when, without warning, Pamela Russell spun about and pointed at her.

'This,' she shouted, *'this,* Sadie Jennings, is all *your* fault.' To Kate's astonished look, Naomi Russell shook her head and raised her shoulders in a shrug. Clearly, she didn't know what her mother was talking about either. 'I *knew* you were trouble. I could see you had no scruples the moment I set *eyes* on you. Well, I won't have it. Not again. Ha! Once bitten, twice shy. *He's a handsome one, Miss Pamela. He's not all stuffy like those young men your mother would have you marry, Miss Pamela. Go on, Miss Pamela. Won't tell a soul, Miss Pamela.'*

Deeply unsettled, Kate shrank back. What on earth was Mrs Russell talking about? Who was Sadie Jennings?

'Mamma—'

But then, collapsing without warning back into the chair, Pamela Russell began to sob. 'I will *not* have it, Naomi. *My* sorry marriage might have been my own doing ... *that* sacrifice might be down to me. But I did not endure ruination and

218

humiliation for you to make the same mistake –
to have you squander *your* chance of making a
decent marriage. I will not go through it all over
again. I will not. I will ... not...'

With Pamela Russell's energy seemingly spent,
Kate tiptoed across the rug to Miss Naomi.
'What can I do, miss?'

'See if you can find Aunt Diana,' Naomi
whispered back, moving quickly to kneel in front
of her mother and take her hands. 'Clearly, she's
overwrought. I need to get her into bed. Aunt
Diana's discreet. She'll help.'

'All right, miss. I'll go now.'

'Thank you. But please, not a word to anyone
else.'

'I promise I won't utter a word to another soul.'

As Kate moved to slip past the slumped form of
Pamela Russell, the aromas of souring perfume,
cigar smoke, and spirits made her wrinkle her
nose, the odour striking her as more befitting of
a cheap harlot from one of the drangs down by
the Smugglers' Tavern than a so-called lady from
London.

'And Kate–'

Wearily, she turned back. 'Yes, miss?'

'After that, you go on to bed. With Aunt
Diana's help, I'll manage.'

Feeling more relieved than she would have
thought possible, Kate nodded. 'Thank you, miss.
See you in the morning then.'

'Yes, see you in the morning.'

Closing the door carefully behind her, Kate
stood on the landing and exhaled heavily. What a
night. What goings-on! And what sore heads and

219

recriminations there would be tomorrow.

Fortunately, on this occasion, she had been but a bystander. Despite what seemed to have got into Mrs Russell's drink-filled head, none of this upset could be laid at *her* door. And thank goodness for that.

Chapter Six

Aftermath

Damp, grey and gloomy. To Kate, looking out from her bedroom window at the mist the following morning, that was how everything appeared. Even her thoughts felt foggy.

Opening her eyes barely ten minutes earlier, her first thought had been that the day was bound to bring doom and gloom: Mr Lawrence and Mr Aubrey would most likely be in disgrace; Mrs Russell – along with many of her guests – would no doubt be regretting the amount of drink she had consumed and, by now, Miss Naomi was probably barred from ever seeing Mr Lawrence again. As for her own position in all of this, she had a nagging feeling about that, too. It had been ridiculous of Mrs Russell to suggest that she had somehow been to blame for the upset. She'd heard about people who were given to nastiness when *in their cups* – not that drunkenness was an excuse for levelling unfounded accusations, not least because, coming from her, people would take it as the gospel truth. All she could do was hope that after she'd left, Miss Naomi had found a way to explain to her that she, Kate, had only been trying to help. At least Ned wouldn't have said anything about her having seen Sybil; he wouldn't have gone to all that trouble to get her an audience only to later give her up. No, she had no complaint with either him or Miss Naomi. It was just unfortunate she couldn't say the same of their mother.

Resting her elbows on the windowsill, Kate sank her chin into her cupped hands. Replaying events from yesterday evening had kept her from getting to sleep. She'd never seen a lady so obviously drunk before and was surprised by how sickened she had felt. Conversely, the time she'd spent talking to Ned couldn't have made her happier. He had spoken to her so ordinarily – not as a servant nor, particularly, even as a woman – just as a person. He hadn't belittled her ignorance, either; he had respected her opinions. Admittedly, he had teased her over some of the things she'd said but it had all been good-natured.

By contrast, her time spent with Sybil had been something of a let-down. This morning, she was even inclined to agree with him that the woman was a fraud. Most likely, she was a member of that theatre company Pamela Russell had brought in to entertain her friends and dupe the more gullible among them.

'Your future is already written,' the so-called prophetess had said to her. 'To learn of it,' she had urged, 'look first to your past, then to your present. From such an examination will your future become clear.' Well, lying awake in the early hours, listening to the pit-pat of the rain on the roof, she had looked long and hard but seen very little. Her past was dull. Her present was dull. As to her future? Well, if she wasn't careful, it would only bring more of the same.

Staring idly out through the window, she frowned. In her mind, a thought was dawning. Perhaps, knowing that her life thus far had been nothing but dull, and realizing that she wanted things to be different, her path *was* already laid out. Perhaps, the future she wanted – indeed, the future she had begun to imagine for herself – *was* there for the taking. Maybe, all she had to do was go after it.

Stepping back from the window ledge, she straightened herself up. Yes, that was it! Madam Sybil had been right; her future *was* there to see. All she had to do was bring it about.

Fired by her new resolve, she turned back into the room. Ned was wrong: Madam Sybil wasn't a fraud at all; she was a very wise woman indeed.

Unable to believe her eyes, Kate stood quite still. Apparently, under cover of darkness, an army of parlourmaids and hall-boys had crept in and set to work; it was the only possible explanation for the cleanliness and order everywhere.

It was a while later that same morning, and Kate was astonished. She had been expecting to find – indeed, had been dreading to find – that after last night's revelries, everywhere had been left in an unholy mess. As it was, not a single trace of the merriments remained. Dumbfounded, she went to inspect the drawing room. There, she found windows opened back, ashtrays emptied, cushions plumped, and vases of fresh flowers – crimson dahlias and deep purple salvias – already gracing the side tables. In the hallway, the floor had been swept and polished and the rugs set back down in perfect alignment. Clearly, Pamela Russell had the power to bring about miracles.

Raising an eyebrow as she glanced about at the scene of perfect order, she wondered what to do with herself. It was still early – too early even for Aunt Diana to be about yet, let alone Ned. But, just in case – and picturing him waking, ravenous for breakfast – she tiptoed towards the morning room. The only signs of life in there, though, were the little spirals of steam escaping from beneath the chafing dishes. If he *was* about, he wasn't at breakfast.

Thinking to make an early start on Miss Naomi's tray, she turned about and made her way below stairs, humming a refrain from the music she'd heard last night and glancing in through the open door of her mother's office as she passed by. 'Morning, Ma,' she called, expecting her mother's customary reply. When the only sound was that of her mother's chair being scraped back over the hard floor, though, she drew to a halt.

'Kate, is that you?'

With a smile, she shook her head: what a daft question. 'Yes, Ma. It's me.'

'Come in here, please.'

Alone in the corridor, Kate pulled a face; Ma's tone sounded short. But then to be honest, that wasn't an unusual state of affairs: she often

223

sounded curt when she hadn't had much sleep. Retracing her steps, she went to peer around the door frame. 'Morning, Ma. Can't stop, I've got Miss Naomi's–'

'Leave that be and come in here, please.' When, to her mother's instruction, Kate gave a weary sigh, it didn't go unnoticed. 'And how many times must I tell you not to sigh like that?'

With a frown instead, Kate stepped into her mother's office. What on earth could have put her mother in such a tetchy mood? And so early in the morning, too? Ordinarily, it was at least nine o'clock before someone made her blood boil. Well, for her own part, she would sound bright and chirpy. After all, it was how she felt. 'Here I am.'

'Close the door, please.'

Thinking it a peculiar command but latching it shut anyway, Kate turned back, only to see that her mother had returned to sit behind her desk. When it came to issuing instructions to either her or Edith, Ma rarely did so from behind her desk. There was family and there was staff. And it was usually only errant members of staff who got the behind-the-desk talk.

She pulled herself upright. *Whatever she's about to accuse you of,* she reminded herself, *feign innocence. Admit to nothing.*

To that end, she persuaded her lips into a smile. 'What is it, Ma?'

'You won't be doing Miss Russell's tray this morning.'

'Is she unwell?' Puzzled, she turned towards the door. 'Only, if she is, I'd best go and see her – see what she wants taken up.'

'Come back and listen to me.'

Still frowning, Kate swivelled about. 'But–'

'Miss Russell isn't sick. Starting from this morning, she will be getting up and joining Mrs Colborne to take breakfast downstairs.'

Downstairs? With Cicely Colborne? What on earth was going on?

'But why?'

'I should imagine because Mrs Russell has told her to.'

To Kate, it sounded nonsensical. 'There has to be another reason.'

'For certain there is. But the whys and wherefores don't concern either of us.'

Beginning to feel uneasy, Kate forced a swallow. Something about all of this wasn't what it seemed. 'Well, if she's intending to come down for breakfast, I ought to go straight up. She'll be needing me to help her dress.'

'That won't be necessary either.'

'What? Why not?'

'Because this morning, I came down to find this.' Reaching to her blotter, Mabel Bratton lifted a sheet of notepaper. On it, Kate could see handwriting. 'It is a note from Mrs Russell stating that with immediate effect, I am to remove you from your duties as lady's maid to her daughter.'

Kate reached a hand to a nearby chair. 'Mrs Russell wrote that?' In answer to her question, Mabel Bratton nodded. 'It was on your desk first thing this morning?'

'Pushed under my door.'

'Then it can't be from Mrs Russell. I saw her late on and she was far too–' On the brink of using the word 'drinky', she checked herself. While there could be no denying that Pamela Russell had been severely the worse for drink, it would be wholly unwise to remark as much. That she *was* drunk, however, made it inconceivable that not only had she been up and about at first light, but that she had also been sufficiently clear-headed to pen such a missive. No, somebody else's hand was at work here. But whose? And why? Aunt Diana? No, she had no reason to do such a thing. Cicely Colborne? Since she barely knew the woman, it seemed unlikely.

'If I were you, girl,' Mabel Bratton interrupted her daughter's thoughts, 'I'd worry less about where the instruction came from and more about ensuring that your answer to my next question is truthful.'

Beginning to sense what might have got her into this mess, Kate nevertheless continued to stare across the desk; there was no sense alerting Ma to Mrs Russell's rantings. It wasn't as though there was any substance to them. 'And what question would that be, Ma?'

When circumstances prevented Mabel Bratton from raising her voice, she had a habit – recognized both by her daughters and staff members alike – of speaking very slowly and enunciating every word with the utmost precision. In anticipation of it happening now, Kate felt her insides twisting. She was about to be on the receiving end of a reprimand. And, if what she had just supposed was right, it was going to be for something she hadn't even done.

'What in God's name did you do, to upset Mrs Russell *so much,* that you left her with no alternative but to demand that I remove you from attending to her daughter? What, I ask you? Because I'm *surely* at a loss to know.'

There. That was it. That was the *how could you possibly be so stupid* tone. Clipped and steely. Well, she wouldn't have it. She would stand up for herself. 'Nothing. I have done nothing to cause either offence or upset. Quite the contrary. Ask Miss Naomi.'

'I'm asking *you.*'

'All I can say is that there must have been a misunderstanding.'

'You were not party to some *fracas* last night then?'

Fracas? Now, not only did she know her supposition was right but she could do as her mother had instructed and answer truthfully. 'I was not.'

'Am I to understand your contention is that Mrs Russell is lying?'

Kate swallowed hard; she knew from experience that sometimes, the truth only made matters worse. And this morning, it wasn't just her position as lady's maid that was at stake: there was her plan for Ned to consider – indeed, her entire future. Frustrating although it was, caution felt to be her best bet. 'I didn't say *that.* But I do believe her to be mistaken. If we could just go and see Miss Naomi–'

'You are to go nowhere near Miss Russell. From this moment forward, I will assign you duties each day as I see fit and in line with whatever needs to be done.'

'Look, Ma, at least hear me out while I–'

'Kate, enough. Mrs Russell, here as a guest of the Latimers, has been so greatly incensed by something in which she claims you were involved that I haven't the least intention of letting you suggest to her that she is mistaken. She writes here that were it not for you being my daughter, and were it not for Mr Latimer speaking so highly of *my* service here, she would be demanding that you be dismissed altogether.'

In her state of astonishment Kate was finding it hard to think, her rapid and shallow breathing only adding to her sense of panic. 'But wrongly – I assure you Ma, she would be insisting wrongly–'

'Kate Bratton,' her mother hissed, in one single movement getting to her feet and moving around the desk. 'Need I remind you that it is only by the grace of the Latimers that the three of us have work and a home. One word from Mrs Russell, or indeed from any other guest who comes to stay here, and we could *all* of us be dismissed. Just like that. Work. Home. All gone.'

'But Ma–'

'You know as well as I do that big houses these days are run with *fewer* staff, not *more*. And you don't need me to point out how this place already stands empty for most of the year as it is. I daresay we're all of us an expense Mr Latimer could do without. So, if you remember only one thing today, let it be this – you're to stay away from Mrs Russell, you're to stay away from her daughter, and you're to stay out of trouble. And don't you dare venture another word on the subject. Let this be the end of the matter. Now, after the upheaval of yesterday, I've more than usual to see to this morning so, take yourself off and reflect on what I've just said. Then, come nine o'clock, report to your sister, cleaned up and ready for service.'

Edith? She was to report to Edith? Ma was banishing her to the kitchens? Oh, but this was insufferable! A glance to her mother's scowl, though, suggested that however unfair the whole business, only someone with straw for brains would be mazed enough to challenge her and risk making the situation even worse.

For the moment at least, then, there looked to be only one thing to do. And that was comply. Or at least, to give the appearance of it. 'Yes, Ma.'

'Very well. Now get out of my sight.'

Go and reflect, Ma had said. Well, after that little shock, she was unlikely to be able to do much else.

Heaving a long and weary sigh, Kate stepped out from the scullery, noticing, with more than a little irony, how the morning no longer looked so gloomy. The deadening mist of earlier was lifting and, as she rounded the corner and looked across the gardens, pale sunlight was picking out the raindrops on the blades of grass in much the same way that, last night, the lamplight had picked out the tiny jewels on Miss Naomi's borrowed tiara. It had looked so lovely, nestled above her ringlets.

Naomi and Ned: it was hard to believe two such pleasant and level-headed people could have come from such a distinctly unlikeable mother. Granted, Miss Naomi's tongue had a sharp side at times, but Ned's temperament bore absolutely no resemblance to his mother's at all. The only possible explanation for the Russell children being so good-natured, was that Mr Russell was a far nicer person than his wife. He *had* to be.

Were it not for the fact that Mrs Russell had been so drunk, she would be convinced beyond all doubt that she was behind that letter: the woman's distrust of her had been obvious from that first afternoon. And then, last night, she had made those wild accusations. But servants always were easy prey: if something went missing, it had to be a servant; if something got broken, it had to be the maid. This, though, felt different. Those accusations had been cruel and mean and un-true. Besides which, who was Sadie Jennings anyway? Sadie Jennings, Mrs Russell had called her. Even Miss Naomi hadn't seemed to know who that was.

If the note to Ma wasn't solely Pamela Russell's idea, it meant that someone else also bore her ill will. But who? She could safely discount Aunt Diana, who, only last night, had thanked her for the discreet route she had taken to obtain her help. And she had no quarrel with the Filling-hams – nor they with her. So that really only left the Colbornes.

Wearily, she leant back against the wall of the house. Being Miss Naomi's lady's maid had come to mean everything to her – and not just because it provided her with titbits about Ned. But, if she was ever to be re-instated, she would need to prove her innocence. Knowing what she did about the Colbornes, she wouldn't put it past them to have had a hand in it somewhere. To her mind, all of the Colbornes – with the exception of Lawrence – had small and shifty eyes. Especially *Mrs* Colborne. *Cicely Colborne*. Yes, that might make sense. If Cicely Colborne was to see her beloved Aubrey wed to Miss Naomi, after the goings-on of last night, a number of things were going to need to be either explained away or else swept under the carpet. At the very least, Aubrey's reputation would need buffing up. He would have to be made to appear blameless, which would mean either sacrificing poor Lawrence or else implicating Miss Naomi as having been in some way responsible – perhaps for leading him on. They couldn't besmirch her character too much but they *could* claim she had fallen under the influence of someone unsuitable. And who better to blame for putting ideas into Miss Naomi's head than her lady's maid, a poor unfortunate who Pamela Russell had probably already admitted to mistrusting. Yes, although in some ways it was difficult to believe, in others, it made perfect sense. Cicely Colborne might look frail but, penny to a pound, behind that feeble appearance beat a cold and calculating heart. Needing to distract from Aubrey's behaviour, she had settled upon the perfect scapegoat, one whose supposed role as a bad influence didn't even have to be specific: she was a servant; no one would question that she had played some part in it, nor would they believe a word she uttered in her defence. She could even imagine Cicely Colborne pressing her case – wasting no time last night in pouncing upon Mrs Russell's already emotional state. *'I blame that maid, Pamela.*

You know what a poor influence servants can be. Allow me to deal with her for you.'

Well, if things *were* as she had just supposed, there was probably little she could do about it – certainly not without risking more trouble. Of greater importance was her plan regarding Ned, which, if she went out of her way to keep clear of further trouble, still stood a chance of coming together. And so, to that end, she would somehow swallow her pride, sit on her anger, and do nothing in haste.

Her course of action decided, she nevertheless heaved a vexed sigh. At least it was still early – an age yet until Ma expected to see her at work in the kitchen. The kitchen. Edith gloating. The prospect alone was almost more than she could bear.

Pushing herself away from the wall, her eyes came to rest upon movement at the far side of the lawn. She squinted. Coming towards her was Aunt Diana, the bottom few inches of her long robe dark with the dampness it had soaked up from the grass. She was drifting serenely, her progress that of someone with nowhere in particular to go and no set hour by which to be there. Well, lucky her.

With no desire to be drawn into making polite conversation, Kate remained where she was and hoped not to be seen. In a minute, she would go down to the cove; this early in the morning it would be lovely and peaceful, a few moments of stillness something she suddenly craved. Somehow, in what felt to be nothing more than the blink of an eye, her existence had gone from being filled with promise to beyond despair. If she was no longer to be Miss Naomi's maid, all sorts of doors – and routes to Ned – would be closed to her. The irony wasn't lost on her: in those first few days after the Russells had arrived, she would have given almost anything to be spared the job. Now, though, she was going to miss it terribly. And the worst of it was that for once in her life, the trouble that had brought about her dismissal wasn't even of her own making.

When, eventually, she looked up from her contemplations, it was to see that Diana Lloyd was coming towards her, her hand raised in greeting. 'Good morning,' she called ahead.

Feeling her shoulders sag, Kate gave a half-hearted wave. Bother. Now she was going to have to make conversation. 'Good day to you, Mrs Lloyd,' she nevertheless summoned a smile and answered.

'I see I come upon a like-minded soul enjoying the beauty and stillness of first light.' At Aunt Diana's incorrect observation, Kate gave a wry smile. 'I can't abide lying in bed on mornings like this.' Again, Kate smiled. 'Still, don't suppose you have much say in the matter. Quick breath of fresh air before you must embark upon your daily toils?'

Unable to help it, Kate made a little scoffing noise. 'I was sent out to *reflect on my behaviour.*'

'Ah.'

There was something about Diana Lloyd's languid movements and soothing manner that made Kate feel less taut in her own limbs. Already, the tension in her neck was softening and she was breathing more slowly. While she didn't know Diana Lloyd, she did have a sense that she would be a sympathetic listener. And, while Ma had warned her to stay away from Miss Naomi and Mrs Russell, she had said nothing about Aunt Diana.

'But it's hard to reflect on *anything* when I know I wasn't in the wrong.'

'It is rather, isn't it?'

'Truthfully, Mrs Lloyd, on this occasion, I *know* I didn't do wrong.'

'Tell me, Kate, do you have time to make a circuit of the lawn with me?'

Feeling less than comfortable to be so openly in the company of one of the guests, Kate glanced back to the house. In this instance, it wasn't a question of having the time – it was more about the risk of being seen. Although, with her mother ensconced below stairs – by her own admission more busy than usual – and Edith supervising the breakfasts, perhaps she would take a chance. After all, how much more trouble was it really possible to bring down on herself?

'I'd like that,' she said. 'But, if we're to go a-walking on the grass, would you mind waiting whilst I take off my shoes? It might be better I didn't go back in with them all sodden from the dew.'

'Not at all, my dear. Were I wearing any, I might do the same.'

Not sure whether to believe that Diana Lloyd was barefoot, Kate glanced down, only to see that her feet – shod or otherwise – were hidden by the bottom of her robe.

'Let me guess,' Diana Lloyd picked up as they started across the lawn. 'You're being implicated in last night's little upset.'

'Yes! And yet all I did was go to Miss Naomi's aid.'

'I know, my dear. Of the various accounts from last night, to my mind, there's only one that bears scrutiny.'

'It didn't help that when I went for help, I came across grumpy old Mr Colborne. If I'd found Ned – *Mr Edwin,* it might all have turned out different. As it was, for reasons I can't put my finger upon, Mr Colborne took straight against me.'

Dangling her shoes from her fingers, Kate was surprised to feel Diana Lloyd reach for her free hand and tuck it under her arm. It was such an unexpected and kindly gesture that she found herself biting back tears.

'Kate, my dear, when it comes to my niece and nephew, many's the occasion I have felt moved to intervene. However, with families being the precariously stitched tapestries that they are, rarely would doing so have made a situation any better. Indeed, often, it would have served only to weaken fraying bonds. And so, where matters of family are concerned, I have long since resolved not to meddle – no matter the apparent injustices of a situation. That said, while you won't find me rushing to take up arms on your behalf, you are welcome to avail yourself of my impartial ear. So, why not tell me all about it – get it off your chest?'

Kate did have a deep longing to unburden herself. And so, with her unexpected confidante either nodding or murmuring her agreement,

Kate recounted what had happened between Miss Naomi and Mr Aubrey, and then between Mr Aubrey and Mr Lawrence. And, just as she had indicated, although stopping short of offering suggestions as to redress, Diana Lloyd did agree that the outcome seemed unfair.

It was then that Kate spotted her chance to solve another mystery – as long as she could muster the courage to speak rather plainly about Diana Lloyd's own sister.

'When Mrs Russell got all upset,' she began, her words chosen with the greatest of care, 'she addressed me by the wrong name – Sadie Jennings, I think she called me. Yes, that was it. Did Mrs Russell get confused because I resemble this woman in some way? Is that what happened?' Pleased with the way she had presented her question, she held her breath.

'My dear, you resemble her only to the extent that you wear the uniform of a domestic servant. Apart from that, not greatly, no.'

'Oh. So...'

'But to answer you more helpfully,' Diana Lloyd continued, her voice lowered, 'Sadie Jennings was a young woman who, for a brief spell, was employed as lady's maid to my sister. It all happened more than twenty years ago, shortly after I had married and gone from home. For that reason, I never actually met her. However, I do know that not only did she behave badly but that she also had a rather unfortunate influence upon my sister – who, needless to say, thought her a breath of fresh air. Miss Jennings didn't last long, a hurried investigation into her past revealing that she had obtained the position under false pretences. More than that, all I feel able to say to you, even after the passing of so many years, is that her influence turned out to be an abiding one. The rest of the story, I leave you to imagine for yourself.'

A lady's maid who'd had an abiding influence upon Pamela Russell? That seemed unlikely; Pamela Russell didn't seem the sort to be swayed or influenced by anyone. Although perhaps, as a young woman, she hadn't been so single-minded. She sighed. Intriguing though this story was, in the overall scheme of things, Mrs Russell's crazed rantings were neither her problem nor, going forward, worth becoming distracted by. In all other respects – and despite her initial reservations – Diana Lloyd had been helpful. She had certainly made her feel less tense – not to mention vindicated. But, even with the matter of last night aired and put to bed, she found herself eager to keep talking. It was, she realized, the first time she'd had the ear of someone open-minded. And, as a result, her head seemed to have flooded with all the matters upon which, over recent weeks, she had grown desperate for advice.

'So, it's all right for me to pay no heed to what everyone else thinks?' she said, the matter of Luke and his long-standing proposal of marriage, the topic to which she turned next.

'Perfectly so. According to the law of the land, you arc of age. When it comes to the matter of taking a husband, you are entitled to exercise free will.'

'And it's all right to want more from my life …

237

and to go off in search of it?' Deep down, she recognized that she was being selective with the truth, despite this being someone whose unbiased opinion she genuinely wanted to hear. But it would be tricky to admit that what she was really seeking license to do, was abandon Luke and pursue her dream of being with Ned. Nevertheless... 'Only, how can I think of getting wed and raising up children – you know, teaching them all about life – when I've done nothing yet with my own? If you ask me, I should see a bit more of things for myself first.'

'You would not be the first woman to anguish over that quandary. But, while many women would readily agree with you, few of them have the luxury of choice.'

Slowly, Kate shook her head. 'No, I suppose not. But it's all right that I don't want to marry Luke and stay here and ... be dull.'

Diana Lloyd smiled. 'Dear girl, there is only one person who can know whether or not something is right for you. And that, of course, is you. That said, there are things that any woman considering a decision of such magnitude would do well to bear in mind. Take fear, for instance. Fear can lead one to put up barriers, can make one find reasons *not* to do something simply because avoiding it feels by far the less daunting prospect. But, whilst a little fear can be healthy, one shouldn't let it hold one back.'

'I do see that.'

'On the other hand, one should never fool oneself, either. One should never blindly pin everything on a dream that has little chance of being realized or that ultimately, might prove just as unsuitable as the alternative – no matter how dull. To strive for something is admirable – just so long as one has a realistic chance of being able to bring it about and then, to abide by the outcome.'

'I do see that too.' Was it possible that Aunt Diana somehow knew what she had in mind to do? Had she seen her talking with Ned? Had she, perhaps, observed the way she behaved in his company? Sometimes when she was with him, she did come over all dewy-eyed: it was beyond her not to. The worry was that if Aunt Diana had noticed, then who else might have? Perhaps Pamela Russell had observed the same thing and was using the events of last night as an excuse to end her association not just with Naomi but also with Ned. Heavens, yes. It was more than possible.

When they arrived at the edge of the lawn and stepped onto the gravel of the driveway, Diana Lloyd released Kate's hand, freeing her to slip her feet back into her shoes.

'Kate, my dear, any life lived to the full will be littered with mistakes. Lord knows, I, for one, have made enough to last me the rest of my days. But you seem like a sensible young woman. Certainly, my niece speaks highly of you. She trusts you and she's going to miss your companionship. So, for what it's worth, I will offer *you* the same advice I would offer to *her* were she to seek it – trust your instincts. If something you are proposing to do is making you feel uneasy – guilty, even – trust those feelings and accept that, perhaps, what you're considering isn't quite right – either

239

for you, or possibly even at all. Rely upon your instincts in the same way that you would a compass: trust what it's telling you and, more often than not, you will arrive where you're supposed to be.'

Kate nodded her agreement to Diana Lloyd's advice. 'Thank you,' she said. 'I'll try an' remember that.'

'Try also not to be *too* hard on your mother. It might not seem so at this precise moment, but hers is surely a life weighed by duty. She alone bears the responsibility for the running of this house, all the while wanting the best for her daughters, one of whom she sees struggling to find her way in the world.'

Although loathe to admit it, Kate could see the truth in Diana Lloyd's observation. 'I suppose it must be so, yes.'

'But she seems to have equipped you well. From the manner in which you are considering what you should do, I have every confidence that you will decide wisely.'

Decide wisely. She wished she shared Aunt Diana's faith. Even if she did decide wisely, it would be no thanks to her mother.

'Thank you, Mrs Lloyd. I shall try to do that.'

'Well, goodbye, my dear. And thank you for walking with me.'

For some long time after their conversation, Kate found it impossible to settle her thoughts. Having started the day feeling gloomy and despondent, she was now beginning to feel eager and hopeful once again – and desperate to advance her plan. According to Aunt Diana, wanting a dif-

240

ferent life wasn't wrong, nor was it – although this was more by her own reckoning – unattainable. But, although she now knew what she wanted, deciding what to do next in order to bring it about felt less straightforward. What she did *not* want, was to go back indoors and take orders from Edith. So, in her new spirit of determination, she wouldn't. Instead, she would go down to the cove, where, following Ma's instructions to the letter, she would *reflect upon her behaviour* – except that she would reflect upon the behaviour she was *going to adopt,* not that for which Ma had (wrongly) held her accountable. From now on, she would stand up to the pair of them – her mother and her sister – and not let them bully her down a path she didn't want to go.

Si-si-si-si-doo, si-si-si-si-doo. From somewhere in the lush canopy, Kate could hear tomtits calling to one another, their chatter switching sharply to calls of alarm when they evidently spotted her intrusion into their territory. Having picked her way through the birch trees to arrive deeper into the woodland, she fell still and looked up – not that she could expect to pick out such tiny creatures from among such dense foliage. Looking back down, she drew in a long breath. It was going to work out all right. She was going to have a different life. She was going to shed her yoke of servitude. Mrs Russell might have taken deeply against her, but now she was more determined than ever to marry Ned.

Now well beyond sight of the house, she lifted her skirt clear of her ankles and scampered

241

through the trees. Despite the lack of a proper path she made rapid progress, able to dodge the stumpy oaks and gnarly hawthorns as easily as a startled roe deer. From almost twenty years of adventuring, she knew which brakes of bracken hid moss-covered boulders to send the unwary sprawling, and which of them concealed heart-stoppingly sudden drops She knew where the paths down the slope became lethal after a fall of rain, and where the stretches beneath the trees became boggy enough to suck your boots clean from your feet. No one, she was certain, could cover the ground as quickly and as unscathed as she could, not even Luke.

Two-thirds of the way down between the gardens and the shore, the land dropped away more quickly and, where the trees yielded to the ferocity of the winter gales off the Atlantic, the cove opened wide before her. Today, it looked idyllic, the hills to either side resembling patchwork bedspreads, the soft green of the springy turf flecked, threaded, and splashed with low mounds of pale pink thrift, golden birds-foot trefoil, and rust-coloured kidney-vetches. She stood for a moment, surprised to find that the mist had now evaporated and that before her, under the boldest of July skies, the sands, slowly baking to a crisp and salty crust under the midday sun, were being lapped by the most benign of seas.

Arriving among the boulders at the head of the cove, she bent low and, pulling off her shoes, began to pick her way carefully down over the rocks to the beach. There, under her bare feet, the sand felt surprisingly cool, the tide having only recently receded and the sun having not yet climbed high enough to warm it up. Setting her shoes on top of a nearby boulder, she continued on to where the waves were gently breaking.

Idly, she traced a line in the damp sand with her big toe. Then she stopped and stared out to sea again. There was not a feature to be seen: no land; no fishing boats; no discernible clouds – just a faint line of deeper blue where the water stopped and the heavens began. With her toe, she once again started to draw, this time inscribing an arc, next to which she drew its mirror image before joining them at the top to form the outline of a heart. Ridiculously lop-sided, the shape of it made her laugh. Anyone with such a limp organ in their chest would surely be at death's door!

'Hie, Kate!' Startled, she quickly dragged the ball of her foot across the sand to leave nothing but a long smudge. 'Kate, up here!'

Fanning her face with her hand, she cast over her shoulder. Ned was wending his way down between the boulders, his sleeves rolled back to his elbows, his trousers turned up to the middle of his shins.

'Hello,' she called lightly back, still fanning at her face as he jogged, barefoot, towards her.

'You're about early,' he observed, coming to a halt a couple of yards away from her.

'Same could be said of you, sir.' *Sir?* Why on earth had she called him *that?* Not that he seemed to notice.

'To tell you the truth, I didn't sleep all that well.'

She gave a wry smile. 'Me neither.' Somehow,

though, she doubted that *his* sleeplessness had been rooted in the same cause as her own. She doubted that *he* had lain awake, troubled by the drunken rantings of his mother.

'In the end, I gave up trying and got up,' he said. 'But it's only now the mist has lifted that I've thought to come down here.' When she dared to look back at him, it was to see that he was stood with his face turned to the sky and his arms held wide. 'Glorious, isn't it?'

Despite the fact that he wasn't looking at her, she nodded. 'It is now.' But then, lest he misconstrue her meaning, she hastened to add, 'Although, as you say, it wasn't earlier.'

'Hard to believe we're on the brink of war.'

When he looked back down, she nodded again. 'Yes.'

'I say, have I disturbed you? Were you hoping to be alone? If you were, I can leave. I don't mind.'

Struck by the irony of his observation, she pressed her lips together against laughter. The only thing from which he was disturbing her was attempting to plot how best to get to know him. 'No, truly, no there's no need,' she said, at pains to sound unconcerned. 'As it happens, I shouldn't mind company.'

'You do not fear being seen talking to me?'

Amused by the topsy-turvy nature of his observation, she laughed. 'Shouldn't *I* be asking whether *you* fear being seen talking to *me?*'

'Goodness, no,' he was quick to reply. 'And in which case, shall we walk a little? It would seem a waste not to enjoy a stroll while we have the place to ourselves.'

He wanted to walk with her? Alone with her? It was as much as she could do to stop herself grinning with delight. 'It *would* seem a waste, yes.'

As he turned to face in the same direction and they started walking, Kate felt certain she saw his hand twitch – flick briefly towards her before being snapped back to his side. Had he been minded to reach for her hand? He *had*, she would swear to it! So, why had he thought better of it? Had he thought she would be startled – or that she would think it improper? Because on that front, he was as wrong as could be. How, now, to assure him otherwise? Could she reach for his? Or would that be too forward? It might be. Perhaps such a confident move would delight him. No, she knew what it was: they were out in the open and he didn't want to risk the damage to her reputation if they were spotted behaving improperly.

As it happened, while she had been dithering, the distance between them had widened. Under her breath, she cursed: through her dallying, she had cost herself the best chance she might ever have.

'Tell me,' he said, the tone of his voice giving nothing away, 'this morning, in the bright light of day, do you still believe that our prophetess had the ability to see the future?'

She tried to drag her thoughts away from the matter of his hand. Did she, in response to his question, admit to having briefly agreed with his view that Sybil was a fraud or did she stick to her guns and say that this morning, much of what the woman had said now made sense?

'I'm not sure,' she settled for saying, groaning,

inwardly, at the woolliness of her response. *So much for vowing to be decisive and determined!*

'No?'

Unless she wanted him to think her dull, she had to do better. 'At first,' she said, 'I thought her very … vague … but on the other hand…' *Hand. Forget about hands! Quell your turmoil,* she told herself, *or he'll think you're crazed.*

'Her vagueness disappointed you?'

'It did, yes.'

'You were hoping to hear something specific – something you might interpret as guidance?' When she didn't immediately answer, he went on to say, 'It would be quite natural.'

Briefly, she looked up ahead; they were following the curve of the cove, no more than a yard or so from where each little ripple of the tide was abandoning a line of bubbles to the sand. Unexpectedly, he had hit the nail on the head; it was *precisely* what she had been hoping for. In the event, her guidance had come in the unlikely form of his Aunt Diana.

'Yes,' she said. 'Sometimes, you just want to be sure of a thing, don't you – before you commit to it, I mean?'

'Very much so.' Surprising her by then dropping to his haunches, he said, 'I say, look.' Watching him poke about in the sand with his forefinger, she smiled 'How pretty this is – the blue of this shell. Or would one more properly call it purple?'

Unable to bring herself to tell him that it was merely one half of a mussel shell, when he held it towards her, she took it, turning it this way and that, ostensibly to examine it in more detail.

'It's a mussel,' she finally felt compelled to say.

'Yes, but just look at the underside of it,' he urged, turning it the other way up on her palm. 'See how the light reflects the different colours?'

'It's nacre,' she observed, pleased to be able to tell him something he appeared not to know. 'More often called mother-of-pearl.'

'Yes, Min has it on some jewellery. But I don't recall having seen it on a shell before – you know, where nature intended it.'

His admission made her laugh. Here was a man who, having been to study at a university, was marvelling over the remains of a dead sea creature. 'No,' she said, 'I don't suppose you see many shells in London.'

'To be fair, there aren't *that* many *here*.' Casting about, he gestured with his arm. 'Not for a beach, there aren't!'

'That's because this cove is mainly sandy,' she explained. 'But go to one of the bays either side of here and you'll see plenty – hundreds and thousands, most of them dashed to pieces on the rocks.'

The matter of mussel shells seemingly exhausted, they walked on. The sun was beginning to feel warm now and, for what had to be the first time ever, she wished she'd thought to bring a hat. Still, better that he could see her hair, which, with any luck, in this bright light would look quite eye-catching.

Ahead of them, apparently marooned on the sand, sat two large and perfectly smooth boulders. As a child, she had always imagined them to have been dragged from higher up the beach by a giant, who, having grown tired of their weight, had abandoned them to their fates at the hands of the returning tides.

'Shall we perch a while,' he said, turning to her for an answer. She nodded. There was nothing she would like more. 'You take the lower one and I'll try and...' With that, he proceeded to try to haul himself up onto the larger of the two rocks, its perfectly smooth and featureless form defeating his attempts to catch hold.

'You can share mine, if you'd like,' she said, trying to conceal her laughter by shuffling further to one side. 'There's room enough.' She knew it was wrong to encourage him into such close proximity. But, by most reckoning, it was wrong to be alone there with him in the first place. Certainly, if Mrs Russell – or indeed, Ma – were to see them, there would be hell to pay. In a flash of guilt, she glanced in both directions along the beach. Thankfully, to be caught this early in the morning, they would have to be very unfortunate indeed.

When he settled beside her, she was unprepared for how it felt to be so close to him. Even the touch of his sleeve as it brushed against the back of her hand set something tingling inside her. She was even convinced she could feel the heat from his thigh through her skirt, which, given that there was at least two inches of space between them, had to be entirely down to her imagination.

'Won't you miss this, if you leave here?' he asked, his own manner perfectly unconcerned.

It wasn't something she had considered. All she had ever thought was that she couldn't wait to get away to somewhere more exciting – to somewhere with some colour and life.

'I doubt it.'

'No? Not all this fresh air? Not the glorious blue of the sea nor the dazzling emerald of these hillsides?'

She shook her head. What was it with men and fresh air? Was the air in London really so filthy?

'You wouldn't say that if you were stuck here in November ... or February, when everything is the self-same shade of grey. Or when to go a-traipsing up the lane towards the crossroads means to see just the one shade of mud brown and to get thoroughly begrimed by it.'

'I suppose there is that,' he said. 'Although I should imagine that here, the air is clean year-round. In London, the winter months are evil, the air thick with smoke, coal-smuts dirtying everything–'

She laughed. 'We have those too, you know. Although, here we call them smitches–'

'*Smitches?*'

'Smitches. Though of course mainly we burn wood.'

'Which *doesn't* give off smitches?'

'Which doesn't give off *so many* smitches.'

'Ah.'

'Was your mother pleased with her party?' she asked after a moment's silence, desperate that their conversation shouldn't fizzle out.

'I haven't seen her yet this morning to ask. I doubt she'll be about until at least midday. But some of it seemed to go well, don't you think?'

Not knowing how much he knew of what had happened after they had parted company, she felt it safest to agree with him. No sense sending him scurrying away for fear of courting his mother's wrath. 'Yes,' she said. 'The music sounded lovely – from what I could hear of it.'

From the corner of her eye, she could see that he was staring out towards the horizon.

'Yes. And Mamma's idea of picnic-baskets was inspired.'

'Yes,' she agreed. 'And the costumes most striking.' Then, summoning further courage, she added, 'Especially you in your blue. You really stood out.'

'Did I? It was rather odd to be in uniform. Made one feel obliged to stand tall and erect. Even though it was a very old one, it felt like a taste of what might be to come – you know, joining up and belonging to a regiment.'

'I did wonder whether you would all feel like real soldiers,' she ventured, reminded, with a sharp stab, of the unease she'd felt at seeing him in military apparel.

'Good job it *wasn't* for real – not with Aubrey and Lawrence getting into that scrap. This morning, as well as having bruised ribs and sore heads, they'd be waking up in gaol. *Conduct unbecoming of an officer* and all that.'

'But Mr Lawrence wasn't to blame,' she said quickly, realizing that he had indeed found out what had transpired. For all Miss Naomi wanting it to remain a secret, an awful lot of people seemed to know. 'He just came to Miss Naomi's rescue.' Into her mind came the thought that the same had been true of her own actions and yet *she* was still having to bear the consequences.

'I'm not sure that would be of the least interest to their superior officers. Details like that seem unimportant where reputations are at stake.'

Yes, Kate thought. How true *that* was turning out to be – her own superior equally unconcerned by the trifling matter of the actual facts. Still, if she was clever, having now got Ned onto the subject, she might manage to persuade him to divulge what had happened afterwards.

'Yes,' she said. 'I suppose so. Fortunate Miss Naomi called out when she did, though – when I just happened to be on my way back to the house.'

'She mentioned that. It was good of you to go to her aid. Of course, Aubrey was an idiot to get so inebriated as to make a fool of himself in the first place. Terribly juvenile thing to do. As indeed it was for him to pick a fight with his brother, who, according to Min, was entirely sober and who, in any event, is far stronger and more athletic than Aubrey will ever be.'

So far so good. 'I trust neither of them was badly hurt.'

'I doubt it. For Aubrey, I should think that this morning, it will be more a case of wounded pride.'

'And a thundering headache, too, I shouldn't wonder,' she said. 'Still, that's preferable to any real harm having been done.'

'Yes. The real harm, as you put it, will come when he has to suffer the wrath of his parents – especially Aunt Cicely. Although diminutive of stature, she can be every bit as fierce as Mamma. Added to that will be the embarrassment of having to apologize to Min for his behaviour.'

'Poor Miss Naomi, I hope she's all right this morning.'

'I say, yes, you're not doing whatever it is you normally do for her at this time of day. Did she ask to sleep in? It wouldn't surprise me. I think she was kept up very late with Mamma – some sort of commotion by all accounts. Aunt Diana came and whispered to me that Mamma was going to retire for the night. When I then enquired whether she was all right, Aunt Diana told me she had become upset about something. I went to see whether I could be of assistance, but Min already had Aunt Cicely there and assured me that every-thing was all right.'

Digesting this revelation, Kate gave a little mur-mur that she hoped he would take as being one of sympathy. Deep down, though, she was seething. She *knew* Cicely Colborne had been involved, and now Ned had confirmed it. *Upset about something*, indeed! Pamela Russell had been drunk and wailing pitifully, disgracing herself in front of her daughter.

Willing that Ned would continue talking, she sat perfectly still, while beside her on the rock, he shifted his weight. That he seemed to have for-gotten his question about why she wasn't attend-ing to his sister was a relief, since she didn't feel inclined to try to explain how things had turned out. When he didn't appear about to volunteer anything further, though, she said, 'Tell me, if it wasn't for the war, what would you be going to do once you return home?'

'*That* is a very good question. And one for

which by now, I ought really to have come up with an answer.'

Drawing her bare feet up onto the rock and tucking her knees under her chin, she looked sideways at him. 'Having to decide something so big is hard, isn't it? When you're a littl'un, grown up folk teach you how to walk and talk and read and write. But no one thinks to teach you how to decide things.'

'I'm not sure they can. Every decision brings its own considerations, doesn't it? Take my situation as an example, although I have an obvious path stretching ahead of me, I find myself wishing for others against which to compare it.'

'Because otherwise, it don't feel like making a choice at all?'

'That's right. It's not a true decision but more a forfeiture of a decision. And therein lies my unease.'

'Hmm,' she said. 'I do see your problem.' With him having admitted that much, how, now, did she encourage him to elaborate, the direction of *his* future having become critical to her own. Lost to know, she gave a little sigh. All she could really do was rely on what little of his situation she already knew. 'I suppose your father would like you to follow him into his business.'

'It's been his dream since the day I was born.'

'But not yours?' she observed, there being no need for him to know what Miss Naomi had already told her.

'Don't get me wrong, I could do a lot worse. And I should imagine that to some, I must appear ungrateful. But the matter is not as straightforward as it might appear.'

'No?' Rather than ask outright, she waited, hoping that he would explain.

'You see, sometimes, I feel something of a fraud.'

'A fraud?'

'It's not something Mamma would ever under-stand – although Father might – but, courtesy of their widely differing backgrounds, I sometimes find myself struggling to be certain who I am. I mix with the gentry and yet, by some of their number, I am viewed with suspicion. Tainted, is how some of them see me. Equally, I'm not truly *trade*, as Grandmamma Alice refers to Father.' Astonished by the frankness of his admission, Kate confined herself to nodding. 'Without rea-lizing it, by clinging to such differing hopes for my future, Mother and Father are pulling me in different directions, both of them wishing only for the best for me, neither of them prepared to concede that their wish might be the unsuitable one. Even were I to decide to follow my father into his business, it wouldn't be without its pit-falls; I have always rather feared that I would be setting myself up for a fall – you know, by not living up to his expectations of me, or by failing to fill his considerable shoes.'

'Mmm,' she agreed, trying to digest what he was saying. No wonder he appeared to lack purpose. And so much for privilege. That aside, she rather warmed to his uncertainty; it helped her to know that he was fallible – just like her.

'People often describe my father as larger than life itself,' he went on. 'And they're not wrong.

254

And, while I know one shouldn't let fear hold one back, where Father is concerned, I'm rather ashamed to admit that I do.'

'I think to be a-feared of something like that is perfectly normal,' she said, remembering Aunt Diana's words but having, anyway, always believed it to be the case.

This time when she glanced to his face, he caught her look and held it. If only he would reach for her hand again ... or better still, decide to kiss her.

Instead, taking her by surprise, he slid from the rock, landing with a dull thud on the sand and then brushing at the seat of his trousers before bending low and rolling them right up to his knees.

'Quick paddle before breakfast, I think.' Wide-eyed, she watched as he jogged towards the water before she, too, slid from the rock and followed in the line of his footprints. But, while he ran, without apparent care, straight into the waves, she held back. 'Not coming in?' he called, laughing, and squinting to where the waves were just breaking over her toes.

'In my uniform?' she shouted back to him, hurriedly raising the hem of her skirt above her ankles as her feet started to sink down into the wet sand.

He laughed loudly. 'Poor you. Rotten luck!'

'And what about your trousers?' Grasping her skirt with one hand, she gestured with her other. 'They're getting wet.'

Raising his arms in a gesture of helplessness, he shrugged his shoulders. 'I'm sure they'll dry quick enough.'

'Not if I do this,' she called, dipping her fingers into the water and scooping a handful of it in his direction. When it splashed just a few inches short of where he was standing, she laughed and did it again.

'No, you're right,' he called back, '*now* I *shall* have to change. And some poor laundrymaid will curse my thoughtlessness as she stands at a sink somewhere, trying to wash the salt from them.'

'*You* were the one who went running in,' she shouted to him, watching as he raised himself above the curling of a slightly higher wave. 'So, what did you think was going to happen?'

'I gave it not a moment's thought!'

With a sense of what he was about to do next, she gathered her skirts higher still, turned quickly about and, with the sound of water splashing behind her, ran back up the sands.

Once clear of the water's edge, she turned back. 'You devil!'

'Takes one to know one,' he called. 'You were the one who started it!' When he then staggered, in exaggerated fashion, out of the waves and up the beach, the effect on her breathing became difficult to conceal, her chest rising and falling far too rapidly to go unnoticed. If he did notice, he passed no comment. 'And you can honestly say you won't miss this?' he asked instead, bending to examine his spattered trousers. Although he couldn't know it, of course, he was missing the point. Ordinarily at this time of day, she wouldn't be on the beach in the first place. And, without him to take her breath away, she certainly wouldn't be enjoying it as much. 'London doesn't have beaches, you know.'

No, she thought, but it has *you*. And between you and this beach, there's no comparison. 'I know,' she said lightly. 'But happen there will be other ways to spend my time.'

'Happen there will, as you say down here.'

''*Appen*,' she corrected him. 'If you're going to use our words, you should at least learn how to say them proper. Elsewise, you risk making yourself a laughing stock.'

''*Appen* I'll learn myself *praa-purr* then.'

At his daftness, she shook her head. 'Now you just sound like the village idiot.'

When he made to start back up the beach, with a sigh, she reluctantly followed suit.

'Seriously, though, I didn't properly splash you, did I?'

She glanced down at her skirt. There were two dark splotches, neither of them his doing. 'Not proper, no. Not so much as to draw attention.'

'Good. Only, I shouldn't care to land you in trouble.' Despite the warmth of the sun on her arms, she shivered. 'I say, are you all right?'

She held off saying she felt as though someone had just walked over her grave. Instead, preferring that he didn't think her fanciful, she nodded, uncertain anyway why the words *land you in trouble* should feel so ominous. 'I'm just fine, thank you.'

'Well, I must away to take breakfast,' he said as they headed further back up the beach.

'Yes, I suppose so,' she replied, disappointed by the casual manner in which he seemed able to take his leave – no suggestion or arrangement

257

that they should meet again.

'Though, *'appen* I'll see you down here again.'

She brightened. 'Aye, *'appen* you will.' *At least, happen you will if* I've *got anything to do with it,* she thought as she let him go on ahead of her up through the boulders to disappear out of sight into the trees. *Although you can be certain that when you do, happenstance will have had absolutely nothing to do with it at all.*

A little while later, making her own way slowly back through the copse towards the house, Kate could barely believe what a morning it had been, especially since judging by the height of the sun, it still wasn't even nine o'clock. After her reprimanding by Ma, the last thing she had been expecting was to have her prayers answered, and end up alone with Ned. It would have seemed so unlikely.

Even before his arrival on the beach, she had begun to feel more certain of herself – more encouraged and purposeful. Aunt Diana had agreed with her that a person should be free to marry whomsoever they chose. And, last night, Sybil had said that to see her future, all she had to do was look inside herself. Taken separately, those two pieces of advice had meant nothing to her.

But now, piecing them together, it felt as though a mist had lifted. Her future had been revealed: no matter who decried it, her dream was hanging there for the grasping.

Swiping a hand at the stiff and crispy fronds of bracken as she moved between them, she picked her way on up the slope, her thoughts about the precarious nature of dreams for some reason bringing her to think of Miss Naomi. Aunt Diana's advice had been to trust her instincts. So, shouldn't Miss Naomi do the same – even if it did mean going against what was expected of her? Either Aunt Diana's advice was sound or it wasn't. And, if it was, then surely it had to apply to everyone equally: Miss Naomi included. If she wanted to be with Mr Lawrence, she should let no one stand in her way.

In the cover of the woodland, she came to a halt. Perhaps she should try to find a way to talk to Miss Naomi and urge her to be true to her heart. Perhaps, given the similarity of their situations, they could find a way to offer each other encouragement and help – if not as a lady and her maid, then as two sisters might. Of course, she harboured no illusions: even should Miss Naomi agree with her, it wouldn't be easy; pursuing their choices of husband would bring considerable opposition. But surely, by going about it together, they would be better placed to overcome the obstacles in their paths.

Glancing up ahead through the trees, she started walking again. What she had to do now, it seemed, was find a way to get to talk to Miss Naomi and convince her that they should join forces. Given that they were forbidden to see each other, even doing that wasn't going to be straightforward. But, in her new mood of determination, she would find a way. In the meantime, where her own plan for Ned was concerned, she would grab any and all opportunities to get to know him better and, almost more importantly, give him every chance to get to know her. After all, if *he* grew to like *her* as much as *she* liked *him,* then surely most of her battle was already won.

Where her path made its way up through a narrow gulley in the rocks, she paused, as she always did, to run her hand over its coat of soft emerald mosses. Pamela Russell and her false accusations be damned. And Cicely Colborne and *her* part in it, too. She knew now that Ned liked her. And, after everything she had been through in the last 12 or so hours, she felt stronger and more determined than ever. Never mind all those narrow-minded people and what they thought: if she and Ned liked each other enough, then it would take something on an unimaginable scale to tear them apart.

Chapter Seven

Secrets...

'Pamela, my dear. Terribly sorry you had to arrive on your own like that. I trust you settled in well enough?'

'Sidney, darling.' *Mwah, mwah.* 'Of course we did. It's all been perfectly lovely. Such a charming little house.'

'Hardly a match for Biarritz and your favourite *Hôtel du Palais.*'

'But wonderful fun, nevertheless.'

'Good-oh. Well, feel free to stay as long you'd

like. Take it from me, this is quite the best place to be at the moment. Whitehall and the city are beset with panic. No, don't look at me like that, you'd be surprised at how quickly things in town have ground to a halt. Old Hugh's in his element, of course. Opportunities left, right and centre, or so he's been telling me on the way down. Isn't that right, Hugh?'

'Hello, Pam, love.'

'Don't you *Pam, love,* me, Hugh Russell – deserting me like that.'

Eavesdropping upon the arrival of Sidney Latimer and Hugh Russell, Kate couldn't help but smile. She had thought that with her husband coming to stay, Pamela Russell's mood might improve. Unfortunately, from the tone of her greeting, she seemed as displeased as ever.

She had also been hoping to see what Hugh Russell looked like – to try and spot any resemblance to Ned – but when, far earlier than expected, the station cab had drawn up alongside the porch, unable to think of a reason for why she should be standing in the hallway, she'd plunged into the cloakroom. And now she was stuck in there, unable to see anything of him at all. Even opening the door just wide enough to look out was taking a chance; she still hadn't been forgiven for her supposed part in what everyone – both above and below stairs – kept referring to as 'the other evening's little upset'. Goodness, how cross everyone had been with her, the censure from her own sister particularly galling. Sisters were supposed to support one another. But hers *never* had. *Hers* had only ever been a buttoned-up and disapproving old spinster. Well, as Ned had so shrewdly observed only the other night, you got the life you deserved. And, where Edith was concerned, it couldn't be more true.

Turning her thoughts back to the arrival of Hugh Russell, Kate pressed her ear to the door and strained to hear what was being said on the other side. Luggage. Rooms. Luggage again. Dinner. She was unlikely to learn much from any of that.

Disappointed, she risked easing the door open just a little.

'Five or six nights only, I'm afraid,' she heard one of the men saying, his voice frustratingly indistinct. 'Then it's off to the Highlands for the grouse. Never missed a glorious twelfth yet and don't intend to start now – threat of war or no.' With that, their voices started to grow even more difficult to hear – presumably as they headed upstairs – the last thing she was able to make out being, 'By the way, do you know the Rattray-Smyths? No? It just so happens they've decamped from town to their cottage on Exmoor for a couple of weeks. Said they might pop down for a day or two. Hope you don't mind.'

When it finally sounded as though the little group had left, Kate exhaled with relief: it was safe to leave the cloakroom. It was annoying to have been in such close proximity to Hugh Russell without actually being able to see his face; she'd been hoping to discover that he looked to be easy-going. Or, better still, to discover that he looked like a man to be charmed by a pretty face, since, if her plan for Ned was to succeed, she was going to need to win over at least one of the Russell parents. And after 'the other night's little upset', that parent was unlikely to be *Mrs* Russell. Very unlikely indeed.

'She must have ruddy great feet. That's all I can say.'

Unable to miss the squeals of laughter coming from beyond the partly-open door to the boot room, Kate peered in. Beyond it were Dulcie and Aggie, two of the day girls, the former doubled over with laughter, the latter parading up and down in a pair of patent-leather ankle-boots.

Stepping quickly inside, Kate pressed the door shut behind her. 'Whatever are you doing?' she demanded of them in a fierce whisper, at the same time taking in the tears running down Dulcie's cheeks and the straightening of Aggie's face.

'Sorry, Kate,' Aggie replied, pulling her feet one-by-one from the boots and then lifting them back onto the bench. 'We didn't mean no disrespect by it.'

In despair of their behaviour, Kate shook her head. 'Whose are they?' she asked, nodding towards the bench and determining from their considerable size that at least they didn't belong to Miss Naomi.

In unison, the two girls shrugged. 'Someone too short-sighted to see a pile of sheep-dung under her nose,' Aggie replied, and to which her partner-in-crime snorted with laughter.

'Give them here,' she said, holding out her hands. 'If you're fool enough to lark about, you ought at least see to it that the door's closed.

What if it hadn't been me coming along there but my ma?' Accepting the pair of ankle-boots, she shook her head. They did at least look clean, if a little lacklustre. 'What did you clean them with?'

'A damp cloth, once I'd scraped off the sh— *muck*.'

'Hmm. Not a complete waste of time. But, if I was you, I'd soak a corner of your cloth in some milk, wipe it *thinly* all over, and then buff them up. It's just the thing to restore the shine to scuffed patent.'

Looking relieved, Aggie nodded. 'Thanks, Kate, I'll do that now.'

Then, glancing over the bench and turning to Dulcie, she said, 'At risk of sounding like my mother, what is it *you're* supposed to be doing?'

The young girl motioned behind her. 'Getting the claret stains from those two silver salvers. I was just waiting for the paste to dry before I scrape it off and give them a good buff up.'

Kate glanced to where the girl had indicated. 'I thought I could smell hartshorn. Well, just make sure an' get it all out of the engravings afterwards. Mrs Russell won't hesitate to complain about shoddy work if she comes across it. And Ma's already in a bit of a fret. So, trust me when I say that you don't need to cause her any more grief.'

'I'll make good an' sure, Kate. Thanks ever so.'

'By way of a return favour,' Aggie began, glancing beyond Kate to the door and then lowering her voice, 'you might want to watch out for Mrs Russell's 'usband.'

Kate frowned. 'Watch out for him?'

'Leery sort. Wouldn't want to get myself caught alone with 'im anywhere. Looked me up and down as though wondering whether I'd do the business with him, if you'll pardon me saying so.'

Feeling her eyes widen, Kate nevertheless nodded. 'Thanks,' she said. 'I'll make sure an' give him a wide berth. But just try an' stay out of trouble, the pair of you. For all of our sakes.'

When she left the room and went back along the corridor, it was with a frown; was she to deduce that Mr Russell was something of a lecher? While neither of those two girls could be relied upon to tell the truth to save their own skins, it would certainly explain a good deal of *Mrs* Russell's constant weariness. But, if they *were* right, then as she'd found herself reflecting barely an hour or so earlier, she might be able to make it work to her advantage: moving forward with her plan requiring any and every ounce of deviousness she could muster.

'Oh, there you are, love. I need you to take up the flowers for the drawing room.'

Inwardly, Kate groaned. This was only her second day of being back at her mother's beck and call but already, her daily routine was proving tedious beyond belief. In fact, she was only now coming to realize just how much freedom the job of lady's maid had permitted her. She *could* have another go at pleading to be allowed to resume the position but, in all likelihood, it would be a waste of her breath. Even if she could somehow overcome *Ma's* objections, she sensed that she would be unlikely to convince Mrs Russell to reconsider. No, unfortunately, where finding out more about Ned was concerned, her days of being privy to snippets of information from his sister were well and truly over. As was her freedom to come and go as she pleased.

'Flowers for the drawing room. Yes, Ma.'

'One of the day girls hasn't turned up this morning and Mrs Channer's legs were giving her so much pain I've had to send her back home. She'd already finished making up the vases, so I just need you to take them upstairs. Edie's about to go and see Mrs Russell with the menus so, if you wait a moment, she can help you carry them up.'

Dutifully, Kate went through to the boot room. This, then, was what she had been reduced to: fetching and carrying. Still, it was better than cleaning the range for Edith. *Thank goodness for Ned writing that letter to his cousin,* she thought, watching her sister come trudging along the corridor towards her.

'You seen Luke lately?' Edith asked, tucking her day book under her arm and reaching for two of the towering arrangements of antirrhinums.

Lifting the remaining two vases, Kate sighed. What was the matter with her sister to keep on like this? Had she nothing else to fret over? 'Couple of days back,' she replied shortly. 'Though what it's got to do with *you,* I can't fathom.'

'And what *I* can't fathom,' Edith hissed once they had crossed the hallway and arrived in the drawing room, 'is what your game is. What I *do* know, is that you'd be better-served spending more of your time with him and less of it simpering at this lot upstairs.' *Simpering?* Such was Kate's outrage that, momentarily, she couldn't even speak. How dare her sister bandy such accusations! She did *not* simper. 'I mean it, Kate. Trust me, Luke Channer is worth ten of these flighty young sorts up here, with their fancy clothes and their oiled hair. Fraternizing with this lot will bring you nothing but trouble. Devote your attentions to Luke – start showing him the respect he deserves.'

'Respect?' What gave her sister the right to lecture her about Luke?

'There,' Edith said, placing her two vases on the runner on the sideboard and acting as though she hadn't even raised the subject. 'Mrs Channer usually puts one at each end of here, and one on each of those side tables.'

Still speechless, Kate shook her head. 'I do know where the flowers go.'

'Seriously, Kate,' Edith once again lowered her voice to add, 'men like Luke don't come along every day of the week.'

Removing one of the vases to the nearest side table, Kate wondered what on earth she had to do to stop Edith interfering. It wasn't even as though where men were concerned, her sister was in a position to judge – something she decided to make plain. 'Not that you'd know.'

Edith, though, wasn't giving up. 'Happen I'm in a better position than you think.'

'You? Huh.' Returning to the sideboard, Kate shook her head crossly: on top of everything else, her sister was deluded.

'Scoff all you like,' Edith replied. 'But it's true.'

About to deride her sister's claim further, Kate checked herself; someone was coming towards the drawing room, their purposeful footsteps echoing around the hallway. Desperate to avoid further trouble, she held back her riposte; it would keep until whoever it was had moved on. The footsteps, though, stopped and, sensing that someone was looking in through the open doorway at them, Kate drew herself smartly upright and proceeded to fuss with the stems of the antirrhinums – anything rather than appear as though she was nobbling and newsing. She wondered whether it might be Ned – it would be typical of her bad luck to have him come looking for her and find her with Edith. In case it *was* him, she turned very slowly to check. But, silhouetted against the brightness of the doorway was a portly figure, who, by the time she had turned more fully in its direction, was already walking away.

'Who was that?' she whispered. Turning back for her sister's answer, she was shocked to see that Edith's face had lost all of its colour. She reached for her arm. 'Edie? You all right? You've gone all pale.' Grasping for the sideboard, Edith lowered her head. 'Truly, Edie, your face is whiter than milk. Ought you to sit down a while?'

'I'm fine,' Edith murmured. 'I just came over … dizzy-headed for a moment.'

'Dizzy-headed? Saw a ghost, more like. Come over here and sit down a mo'. Come on, I'm worried you'll fall elsewise.'

Raising herself upright again, Edith appeared to try and pull herself together. 'I'll do no such thing – and certainly not in here, of all places.'

'But Edie,' Kate persisted, 'even your hands are trembling. Look at them. Come on, surely you can see something ain't right. If you won't sit down *here*, at least let me help you back downstairs. Mrs Russell's menus will keep a moment longer.'

Edith, though, was not to be persuaded. 'For the last time, Kate, there's nothing wrong with me. I just had a funny turn. And I'll thank you to leave it at that.'

In response to her sister's dismissiveness, Kate shrugged. 'Suit yourself. I was only trying to help.'

'Just stop your fussing and get these vases put out. And another thing, try and stay on the right side of Ma for once. Keep your head down and get on with your work like the rest of us. And just sort things out with Luke, too. Far too long you've been leading him a merry dance–'

Unable to help herself, Kate rounded on her sister. 'Patient saints, Edith, stop telling me what to do! Truly, stop it. I've had my fill of you and Ma keep poking your noses into my business. Luke is my matter to see to, not yours.'

'Well, *I've* had *my* fill of *you* keep rocking the boat,' Edith hissed back. 'What you overlook is that with Mr Latimer back here, he's well-situated to learn of your transgressions first-hand. Try remembering *that* next time you're minded to open your mouth and speak out of turn. Give him grounds to throw us out on our ears and we're done for. Be quick enough to traipse up the aisle with Luke Channer then, wouldn't you?'

'For God's sake, Edith, whether I wed Luke or

whether I don't has nothing to do with you. And quite why you'd think I'd take advice from a lonely old spinster is beyond me anyway.'

'You take that back, Kate Bratton.'

'Take what back? The truth? Ain't my fault it's hard to hear. Tell you what, if you're so fond of Luke Channer – if you think him such a good catch – *you* marry him! Marry him with my blessing.'

What *had* come over her sister all of a sudden, Kate wondered as she lifted the remaining vase from the sideboard. Crossing the rug and plonking it down on one of the occasional tables, she purposely didn't turn back to look at her. Instead, she stood, teeth gritted, tweaking the stems of the blooms as though caring how they looked until eventually, hearing her sister heading away, she let her arms drop to her sides and gave a long and weary sigh.

Her sister was right about one thing: some matters did need sorting out. For a start, Luke needed to stop naysaying how she felt; he needed to respect her feelings and be in no doubt about where he stood. She had a plan to further and it didn't involve *him*. Furthermore, to bring it about, she was going to need a clear head. So, yes, where Luke was concerned, on this occasion, Edith was right: the time had come to sort things out. Once and for all.

She had to go through with this. Despite feeling sickened by the prospect, she had to see it through.

It was later that same morning and, having

somehow made it all the way to the far side of the stable yard without caving in to second thoughts, Kate found herself standing a few feet from the door to the workshop, trying to summon the courage to go inside. Whoever was in there was sawing wood – she could hear the saw rasping back and forth. Having worked herself into a state of high anxiety, all she could do was hope that it was Luke.

Drawing a deep breath and taking the last few steps to the partly open door, she peered around it. The air was thick with sawdust, a single shaft of brightness from the roof light illuminating him bent over the sawing-horse. From across the dusty room, he looked so manly and purposeful that her legs wanted to carry her away to save her from doing something foolish. But, coming just as vividly to her mind was a picture of Ned, trying to splash her with sea water. *One or the other,* she reminded herself: *Ned or Luke – you can't have both.*

If she was honest, she was still struggling to believe how easily she had reached this point – two supposedly separate matters having somehow collided to present her with the most incredible of opportunities. So, why the hesitation? Her desire to leave Woodicombe was unchanged; she only had to recall the fate of poor Liddy Tucker to reassure herself on that point. That she had fallen for Ned Russell and his lovely attentions was also beyond dispute. The problem lay with what was required of her next: that she break Luke's heart.

Feeling how parched her throat felt, she swallowed uneasily. Yes, it was going to be awful, but there was no way around it.

'Luke?' she called tentatively across to him.

Straightening up, he wiped a hand across his brow. 'Kate.'

Briefly, she looked down. Then she forced herself to look back up. *This has to be done. You have to go through with it.* 'Spare me a minute ... to talk?'

Setting the quivering saw on top of the length of timber he'd been cutting, Luke brushed his hands down the front of his overalls. ''Course. What brings you out here?'

Trust your instincts had been Diana Lloyd's advice. Easy for *her* to say; she wasn't about to break the heart of an innocent man – a good man. But, as she kept reminding herself, anything less would amount to treachery. *You don't want to marry him. And he has to know that.*

'I've decided I don't want to stay in Woodicombe.' There. She'd said it. Sort of.

The look he gave her was a weary one. 'Kate, we've been through this–'

'Aye, I know I've said it afore. But, lately, I've been thinking about it proper. Long and hard, I mean. And it's not what I want. I've not come to ask you to go with me because I know you don't want to. All I've come to say is that I'm going to London. And so you can stop going on about getting wed.'

To her relief, he didn't try to approach her. In fact, he didn't move.

'You're going to London.' In response to his statement, she gave a single nod. 'On your own.'

Wishing she felt able to meet his eyes, she

nodded again.

'Yes.'

'You've got work there.'

'I have.' More lies. 'Someone I know there is seeing to it.'

Still he didn't move. '*You* know someone in London. Since when?'

Now what did she say? She hadn't expected him to challenge her – at least, not to challenge the details. 'Well, I don't actually *know* them but–'

'Kate, don't lie to me. After all this time, I deserve better than to be lied to. It's the Russells, ain't it? You're going to London with the Russells. That girl – your Miss Naomi – she's spoken for you somewhere, hasn't she?'

At least that was *something* she could deny with a clear conscience. 'No. It's got nothing to do with Miss Naomi.' In a way, it might have been easier if it had.

'Well it's not her mother speaking for you, that much I do know. There's no love lost there. It must be him, then – the son.' With his expression suddenly changing to one of sickly recognition, Kate felt something in her stomach knotting tightly.

'Christ, Kate, it's him, ain't it? You're going to London with *him*.'

'Huh, if you think he'd take *me* to London with him, you're more mazed than I had you down for.'

'Christ. That's it. I've seen you talking to him, you know.'

She shuddered. How had he? And when? Without knowing what he'd seen or heard, she'd have

273

to be careful about what she said next. 'Well, yes, I've spoken to him, of course I have. He's Miss Naomi's brother. He's often ... about. We even saw him that day in Westward Quay.'

'Handy.'

'Chance. Truly. Ask Miss Naomi. Even *she* didn't know he was going to be there.'

'Huh.'

'For the last time, Luke, I am *not* going to London with N– Mr Edwin.'

'If you say so.'

'I do.'

'Go with whoever you like Kate, I can't stop you. But, if we're no longer to be wed, then I'd best be getting back to my work. Ain't nobody going to find *me* a job elsewhere.'

Feeling utterly wretched, Kate stared down at her shoes. Then, with seemingly nothing more to be said, she turned away. Having expected to feel light-hearted and relieved – her problem dealt with – she was surprised to realize that what she actually felt was an overwhelming sadness. There, in that dusty old workshop, all their years of friendship, and of mischief and laughter, had come to an end – seemingly without so much as a bat of an eyelid from either of them.

Bewildered – and not that far from tears – she stepped back out into the daylight. By rights, she ought to feel relieved that he had made it easy for her and yet, in truth, she felt distraught by the recognition that he hadn't tried to get her to change her mind – hadn't begged her to reconsider. Well, the fact was, he hadn't: with no more than a few cross words passing between them,

274

she had got what she wanted.

Unable to think what else to do, she made her way slowly back to the scullery. But, upon nearing the back door and thinking she might be sick, she doubled over. She pressed a hand to her chest. What had she done? What *had* she done? What she had *done,* she reminded herself, reaching to the doorframe for support, was take a step closer to realizing her dream. Now, with Luke no longer misunderstanding the situation between them, she was free to bring about the life she craved. Carefully, she stood up. As Diana Lloyd had so clearly advised, and as Sybil the seer had somewhat more vaguely intimated, she was bringing about the future she wanted. And, once she stopped feeling so guilty, she would appreciate what an incredibly brave thing she had just done.

Beginning to feel a little less sick, she forced herself to draw several long breaths. Of course, now, she had to hope that Luke didn't stir himself into a fit of jealousy and decide to confront Ned. Or, equally disastrously, decide to join forces with Edith and Ma and hatch some sort of plot to get back at her for jilting him; it wasn't altogether impossible. She sighed heavily. No, Luke wouldn't do that. Not to her, he wouldn't. It was like Edith had said earlier: Luke Channer was a good man. Always had been. And, despite what she had just done to him, always would be.

'Truly? She's willing to do that? For *me?*'

In response to Kate's question, Ned nodded. 'That's what she said in her letter – that she would be happy to see what she could find out.'

275

It was a couple of days later – Monday the third of August – and, having earlier seen Ned heading away over the lawns with the attitude and apparel of someone setting off for a walk, she had tried to gauge when he would return. To her astonishment, she had guessed correctly, slipping out of the house and down to the cove with unbelievably perfect timing. And now, in the bright afternoon sunshine, the two of them were seated on what she had come to think of as *their* boulder, holding a conversation that felt neither uncomfortable nor inappropriate. That he had heard from his cousin was a relief; that this unknown woman was prepared to make enquiries about permanent positions for her, thrilling.

'It sounds better than I could have hoped,' she said, almost afraid of jinxing the way this was turning out.

'It's certainly encouraging,' he agreed. 'If Cousin Elizabeth didn't think there was a chance of finding something for you, she wouldn't have offered to talk to her friend. As soon as she writes again, I shall of course let you know.'

'Thank you,' she said, still struggling to believe her good fortune.

'Now we just need to wait and see how events over these next few days turn out.'

She knew, of course, that he was referring to the likelihood of war. Sitting there so peaceably, it was something she would rather not think about. The trouble was, her plans were inextricably linked to its coming; without it, there would be less need for the very people whose ranks she was hoping to join. Without a war, she had next-to-no chance of escaping from Woodicombe.

Distractedly, she traced a finger backwards and forwards over the surface of the rock while, a few yards in front of them, the tide lapped lazily at the smaller pebbles, barely bothering to disturb them from their slumber.

Unwittingly, she sighed. 'Is war certain now, do you think? Is there nothing to be done to prevent it?' More than anything, she wanted things to stay just as they were at that very moment: the sunshine warm; his company easy; real life suspended. In other words, perfect.

'All the while the government can't decide what to do, there is still *some* hope, I suppose.'

In disbelief, Kate shook her head. *'Can't decide?* About *going to war?* But that's madness. Not being able to decide whether to put pickles on your bread and cheese is one thing. Not being able to decide whether to go to war seems plain preposterous.'

He laughed. 'Preposterous. I like that. But yes, it does rather, doesn't it? In the newspaper this morning, it said that the Cabinet met yesterday – on a Sunday, no less – but that they are still split between those in favour and those against, with many ministers threatening to resign if the other side gets its way. Apparently, even in the streets, there are as many people demonstrating in support of war as there are attending peace meetings.'

'So, what *will* decide it – whether or not there's a war, I mean?'

'Events beyond our control, I'm afraid. If Belgium resists Germany's ultimatum to allow them to move forces onto their territory – supposedly

277

to prevent a French attack – then to my mind, war becomes inevitable. If Belgium agrees, however, then the threat might recede – for now, at least. No doubt tomorrow morning's newspapers will tell us more.'

With that, he slid from the boulder and bent to reach for his duffle bag. Following suit, Kate, too, slipped back down to the sand.

'Would you mind if I ask you tomorrow what that news is?' she said, watching him wipe a hand over his trousers. If nothing else, it seemed a good way to keep herself at the front of his thoughts – especially if there was a chance he might need to depart without much warning.

'No, of course I don't mind. It's good that you wish to keep abreast of things.'

Since opportunities to see him were so few and far between, she knew that more definite arrangements were called for. To that end, she said, 'Oftentimes, I can get away for a few minutes once upstairs breakfast has been cleared away.' *Trust your instincts.* 'I could go to the stables and wait, you know, on the off chance.'

He slung his duffle over his shoulder, his movements loose and relaxed. 'All right. I'll try and remember. Just don't think badly of me if I forget.'

She smiled warmly. And, as she watched him picking his way between the giant boulders towards the path up through the trees, under her breath, she murmured, 'There's nothing you could do that would make me think badly of you.'

For Kate, the next morning couldn't come soon enough. And, when it did, she darted about the kitchen, trying to do things before she was asked: she kept watch over the fillets of smoked haddock for the kedgeree to ensure that they simmered rather than boiled; she upturned the timer for the eggs rather than guess at how long they had been cooking; instead of wiping her hands down her apron, she washed them under running water and ensured that they were properly dry. Her only disappointment was that, unusually for her, Edith didn't seem to notice. Ordinarily quick to comment upon her sluggishness, today, her sister didn't even seem aware that she was there.

'You feeling peculiar again?' she enquired of her at one stage.

'No, I'm perfectly all right,' Edith responded. 'Just didn't sleep well.'

'I know the feeling,' Kate replied, glad that there was no need for her to enquire further but sensing that, unlike her own situation, the reason for Edith's poor sleep had nothing to do with feeling excited. 'Maybe try and get some fresh air.'

'Mmm.'

Eventually, with the bustle in the scullery quietening down and activity in the kitchen turning from breakfast to luncheon Kate spotted her chance to slip away. There was no time to go and check on her hair or her face but then Ned never seemed overly concerned by how things looked: another reason to like him.

She went first to the old tack-room; if anyone had spotted her, at least she wouldn't be leading them directly to Ned. Once there, she stood for a moment, wanting to be sure that she hadn't been followed, the air feeling warm and still, the only discernible sound the cheeping from a family of house sparrows echoing around the yard as they picked about in the straw. Eventually, satisfied that she was alone, she slipped through to the stables. And there, she waited.

To pass the time, she turned her thoughts to Ned. Although he could depart Woodicombe at almost any moment, she knew she couldn't rush him. He liked her, of that she was sure. But it was going to take caution and patience to get him to let his feelings be properly known. So, for the moment, she would aim only to strengthen their friendship, letting it blossom, naturally, almost without him noticing, until – hopefully – it turned into something more.

Exhaling a long sigh, she noticed a flicker of movement away to her right. She stiffened. Although she hadn't heard anyone approaching, she felt certain she'd seen something akin to the flick of a skirt – the flick of a *pale grey* skirt, like the one Edith wore. She frowned. What business could Edith have out in the stable yard at this time of day? Where could *she* be going? Even had she taken her advice about getting some fresh air, she wouldn't come all the way to the stables to get it – she would take a few steps close to the back door. There could be only one explanation: her sister had followed her. She must have. Somehow, she must have become suspicious. Either that, or Luke had been to tell her what had happened. It would be just like the two of them to get together and spy on her. Well, she would turn the tables on them. She would catch her sister lying in wait – see how she explained herself. And then she would decide whether to risk alerting Ned to the possibility that they were being followed.

On the toes of her shoes, she crept past the empty horse-stalls, reaching to the rails and posts to steady her balance. Her heart pounding, she found the prospect of creeping towards something no less disquieting than when she so frequently found herself creeping away from it.

'*Remember* you? Why on earth would I remember *you?*'

She froze. She'd been right to think someone was there, although, since the voice was unmistakeably a man's, wrong to suppose it was Edith.

'It *has* been a long time since you were here. That much I'll grant you.'

What? Edith *was* there? What on earth could *she* be doing in the stable yard, talking to a man – a man whose voice she couldn't place? It seemed such an unlikely thing. Edith didn't *know* any men – certainly not the sort she would have cause to sneak away to meet.

'Clearly, you mistake me for someone else. I have never been here before this week. And so, if you will excuse me–'

'It is *you* who are mistaken. In the days when the place was still owned by old Mr Latimer, you came a-visiting with his grandson, Mr Sidney.'

'No, as I say, you are mistaken–'

Who the devil was Edith talking to? Who would *she* have the nerve to address in such a forthright manner? And what were they talking *about?* Perhaps, rather than trying to identify the man's voice, she might be better served by listening for clues in what they were saying.

''Course, in *those* days, you went by the name of Bertie.'

Bertie? Who the devil was Bertie?

From the man, there came the sound of coughing.

'And as *I* say ... you are mistaken–'

'And back then, you weren't wed, neither. Although, seems to me now, you must have scampered up the aisle with some haste, certainly before that year was out.'

'Now look here, I don't know what you're alleging–'

'And yet it seems you do. It was the resemblance that stopped you dead in your tracks, wasn't it? I mean, if the likeness struck *me*, then it can't have failed to strike *you*.'

Hidden behind the stable door, Kate hardly dared to breathe. She'd never known Edith be so plain-spoken.

'Now look here, missy,' the man continued, 'I don't know what your game is, but it would serve you to remember how I can land you in a lot of trouble.'

'Trouble. Huh. There's irony for you. You really *don't* remember me, do you? Don't remember all those hot afternoons? Don't remember how–'

'Look, what is it you want from me? Money? Is that it? You think to blackmail me? Threaten to tell my wife if I don't pay–' *Blackmail?* What the devil was Edith mixed up in?

'It's too late for your money–'

'Well, I shan't be blackmailed. *Can't* be blackmailed. Not only would my wife see right through your scheming, but my marriage is well beyond being harmed by tawdry scandal. So, my advice to you would be to save yourself the ignominy.'

'You don't listen, do you? It's not your *money* I'm after.'

'Then what, damn you? What the devil *are* you after?'

'I'm after having you bring an end to something. Something that otherwise left alone, could see you and yours up before the constabulary–'

'All right, all right. But for Christ's sake, woman, not here–'

With the conversation beginning to fade from her hearing, Kate let go of the breath she'd unwittingly been holding in her chest. Whatever had *that* been about? What on earth had her sister been doing? And with whom? As much as she wanted to know, she hadn't dared to peer around the doorway to find out. And it hadn't sounded like the sort of conversation she could just ask Edith about next time she saw her, either. So, how was she to find out?

'Sorry I'm so late!'

Turning away from the brightness, Kate squinted in the direction of Ned's voice. She'd clean forgotten about *him*.

'It's all right,' she said, her head filled with so many questions that she felt in completely the wrong mood for talk of war.

With an easy smile, he waved a rolled-up newspaper. 'Here to report on the latest news.'

'Yes,' she said, her mind still on Edith. 'Thank you.'

'I say, is everything all right? You seem ... troubled.'

She shook her head. 'Sorry. I was just thinking about something. Maybe you could help.'

'Help with what? What would you like to know?'

There seeming no sense in beating about the bush, she said, 'Have more guests arrived?'

The expression that came across his face was one of puzzlement. 'More guests?'

'I know Mr Latimer came with your father – although I haven't seen either of them yet – but did anyone else come with them?'

'Not *with* them, no. Separately from them, the Rattray-Smyths arrived. They've been staying on Exmoor and decided to pop down for a few days. Although it rather looks now as though they might be heading straight back to London. Donald Rattray-Smyth is a Whitehall solicitor.'

'Has he been here before?'

Ned pulled a face. 'It's possible. He's clearly an old friend of Sidney Latimer.'

Then it had to be him, Kate decided of the mystery man. She'd overheard Edith say he'd previously come to stay with the Latimers, although it still didn't explain what they'd been talking about in such agitated fashion.

'Why do you ask? Has one of the guests bothered you in some way?'

Quickly, Kate shook her head. 'Oh, no, nothing like that. No, it's just that I heard a voice and didn't know whose it was. That's all.'

'I see. All right. Well, if nothing's wrong, then to the subject of war!'

'Yes,' she said, determining to get the bottom of the mystery by some other means. 'To the subject of war.'

Kate drew back the curtain. From her bedroom window the following morning, everything looked much the same as it did at this early hour on any other summer's day: beyond the far hedge, Abe Pardey's cow-boy was calling the animals up for milking; in the yard, the kitchen tabby was slinking about in search of an easy breakfast; circling the chimney stacks, house martins were plucking insects from thin air. All of that was the same as it ever was. And yet, last night, in London, the Government had declared war on Germany.

The news had been relayed to them by Mr Latimer. Late into the evening, he had received a telephone call, after which he had gone straight to the drawing room to inform his guests. A little while later, he had appeared in the servants' parlour, where he had conveyed the information to those members of staff still there. Digesting the news, Kate had felt a sort of betrayal; for all of their supposed intelligence, the old men of the government had somehow made the wrong decision, the news leaving her feeling numb and struggling to work out what it would mean for them. The only real certainty was that Luke would now take himself off to join the army but, by that same token, so would Ned. As for the effect upon her own position and that of everyone else left behind, she supposed that only time would tell.

Now, with the breaking of the new day, she felt no less shocked. But, since presumably, for the moment, her own days would be unaffected, all she could do was carry on as usual and wait to hear from Ned's cousin Elizabeth. And so, she stripped off her nightdress and splashed her face with water. Then, slowly, she pulled on her undergarments and her slip. Returning to stare out of the window, she buttoned her uniform and then, reaching for her apron, tied it about her waist. More than anything, she needed to see Ned. She needed to know how soon he might leave – to discover how little time she now had to get him to feel as strongly about her, as she did about him.

Silently, she went along the landing and down the three flights of stairs to the basement. It was still early, but, as she neared the kitchen, she could hear the sound of breakfast being prepared. Dare she slip outside – just in case Ned was taking an early morning stroll? She peered along the corridor towards her mother's office. It would be tricky: Ma would already be at her desk, going over arrangements for the day ahead. Undecided, she ventured a couple of steps further.

'Ah, Kate, there you are.'

Damnation. Faced with her mother choosing that moment to leave her room, Kate tried to persuade her scowl into an unconcerned smile. 'Morning, Ma.'

'I've just had word from Luke that Mrs Channer won't be up at all today.'

'No? She must be took real bad, then.'

'It would seem so – stiffened right up and can't barely move, poor soul. They've had Dr Brinsworthy out to her, though why they bothered with *him* I can't imagine – never could tell the breathing from the departed. Anyway, since she won't be up to change the flowers, you'll have to do it. According to her list, today is the turn of the morning room, the entrance hall, and the landings. Obviously, you won't be able to do the morning room now until after breakfast but you can still make ready with the arrangements–'

As it dawned on Kate that her mother was serious, it was as much as she could do not to laugh out loud. 'You're wanting *me* to do the *flowers?*'

'I've no one else to do them, love. And it's been that warm they won't last another day.'

'But you *know* I'm hopeless with that sort of thing – fiddly stuff.'

'Then stay away from fiddly. Salvage the greenery from the vases, go out and cut some big and colourful blooms from the border, and then just ... do your best. I'm sure they'll turn out fine.'

With a long and weary sigh, Kate shook her head. 'Yes, Ma.'

'But don't go messing about in the morning room until breakfast has been cleared away.'

'No, Ma, you said.'

'And I mean it.'

Flowers. It beggared belief. But, bubbling up through her incredulity came a thought since she would have to go around to the cutting-border, the tedious flower arrangements had just given her the perfect excuse to be outside. She would have to be clever, though; not knowing whether or not Ned was up yet, she would need to leave it as late as possible. In the meantime, to satisfy Ma that she was doing as she'd been told, she would collect the vases from the hall and the landing and make great show of emptying and cleaning them. Then, once it was more likely that Ned was up and about, she would go out into the garden. Dear old Mrs Channer: may the Lord be praised for the decrepit state of her legs!

Wasting no time, she set off up the stairs, pausing for a moment at the top to run a hand over her hair and drag her teeth across her lips in the hope of making them look plump and rosy – just in case he *was* about. When she carefully opened the door to the hallway, though, much as she had been expecting, it was deserted. Unseen by anyone, she came and went, ferrying the wilting flower arrangements down to the sink in the boot room. There, following her mother's advice, she set aside those fronds of ferns and stems of laurel that were still presentable, scoured the vases with bicarbonate, and then carried the spent blooms to the waste heap in the yard. That done – and with a quick glance to the clock – she folded her arms and leant back against the sink. Now she would wait.

She listened to the sounds of breakfast being prepared: Edith chiding the daygirls as they prepared the chafing dishes for the morning room; Ma chastising a latecomer; feet scurrying across the floor tiles. She glanced again to the clock. Very shortly now, the guests who liked to take their breakfast early would start coming down: Aunt Diana would be in from her walk; Mr Lawrence, already smartly attired, would be reading the *Daily Telegraph*. And Ned would be ... well, that was the problem. Ned's movements were difficult to predict. But, wherever he was, she *had* to get to see him. With war having now been properly declared, he might be thinking about changing his plans, something she might not discover until it was too late and he was on the verge of departing. Damn the daft old men in the government; until they'd declared their stupid war, her plan had been going along nicely.

Eventually, growing bored of dallying in the boot room, she made her way to the flower border, one eye out for Luke, the other for Ned. Once there – and with no sign of either – she took her time selecting and cutting the showiest of the fiery zinnias, some of the longest-stemmed Shasta daisies, and a dozen or so of the globe thistles so favoured by Mrs Channer, before reluctantly, making her way back indoors. In all of the time she had been out there, she hadn't seen another soul.

Later still, having made up four vases of what she felt might loosely be termed *arrangements,* she lifted the first two from the bench and set off for the landing. On the other side of the door into the hallway, though, she was sent lurching sideways by something in her path. Cursing rather too loudly and with water slopping from the vases, she cast over her shoulder: two suitcases. What sort of hare-brain left two suitcases *right* behind a door? *Suitcases.* She stared down at them. Someone was leaving? So soon after last night's announcement? Or was that simply coincidence? Either way, who would have chosen to leave so suddenly?

With the two vases of flowers now slippery in her wet hands, she padded up the staircase, her eyes drawn back over the bannisters to the two pieces of luggage. They were small and matching – something about the battered leather suggesting they belonged to a man rather than a woman.

Arriving on the landing, she placed the first vase on its plinth and then, to set off its best side – in truth, its slightly less messy side – she gave it a half-turn. From there, she went on to the next plinth and set down the second vase. Then, going to stand between the two, she looked from one to the other and gave a helpless shrug. They were flowers in vases. She'd seen worse.

Below, in the hallway, the owner of the luggage still hadn't appeared. And, from the look of them, the cases didn't have any labels. Feeling uneasy to be loitering, she stole back down the staircase. Fortunately, the remaining two vases gave her a genuine reason to return and, with a bit of luck, by then, it would be apparent to whom the luggage belonged. *Please Lord, don't let it be Ned.*

Once back in the boot room, she leant against the sink and chewed on a thumbnail. No matter her feeling of panic, there was no sense rushing back: the longer she left it to return, the better her chances of finding out what was going on. After a couple of minutes, withdrawing her thumb from between her teeth, she picked up a single vase and set off back along the corridor.

In the hallway, the first thing she noticed was that there were now four suitcases, two larger, non-matching ones having appeared. Feeling conspicuous, she crossed the hall and set down the vase on the side table where she proceeded to tweak the blooms. But, as time passed, the only sounds to reach her ears were those from the morning room – the gentle murmur of conversation broken by the occasional clatter of cutlery.

Drawing a long breath, she urged herself not to panic. There was no reason to suppose it was Ned who was leaving. The suitcases could belong to anyone. Perhaps Mr Latimer had chosen to return home, or even Mr Russell. By all accounts, he had been hoping for this war, rubbing his hands at the prospect of the opportunities it presented for his business. Maybe, then, he couldn't wait to get back to it, even if he had only been away for a couple of days. Perhaps *Mrs* Russell would even go with him. *Please* let Mrs Russell go with him!

After a further couple of minutes, during which time *still* nothing happened, Kate had no choice but to go back to fetch the final vase. When, eventually, she returned with it, it was to see Sidney Latimer and the back of what she imagined to be Hugh Russell, deep in discussion alongside the luggage. When neither looked in her direction, she went straight to the side table, put down the vase and blew out a long stream of breath. Thank goodness: it was those two who were leaving! *See,* she told herself, already breathing more easily: she had been right – there had been no need to panic.

Careful to remain turned towards her flower arrangement, she swivelled her eyes towards Mr Russell, this being her first chance to study his appearance. From the look of his waistband, he was fond of his food. Fond of his drink, too.

291

Although, to be fair, the redness of his nose might more properly be down to an hour or two spent in the recent sunshine. Although distant from him by several yards, she could still make out that his eyes looked crinkly and might, under other circumstances, flash with mischief. In that regard, they reminded her of Ned's. Father and son shared a similar light-brown hair colour, too. There, though, the similarities appeared to end. Mr Russell's nose was stubbier and his mouth flatter than his children's, both of whom shared the shape of their features with their mother. All told, especially standing as he was with his hands in pockets, Hugh Russell looked like a man who didn't hold with too much ceremony – another trait he had passed to his son. Not altogether off-putting – as old men went – he indeed looked like a man for whom a come-hither look from a young woman might prove irresistible. Yes, when the time came to win him over, she would play to what was almost certainly his weakness. At that very moment, though, her most pleasing dis-covery was that it was him, and not Ned, who was leaving.

At the sound of wheels approaching over the gravel, she switched her attention from Mr Russell to the open front door, beyond which she could see the out-porter's van pulling up. Soon, they would be gone. Then, perhaps, things would return to normal.

Turning back to her flower arrangement, she caught sight of the long case clock: not long until it was time to meet Ned. With war having now been declared, she no longer felt the same need

292

to understand the news from London, but there was no need for him to know that. He might not have made any proper overtures towards her – *yet* – but they were certainly getting along nicely together. They seemed to understand one another. And from that she drew comfort because, from a footing of respect and shared views, love and romance could be encouraged to follow.

With the departing guests of no further interest to her, she headed back to the boot room, where, while gathering up the debris from her flower-arranging, she hummed a tune. She could relax. She was about to see Ned.

Out in the yard, she cast the waste onto the heap, wiped her hands down her apron and went quickly out through the gate. Arriving in the stable yard, she made a quick check for signs that anyone else was about before slipping in through the door and going to lean against the centre-most stall, where she stood composing herself for his arrival. And then she waited: she twiddled with her hair; she straightened her apron; she sang softly. She heard the clock chime the half hour. She began to grow worried. Her stomach tightened and a bitter taste rose in her throat. He had forgotten their arrangement.

With a quick look in either direction, she started back the way she had come, except that, when she reached the yard, she continued along the side of the house to the front corner, where she peered around. In place of the out-porter's van stood the station cab. She tried to think. Even just a glimpse of Ned – perhaps seeing his father off – would reassure her that, in the upheaval, he had simply forgotten their arrangement to meet. Although a disappointing thing to discover, it would be by far and away preferable to the other possibility beginning to gnaw away at her.

As she stood trying to decide upon her best course of action, her eye was caught by movement further along the drive: the postman was coming, the scarlet piping on his navy uniform standing out in the bright light. Watching his progress towards the house, she saw him remove from his bag a single envelope. Ned's cousin must have written back. Now she *had* to find him because, in that little envelope, could be news of her way out of Woodicombe! *Think,* she urged her woolly head as she shrank back out of sight: *where would he be?* The trouble was, she hadn't the least idea. But then it occurred to her: Miss Naomi might know. Although warned by Ma to stay away from her, she would go anyway, the risk on this occasion worth taking.

Galvanized by a sensation that felt worryingly like doom, she turned and ran to the back door. Once inside, she took both flights of stairs two at a time, pausing on the landing for just long enough to straighten her pinafore. Easing open the door, she looked along the corridor. Thankfully, all was quiet and so, drawing a long breath, she stole towards Miss Naomi's door where, before she could lose her nerve, she tapped lightly.

'Come in.'

Opening the door just a fraction, she slipped into the room. 'Sorry to trouble you, Miss Naomi–'

Setting her magazine down on the window seat,

Naomi Russell got to her feet, her face brightening. 'Kate! How lovely to see you. But what are you doing here? I thought you'd been dismissed from my service.'

Deciding to remain close to the door, Kate smiled warmly back. 'I have. I shouldn't be here.'

'Yes, I'm sorry about that. When I heard what had happened, I was livid. I just hoped you knew it wasn't *my* doing.'

'I didn't think it for one moment, miss.'

'The whole thing got rather out of hand, I'm afraid. I wanted to try and find you to explain but, do you know, since the events of that evening, Mamma has seen to it that I'm hardly ever left by myself. Honestly, you'd think I'd been caught *in flagrante* with the groom rather than having been set upon by a drunken Aubrey. She still doesn't believe my version of events, you know. She still thinks I did something to pit Lawrence and Aubrey against one another. And, all the while it plays to his advantage, Aubrey doesn't seem about to disabuse her.'

'Mrs Russell is still intent on forcing him upon you, then?' Kate said, her thoughts momentarily distracted from her own plight by that of Miss Naomi

'To my deep regret, yes. I've told her, repeatedly, that she's wasting her time. I've said again and again that I shan't marry him. I can only think she hopes to wear me down. You know, the other day, I overheard Aunt Cicely talking to Uncle Ralph. "Ralph," she said to him – obviously not knowing I was there – "I'd quite forgotten how vulgar Hugh Russell is, with his talk of business deals and just how much they're worth." To which Uncle Ralph replied, "And yet, my dear, that very same *something-or-other* is the reason we're here." And then they moved off, and I was unable to hear the rest.'

'Money,' Kate said. 'They're after you because you have money.'

To Kate's reply, Naomi Russell's expression changed to one of puzzlement. *'My* money? My little trust? Or did you mean *Papa's* money? Not that either makes any sense. The Colbornes' wealth is far greater than Papa's will ever be. For a start, they own Avingham Park. Heavens, not *so* very far back, they owned the whole of Avingham Ducis. They're *old* money, like Mamma's family.'

'Then happen I'm wrong,' Kate remarked, remembering then why she was there. Somehow, though, she couldn't summon the courage to ask what she wanted to know. And so, aiming to build up to asking, she said, 'Is it right that Mr Russell's leaving us?'

Naomi nodded. 'It is. And what a fuss *that* caused when he told us last night. Mamma accused him of using this declaration of war as an excuse to return to London. She was utterly beside herself with rage – still is this morning, by all accounts. Barely five minutes ago, Aunt Diana came in to suggest I steer clear of Mamma for a while. *Apparently,*' she went on, lowering her voice, 'she and Papa were shouting at one another for all they're worth. I can only imagine poor Papa was trying to explain that for him to remain down here any longer would be costly for the business, which, trust me, would only make

296

Mamma even more incensed.'

Listening patiently, Kate nodded. 'Oh dear.'

'Quite. It's why I'm doing as Aunt Diana suggested and lying low for a while. Anyway, I don't imagine that's what brought *you* to my door.'

'No, miss,' she said, unable to put off asking any longer. 'I came to ask if you know where Ned is.'

'Ned? I should imagine he's in his room, seeing to last-minute packing.'

Last-minute packing? Had she just heard Miss Naomi correctly? Feeling as though all of her breath had been squeezed from her chest, she tried to get her mouth to work. 'You mean ... he's leaving?'

'Him, Papa and Uncle Sidney. They're all travelling back together. Why are you looking for him?'

Ned was leaving. Today. He was leaving today! Struggling to grasp the fact, she had no idea how to respond, feeling as though she had become engulfed in a thick and woolly fog that was preventing her from thinking straight.

'Umm...'

'Kate, is everything all right?'

'There's a letter come for him,' she blurted, grateful for the thought that shot into her head. 'He asked me to look out for it. Yes. And since I just saw the postman coming up the drive ... I wanted to let him know.'

'Oh, I see. Well, hopefully, he will pick it up from the hall–'

Realizing that she had to act quickly, Kate turned sharply towards the door. 'Forgive me, miss,' she said, reaching for the door handle, 'but

... perhaps I'd best go and make sure that he does.'

'Very well. Don't let me detain you.'

'No, miss.'

Closing the door behind her, Kate stood for a moment trying to decide what to do for the best. In her chest, her heart was beating terrifyingly fast. Ned was returning to London. She *knew* she'd been right to feel uneasy. She *knew* she should have trusted her feelings – she had a sense for these things. Instead, by dithering, she had wasted precious moments. But what to do now? Seemingly, there was only one thing she *could* do.

Taking the stairs at an unladylike canter, she arrived in the servants' corridor and ran full pelt towards the hallway where, not caring who might be on the other side, she threw back the door. Quite by chance, there was no one there. Outside, though, a motor was running and so she ran to the front door, arriving in time to see Hugh Russell climbing into the station cab. Through the window, she could see the backs of two heads.

'Ned!'

At her shout, Mr Russell turned sharply. But then, looking her quickly up and down, he hastened into the cab, grabbed for the door and, before he had even pulled it properly closed behind him, was shouting to the driver. 'Go, man. For Christ's sake, drive on. Quickly!'

In disbelief, she shouted after him. 'Mr Russell, please! Ned!' But, despite her distressed shrieking, not one of the heads inside even turned towards her.

With the cab starting to pull away, she lunged

towards it, only to be left with her arms flailing as she battled to remain upright. Determined they shouldn't get away from her, she bunched her skirt against her legs and started to run after them. With the cab gathering more speed, and heedless of the widening distance, she trailed in their wake, gulping for breath, her legs becoming leaden beneath her. Even as it became obvious that she wouldn't catch up to them, she continued to run anyway, sobbing loudly, while, inside the cab, not one of the three heads turned to look back.

Eventually, her breath spent and her lungs burning, she stumbled to a halt, clutching at her side. Then, gasping, she dropped to her knees, the gravel stabbing at the palms of her hands as she doubled over, gulping for breath.

Behind her, footsteps scrunched heavily. Then, with two arms reaching around her waist, she felt herself being lifted from the ground.

'Kate, Kate, I've got you. It's all right. I've got you.'

Chapter Eight

...And Lies

'Kate, please, try an' draw some deep breaths.'

Kate was tired of Luke's pleading. She didn't want to take deep breaths, she wanted to rant and shriek and rage at what they had done. Since having caved to his plea to be allowed to bring her indoors, she had sat in her mother's office and refused to move. Ma and Edith had repeatedly tried to persuade her to go upstairs and lie down but she had no intention of doing anything of the sort. One of them – if not all of them – *had* to admit to being responsible for Ned's sudden departure, and she was going nowhere until they had. She would not be silenced. She hated them. All of them. Because of them, Ned had left without even telling her he was going, let alone saying goodbye. And that had been *their* doing. *All* of them.

'*You* did this!' she shouted yet again, pointing a trembling finger at her sister. 'Yes, you,' she went on, still pointing to where Edith was standing against the closed door, her arms wrapped across her chest and her face with even less colour than usual. 'You, you evil witch! You did this.'

'Come on, Kate,' Luke again tried to reason with her. 'You know that ain't true. How could it be?'

'It *is* true,' she wailed. 'She did ... something. Told ... someone. I know it!'

Unable to bring herself to look at Luke's face as he crouched beside her, Kate hung her head. Her temples were throbbing, her hair was damp against her face and her throat felt dry and hard. She had been crying for ages and it was making her head ache, but she wasn't going to let them calm her down. *They* had done this to her. And *they* would pay. She would not be led, quietly, up to her room; she wasn't going to let them have it that easy.

'If you're suggesting I had any part in that boy's departure,' Edith began, unfolding and then immediately refolding her arms, 'you're wrong. It was nothing to do with–'

'*That boy?*' Kate spat, leaping from her chair to stand just inches from her sister's face. '*That boy* is called Ned. Or to you, Mr Edwin. And don't you dare deny your part in it. Your petty jealous handiwork is plain for all to see. I *know* it was you.' When Luke stood up and reached towards her, she swung to face him. 'And *you* put her up to it. *You* betrayed me to her,' she said. But then, momentarily startled by the blankness of his expression, she faltered, only the ache in her chest forcing her to continue. 'You *knew* she would try an' put a stop to it, so you told her. Yes, you did.'

'Kate,' he said wearily, his shoulders slumping and his head shaking slowly from side to side. 'I've not spoken so much as a single word to your sister since you came out to see me in the work-shop.' Marking a cross on his chest with his forefinger, he added, 'And I'll swear to it howsoever you wish.'

'Then she did it on her own,' she said, nodding her head in the direction of Edith, 'the shrivelled-up and jealous old shrew.'

Having so far done nothing but sit behind her desk and listen, Mabel Bratton rose smartly to her feet, her face stony. 'Kate, that's enough. I will not have you speak to your sister in this way. That you've worked yourself up into a lather over something is no reason to take it out on the rest of us. I've put up with your waywardness these last weeks but now, it's got to end. Your behaviour this morning has been beyond the pale.'

'But Ma–'

'I'm still speaking. So have the good grace to remain quiet and hear what I should have said to you before now. Not for the first time this last month, you've disgraced yourself and brought shame upon the rest of us. Not for the first time, you've got some mazed idea into your head and behaved with no thought as to the consequences. And now that it's all come a-tumbling down about your ears, you're looking to lay the blame at someone else's door. Well, I will not tolerate it. I will not have you carry on like it. Nor will I stand by while you call Edith such wicked names. Luke,' she said, turning stiffly towards him, 'before I ask these two to account for themselves, tell me, what do *you* know of what happened?'

Beyond caring how Luke might respond, Kate sank back down onto the chair. So what if he relayed what she'd said to him about leaving? What did it matter now? Her situation couldn't be any worse than it already was, so what did it matter? Pulling her already sodden handkerchief from her pocket, she dabbed in futile fashion at her eyes. They felt swollen and achy and she could only guess at how awful she must look.

'Honestly, Mrs Bratton? I know nothing of any of it.' From behind her dishevelled hair, Kate flicked her eyes to his face. In apparent emphasis of his point, he was standing with his hands outstretched, palms uppermost. 'I was going about a repair to the bench under the cedar tree when I heard a commotion. When I put down my hammer and went to see what was going on, I saw

302

Kate, dropped to the ground, sobbing her heart out. But as to what had gone on before I got there, I couldn't say.'

Why was he doing that, Kate wondered? Why wasn't he telling them what she'd said to him? Why was he protecting her? It wasn't as though it would change anything between them; she still wasn't going to marry him.

'Hmm. And you, Edith, what's your involvement in all of this?'

This time, Kate pulled her hair back from her face and stared openly at her sister. The manner with which Edith was wringing her hands almost certainly spoke to her guilt.

'Nothing, Ma. I've not the least notion *what's* behind her wild accusations.'

'Liar!'

'Kate, be quiet!'

'Well, she *is* a liar! She stands there, all saintly and innocent-looking, all the while hiding a secret of her own.' When she saw the panic that flashed across Edith's face, Kate didn't miss her chance. 'That's right. Didn't know I knew about that, did you? Thought I'd never find out about your secret trysts with one of the guests.'

'One of ... the guests?' The fractured nature of Mabel Bratton's observation – as though struggling with either fear or disbelief – turned all three of them towards her.

'Yes, Ma,' Kate said, her own manner suddenly calm. 'Ask her who she's been meeting behind the stables. And *then* ask her what's she been threatening him with.'

Very slowly, Mabel Bratton sat back down, her

303

hands coming to rest in her lap. 'Edith what did you do?'

'She's making it up, Ma, she's ... desperate. She's desperate to distract us from her own wrong-doings.'

'Or is it the other way around?' Kate said, struggling anew to contain her rage. 'Is it that having made advances to some man and had them spurned – laughed at, most likely – she set out to ruin first *him* and then, in a fit of jealousy, *me* and *my* chances of happiness with Ned. That's more like it.'

'If you did but know it,' Edith said quietly, reaching to the door handle for support, 'I didn't *ruin* anything, I saved you–'

'Saved me? Saved me from what? A better life? Happiness? Love? All the things you'll never have?'

On the other side of the desk, Mabel Bratton gave a strange little cry. 'Edith,' she said, her face drained of all colour, 'I'll ask you again, what did you do?'

When Kate turned back to her sister, it was to see that she was shaking.

'I did ... what had to be done. What only you or I could.'

'Oh, Edith, we talked about this. You swore to me you would leave well alone. We were keeping good watch over her.'

'I had no choice–'

'Then we must tell her. With the ways things have turned out, we have to. She should know.'

With a very different sense of unease now, Kate looked back and forth between their two faces.

She should know what?

What was all this? 'Ma … what–'

'Edie, love, you know it's the right thing to do. There's no way round it now.' At her mother's entreaty, Kate saw Edith hang her head. 'Why don't you pull up the other chair,' Mabel Bratton went on, moving around her desk to take hold of Edith's hand. 'Come on. Let's you and I lay the thing to rest, once and for all.'

'Lay what to rest?' Kate asked, her insides knotting hard.

'Luke, lad, go out and fetch yourself another chair. And when you come back in, turn the key behind you. What you're about to hear is nobody's business but our own.'

When, with a rather uncertain nod, Luke left the room, Kate simply sat where she was, trying to make sense of what was happening. Edith really *did* have a secret? She really *did* know something with which to blackmail someone? How was that possible? She pulled herself more upright on the hard-wooden chair and, with a loud sniff, reached again for her handkerchief. Well, whatever it was, seemingly, she was about to find out.

Moments later, Luke returned. Carrying a chair from the staff parlour, he set it down next to her own. When he then went back to turn the key in the lock of the door, she wrapped her fingers around the edge of her own seat and drew a long breath, exhaling it from her body in a series of uneven judders. How had she lived so close to Edith without knowing that she had been hiding something?

'You tell it, Ma,' Edith said, her face turned

305

aside and her words barely audible. 'I don't think I can even see where to start with it.'

'Very well,' Mabel Bratton agreed. 'If you're certain.'

'I am. It's what I want.'

'Well, two-and-twenty summers back,' Mabel Bratton announced without further ado, 'as was their habit at that time, the Latimers came to take their holiday. Some weeks into their stay, their grandsons came a-visiting. They'd been up at university and had brought with them a couple of friends – nice lads, clean and well-mannered for the most part, if not a touch ... spirited. One of them was a lad the others called by the name of Bertie.'

At the mention of that name, Kate stiffened. 'So ... when I heard–'

'Kate, please child, let me tell it the only way I can think how.'

Checking her impatience, Kate nodded. 'Sorry.'

'Anyway, this Bertie had an eye for a pretty face and a smooth tongue in his head. And your sister, well, like most any girl of her young years, she was ... well, let's just say she was easily impressed.'

Glancing to her right, Kate frowned. Then she drew her hand to her mouth. 'Oh, good Lord,' she said, the embarrassment enough to make her wriggle on her seat.

'Anyway, not far short of Christmas that same year,' Mabel Bratton resumed her tale, 'Edith went down with what I thought to be a bout of winter sickness. But, as time went on, the nature of it came to give me cause for concern. And, soon after, putting two and two together, I fathomed it was more properly down to her being with child–' As one, Luke and Kate drew sharp breaths. '–leaving me an' my Thomas to pry out of her what had gone on.'

Edith? Pregnant? Unwed and pregnant? 'So was–'

'Please, Kate, let me tell it through to the end.'

'Yes. Sorry.' But to Kate, the story even thus far defied belief: if what her mother had just said was true, then while nothing more than a girl, her prudish old-maid of a sister had been with a man? For so very many reasons, it was impossible to credit. For a start, Edith didn't have a passionate bone in her body, nor had she ever exhibited so much as an ounce of tenderness. It couldn't possibly *be* less likely.

Regardless of Kate's disbelief, Mabel Bratton picked up her tale where she had left off.

'As you might imagine, me an' my Thomas were beside ourselves with worry. With a baby well on the way, and with the remedy of a hasty marriage denied us, we were lost to know what to do. Edith was never going to find a husband, not around these parts and not with her *that* far gone. And we could hardly complain to the Latimers. It was only by their grace that we each of us had work and a home, something we could nary afford to risk. Even had we gathered all our courage and gone to them and explained, as sure as eggs is eggs, this Bertie fellow would have denied it. It would have been Edie's word against his. And, in the meantime, Edie's reputation – and no doubt ours, too – would have been dragged through the mud. We could see well enough how *that* would work out. So, what were we to do?'

Unable to take it all in, Kate tried to get her tongue to ask the only question that seemed to matter. 'So ... what *did* you do?'

'The only thing we could think of, we came up with a plan to try an' cover it up.'

'Cover it up? A baby?'

'It was our only remedy. With the house all but shut up for the winter, I took Edith and went to my mother's in Torrington. Thomas stayed behind to keep things up together and told anyone who thought to ask that I'd gone to look after my mother. It wasn't that far from the truth – by then, she was proper ailing.' Desperate to unravel events from there on, Kate couldn't wait any longer. 'And the baby – you gave it up? For adoption? You gave the baby up for adoption?'

'No. No, love,' Mabel Bratton said calmly. 'We didn't give it up for adoption. We thought of it, of course we did, but we couldn't none of us bring ourselves to go through with it. No, we ... we brought her home with us and I ... well, *we* ... passed her off as mine.'

'*Yours?*'

To Kate's surprise, she felt Luke grasp her hand. His fingers felt hot and big and familiar and, engrossed by this most unlikely of stories, she didn't pull away from him. 'A late surprise, that's what we told everyone.'

'No one ever thought it odd?' Kate asked.

'Odd? Why should anyone think it odd? A fair few women get caught with late babies.'

Of all the things in this tale that were hard to believe, the one Kate found most incredible was that no one had been suspicious. 'But surely, it would seem so unlikely.'

'Well, it didn't. Perhaps, in a way, it helped that my Thomas didn't have to live long with the deceit, what with him being taken scarcely ten months on. And old Mr Latimer didn't last long, either, God rest his soul. Course, with his only son having gone before him, there was a tremendous to-do over the passing of the estate – you know, to his grandson, Mr Sidney. Dragged on for years, that business did. And, by the time it was all sorted out, Mr Sidney had wed and it was several more years before he – or any of the family, for that matter – came here again. So no, no-one challenged the story. Before long, there was no one even left to care.'

Kate stole a look at her sister. By rights, she ought to look different – at the very least, she ought to look sullied. But she didn't. She was sitting, her hands in her lap, her eyes directed straight ahead and her mouth pressed into a flat line. She'd taken no part in the telling of the tale – indeed, seemed to have cut herself off, dissociated herself from what, all of those years ago, she and their mother had done. As a result, Kate didn't know whether to despise her or to pity her; neither seemed wholly appropriate, both felt beyond her. Dumbfounded. Betrayed. *Angry.* Those were the things she felt. All the while criticizing her treatment of Luke, her sister had been hiding a shameful secret of her own. Well, after this, Edith Bratton had lost all right to criticize anyone. People in greenhouses did not get to throw stones.

With her mind moving from the matter of her sister's duplicity to the unfortunate child, Kate was struck by something. 'What happened to the baby then? Eventually, I mean,' she added when her mother seemed puzzled that she should ask. 'Did it die?' In a way, it felt like the kindest outcome. Safely covered up or not, there were no two ways about it: the poor child had been a bastard – the upshot of the sordid seduction of a silly young girl by a man with no care but the satisfaction of his own urges. Although, perhaps, she shouldn't be so quick to judge: *there but for the grace of God* and all that.

'No. No, love, she didn't die.'

Feeling Luke squeezing her hand so tightly as to almost crush her knuckles, Kate yelped with pain. But, when she tried to wriggle free from his grasp, he simply tightened his grip further still.

'Kate,' he said, his voice little more than a hoarse whisper, 'Edith's baby ... I think it's you.'

Wrenching more firmly at her hand, she stared back at him. 'Don't be ridiculous. Why on earth would you say such a thing? Of course it's not me!' At the sight of his expression, she turned to look across the desk. Rolling down her mother's cheeks were tears. In disbelief, she spun to look at Edith. She hadn't moved. She was simply staring ahead, her hands still at rest in her lap as though merely listening to a long and rather boring Sunday sermon. 'Ma?' she said, shaking as she turned back to look at her. Why was no one contradicting Luke? Why weren't they telling him he was wrong? Slowly, everything around her started to look smudgy and indistinct, as though someone

310

was wiping across her eyes with a dirty dishcloth. With her free hand, she reached to the edge of the desk. 'Ma?'

When it eventually came, Mabel Bratton's answer was little more than a whisper. 'He's right, love. He's right. It's why I'm telling you all of this. You were the baby. You're Edith's little daughter.'

She sprang to her feet. 'No!' she shouted, gulping for air and whirling about so fast that her hand finally came free from Luke's. 'No! You're lying! All of you. I'm not ... she's not...'

Beside her, Luke also got to his feet. 'Kate—'

'Did you *know?*' She rounded on him. *'Did you know?'*

He shook his head. ''Course not.'

'What – you just ... guessed? Is that what you're telling me? Is that what you expect me to believe?'

He nodded slowly. 'I did guess it, yes. I can't say for certain why, but, as your Ma... I mean as, well, as Mrs Bratton was telling it, I had a feeling I knew what was coming.'

'Is that true?' she turned back to demand of the woman she had always called Ma. 'Did he not know?'

'He knew none of it,' Mabel assured her. 'No one did. Until this very moment, no one but me and Edith knew a thing. And they still needn't, love, truly.'

'Don't call me *love!* You're not my mother!'

Slowly, Mabel Bratton pushed back her chair and got to her feet. 'No, I'm not. But I do love you, dear, just as surely as though I was. From the moment you were born, I took to you as if

311

you were my own. I never thought of you as anything but.'

'While *I* never had the chance to.' To Kate, Edith's admission was so soft and so startling that she spun, wide-eyed, towards her. 'I had a daughter. And yet I didn't. I could have loved you—'

'We all of us agreed it was for the best—'

'No, Ma,' Edith said softly. 'You and Pa did. *I* was given no say.'

'You were sixteen. You were unwed. Without a husband you were still your father's responsibility—'

'Stop it!' Kate shouted, throwing up her arms. 'Stop it, both of you.'

For a moment, all that could be heard in the ensuing quiet was the sound of ragged breathing.

'Anyway,' Mabel Bratton eventually resumed, her tone recovering some of its more usual steadiness. 'The facts of the matter change nothing. I have loved you since the moment you were born – me and Edith both have. And that need be no different now.'

Although Kate shook her head, her thoughts weren't to be stilled. *The facts of the matter change nothing?* How could anyone in their right mind even *think* of saying such a thing? Supposedly, Edith wasn't her sister but her mother. And Ma, well, the woman she had always *called* Ma, wasn't her mother at all but her grandmother. And Thomas, the man she couldn't remember but who she had always thought to be her father, now turned out to have been her grandfather. How could anyone in their right mind say that nothing had changed? *Everything* had changed.

Staring down at the floor, she continued to shake her head. But then, with her eyes given to contemplating a particularly swirly knot in the floorboards, she was struck by the realization that the tale wasn't yet complete. There was still a piece missing. She looked back up. 'So, what do you know of this Bertie? What happened to *him?*' When she glanced across the table, Mabel Bratton, with her head in her hands, was weeping softly. To her right, Edith was also now crying. 'Damn it, who was he? I've a right to know!'

As she stood, rigidly, continuing to look between the two sobbing women, the only person to move was Luke. And, even then, as he took her hand and held onto it, it was some time before he seemed able to bring himself to say, 'Kate, I think the fellow Edith knew as Bertie was more properly called Hubert – the man *we* now know as Hugh Russell...'

'*Please*, Kate, love, you *must eat.*'

To Mabel Bratton's plea, Kate responded firmly. 'No,' she said. 'There's no *must* about it. Whether I eat or whether I don't, is my own business. I don't have to take instruction from *you* ever *again*.' And she meant it, too. To her mind, the woman standing before her had, by virtue of her deceit, given up any and all rights to offer advice about what she should or shouldn't do.

It was early afternoon that same day – a day that, to Kate's mind, had started out much like any other, if not a good deal more promising than some. Granted, she should probably have been more suspicious when Ned hadn't arrived at their meeting in the stables but, with the post-man bringing a letter, she had been convinced she was about to learn what sort of work his cousin Elizabeth might have found for her in London. Bit by bit, her plan had slowly been coming together. Yes, it had needed more work and yes, the unfortunate declaration of war had brought even greater urgency to her aim to make Ned fall in love with her. Even so, she'd still had a chance – a *good* chance – of succeeding. But then, with no warning whatsoever, her plans and dreams had gone the way of the morning's mist and evaporated into thin air. Worse still, everything she had ever held to be true had turned out to be a lie: her mother wasn't her mother; her sister wasn't her sister. And a man she hadn't heard of until a few days previously had turned out to be her father. She wasn't even properly Kate Bratton but Kate Russell. But – and here was irony – she hadn't become Kate Russell by virtue of succeeding with her plan to marry Ned, but because *his* father and *hers* were one and the same, the object of her affections emerging from all of this as her half-brother.

'But you didn't touch a mouthful of your dinner.'

From sheer frustration, Kate shuddered. Dinner? Her world had been upended and all her so-called mother was concerned about was that she hadn't eaten her *dinner*? The woman defied belief, she truly did.

'And you wonder why, Ma?' At this latest slip of her tongue, she growled with exasperation. 'Huh!

I don't even know what to call you any more. Granma, perhaps? Or Mabel? Or how about Mrs Bratton, *ma'am?*'

To her tirade, she saw Mabel Bratton flinch. There was no need for such cruelty, she knew that, but fermenting inside her was a desire to lash out and cause pain of the sort she had been made to feel.

'You can still call me Ma, love. You could think of it as being short for Granma.'

'No, Ma, I can't do that.' At her complete inability to cease addressing the woman as mother, Kate curled her hands into fists, furious that the habit should be so ingrained 'Oh, for heaven's sake this is mazed, utterly mazed,' she said. 'I can't bear it a moment longer. I need some air. I'm going for a walk.'

'Yes, of course, love. Why not go and see whether Luke will go with you – keep you company?'

'Because I don't *want* company. Especially not *his.* After everything you've done to me, I want to be alone!'

'All right, dear. I understand. And when you come back, Edie will make you a nice bite to eat. Happen you'll have more of an appetite after a walk.'

Feeling as though she might burst, rage spewing out from her very core, Kate fled along the corridor, her head ducked against what she imagined would be enquiring looks from the kitchen. With Edith having gone to lie down, and with her mother – her *grandmother* – having spent most of the morning shut away in her office, the place had to be thick with supposition and gossip. Well, they could suppose all they liked. They wouldn't get a word out of *her;* this shambolic affair was nobody's business but her own.

Once beyond the back door, she opened the gate and stepped out, the sight of Luke pacing backwards and forwards over the same half-dozen or so yards of gravel making her close her eyes in despair.

'Kate,' he said, the sound of the gate-latch bringing him hurrying across. 'Kate, how are you?'

Preferring that his well-meant enquiry didn't launch a fresh round of tears, she stared down at her shoes – not that there was any way around it: she at least had to answer him; if she tried to walk on without saying anything at all, he would only follow her. Better to deal with him now and be done with it.

'How do you *think* I am?'

'Beside yourself, I shouldn't wonder.'

Slowly, she raised her head to look at him. It was the first remotely fitting thing anyone had said to her. By chance or otherwise, he had happened upon the perfect description of her mood. *Beside herself* – as though her mind had separated from her body to leave her staring back at an empty and unfamiliar version of herself. She looked the same; she sounded the same. Inside, though, she felt anything but the same. She felt detached. Disoriented. Not even sure who she was any more. She also felt stupid – not that she was about to admit as much to Luke.

'I need to be by myself a while,' she said, unable to bring herself to witness the look of concern she knew would have come over his face – those soft, pleading eyes and the sympathetic line of that mouth of his.

In the event, all he said was, "Course.'

At that very moment, in response to the tenderness of his concern, she felt as though something inside her broke – snapped clean in two. But, deciding to ignore it – *and* the welling of fresh tears – she forced herself to continue across the yard. Breaking down in front of him would be a mistake, allowing him to console her, even worse. Instead, letting herself out through the gate in the wall, she made it all the way to the far side of the lawn before finally giving in to tears. This time, though, they weren't the outpouring of anger they had been earlier but tears of grief. Indeed, she found it hard to imagine that her pain would be any greater had someone told her that Ned had *died.* By most reckoning, she ought to feel sickened at having fallen for someone to whom she was so closely related – and, now and again, fleetingly, she did – but, for the most part, she felt as though someone had snatched her dreams and dashed them, like a bone china tea service, on the scullery floor.

Not knowing what else to do, she walked on, rounding the end of the lawn and sniffing loudly, thinking only then to check whether anyone was about. Thankfully, she seemed to be alone. Perversely, now that she was, she didn't want to be; she wanted someone to talk to. She glanced across the gardens to the side of the house. The sunblind at Miss Naomi's window was raised and the curtains tied back. And there seemed to be

317

someone on the window seat. Was it Miss Naomi? The reflections on the glass made it impossible to tell.

Leaving the path, she made her way across the newly mown lawn, stopping a couple of yards short of the herbaceous border under the downstairs windows to peer upwards. The dark outline in the bottom left-hand corner *could* be Miss Naomi. On the other hand, it could also be just about anyone else. She took a couple of paces backwards. The shape moved. And then it moved again. Not daring to wave, Kate remained where she was, crossing her fingers that she wasn't about to get a tongue-lashing from Cicely Colborne or worse still, from Pamela Russell.

With a succession of jerky and reluctant movements, and with the sound of wood grating against wood, the lower sash was heaved upwards. 'Kate?'

'Yes, miss, it's me.'

'Go and wait for me around the corner. I'll try and get down to you.'

Doing just that, Kate waited, her thumbnail between her teeth. Why she felt driven to seek Miss Naomi's company, she didn't know. She didn't even know whether she'd been told the news by anyone – or indeed, how she would react to learning of it if she hadn't. Was it even her place to tell her? In her muddled state, so many things felt beyond her to decide.

'Cicely Colborne's gone for a nap,' Naomi Russell announced without preamble as she stepped quickly through the French doors and out onto the terrace. 'I told her I would sit and read for a while, but it would still be best that we keep out of sight.'

Surprised by how matter-of-factly Miss Naomi was behaving, Kate nodded her agreement. 'We can go to the stables,' she said. 'If we keep to the main path, you won't get your shoes all grassy.'

Naomi Russell nodded, going on to remark, 'I can see from your face that you've been told.'

Catching her shoe on the raised edge of a flag-stone, Kate lurched forward, regaining her balance to turn about and say, *'You knew?* You knew *all along?'*

'Shush,' Naomi Russell urged, glancing over her shoulder and then quickening her pace.

'You *knew* but you said nothing? You saw fit to entrust me with the safe-keeping of *your* confidences while all the time keeping the most tremendous secret of all to yourself? How could you! How could you be so cruel?'

Catching hold of Kate's arm, Naomi Russell whisked her on along the path. 'Of course I didn't know!' she hissed, propelling Kate further from the house. 'Of course I didn't. And I'm hurt you would even think it of me!'

Freeing herself from Naomi's grasp, Kate walked on, reaching the entrance to the stable yard and then slipping in through the nearest door. Once inside, Naomi Russell stood glancing about at the dusty room and its disused contents.

'I'm sorry,' Kate said softly. 'But I don't know who to trust. You can't know how it feels to have everything about your life dashed to pieces – and by your own family, at that.'

'No,' Naomi Russell agreed. 'You're right. I

can't imagine it. For me, learning of the news was different – a shock, of course, but different.'

Going to lean against one of the old saddler's benches, Kate let out a long sigh. 'So, you *didn't* know? When I came to you earlier, looking for Ned, you had no notion of any of it?'

'Kate, I assure you, I had no idea. Until this morning, neither Mamma nor I – nor Ned, for that matter – had any idea that Papa had even *been* to Woodicombe before, let alone … well, let alone carried on with one of the staff here. But it was such a long time ago – before Mamma had even met him – that why would we? We knew, of course, that he'd known Sidney Latimer since their time at school together. It's how we came to have the loan of this place.'

Kate sighed heavily. In Miss Naomi's presence, she didn't feel quite so stiff with rage. But, the fact remained, there had to be something she was missing. 'So … what did Mr Russell tell you? How did he explain Edith an' me away to you?'

'*He* didn't tell me. Mamma did. And then, once she'd left my room and I was trying to understand, I realized it must have been what the two of them had been arguing about earlier – you know, when Aunt Diana warned me not to interrupt them.'

Absently, Kate ran her fingers along the edge of the workbench and then examined the coating of grey dust on her fingertips. Had she heard that correctly? 'Your father didn't come an' tell you *himself?*' It seemed beyond belief, even for someone as errant as Hugh Russell – or whatever his real name.

In response to her question, Naomi shook her head. 'No. Mamma came in, absolutely seething, relayed the bare bones of it, and warned me never to speak of it again – not to anyone, ever.'

'And that was just this morning.'

'No more than a few moments after you'd gone off in search of Ned. I would have gone after you, but Mamma called Cicely Colborne in to sit with me. I imagine she wanted to ensure I didn't do precisely that – set off to try and find you.'

'But whatever must your mother have thought to learn such a thing of her husband?'

'She was livid, fuming, much of her response beyond repeating. Apparently, when Papa confessed, she demanded of him *how many more times am I to be humiliated by your sordid past?*'

Staring back at Naomi Russell's untroubled face, Kate frowned. How many *more* times? This had happened before? 'So are you saying–'

'Oh, this isn't the first time we've been presented with such news. Ned and I already know we have another half-sibling somewhere, the result of another of Papa's ... *dalliances* – albeit one from a time *after* he married Mamma.'

In utter disbelief, Kate blinked several times. This was growing more and more murky. 'For truth?'

'Sadly, yes. It came to light a while back. Don't ask me how. Neither Ned nor I have ever been privy to the finer details. We don't see him. Or her. The other half-sibling, I mean.'

'Then no wonder your father left in such a hurry. He must have feared for his safety.'

Naomi Russell shrugged. 'The two don't

321

necessarily go together. I'm fairly certain Papa was intending to leave today anyway – this declaration of war no doubt only adding urgency to some prospective business deal. Although doubtless, this latest matter hastened his departure.'

'Doubtless.'

'According to Mamma, he made a fleeting confession, they exchanged words and then he left, claiming he couldn't risk missing the train.'

'Heavens.' What a dreadful man she had for a father! And what a family.

'I know we must sound like truly dreadful people, Kate,' Naomi said, 'but please believe me when I say that we're not. Find it in your heart, if you can, not to think too badly of us, especially of Papa.' Slowly, Kate shook her head; it was as though Naomi Russell had been reading her thoughts. 'That he behaved recklessly when he was younger, I won't deny. Nor, I doubt, would he. That past mistakes on both sides are to blame for the awful mess in which you now find yourself is beyond dispute. But he's not a bad man *per se*.'

Not a bad man? To Kate, he was nothing short of villainous.

'If you say so.'

'For what it's worth, *I* don't think badly of him. Although I can quite see why you wouldn't care for *my* opinion – not after what you've just found out.'

No, she didn't care for it, not really. This wasn't about Naomi. Nor, in this particular instance, was it about Hugh Russell. It was about the up-ending – the complete destruction – of her own life.

'Do you know the worst thing about all of this?' she asked, desperate to voice some of her darker thoughts.

Naomi Russell shook her head. 'I wouldn't presume to, Kate. I simply can't imagine.'

'It's to learn that my whole life – my entire being on this earth – came about only through a mistake. I wasn't born to a mother and a father who loved each other. I was born because my holier-than-thou sister was too besotted – or too stupid or even too wanton – to resist the attentions of a man, to see through the false flattery and the sweet words. Worse still is the way that, even though this mess was her doing in the first place, she carries on as though perfectly entitled to lecture *me* about *my* behaviour!'

'It must be so difficult for all of you. I can't begin to imagine.'

'What's difficult, I'll tell you, is the realization that I'm only here at all because of Edith's foolishness. I'm here because – and only because – she made a mistake. And you'll never know how worthless that makes me feel.'

When Kate started to cry, she felt Naomi Russell's arm settle around her shoulders.

'Dearest Kate, don't feel worthless, for if you are a mistake, so am I.'

'You? Hardly.'

'No, it's true – Ned and I are Mamma's mistake. And, when she is having one of her *poor me* days, or when she is particularly cross with Papa over something he's done, she's not slow to remind us of the fact, either.'

From where her face had been hidden against

Naomi's shoulder, Kate looked up 'Remind you? I don't understand.'

'Well, although Mamma will never forgive me for telling you this, she too was unmarried when she fell pregnant with us. And we know this because Ned and I were born less than six months after she married Papa. So, if *you* are a mistake, then so are we. It wasn't only your poor Edith who fell for young Bertie Russell's charms. It's just that Mamma was the one forced to marry him.'

Trying to digest this revelation, Kate frowned. Into her mind came a picture of Pamela Russell, drunk and wailing something about sacrifices. And then there was what Aunt Diana had told her about that Sadie Jennings. Slowly, it all started to fit together – not that it helped her own situation.

'Well, even though that might be true, it don't help me to know it. At least your mother and father *got* wed. And at least neither of them lied to you–'

'No,' Naomi Russell agreed. 'We've always known who we were. Anyway, setting that aside, just for a moment, I for one couldn't be more delighted to discover that you and I are half-sisters. It certainly explains a thing or two, doesn't it?'

At Naomi's unexpected change of direction, Kate took a step away from her. She could almost feel her brain struggling with something, its cogs and teeth whirring, much in the manner of the long case clock in the hall as it worked its way up to announcing the hour. 'Explains what...?'

'Well, you know, our shared sense of humour: the uncanny feeling that we're of the same mind on certain things. How easy it felt for me to trust you. I must remember to ask Ned if he noticed it too...'

With that, Kate's breath seemed to catch in her chest. Reaching to the workbench, she suddenly realized what had been clogging her thoughts: the matter of whether, before all of this had come to light, Miss Naomi had known of her meetings with Ned. Judging from her last remark, it now seemed unlikely. She had mentioned discovering they were half-sisters, but had made no reference whatsoever to the implications for her friendship with Ned.

In her throat, a lump had formed. She tried to swallow it down but it wasn't to be budged. Naomi was proud of how close she and Ned were – about how the two of them knew everything about one another and shared every confidence. And yet, it seemed now that Ned *hadn't* told his sister of their secret meetings. How could that be? How, if they shared their every thought, had he not told her?

Careful not to move too quickly and draw Naomi's attention, she stepped further backwards until, behind her, she could feel the support of the workbench. She felt panicky and sick: hot and cold at the same time; one moment prickling with humiliation, the next, shivering with foolishness. Had she misread the extent of Ned's interest in her? That he had said nothing to his sister suggested she must have. But he seemed to have enjoyed their meetings – seemed to have enjoyed talking with her. Perhaps, though, that was *all* he had done. Perhaps he had only ever looked upon her as someone with whom to pass some time – as someone with whom he felt inexplicably comfortable. Oh, dear God, how mortifying if that turned out to be true!

She cast a glance to Miss Naomi. She was examining one of the tools from the bench – a thin iron rod, its end sharpened to a point.

'Miss Naomi, I wonder, did–' Partway through asking the question burning away at her, Kate faltered. Her mind and her mouth seemed unable to agree upon how to go about it, her mouth wanting to simply blurt out her concern and get it over with, her mind urging caution.

'Look, Kate,' Naomi Russell turned unexpectedly towards her to say, 'I'm terribly sorry to desert you like this, but I can't afford to have Cicely Colborne discover I'm not where I said I'd be. It's a fuss I could do without.'

'But I just wanted to ask–'

'Fear not. Just because I must return indoors doesn't mean I'm abandoning you. I shan't do that.'

Kate felt her breathing getting faster and faster. Miss Naomi couldn't leave. Not now, not before she had asked her. 'But–'

'What if I were to try and sneak away after dinner? How would that be? From a purely practical consideration, it's probably the easiest time for me to give Cicely Colborne the slip. We could meet in here again – if you think it would be safe to do so.'

In a way, if she let Miss Naomi leave, she would

be giving herself the chance to think. Part of her *had* already begun to wonder as to the wisdom of baring her soul. At least this way, she could reflect for a while and *then* decide whether or not to ask her about Ned.

'Yes,' she said, beginning to breathe more freely. 'For certain we'll be safe here.'

'All right. Then I'll see you again after dinner.'

With Naomi going carefully back out into the yard, Kate stood, deep in thought. Doubting Ned's feelings for her had made her feel sick – a good part of that discomfort seeming to stem from the recognition that perhaps she had got it all wrong. That being the case, did she really have it in her to hear the truth? If she was ever to feel less awful, surely, she had to know, even if it did mean discovering that she had been guilty of a colossal misjudgement, the mortifying extent and nature of which was only now becoming apparent.

'He never mentioned me at all, then.'

True to her promise, later that evening and with the cover of dusk to shroud her movements, Naomi Russell stole away from family and guests to stand stiffly, her dark gown in peril of becoming soiled by the dusty and disused state of their surroundings. On her face was an expression of disquiet.

'My dear Kate, no. Not once. Until this very moment, I had no idea that my brother had even been meeting with you.' For Kate, reaching to the bench for support, Miss Naomi's incredulity told her all she needed to know. Her consternation

327

had been well-founded: Ned hadn't had feelings for her at all. 'On the days when I could never find him anywhere,' Naomi picked up again, 'I assumed he was just out walking. He loves to walk and to explore new places.'

'Yes,' Kate replied, 'I know.'

'Yes, I suppose you would. Look,' Naomi Russell said, clearly uncomfortable, 'you'll have to forgive my astonishment. But, while on numerous occasions over this last week *I* confided to *him* my displeasure about Aubrey and Mamma, not once did Ned mention – even in passing – that he'd been spending time with you. And he tells me everything, particularly matters that either concern or delight him. So, to now learn that you had been spending time together has taken me completely by surprise.' More than anything, Kate longed for the power to wind back time – to withdraw her hastily-made confession. Not only did she feel no better for supposedly unburdening herself, she had probably ruined Miss Naomi's opinion of her. How much better to have just drawn her own conclusion about Ned's feelings and then suffered in silence. It wasn't as though knowing how he had – or hadn't – felt about her was going to change that she was related to him.

'It's my fault, miss,' she said quietly. 'Clearly, I was wrong to think he liked me. It was just my mazed imaginings and I should never have troubled you with them. I was wrong about the whole thing. Wrong and foolish.'

'Oh, my dear Kate, no. Please don't think that way. I can quite see why you might fall for him. People often remark upon how terribly easy he is to like. He's one of the few people who is entirely without nastiness. And that's without considering his lovely looks.'

Already knowing all of that, Kate sighed heavily. 'So why, then, did he leave without even saying goodbye?'

Although a largely pointless question, to her mind there were only two possible reasons: either, when he had learned of her parentage, he had been so sickened that he had wanted only to get away as quickly as possible, or else – and in a way, she preferred to think of this as the more likely – when it became evident what had been going on, his parents had forbidden him to go anywhere near her. It did feel like the sort of thing they would do – brush it under the carpet for the sake of appearances.

Recalling her last sighting of him – sitting in the back of the station cab, staring fixedly ahead – Kate felt her grief finally overflow. She started to cry, making no effort to stop, even when she felt Naomi's arm about her shoulders.

'Oh, my dear Kate, I am so truly, truly sorry. You must be heartbroken.'

Somehow, Naomi's kindness only made her feel worse. 'I ... am,' she mumbled between sobs. 'Though he might not be dead, I do feel the grief as surely as though he were.'

'Yes, I imagine you must.'

'He liked me. I know he did.'

'I'm sure he did ... does.' Withdrawing her arm from Kate's shoulders, Naomi Russell reached into her evening bag and pulled out a pristine handkerchief. 'Here, take this.'

'Thank you, miss.'

'I do wish there was something I could do. I hate to see you so upset.'

'Grateful though I am for the thought, miss, there's nothing to be done – not by you nor anyone. Right this very moment, I curse my sister for her – I curse *Edith* for her stupidity and wish I'd never been born.'

'Come,' Naomi said, once again raising her arm to Kate's heaving shoulders. 'I know it feels that way at the moment ... and I know you didn't choose for any of this to be brought upon you – but one advantage of having my father's blood in your veins is that with it comes his strength and determination. That very wilfulness of yours will help you to one day look back upon this and see it for the upset that it is. Not immediately, I don't mean, but soon. I just know it.'

'But that's just it! I don't *want* to see it as an upset. I want things to go back to the way they *were*. To feel the joy ... and the hope.'

Against her shoulder, Kate heard Naomi give a long sigh. Then she felt her removing her arm.

'Kate, dear Kate, look at me for a moment.' When she made no effort to raise her head, Naomi Russell went on, 'Do, please.' She gave in and looked up. What did it matter? What did *any* of it matter? 'I wish I had known how you felt about Ned because I might have been able to spare you some of this dreadful pain. You see, the fact is, even had you not turned out to be related, there would have been other, equally insurmountable obstacles–'

'I know that,' Kate interjected. 'But I thought

that if he liked me, we would be able to overcome all sorts of things.'

'And I'm sure some of them, you would. But, even had Ned fallen head-over-heels in love with you, it's highly unlikely anything would have come of it. I know we're not in the dark ages any more but some things haven't changed. We might not be a titled family, nor even a landed one. Even so, with the differences in your stations in life, the two of you would never have been able to marry. And, deep down, Ned would have known that.'

It wasn't what Kate wanted to hear. But who *would* want to hear the truth if it was going to hurt so very much? 'We might have been able to,' she said, determined not to let go of the vestiges of her dream just yet.

'No, Kate. Believe me. At the first whiff of such a thing, Mamma would have gone all out to prevent it. And Papa, for all he can be open-minded at times, would have fallen in line with her wishes. Yes, I know that both of you would have been old enough to marry without needing consent but, denied the money from his trust – because that's what Mamma would have ensured, the funds coming largely from *her* family's wealth – Ned would have faced a very difficult choice. Mamma would also have seen to it that he didn't get to follow Papa into the business. Now, that might not seem a great loss – especially since I know Ned is undecided on that as his future course anyway – and yes, I also know everyone says that money doesn't buy happiness. But glib sayings don't alter the fact that it would have been very hard for him. Were he to one day find himself struggling to provide the sort of life he felt you and his family deserved, it would only be natural for him to look back and remember all he'd given up for you. From there, it would be but a short step to resentment, which, trust me, is enough to ruin any marriage. One only has to look to Mamma to see that. Love might have tremendous power, Kate, but, when faced with hardship and resentment on that scale, it can dissolve quicker than a lump of sugar in a cup of coffee.'

'But–'

'I know it isn't what you want to hear. I also know it's moot – one can't marry one's brother, half or otherwise.'

'No,' Kate persisted. 'I know that – all of it. But that don't stop me from wanting to do harm to those who kept the secret from me. Because, had I known, then I would only ever have looked upon him as a family member. I would never have let myself get carried away with *what ifs*. More than anything, I would never have been made to feel so ... so ... foolish!'

When Naomi reached for her hand, Kate let her take it.

'Kate, you've no need to feel foolish. Were our fortunes reversed, I could just as easily have made the same mistake. Why, for instance, would I ever think to wonder whether Lawrence might be my half-brother?'

With a little scoffing noise, Kate raised an ironic smile. Naomi was right, of course. Not that it eased her pain. 'I see that. But–'

'Kate, I know. It doesn't make the outcome any easier to bear. You've no need to tell me that. But, one way or another, I shall try to think of a way to make it up to you.'

At Naomi's thoughtfulness, Kate sighed. 'It's not *your* doing to make up for, miss.'

'No, and I know that too. But it *was* my father's. In *his* shoes, I doubt *I'd* have had the gall – knowing what I'd done all those years back – to come here again, chance of a holiday on the coast or no. So, one way or another, I will try to think of something that will help you.'

At this, Kate gave a rueful shake of her head. 'I don't see what, miss. You can't make me un-hate my family. And believe me, I hate them with a passion that quite frightens me. They told a lie – a most tremendous lie – and then they let me grow up never doubting it to be anything but the truth.'

'I know.'

'I never knew Thomas Bratton. I have no memory of him at all. By all accounts he was a gentle and a placid man, hardworking and as honest as the day is long. My anger has nothing to do with having been led to believe that *he* was my father. It's not even, in itself, that my real father has turned out to be Hugh Russell. It's that through allowing the lie to persist – long after it need have – they've brought me pain of the sort I would never have thought it possible to feel. And please, if you really care for me at all, don't spout the sort of nonsense Edith would – words such as "that which don't kill you makes you stronger".'

'Kate, I wouldn't–'

'Because even were that true, which, after this,

I highly doubt, it doesn't help. I hate what they did to me and I hate them too.'

'And I understand, truly, I do,' Naomi said, gently letting go of Kate's hand. 'But might you not feel differently, were you to picture how it must have been for them?'

'Why should I? It was *their* doing.'

'Well, because, through very little fault of her own, there was a young woman, barely out of girlhood, who fell for a sweet-talking stranger. And there was her family, with little or no recourse for the fix in which she ended up. If *I* try stepping into their shoes, I see only heartache. And shame. So, I choose to believe they did what they felt was for the best. They clung to what was important – their family, their home, their work, and their good name. And, with nothing more than love and affection, they raised the child who had been foisted upon them. Yes, they concealed your true identity and yes, perhaps, once you were old enough to understand, they could have explained some of it to you. But when? When was there ever going to be the right moment to tell you something like that? You're an adult now, yet *still* you struggle to understand how they could have fostered such a lie. And that's *without* considering that they couldn't possibly have foreseen what would go on to happen more than two decades later.'

Kate remained silent. While it didn't sit easily with her, Naomi had a point. There were even chilling similarities between Edith's position all of those years ago and her own now. After all, had Ned returned her feelings – had he responded amorously towards her – would she have found the will to refuse him? Would *she*, thinking herself on the verge of making her dreamed-of marriage, have managed to keep *Ned* at bay? Might she not, instead, have ended up the same as Edith? Hand on heart, she couldn't say no. And, even had they *not* turned out to be siblings, once she had found herself with child, she had to concede it unlikely that Ned would have married her. So, above everything else – and she really couldn't believe she was even thinking this – thank goodness Edith *had* intervened. Thank goodness, she *had* spotted the resemblance and *had* gone on to work out that Hugh Russell was the same Bertie for whom she'd fallen all those years previously. And, while she couldn't bring herself to muster any compassion right now, she did wonder how on earth Edith must be feeling to have the details of her sordid mistake raked up and picked over.

Surprisingly, the realization left her feeling a little calmer. 'Yes,' she said eventually. 'You're right. Although it'll be a good while yet afore I can find it in myself to forgive them.'

'Of course it will be.'

'As regards the rest of my life, well, I don't see now what I shall do with it. I thought to have it all worked out–'

'And one day, you shall have it all worked out again, I'm sure of it – a strong-minded young woman like you–'

'–I was going to London to do something important for the war.'

'–with that streak of Russell determination.'

'But now I fear ending up like Edith – sour and

335

bitter at the hand life has seen fit to deal me.'

'But you needn't, Kate. You're not Edith. Nor are you in her position.'

'Hmm.'

'And, while we're talking of forgiveness, don't you think perhaps you could find it in your heart to apologize to that young man of yours?'

'Luke?'

'I've seen him about the grounds. Terribly handsome, isn't he?'

'I won't deny he's handsome, but he's not my young man – not no more. And I don't see why you think he warrants an apology. You know nothing about it. Or him. Or us.'

'That's true, I don't. But I do remember some time back, you told me how much he cares for you – how he would do almost anything for you.'

'He would. And I won't hear no one say other-wise.'

'Then just tell him you're sorry for the way things have turned out.' When Naomi smiled, Kate tried to do the same. 'If he's the decent man you say he is, then he deserves a little graciousness in return, wouldn't you say?'

Minded that Naomi was right, Kate made a little huffing sound. 'I suppose. But only so long as that's *all* you're expecting. As long as you're not angling to get us back together, because I'll tell you now that won't be a-happening.'

'If you say so.'

'I do.'

'Very well then.'

Exhaling a long breath and beginning to feel less fraught, Kate realized this was her opportunity to make known her views on another matter that had been playing on her mind. 'On the subject of things not happening, miss, I do think you should find a way to be rid of Mr Aubrey, once and for all, and to be with Mr Lawrence. It's one thing to escape marriage to a man you don't want, but quite another to secure for yourself the man you do.' *And trust me,* Kate thought, *I should know.*

When Naomi responded, it was with a wry smile. 'I quite agree. And so it should please you to learn that even *without* you here to chide me, I haven't been letting the grass grow under my feet.'

Kate frowned. 'I'm not sure I understand, miss.'

'Well, with Aubrey forced to maintain a respectable distance these last few days, I've found myself with rather more opportunities to talk to Lawrence. He's positively charming, you know – so unlike his brother.'

Although pleased to learn of Miss Naomi's progress, Kate was surprised to feel a tinge of jealousy. Nevertheless, she raised a smile and said, 'Well, good for you, miss.'

'In addition to which,' Naomi went on, 'I draw comfort from the words of our friend Sybil, the prophetess.'

Wide-eyed and disbelieving, Kate shook her head. 'For truth? You believe *her?*'

'I didn't say I *believed* her. But I do think she's right to say that things have a habit of turning out precisely how they are meant to.'

'Hmm,' Kate replied, remembering snatches from her own reading with Sybil. *Your true path is already known to you. Look into your heart and you will see it for yourself* – or thin words to that effect. Clearly, on this occasion, Miss Naomi's faith was badly misplaced because, as it had turned out, that so-called prophetess couldn't possibly have got it more wrong.

Chapter Nine

Family Affairs

Kate ran her eyes back over the loopy handwriting. It was the following evening, and in her hand, was a note from Miss Naomi, the folded sheet of paper having been slipped to her by Aunt Diana a few hours earlier. It beseeched her to be at the summerhouse after supper, there being a *proposal* she wanted to put to her – one that she was certain would be of interest.

Folding the note back in half and pushing it to the bottom of her pocket, Kate peered across to her little clock. It would be at least another hour before supper was over and done with – time enough for her to decide what to do. She tried to picture what Miss Naomi might mean by *a proposal*. In her experience, proposals were what people made when they intended an arrangement, usually in connection with either a matter of business or else a marriage – which, in some cases, she had lately come to decide, seemed to amount to much the same thing.

Looking out through her window, she wondered whether to do as the note urged. What could Miss Naomi's proposal be? She sincerely hoped she wasn't intending to meddle. Having come to know her, it was apparent that Miss Naomi liked things tied up all nice and neatly. But life, as she had so recently learned, rarely fell into line. She wouldn't entirely put it past Miss Naomi to have decided that she should take up with Luke again. Well, as she'd told her on more than one occasion, that wasn't going to happen. Luke wouldn't have her now, anyway; she'd ruined her chances there. She'd lied to him and disappointed him. Where a future with him was concerned, she had well and truly burnt her bridges. But what else could Miss Naomi have in mind?

Turning away from the window, she let out a long sigh. It had been a day of departures. The Rattray-Smyths had set off back to their cottage on Exmoor, from where, by all accounts, they intended heading straight back to London; their tramping holiday curtailed by the announcement of war and the need for Donald Rattray-Smyth to return to Whitehall. The Fillinghams, too, had left. Unlike Mr Rattray-Smyth, Dr Fillingham couldn't claim to have urgent war business – a fact Pamela Russell had pounced upon, having been overheard begging them not to cut short their stay.

'With all the gloomy grumps gone,' she had entreated, 'we shall once again be free to make merry. Just you see.'

To the dismay of their hostess, her guests had

held fast to their plan, Cordelia Fillingham muttering something about 'needing to see to family matters'.

And so, the household had come full circle: just Pamela and Naomi Russell, Aunt Diana and the Colbornes, the same as it had been at the outset – although obviously, without Ned. Oh, how she missed looking forward to seeing him! Despite everything, the loss of his companionship was still hard to bear. And that was on top of the pain of losing her dream.

Eventually, with the sun starting to slip towards the westerly horizon, and her curiosity making her restless, Kate decided she *would* go and meet Miss Naomi: in truth, she had nothing to lose.

On her way to the door, she glanced in the mirror, her dishevelled state causing her to cast about for her hairbrush. But then it struck her: it didn't matter. She no longer had anyone to impress. There was no one to care how she looked. There was no point.

With a scowl on her face that she had no care to soften, she made her way out of the house and across the lawns. She *had* been hoping to find Miss Naomi already there; that she wasn't, was mildly irksome. As she drew closer to the summerhouse, she thought it a peculiar choice for a secret assignation, the little cabin sitting as it did on a bank above the lawns, in plain view of most of the house and much of the grounds. Not that anyone else appeared to be about.

Stopping a few yards short, she turned to stand and stare out over the gardens. Nothing was moving: the breezes that came off the sea every

340

afternoon to ruffle leaves and flirt with the brims of hats had already dropped; it was too early for the rooks to be chattering and settling into the tall trees for the night, and the tide had withdrawn to its lowest, meaning there was no rushing sound from the cobbles in the cove, there being no waves to tug them back and forth.

Out in the open she felt conspicuous and so she took herself around the corner of the little building, intent upon waiting somewhere less exposed. But, once there, with a sense that she was being watched, she turned sharply. A little way into the trees, with his arm reaching to the trunk of a holm oak, stood Luke. Out of his overalls, he looked less shambling and more purposeful. He also looked to be waiting. Holding back a groan, she hung her head in dismay. She should have known this would be a trap.

'You been summoned here, too?' he asked, his expression giving away nothing of his mood.

Reluctantly, she nodded. 'I'm meeting Miss Naomi.'

'Mr Lawrence,' he said in explanation of his own presence.

'Oh.' Inside, she was seething, her disappointment with Miss Naomi such that she could cheerfully have throttled her. 'I don't think I'll wait,' she said, trying to sound more decisive than she felt.

'Fair enough.'

'I wasn't sure about coming anyway.'

'I'll tell her.'

'All right.'

Before she had even moved though, with a nod

341

of his head he gestured beyond her. She turned to look. Making their way across the lawn, and walking to either side of Aunt Diana, were Miss Naomi and Mr Lawrence, the latter in evening dress, the former in the pale blue silk that made her look as though she'd stepped out from a fairy tale. Well, whatever sort of trap they thought they'd so cleverly set, she was not about to step into it. She would make a point of letting them see her leaving. She didn't care.

'Kate, please wait.' Coming to an indecisive halt, Kate stood for a moment, unable to decide whether or not to comply with the request Miss Naomi called towards her. '*Please* wait. We've something to tell you.' And then, lifting the hem of her gown and accepting Mr Lawrence's arm as he assisted her up the grassy rise, she added, 'Please, do wait.'

With her shoulders sagging, Kate turned back; she would stay and listen. But that was all she would do.

'Good evening to you, Luke.'

'Evenin', Mr Lawrence. 'Ow be?'

'Fair to middlin', as I've come to learn is the correct response to that enquiry.'

Astonished by the easy way with which the two men exchanged greetings, Kate turned to look at them. How had Luke come to be on such comfortable terms with Mr Lawrence?

'*I* shall withdraw for a moment,' Aunt Diana announced. 'I shall take a stroll along the border to see whether that *Matthiola* has any fragrance this evening.'

'Thank you, Aunt. We won't be long.'

With Aunt Diana's departure, Kate felt her pulse quicken. *Won't be long* suggested this was to be nothing more than a straightforward announcement. But if so, why was Luke there? Presumably, any moment now she would find out.

'Announce away,' Mr Lawrence said with a smile and a gesture to Naomi.

Naomi wasted no further time. 'Lawrence has asked me to marry him. And I've accepted.'

Although, at the sight of Miss Naomi flushing pink, Kate's mouth formed into a smile, behind it, she could feel her throat constricting. Miss Naomi was to marry Mr Lawrence. But that was the way of the world: people of good fortune begot more good fortune; princesses married their princes. Ordinary people like herself, on the other hand, rarely had such luck.

'Congratulations, Mr Lawrence, sir.' At Luke's hearty response, Kate looked up. He was shaking Mr Lawrence's hand. And he was doing so warmly, the smile on his face seemingly genuine.

'Thank you, Luke.'

'Congratulations, ma'am.'

'Thank you, Luke.'

'That's ... lovely news,' Kate felt the need to add, her remark rather less assured. 'Congratulations to both of you.'

Miss Naomi stepped towards her, fixing her look as she did so. 'Thank you, Kate, from both of us.' But then, from within the secrecy of an embrace, she whispered, 'I told you I hadn't been letting the grass grow under my feet! And don't worry, although Mamma is beside herself and Aunt Diana has warned me that the Colborne coffers are bare – the result of a scandal of some sort, I'm led to believe – I want to marry him anyway.'

In a bid to stop herself crying, Kate bit hard on the side of her tongue. While there was no shame in shedding tears of happiness, she couldn't be sure that was what hers were – even though happiness was what she genuinely wished for the two of them; they were nice – for people of their sort. No, the twisting of her insides felt to have rather more to do with the unfairness of life.

'The wedding won't be a grand affair but it will be soon,' Mr Lawrence picked up. 'I'm going up to see my grandfather's regiment next week. Seems they're keen to have me.'

'That's good news, sir.'

'It is, Luke. Having a family connection and volunteering early ought to bring rewards, which leads me to another proposal I wish to make.'

Kate bowed her head. Had she misunderstood – again? Had she been mistaken in her thought that Miss Naomi had a proposal to put to *her*. She was sure that was what her note had said. But here was Mr Lawrence making a proposal to Luke.

'Yes, sir?' Luke, evidently, was all ears. Well, good for him.

'This war is going to bring opportunities for men who are prepared to put themselves out. It is, in part, why I have been so quick to volunteer. And so, with your agreement, I should like to put in a word for *you* – see if they'll have *you, too*. All those evenings when you stuck it out, endeavouring to master the maintenance of Father's infernal motor and learning how to drive it, will have set you in good stead. Get in early – to the right battalion – and you have a good chance of advancing rapidly.'

Luke blew out a long stream of breath. 'Much obliged, sir.' And then, after a mere moment's hesitation, he stepped forward and reached to shake his benefactor's hand. 'Thank you, sir. I'd like that very much.'

In Kate's stomach, something twisted further. Luke was going to join up. He was going to war. *He was leaving Woodicombe.* How unfair was *that?* The man who hadn't wanted to go anywhere, was now, without very much effort at all, going to do the very thing for which she herself had strived so hard but failed.

'I should also like to make it known, Luke, that while none of us can say how things will turn out, I very much hope that once this war has been won, you will permit me first refusal upon your service in our household.'

Standing a little aside, Kate curled her hands into fists. Was Luke now being offered a job as well – a future after the war? Just how wicked must she have been to have missed out on such good fortune?

'Thank you, sir,' she heard Luke reply, the delight in his voice impossible to miss. 'I'd be honoured.'

'Good man. Then that's settled.'

Somehow, before she took her leave of the happy little gathering, Kate knew she ought to wish Luke good luck. It was only right and proper. While it pained her to admit it, he deserved this turn of good fortune. He was decent.

He was honourable. And, but for her own foolishness, *she* might now be contemplating a future with him – in London, of all places! As it was, he would now go on to find someone else with whom to share his new and exciting life. Well, therein lay her bitter lesson: sometimes the grass on the other side *wasn't* as green as it looked. And there had to be some parable in there about inspecting the mouths of gift horses, as well.

'Now, Kate, don't feel left out. I too, have a proposal.' From where she had taken to staring out towards the horizon, biting back tears, Kate turned her attention to Miss Naomi. 'When Lawrence and I marry, I shall become eligible to receive an income from my trust, from which I shall be able to pay a small salary, should I so choose. To begin with, Lawrence and I will rent a house – a modest one, of course, nothing on the scale of Clarence Square, but then neither of us wants anything grand. Anyway, my point, is that in our new home, I should like to propose a position for *you*.'

Kate stared back at Miss Naomi's light smile, eventually finding her tongue to respond with, 'A position, miss?'

'Yes. I haven't decided what – well, I wouldn't, not without discussing it with you first. But I *have* spoken to Lawrence and … explained your situation … and he said that it's my money to do with as I please. And what *would* please me, would be to have you in our home.'

Eventually, Kate remembered to breathe. 'In your home?'

'What I would *prefer*, of course, is simply to

have your company. But, since I've learned enough about you to know that you wouldn't settle for being something woolly like a lady's companion, I thought perhaps you might like to become our housekeeper.'

A housekeeper? Her? 'You want me to be your housekeeper, miss?'

'If you think you'd be happy in that position, yes. Also, since Lawrence will be away giving orders on a battlefield somewhere–'

'And *taking them*, darling.'

'–leaving me largely alone, it occurs that I should like to become involved in some sort of voluntary work.'

'Like with the Voluntary Aid Detachment, did you mean?' Remembering then how it was only through Ned that she even knew of it, Kate winced.

'Perhaps. Or perhaps with another organization. Either way, since it was you who put the thought into my mind in the first place, I should very much like it if you would join me.'

How different the world suddenly looked! Miss Naomi was asking her to keep her house for her. And she wanted them to volunteer together, as well. It was almost too good to be true. Things like this didn't happen to her. And Luke: Luke was being given the chance to go with Mr Lawrence and become a driver – the very thing he'd once said he would like. Heavens. Now all she had to do was find a way to stop grinning long enough to give Miss Naomi her answer.

'Yes, miss,' she said, it proving completely beyond her to stop smiling. 'I should like that very much.'

'Good. I didn't *think* I would be asking out of turn. Well, now we all know where we stand. And Lawrence, you and I can make plans with that in mind.'

'Aren't you forgetting something?' Lawrence asked, his tone such that both Kate and Luke turned to look at him. 'We need to check they are both willing to be bound by our condition. Remember?'

Briefly, Naomi Russell looked taken aback. 'Oh, my goodness, yes,' she said, nevertheless stopping short of explaining further.

Across from her, Kate noticed that Luke was frowning. 'A condition, sir?'

While Luke asked the question on her own tongue, Kate felt her heart miss a beat. *Now* what unforeseen cloud was about to darken her horizon? What spanner was *now* about to fly into the works?

'Well, you must understand that while we're more than happy to have you both in our household and in our employ, we cannot afford ... shall we say ... any whiff of impropriety–'

Puzzled, Kate looked first to Luke's face and then to Miss Naomi's. *Impropriety?* What did that even mean? Didn't it have to do with scandal? 'I don't understand,' she blurted, hoping desperately that this incredible opportunity wasn't about to slip from her grasp. That would be just too mean for words. 'Is it to do with my ... your ... our ... father?'

'No, silly, of course not,' Naomi replied, reaching to touch her arm. 'No, what Lawrence is saying, in his round and about way, is that if the two of you are going to be together in our home, then we ask only that you be married.'

'To one another?'

'Yes, Kate,' Lawrence said, clearly struggling not to laugh. 'Since the two of you are clearly meant for each another and, since you'll be together under our roof, it would seem only proper.'

Feeling all of their eyes upon her, Kate spun away, her fists curled tightly and her eyes narrowing with mistrust. She should have known there would be a trap. Anything that sounded too good to be true usually was. But surely, if Miss Naomi had told Mr Lawrence of her infatuation with Ned and how she had, in the process, trampled all over Luke's feelings, he would know that what he was asking was impossible. She had behaved appallingly – well beyond anything Luke would feel able to forgive. In particular, he would know that the only reason she had given up her pursuit of Ned, was because he'd turned out to be her half-brother.

Seemingly then, she had cost herself not only the job and the home of her dreams, but the man with whom truthfully, she would once have been more than happy to share them. Before setting out so single-mindedly on her doomed pursuit of Ned, everything about this proposed arrangement would have felt utterly right.

Unable to turn back and face the three of them she heaved a very long sigh. There was only one thing for it: if Mr Lawrence's condition meant that only one of them could accept the proposal, she would let it be Luke. He was being offered the most incredible opportunity and, now that it was far too late, she knew that she loved him too much to stand in his way. Somehow, she would find it within herself to let him go.

But, when she forced herself to turn about, it was to see that Mr Lawrence and Miss Naomi were grinning – and that Luke was down on one knee.

'What do you say then, Kate?' he asked, reaching for her hand. '*Now* will you name the day, you bloody obstinate woman?'

Dialect Words Used in This Book

Bellyharm: Stomach ache
Culver birds: Wood-pigeons
Dimpsy: Dusk, twilight
Drangs: Alleys or narrow passageways
Fadge and find: To toil for one's daily bread
Mazed: Mad, crazy (of a person)
Nobbling and newsing: Gossiping
Stickle: Used to describe a hill or path that is steep in gradient
Taffety: Fanciful, without substance
Tallet: A hay-loft

The publishers hope that this book has given you enjoyable reading. Large Print Books are especially designed to be as easy to see and hold as possible. If you wish a catalogue please ask at your local library or write directly to:

Magna Large Print Books
Cawood House,
Asquith Industrial Estate,
Gargrave,
Nr Skipton, North Yorkshire.
BD23 3SE

This Large Print Book for the partially sighted, who cannot read normal print, is published under the auspices of

THE ULVERSCROFT FOUNDATION

THE ULVERSCROFT FOUNDATION

... we hope that you have enjoyed this Large Print Book. Please think for a moment about those people who have worse eyesight problems than you ... and are unable to even read or enjoy Large Print, without great difficulty.

You can help them by sending a donation, large or small to:

**The Ulverscroft Foundation,
1, The Green, Bradgate Road,
Anstey, Leicestershire, LE7 7FU,
England.**
or request a copy of our brochure for more details.

The Foundation will use all your help to assist those people who are handicapped by various sight problems and need special attention.

Thank you very much for your help.